ENDTIME

Andy Secombe acquired his love of fantasy at an early
age, but he had to overcome a natural talent for pre-
varication, and an acting bug that lasted thirty years
(including appearances in two of the Star Wars films),
before he was able to settle down to writing his first
novel, *Limbo*. He now lives with his wife and two sons
in Cornwall, and this is his fourth novel.

*Also by Andy Secombe*

*Limbo*
*Limbo II*
*Last House in the Galaxy*

# ENDGAME

## ANDY SECOMBE

**TOR**

First published 2006 by Tor

This edition published 2007 by Tor
an imprint of Pan Macmillan Ltd
Pan Macmillan, 20 New Wharf Road, London N1 9RR
Basingstoke and Oxford
Associated companies throughout the world
www.panmacmillan.com

ISBN 978-0-330-43998-5

3 5 7 9 8 6 4 2

A CIP catalogue record for this book is available from
the British Library.

Typeset by Intype Libra Ltd
Printed and bound in Great Britain by
Mackays of Chatham plc, Chatham, Kent

Visit **www.panmacmillan.com** to read more about all our books
and to buy them. You will also find features, author interviews and
news of any author events, and you can sign up for e-newsletters
so that you're always first to hear about our new releases.

For Peaceniks everywhere

# *Acknowledgements*

Thanks to Tom Kiely for giving up his valuable time to introduce me to the wonderful world of computer gaming; thanks also to Michael at Blue Screen I.T. in Plymouth for his technical help, and to Barbara Gatehouse for her advice on all things religious.

# *In the beginning . . .*

Of course, it was inevitable that the Devil would find out about the Garden of Eden bash, and what was also a dead cert was his wrath at being left off the guest list. But when the long-awaited gold-embossed invitation with clouds and cherubs in the top left-hand corner didn't plop onto his welcome mat, the depth of his rage surprised even him. He stomped angrily around his basement kitchen, hurling pots and pans.

'The bastard! The cheap, mean-spirited bastard! Has he forgotten me so soon? I, who was the brightest, most favoured of all!'

The truth was, the Devil was desperate to get back into Heaven. Creeping around underground was no life for a being of his sensitivity and taste, not to mention his height – he kept smacking his head on stalactites.

'Well, I'm not going to take this lying down,' he snarled, rubbing a newly risen lump on his forehead. And, gathering his leathern wings about him, he made for the front door. He was about to open it when he caught sight of himself in the long hallway mirror. How he'd changed since his fall. The creature that stared back at him was almost unrecognizable as the angel Lucifer: God's favourite, adorning Heaven with his brilliance. 'Ah me,' he sighed. His beauty was now in ruins: his once bright, clear eyes were angry and bloodshot, his face was lined and wrinkled like an old wineskin and his body, which had been so fine and upright, now hunched and twisted.

'Look what he's done to me!' he howled in self-pity. 'One mistake! I make one mistake and he casts me aside like a used handkerchief! Well I'm going to make him pay; you can't treat people like commodities. I'm going to crash his little party. Let's hope he's ordered enough canapés.' And, clambering out of the pit, he set off for Eden.


It was a glittering affair: anyone who was anyone in the heavenly host was there and, happily, so far no one had got drunk, nor were there any cigar burns in the fresh green turf.

Eden looked stunning. A young angel called Blaine, who had a flair for design, had taken charge of the decor. Taking the theme 'genesis', Blaine had planted thousands of daffodils and crocuses which, during the party, pushed their green shoots miraculously through the soil and burst into flower, creating soft clouds of heart-warming yellow, white and blue flowers. Above the heads of the partygo-ers tumbled laughing cherubs (cherubs were very 'now') and young dolphins cavorted in a lake with a working vol-cano at its centre which continually spewed molten lava to form a small but ever-growing island. Blaine had also imported hordes of juvenile animals, which snuffled charmingly around the feet of the guests, snaffling any dropped cocktail sausages.

The centrepiece was a magnificent fruit tree heavy with large, tempting, rosy-red apples, and under this stood the stars of the show: Adam and Eve. They were not at all what most people had expected; indeed, many found them a disappointment. Billed as 'made in God's image' they seemed to have none of the heavenly father's urbanity which made him such a hit on the dinner-party circuit. They knew nothing of the latest gossip; indeed, they seemed to have no conversation at all. To be frank, most of the guests found them a little dim.

But no one could fault how they looked. Their skin had a golden lustre and their bodies shone with health. Eve's long hair tumbled over her shoulders, brushing the slightly upturned nipples of her full and rounded breasts. Her hips were invitingly curvy and her legs long and smooth, tapering to slender ankles. Adam had broad shoulders, a perfectly defined but not over-developed torso and strong, muscular thighs.

God, needless to say, was thrilled with them, shrugging off suggestions that they might be a trifle under-powered in the cranial department by saying that it was precisely their naive innocence that made them so attractive. Yes, the big man was thoroughly enjoying himself, discreetly pleased at how well things were going – prematurely as it turned out.


The first most people knew of the trouble was the sound of raised voices at the garden gate.

'What do you mean I can't come in, you piece of shit?'

'I'm sorry, sir, but I have strict instructions—'

'I don't give a fuck about your instructions!'

An embarrassed hush descended on the guests when they realized who it was.

God groaned inwardly when he was acquainted with

the news but, being a responsible host, wandered down to the gate to take control of the situation.

The Devil, having tried, and failed, to get past the door angel, was now jumping up and down and screaming, 'Gabriel is a personal friend of mine!'

'I'm sorry, sir, but I still can't let you in without an invitation,' the angel replied, quietly but firmly.

When the Devil saw God pushing through the throng towards the gate, he called out to him, 'Hello! It's your downstairs neighbour come to complain about the noise!'

God nodded to the door angel and the gate was opened.

'About time.' The Devil walked straight up to God. 'Remember me? Long time no see!'

'Come and have a drink,' said God, placing a hand on the Devil's shoulder and steering him towards the bar.

'Why not? Let's get stiffed!'

God squeezed the Devil's shoulder. 'Please, for my sake, don't make a scene.'

'Oh, *you're* the one that's upset now. May I remind you it's *me* who's been stumbling around in the dark for the past few millennia!'

'I'm sorry if you find your new accommodation disagreeable, but it's your own fault. Here.' God seized a glass of Buck's Fizz off a tray and handed it to the fallen one.

'You're still angry at me, aren't you? You're still holding a grudge because of my little joke.'

'I don't call usurping the heavenly throne a little joke.' God sniffed.

'I wasn't trying to usurp the throne; I was just fooling around.'

'That's not what it looked like to me.'

The Devil knocked back his drink and grabbed another from a passing tray. 'You know your trouble? You never have any fun. You never let your hair down and let it all hang out.'

'As creator of the universe, I have great responsibilities – I don't have time for "fun".'

'Pity.' The Devil emptied his glass and reached for a third. 'You know, you and me, we could have had a great time. With your power and my . . . good looks, we could have blazed a trail across the cosmos.'

'And who would have looked after the shop?'

'Michael – he would have loved to play God for a while. He's even more anal than you are.'

God plucked the Devil's glass from his hand. 'Come on, there's something I want to show you.'

'I hadn't finished that!' The Devil wailed.

'You can finish it later; I just don't want you spilling anything on my new toys and making them all sticky. Come on.'

The Devil sighed and reluctantly followed God as he weaved a path through the press of guests.

'Lucifer, I want you to meet my newest creations: Adam and Eve.'

The Devil looked up at God with big, round eyes. 'You haven't called me Lucifer in such a long time.'

Ignoring him, God continued: 'He is a man and she a woman. I have created them to be custodians of the earth; they and their offspring will populate the world and have dominion over the birds of the air and the beasts of the field, and over all of the fish in the oceans. I like to think of them as planetary caretakers; they will cherish the earth in my stead.'

The Devil studied them closely, walking round them,

nodding appreciatively. At one point he reached out a hand to stroke Eve's behind, but was restrained by a disapproving 'Ahem!' from God.

When he'd finished his appraisal, he turned back to his host. 'Not bad. I mean, the – what do you call her – woman? She's a babe. Long hair, nice tits, great arse – good job. But as for the guy . . .' he leaned in conspiratorially to God, 'is he all there – up here?' He tapped his head. 'He looks a little shifty to me – his eyes are too close together. And *that*.' He pointed to Adam's genitals. 'Is that a joke? When he sees what you've given the horses, he is *not* going to be happy.'

'You disapprove?' God tried hard to conceal his burgeoning anger, but the Devil knew him well enough to know he was needled.

'Yeah, I disapprove. Personally, I'm not so sure it's such a good idea to leave the earth in the hands of two people who really were born yesterday. They may seem dumbly compliant now but, let's face it, you hardly know them. What if, the moment your back's turned, they turn into a couple of party animals and trash the place? If you want my opinion, I wouldn't trust these particular individuals further than I could throw them.'

'I made them in my image!'

'And you never had an off day?'

The argument was beginning to attract the attention of the other partygoers, who huddled round eagerly.

God could no longer hide his rage. 'They are my creation and they will do my bidding!'

'You want to bet?' The Devil fired back. 'You want to put your creation where your mouth is?'

'Er, I . . .' God paused, looking round at the expectant faces of his guests.

'Come on,' the Devil persisted, 'or is the truth that you don't have that much confidence in your precious Adam and Eve?'

Those clustered round God leaned in closer, staring hard into his face. He knew he shouldn't let Lucifer get to him like this, but how could he back down now in front of everybody?

'Well, all right. Yes, I accept!'

'OK.' The Devil plunged his hand into a nearby ice bucket and pulled out a handful of ice cubes, cigar butts and bits of old cheese, squeezing them together between his palms to form a sort of dirty snowball. Then he hurled the snowball high into the air and it soared off across the sky, trailing a milky-white tail as it began its long looping journey around the sun. 'Now, here's the deal: when that little comet reappears in the skies above earth, if Adam and Eve have been keeping house nicely, pruning the roses and living like additive-free vegetarians, I'll retire happily into outer darkness for eternity and never trouble you again. *If*, on the other hand, they and their kids start having their own ideas of what constitutes a good time: killing all the plants and animals; turning your beautiful blue-green planet into a lifeless rock and in the process wiping themselves out, I get my place back in Heaven. Deal?'

'Deal!' God roared.

Satan spat on his hand and they shook.

'And while we're about it, why don't we throw in the earth as well?'

'Very well,' God replied. 'Winner takes all.'

'Well, winner takes what's left.'

Mightily pleased with himself, the Devil turned to go, but God called him back. 'Just one rule,' he said.

'Here we go,' the Devil muttered. 'What?'

'There must be no interference from either of us. I have granted man the gift of free will; he must be allowed to succeed or fail completely on his own. Agreed?'

The Devil grimaced and sighed irritably.

'Sorry, I didn't quite catch that.'

The Devil spun round angrily. 'I said, I agree!'

'Good, good. Well, please feel free to stay and enjoy the party.'

But the Devil was eager to get away; he had to plan. 'No, I think I'll make it an early night. I've . . . got a few things to do. But it's been great to see you again. *Really* great.' And he meant it. Despite himself, Satan couldn't help liking the big guy. 'I'll see *you* later.' He winked salaciously at Eve, who immediately turned bright pink, although she didn't know why. Likewise, Adam felt a tightening in the stomach and a strange tingle up the back of his neck, but as he had no prior experience of these sensations, had no way of attributing them to jealousy.

Unlike his old friend, God harboured no residual feelings of affection for Satan, other than those of a creator for his creation, and was relieved to see the back of him.

Satan's exit from the party had a sting in its tail. Approaching the angel on the gate, he looked down. 'Oops,' he said. 'Loose shoelace.' As he crouched to tie it up, something slithered sinuously from his sleeve and slipped away to hide in the long grass. And so it was that the worm infested Paradise.

'You have a nice day now,' the Devil said cheerily to the door angel as he left and, whistling, the fallen one strolled happily off down the path to Hell.

# Chapter 1

There was nothing remarkable about Martin Gray. His eyes were an understated brown, his hair was unobtrusively mousy and his nose and mouth occupied the usual spaces and fulfilled their required functions without advertising their presence too forcefully. His life too was straightforward and uncomplicated, or at least it had been until quite recently. He was a dentist, and he enjoyed his work. There was nothing messily vague about dentistry: you saw a hole and you filled it. It demanded a certain amount of artistry in the handling of polymers and precious metals, granted, but Martin regarded himself first and foremost as a craftsman. He wasn't interested in inventing a new flossing technique, nor in exploring novel approaches to plaque removal. Whether he was lovingly sculpting a new porcelain inlay, or deftly excavating a root canal with a hair-fine drill, he was happy to follow the tried and tested procedures laid down by the British Dental Association. Dentistry had been good to him: it had given him a certain amount of respect in the local community, bought him his beautiful old farmhouse, Windyridge, and put his son Luke through public school. It gave his life a framework – borders within which he was perfectly safe and knew exactly what he was doing.

But now, in the short space of a year, the framework

of his life had been blown apart. His wife had left him, he was in debt up to his eyeballs, and to top it all he was being aggressively investigated by the Inland Revenue for suspected tax fraud. He was drowning, and he'd had enough.

He looked out over the deep scar of Blackenstone quarry on Dartmoor towards the rising sun. It was going to be a beautiful day. *At least I'll take a pleasant last memory with me into the afterlife*, he thought. *Ah well, no use in putting it off any longer*. He revved the engine. In several short moments he would be making the long trip to the unforgiving granite floor of the quarry by the shortest possible route. His vehicle would be wrecked beyond repair and Martin would be identifiable only from his dental records. His fist tightened on the gear lever and he grimly clunked the Range Rover into DRIVE. The big car lurched forward and stalled.

'Shit! Shit! Shit! Why can't I do anything right?' he groaned, and slumped miserably forward, resting his head against the rim of the steering wheel.

Across the great open wound of the quarry, Martin could see the red rim of the sun just starting to peep over the horizon. But its cheery rays only served to highlight his dark and desperate mood.

'Bugger it,' he said, turning the key in the ignition. The engine burst into life and, before he had a chance to change his mind, he snicked the lever back into DRIVE. His life insurance policy would more than cover the mortgage on the house and give Helen and Luke a substantial chunk of money on top of that. As for the practice, that would now be solely Westerham Wilding's responsibility. Martin smiled grimly at the prospect of his colleague having to deal with the messy day-to-day running of the place.

Now it was time. Focusing his mind on the task in hand, he blocked out anything that might distract him from his purpose. Taking one last look at the sky, his eyes flicked past the rearview mirror and as they did so he saw Frank Sinatra and Peter Lawford leaning nonchalantly against a fence post. He blinked and looked again. There was no one there. It was strange, but not unnatural, perhaps, to be having hallucinations at this particular moment, but why members of the infamous Rat Pack?

'It doesn't matter,' he told himself. 'Now, focus, Martin. In seconds this will all be over. It is the only way. OK, on three. One. Two. His foot twitched on the brake pedal. Thr—'

*Ring-ring.*

He stared in disbelief at his phone on the seat beside him. It might be Helen, his wife, wondering how he was, but it was unlikely; she'd given up wondering about him some time ago.

*Ring-ring.*

A much more likely explanation was that this was an emergency. Someone, somewhere was in pain and desperately needed the services of a qualified dental surgeon.

*Ring-ring.*

But were they really his concern any longer? After all, *he* was in pain, the sort of pain that novocaine couldn't reach.

*Ring-ring.*

Martin glared at the phone. Why the hell hadn't he turned it off? His right leg quivered with the strain of holding down the brake pedal while he wrestled with the infuriating professional attitude that couldn't let a patient down.

*Ring-ring. Ring-ring.*

Slamming the gear stick into PARK, he pulled on the handbrake.

'Arrgh! Arrgh! Arrgh!' He pounded the steering wheel with his fists, then picked up the phone. 'Martin Gray speaking,' he said in a well-modulated tone.

He didn't recognize the man's voice at the other end, but it seemed that he had cracked a tooth and was in agony.

'Are you registered with me?' Martin asked.

The man said he'd just moved into the area and hadn't yet registered with anyone.

Martin could already feel his resolve weakening, and if he didn't do the deed now, the moment would be gone. 'Surgery starts at nine o'clock. My colleague, Mr Wilding, should be able to see you then.'

But the man was insistent, howling with pain down the phone, saying he couldn't wait and pleading pathetically with Martin to come to his aid.

Martin didn't owe this new patient anything. It was simple: all he had to do was put the car back into DRIVE, release the handbrake and . . .

'Very well!' he barked into the phone. 'Meet me at the surgery – you know where that is? . . . Good, I'll be there in about –' he looked at his watch: 6.15 '– fifteen minutes.'

He clicked off the phone and slung it on the passenger seat. Then he threw back his head and screamed. Before long the screams had turned to sobs and soon he was crying like a baby.

Reversing determinedly back along the track away

from the quarry, Martin eventually hit the road and heaved the big car round in the direction of Exeter.

Frank Sinatra and Peter Lawford watched him go, the morning sun glinting off their suits, its golden rays reflected in the peaks of their red caps.

'*Now* what did you do?' Sinatra snapped, angrily throwing his cigarette to the ground.

'I didn't do anything,' Lawford replied in his lazy English drawl.

'No? Then why the hell did the guy shoot off like that?'

Lawford shrugged. 'Beats me. Maybe he changed his mind.'

'Changed his mind? Are you telling me Head Office made a mistake?'

'They're not infallible.'

'No, but I trust them more than I trust you, which is not at all.'

'That's a fine thing; what have I ever done to you?'

'I'll tell you what you've *never* done, and that's buy me a drink.'

'Here we go again.'

'Yes, here we go again. Old Mr Tightwad with his charming English ways and tight-assed aristocratic friends – you make me sick.'

'Me and my tight-assed friends were good enough when you were desperate to cuddle up to Jack Kennedy.'

Sinatra grabbed hold of Lawford's lapels. 'You two-faced, toffee-nosed pimp, I ought to—'

'Hi, Frank, Peter!'

Sinatra jumped and turned round, but he relaxed

when he saw a figure in a cashmere coat. 'Jimmy. Jesus, you scared the crap out of me.'

'What are you two doing out here?'

Sinatra jerked a thumb at Lawford. 'This bum frightened away our client. He's going to have a lot of explaining to do when we get back.'

Lawford put his hands in his pockets and leaned against a fence post. 'We were waiting for a suicide, but the guy simply changed his mind. I had nothing to do with it.'

Jimmy placed a hand on Sinatra's small but immaculately tailored shoulder. 'How're you finding the working conditions, Frank?'

Sinatra looked gloomily at the ground. 'It's not like it was advertised in the brochure.'

Jimmy shook his head sadly. 'No. And how about you, Peter?'

'Things could be better.'

'Of course they could. Now, I want to put something to you . . .'

The North Road Dental Practice was housed in two large white Victorian terraced houses in one of Exeter's more select neighbourhoods. Originally, the surgery had occupied only one building, but when the house next door became vacant, Westerham came up with a plan to buy it, knock through and create a huge American-style super-surgery offering cosmetic dental treatment, a dedicated round-the-clock bite restoration service and a supermarket selling the latest, cutting-edge imports from the USA: everything from tongue cleaners to green-lipped mussel extract toothpaste. Martin had argued lamely against it, saying that Exeter was full of students who had no money to waste on getting the Hollywood smile. But when Westerham had the bit between his teeth he was a force to be reckoned with and, as had happened on so many other occasions, Martin's objections had been simply pushed aside.

The property was duly purchased on a mortgage signed by both dentists, and building work commenced. Almost immediately they hit trouble. The old house was riddled with rot and needed to be completely gutted.

When the place was eventually finished, six months late and more than twice over budget, the expected rush of patients eager to avail themselves of the constantly on-call tooth-whitening operative never materialized. Likewise, the tills in the gleaming dental hygiene super-market remained silent. The place was haemorrhaging money faster than a severed carotid artery.

It was all right for Westerham, of course, his family was loaded, but for Martin it was a disaster. Financially overextended by the unplanned-for building expenses as well as the burden of the extra mortgage, he might have been tempted to cut his losses, hand the whole business over to Westerham and start again somewhere else, if it hadn't been for the jeers of his father-in-law – a lame, one-eyed *Daily Express* reader – who accused him of being 'frightened of success'.

Instead, Martin shouldered the burden and worked like a dog to keep up the payments, starting early in the morning and sometimes not finishing until late into the night. This impossible schedule soon took its toll, both on Martin and his marriage. What made matters worse was the fact that around this time Helen's father had a mild stroke and, although her parents could well afford a nurse, Helen insisted they move in with them. It was a recipe for disaster.

In front of the surgery, where the small formal front gardens had once been, was a smart and businesslike gravelled parking area. The Range Rover's tyres scrunched on the gravel as Martin pulled up in front of a sign which read: RESERVED FOR MARTIN GRAY. Next to this stood another notice: RESERVED FOR WESTERHAM WILDING. Of course, it was far too early for *his* latest shiny new vehicle to be there, with its silly personalized number plate: W1. Westerham thought it looked very professional, very London. But every time Martin saw it he couldn't help thinking: *Women's Institute*.

Trudging wearily up the front steps, Martin unlocked the door and turned off the burglar alarm.

Flicking on a few lights in the bright, fresh, newly refurbished reception area, he found a consent form behind the reception desk, inserted it into a clipboard from a stack in the corner and strolled into his treatment room. He looked up sharply as he heard someone moan.

A man, a rather tall man, was already seated in his chair. He gazed at Martin and moaned pitifully.

Martin stepped back in shock. 'Ah! Who are you? How did you get in here?'

The man shook his head, still moaning.

Finally the penny dropped. 'Did you just phone me?'

More moaning and nodding.

'How did you get past the burglar alarm?

An extra loud moan.

'Well, you can't just walk in here and make yourself comfortable. This is a surgery; I have sterile instruments.'

Loud moaning accompanied by writhing.

'All right, all right. But before I start, I'm going to

have to ask you a few questions. You'll have to fill out this form.' Martin thrust the consent form at him.

Doing a very good impression of a wounded bear with irritable bowel syndrome and piles, the man went into such paroxysms of agony that Martin chose the path of least resistance and decided he'd investigate first and ask questions later. Sighing, he put the consent form down and gloved up. Lowering the dental chair until the man was virtually prone, Martin sat on a stool at his patient's head, clicked on the examination light and manoeuvred it into position.

'Open wide, please.'

Martin was amazed; the man had the most perfect set of teeth he'd ever seen – not a filling, not a spot of rot anywhere. *And* he had all his wisdom teeth, intact. Even his breath smelled good: faint aromas of cinnamon and honey. *If this man has toothache*, Martin thought, *I'm the Sugar Plum Fairy*.

Martin angrily pushed the examination light aside and stood up. 'Now look here,' he began. He was about to give the man a severe telling-off, not only for wasting his time but also for interrupting him when he could have been much more usefully engaged in the business of killing himself. But before he could continue, his receptionist, Donna, stuck her head round the door.

'Your first appointment's here, Martin.'

Martin looked up. 'Erm . . . I'm with a patient, Donna.'

'Sorry?' Donna frowned.

'I said, I'm with a—' Martin glanced back at the chair; it was empty.

He stared dumbly at the leather upholstery of his dentist's chair for some moments, remembering, bizarrely, exactly how much it had cost and wondering whether his patients ever realized that it was genuine, hand-finished Connolly hide. Looking back at Donna, standing in the doorway, she suddenly seemed an awfully long way away. 'Did you see . . .' But then Martin felt his legs begin to go and had to grab the padded leather chair for support.

'Are you all right, Martin?'

'Er . . . I'm fine,' he said, lowering himself gently into the upholstery. After a few moments, when the ringing in his ears had subsided, he asked, 'Who . . . who is it, Donna?'

'It's Mrs Beacon.'

'But her appointment's not until eight fifteen. And I'll need Vicky.'

'I'm here, Martin.' Vicky, Martin's dental nurse, had appeared and was standing next to Donna in the open door of the surgery.

Martin's eyes went to the clock above the door. It read ten minutes past eight. But that was impossible; he'd arrived at the surgery not five minutes ago, at 6.30. How had he lost over one and a half hours? Did he fall asleep? That was a possibility – after all he had been working a seventy-hour week for some time now. But if he'd fallen asleep on his patient, he would have woken him up, wouldn't he?

'I, erm . . . Perhaps a coffee?' He gazed beseechingly at Donna.

# Chapter 2

At the funeral of Mrs Enid Brown, for many years a valued member of the meat products spillage and disposal team at the local Tesco, Stalin and Trotsky were arguing – again. As the mourners filed out of the church and Enid herself sat patiently on a tomb, the two revolutionaries stood amongst the gravestones, hurling insults at each other.

'If you hadn't betrayed the revolution, Russia could have had a communist system that would have been an example to the world! Instead of which, what did we end up with? A self-serving bureaucracy which only gave the capitalists fuel in their war against us!' Trotsky yelled.

'Did you really think that the demoralized and un-educated Russian peasantry could have stepped straight out of the fields, with earth still clinging to their finger-nails, and taken over the reins of government? Live in the real world, Leon. Bureaucracy may be a bourgeois inven-tion, but it was necessary to the goal of maximizing production, which, as even Lenin would admit, is the starting point of socialism.'

'But what Comrade Lenin did not advocate was using the bureaucracy to line the pockets of a political elite!'

'Nor did he advocate flabby thinking and a rose-tinted view of the proletariat!'

'I'm sorry to interrupt, gentlemen,' said Enid, 'but I'm assuming you've come to take me on to wherever it is I'm to go, so . . . could we get going, please?'

The two revolutionaries turned and looked at her.

'Do you mind?' Trotsky barked. 'We're having a serious discussion here!'

Stalin's breast pocket began to play the Internationale. 'Excuse me.' He reached inside his jacket and pulled out a phone. 'Comrade Stalin speaking . . . Have we really? . . . Right away . . . Yes, and you too!' He put the phone back in his pocket. 'Head Office. We're late. We're to take the old woman back straight away or face the consequences.'

'What could be worse than this?' Trotsky moaned. 'Doomed to spend eternity with you.'

'Come on,' Stalin growled. 'Grab hold of the old crone.'

'Charming,' said Enid as the two men linked arms with her.

'You know, Leon,' said Stalin, 'instead of arguing amongst ourselves, shouldn't we be galvanizing the workers into a revolutionary force for change? Remember the heady days of 1917?'

Trotsky looked wistful for a moment, then shook his head. 'In 1917 we merely rode the crest of a wave; revolution was everywhere. The situation has changed: apathy rules. We'd never be able to stir this lot to anything approaching such a pitch.'

Another figure appeared as if from nowhere, his smartly tailored cashmere coat seeming rather flashy in comparison to the drab outfits of the two communists.

'Gentlemen, I couldn't help overhearing your discussion. Do you think I could have a word?'

'And who might you be?' Enid asked.

'Just a friend. Now, Leon, Joe – can I call you Joe?' Stalin shrugged.

'Good. I understand you're in a hurry, so perhaps we can talk as we walk?'

After a decidedly shaky but thankfully easy morning – three loose crowns, a fitting for replacement dentures, a couple of broken fillings and a particularly juicy buccal occlusion – Martin decided that he needed a settling lunchtime pint.

There was the usual bustling crowd in the pub on Cathedral Yard, the narrow street running along one side of the patch of green in front of Exeter cathedral, and Martin had to fight to get inside. With the judicious use of his elbows, he battled his way to the bar and, after several fruitless attempts, eventually managed to catch the barmaid's eye. Cradling his hard-won pint of Otter, he scythed his way back through the crush and re-emerged into the summer sunshine. With a sigh, he sat down on the wall around the cathedral precinct and took a long draught. Drinking in the middle of the day was asking for trouble, especially in his fragile condition, but these were exceptional circumstances. *It certainly couldn't hurt*, Martin thought. And he was right: the beer instantly soothed his troubled mind, softening the jagged edges of his morning experience. *I'm not losing my mind*, he told himself, *I'm just tired*.

The final event which had figuratively driven Martin over the edge, and literally very nearly done the same thing, had been Helen's exit with her parents back to their bungalow outside Rock. This had left him feeling dizzily unstable and, without his wife to perform her usual function of existential counterbalance, the Martin Gray cardigan had completely unravelled – although he had to admit it was a relief not to have to listen to her father's reactionary ideas, such as introducing limb amputation for double parking.

John, Helen's father, cut a terrifying figure: he had a stiff leg, wore an eyepatch and liked to call his injuries 'war wounds', giving the impression he'd received them serving in the Falklands War. But Martin knew the truth: the nearest John Sullivan had ever been to the South Atlantic was the penguin enclosure in London Zoo. Martin knew the real reason for his injuries, but Helen had made him promise never to divulge this to anyone, least of all her father. Her mother too had a skeleton in the closet, but the mere mention of it would have been grounds for divorce.

Martin took another sip of his pint and looked around at the bodies sprawling over the green, basking in the summer sunshine. He couldn't quite believe that this morning he'd been about to kill himself, to '*end the heartache and the thousand natural shocks that flesh is heir to*'.

He'd been a dentist for nearly twenty years and studied his profession for five years before that, but after a drink it was never, surprisingly, chunks of dental surgery textbooks that came to mind, detailing the correct use of gingival margin trimmers or the properties of zinc polycarboxylate cement, but always lyrical passages from his A-level English syllabus, usually Shakespeare.

The beer carried on working its magic. '*And all the clouds that lour'd upon*' Martin's '*house*' began to lift. Draining his pint, he stared hard at the frothy residue clinging to the inside of the glass. His reasoning was that if one pint could make him feel this much better, two would make him feel marvellous. But claiming a refill would mean a bruising return to the bar. *'Stiffen the sinews, summon up the blood, disguise fair nature with hard-favoured rage . . .'*

'Can I get you another?'

Martin looked up into a pair of sky-blue eyes, the eyes of the man who'd been in his chair that morning.

'You!' he said, leaping up.

The man smiled, revealing his perfect teeth. 'All my own.'

'I know. Where the bloody hell did you go?'

'I'd accomplished what I'd set out to do, so I left.'

'You'd accomplished what?'

'I'd stopped you from taking *"arms against a sea of troubles"*, if you like, as we seem to be in a Shakespearean mood.'

Martin's jaw dropped open.

'Look,' said the man, 'we need to talk. Let me get you another and then we can discuss this in a calm and civilized manner.'

Before Martin could protest, the man had taken his glass and disappeared into the crowded bar. Moments later he reappeared, carrying two full pints. 'Take, enjoy.'

'How did you do that? It takes me ages to get served at lunchtime – well, any time, really.'

'I've been at this game a long time. Cheers!'

They drank. Martin could feel the beer flooding through his system, bringing joy to all parts.

'So, what is your "game" exactly? And how do you know what I was doing this morning?' Martin asked.

The man extended a hand. 'Forgive me, I haven't introduced myself. I'm Gabriel.'

Martin took it. 'Gabriel? Gabriel what?'

'Just Gabriel.'

'Like the angel?'

'Precisely. Look, we may not have a lot of time—'

'Who are you?'

'Just someone who wants to help.'

Martin was feeling distinctly uneasy.

'Do you know the film *It's a Wonderful Life*?' the man asked.

'Ye-es.'

'Well, if you think of yourself as Jimmy Stewart and me as Clarence you'll get the idea.'

Martin frowned. 'Clarence was an angel who prevented the Jimmy Stewart character from committing suicide.'

'Exactly. It's one of God's favourite films; we watch it every Christmas. He's also a great admirer of the work of Powell and Pressburger. He considers *A Matter of Life and Death* a masterpiece, but feels *The Red Shoes* is a bit of a disappointment.'

Martin felt the hairs on the back of his neck stand on end. Maybe the beer hadn't been such a good idea after all. He put down his pint and began to rise. 'Look, it's been very nice, but I really must go.'

'I know what you're thinking, but you're not mad, and neither am I. How did I know what you were up to this morning? If it helps, you can even call me Clarence.'

Martin shook his head vaguely. 'It . . . I don't think . . . er . . .' He was losing it. He was hallucinating, that was it. This figure didn't exist, it was merely a projection of his unconscious mind brought on by extreme stress. In reality he was sitting on this wall talking to himself. He had often seen drunks and mad people doing the same thing, attracting the pitying glances of passers-by. Martin closed his eyes and opened them again, but Gabriel was still there.

'No, you're not hallucinating,' Gabriel said softly.

Gabriel laid a hand tenderly on Martin's knee – it felt disturbingly real.

'Martin, believe me, I *am* the Angel Gabriel, and I'm here to help, if I can.'

'But . . .but . . .'

'But I also want you to do something for me. Finish your pint and let's go for a walk.'

Martin felt a strange emptiness in his stomach. If he hadn't been feeling quite so deranged in the first place – from that classic trio: worry, lack of sleep and alcohol – he might have fought harder but, as it was, he didn't have the strength. He let himself be led across the green and into the cool half-light of the cathedral.

As the pair of them strolled around the great religious edifice, Gabriel talked. Martin didn't really listen – he couldn't, his mind was in too much turmoil – but he let the angel's calm, mellifluous voice roll over him nonetheless. Gabriel was a comforting presence: over six feet tall with a wide, open face and startlingly blue eyes that looked like the sky. Like his teeth, his skin was blemish free, and his hair was as spun gold. The only slightly strange thing about his appearance was that he was wearing an ankle-length raincoat, and this was a warm dry day.

Eventually some of what Gabriel was saying broke through into Martin's consciousness. 'Just a minute,' he interrupted.

Gabriel looked down at him. 'Yes?'

'You just said, "the Devil's bet with God".'

Gabriel nodded. 'That's right. The Devil made a bet with God that mankind would destroy the earth.'

'You're saying that God made a bet with the Devil?' Martin was aghast.

'Well, strictly speaking it was the other way round, but it amounts to much the same thing.'

'God made a bet with the Devil?' Martin repeated.

'Don't you think this conversation is becoming a bit one-dimensional?'

'Does God often hang out with the lord of the under-world?' Martin spluttered.

'Not if he can help it, but the situation is quite difficult for the Almighty. He and Lucifer used to be very close, you see, and although he was quite justified in doing what he did, all the same it's not easy for him.'

'But gambling? Isn't that supposed to be some sort of sin?'

'This was a special circumstance – provocation beyond endurance.'

'I thought God was supposed to be above such things?'

'Normally, yes, but he was feeling rather put out that day.'

'Put out?'

'The Devil had spoiled the party: Adam and Eve's coming out. Then he had the nerve to challenge the deity to this bet. God couldn't refuse, of course, not in front of all his guests; he would have lost face.'

Martin held up his hands. 'Stop! Just stop!'

A nearby party of Japanese tourists who had been admiring the ornately carved Pulpitum Screen all turned to look.

'I'd never pictured God with a guilt complex and a fragile ego,' Martin continued in a hoarse whisper. 'You make him sound like everybody I know. Next you'll be telling me that he shops at Tesco.'

'Waitrose.'

'What?'

'Only kidding.' Gabriel put an arm around Martin. 'Look, I know this is very difficult for you, but you have to believe me,' he said gently.

Martin narrowed his eyes and looked into Gabriel's open face. 'You really are an angel?'

Gabriel glanced up and down the cathedral nave. 'Come in here,' he said, beckoning Martin towards the chapel of St Edmund the Martyr. 'Nice chap, Edmund, as long as you don't get him onto the subject of his execution. He will insist on giving you all the gory details.'

Stepping into the empty chapel, Gabriel unbuttoned his long raincoat and handed it to Martin. Underneath he was naked save for a small loincloth to preserve his modesty. He turned his back slowly to Martin.

'Ah!' Martin gasped at what he saw. Two large white wings, like those of a swan, sprouted from Gabriel's shoulder blades. They were folded close to his body, the points reaching almost to his ankles – hence the mac.

'You . . . you . . . you . . .' Martin stammered.

'Yes,' Gabriel said, turning back to face him. 'You want to see more?' Without waiting for Martin's reply, the angel unfurled his magnificent pinions, and with several powerful beats, which whipped up the dust and billowed the altar cloth, began to rise into the air.

'All right, all right!' Martin hissed. 'I believe you, I believe you!'

Gabriel descended gently to earth and took back his raincoat. 'Now will you help me?'

*

Once settled into the comfortable sofa in the window of the Carved Angel – a cafe overlooking the cathedral and the pigeon-streaked statue of Richard Hooker – Gabriel and Martin continued their conversation.

'So, why me?' Martin asked, when their coffee and cakes had arrived.

'You have nothing to lose.' Gabriel took a sip of his vanilla latte. 'Luckily for us, you decided to take your life at exactly the right time.'

'You've got froth on your upper lip,' Martin informed him.

'Oh, thank you.' The angel wiped his mouth with a paper napkin.

'What do you mean: "exactly the right time"?'

Gabriel put down his coffee and gazed earnestly into Martin's face. 'We think the Devil's up to something. Word at the Interface is he's trying something big.'

'The Interface?'

'The Universal Life–Death Interface: the entrances to Heaven and Hell.'

Martin looked puzzled.

'The gateways to Paradise and eternal torment are side by side, so snippets of news about what's happening down below sometimes cross the divide.'

'Oh.'

The idea of collaboration between angels and devils was a new one on Martin.

'The thing is,' Gabriel continued, 'if Satan is preparing something it would be very timely. You've heard about the Slapton-Azimuth comet?' Gabriel asked.

Martin frowned. 'No.'

'It's a theoretical body, posited by Sir Henry Slapton, the astronomer, to explain the slight wobble in the orbits of the outermost planets of the solar system. No one has actually seen the comet because they've never known exactly where to look, but Sir Henry's theory is about to be proved right. The Slapton-Azimuth comet is hurtling back towards earth and will make its reappearance in the next week or so in the constellation Cygnus.

Martin shook his head. 'I don't understand.'

Gabriel leaned a little closer. 'If astronomers were to analyse the comet's make-up they'd be shocked to find traces of Havana tobacco leaf and Cambozola.'

Suddenly Martin understood. 'It's the one the Devil launched back in the Garden of Eden!'

Gabriel nodded and settled back in the sofa, cradling his coffee.

'But if you know all this, why do you need me?'

'We're not allowed to interfere in the affairs of men.'

'What?'

'Strict instructions from himself. God has to be seen to be occupying the moral high ground and is scrupulously adhering to the terms of non-interference in the bet.'

'But *you're* here.'

'In an unofficial capacity. If God found out he wouldn't be pleased.'

Martin frowned. 'But he'll know, surely. I thought he was supposed to be everywhere.'

'Not since he took up golf.'

Martin nearly choked on a piece of candied apricot. 'God plays golf?'

Gabriel spooned some froth from the top of his latte and slurped it noisily. 'Mmhmm. He's forever striding down the celestial fairway, whacking little white balls around – it's become an obsession.' He put down his spoon and sighed. 'Another problem is that God thinks he's already won.'

'How come?'

'He's sure the Devil doesn't have any time left to do anything now.' Gabriel looked gravely into Martin's eyes. 'I'm worried. The thing is, God won't listen to me any more; he thinks I'm just being paranoid, so I'm afraid the fate of the earth is up to people like you.'

Martin blinked. 'Me?'

'You see, although God may always play fair, the Devil, being the Devil, is not above bending the rules slightly from time to time. Throughout history he's recruited people on earth to do his bidding, so determined is he to win the bet.'

'Who?' Martin asked.

'I beg your pardon?'

'Who has the Devil recruited?'

'Oh, all sorts. Hitler was a biggie.'

'Wow. So the Devil really *was* behind the Second World War?'

'Oh yes. Conflict was one of his earliest ideas. He started small with sticks and stones, but he's been upping the ante ever since: gunpowder, atomic fission, Chelsea fans . . . It's been a steady progression.' Gabriel picked up a discarded *Telegraph* from a nearby table. 'He's also introduced all manner of subtle torments into the world. Envy was one of his, taxes another. And he was extremely pleased with mortgages, which he swiftly followed with interest rate rises. It's all about sowing discontent. Open a newspaper these days and you'd be hard-pressed not to find some new thing with which Satan is trying to torture poor old mankind.' Gabriel scanned the inside of the

*Telegraph*. 'Ah, here we are – "Anger at Speed Camera Hidden in Hedge".'

'I thought he must be behind them,' Martin murmured.

'And then there are mobile phones, pair-trawling, reality TV . . . The list is endless. And of course he's managed to keep the Middle East simmering away nicely for centuries. But whatever he's tried has not had the desired effect: of completely trashing the planet. So far, reason has always prevailed – look at the Cold War. For a while it looked as though Satan might have found the answer with pollution, but then along came recycling. Global warming is another of his, but it's a very slow process and he has only days left. And, as God still maintains, man, created in his image, will always pull himself back from the brink.'

'So, what's the problem?' asked Martin. 'The comet's about to reappear – time's almost up. The Devil *has* lost, hasn't he?'

'It's not over till it's over. Satan has always had an overdeveloped sense of the dramatic and may just be biding his time. Making one final throw of the dice at the eleventh hour would be just his style. We have to be more watchful than ever. Now is the danger time.'

Something didn't make sense to Martin. 'But if the Devil's been interfering in the affairs of man, that's cheating.'

Gabriel shrugged. 'He's the Devil.'

'Yes, but he's contravened the terms of the bet, so surely it's null and void?'

Gabriel finished his cinnamon swirl and took another sip of coffee before replying. 'It's a moot point. The thing is, it could be argued that by using human agents he hasn't interfered directly. To be honest, Heaven hasn't been completely kosher, either. Strictly speaking, I shouldn't be talking to you.' Gabriel eyed Martin's half-eaten apricot Danish. 'Have you finished with that?'

'Er, yes.' Martin slid the plate towards him.

'Thanks.' Gabriel devoured the sticky pastry in two bites. 'I love the food they do here,' he mumbled, covering Martin in crumbs.

There was a lull in the conversation while the archangel savoured the last of Martin's Danish. Eventually he swallowed, then washed it down with the rest of his coffee. Wiping his mouth with his napkin, he turned to Martin and fixed him with his sky-blue eyes. 'The point is, Martin, we need you. What I'm asking you to get involved in is extremely dangerous, but as you've already gone so far as to want to end it all anyway . . .'

'You thought I might be prepared to take a risk?'

Gabriel smiled. 'I knew you'd understand.'

'But what can *I* do? I don't know anything about anything – I'm a dentist.'

'Exactly – you deal with people all the time. Listen to them, and keep your eyes and ears open for anything . . . strange.'

'That's it?'

'That's it. Well we do have *something*, but it's not much.'

'What?'

'One word: *Endgame*. No one seems to know what it means, not even the poor soul we got it from.'

'*Endgame*? That's a Samuel Beckett play – I studied it for English A level.'

'Yes, but I believe it also refers to the closing stages of a chess game.'

'And this came through the Interface?'

'Yes. Of course it could be nothing; things that get passed around the Interface tend to get rather garbled, a bit like Chinese whispers.' Gabriel smiled. 'Now I must be going. If you need me, just call.'

Martin glanced down at his watch. It read ten past one, but that was impossible, he'd started his lunch break at one and they must have been sitting here in the cafe for at least half an hour. He looked up sharply at the place on the sofa where Gabriel had just been and found himself staring at an empty cushion. He searched the cafe, but the angel was nowhere to be seen. He was once again tempted to dismiss the whole thing as an hallucination, until he called the waitress over only to be informed that the bill had already been paid.

'By that nice tall man.'

Martin staggered to his feet and walked unsteadily out into the sunshine, his mind whirring with possibilities. He'd been talking to an angel. His rational mind was reluctant to accept the fact, but what other explanation could there be for the compression of time, the paid bill?

Admittedly, the vision of Heaven that Martin had glimpsed from Gabriel was hardly the traditional view, but it was its very originality which supported its authenticity. Martin was sure that not even his fevered brain could come up with a version of the creator of the universe as a golf-mad film buff who took bets with whoever happened to challenge his fragile ego.

In a strange, dreamlike state after his meeting with Gabriel, Martin headed back to the surgery through the crowded streets, seeing angels and demons wherever he looked.

*

Frank Sinatra and Peter Lawford sat on the steps of the Albert Memorial Museum and watched him pass.

Sinatra shook his head. 'It's not going to happen.'

'For once I agree with you,' said Lawford. 'We could end up trailing this guy for months.'

'I'm not talking about this guy; I'm talking about Jimmy. He'll never pull it off.'

'Oh.' Lawford pondered a moment. 'I don't know though. After all, it's a good idea.'

'Since when have you been a champion of the people?' At that moment, Sinatra's phone rang. 'Just a minute,' he said, pulling it out of his breast pocket. 'Yeah? . . . Well if he had we'd have brought him in, wouldn't we? . . . Thanks for nothing.' He put the phone away and turned to Lawford. 'They're calling us back in. Apparently this guy's been rescheduled.'

Back at the surgery, Martin looked in on reception and was disconcerted, but not surprised, to see the burly figure of Gifford Wilkinson going through the appointments register with Donna.

'Oh, God,' he groaned.

Donna looked up as Martin came in.

'I'm sorry, Martin, but he insisted.'

'That's all right, Donna.' He gave her a wan smile.

Gifford Wilkinson was a large, unpleasant man with close-cropped hair, who was fiercely proud of his reputation as one of Her Majesty's Inland Revenue's hard men. Wolverhampton-born to strictly Catholic parents, he was the seventh of nine children, but despite his extensive knowledge of the Gospel, beaten into him by his abusive father, Gifford was far from sympathetic, seeming instead to take a perverse pleasure in his victims' distress.

Martin's only defence in the face of such a nastily persistent enemy was to make fun of him behind his back, and so he had secretly christened him Revenue Ranger, kitting him out in his imagination as a superhero, complete with eye mask, flowing cape and bright yellow underpants. Martin tried to visualize him now, standing by the reception desk in full costume.

'What a lot of patients you've got, Mr Gray,' said Revenue Ranger, his fictional cape flapping in some imagined breeze. 'How much do you charge for an appointment?'

Martin sighed. What little joy the superhero image afforded him was fading rapidly. 'You know very well how much I charge. Donna, give him another tariff sheet.'

Donna opened a drawer and handed the man a piece of paper, but he waved it away.

'No, I want to hear it from you, Mr Gray.' He fixed his small eyes on Martin. 'I want to hear from the horse's mouth exactly how much you are fleecing each of your patients.'

Martin groaned. 'I do not "fleece" my patients. Compare my charges with any other dentist in town and you'll find they're about average.'

Gifford's eyes widened. '*About* average? That sounds a little vague, Mr Gray. And I like things to be neat and tidy and precise. Above all, precise.'

'Look,' Martin snapped. 'I have given you complete access to my books. I have nothing to hide; you can see for yourself how much I charge. I'm a dentist, not an accountant!'

'That's self-evident from your books. I've already found several errors.' The joy this had given Gifford was palpable. 'You and I are going to have to sit down and go through your accounts, item by item.' He gave Martin a tight, reptilian smile.

Martin's legs finally gave way and he flopped into a chair. 'But I . . . I don't have time for that. I barely have time to sleep. I'm very busy at the moment . . .'

'You need to organize your time a little better, Mr Gray. I know how difficult it is for your sort, what with all the holidays, lunches and tennis tournaments you have to fit in, but from the look of you, I'd say you'd benefit from dropping a few patients. But then that would mean taking a cut in salary, and I doubt very much that would appeal.'

What did appeal to Martin was the idea of performing leisurely root canal surgery on Gifford Wilkinson with dirty instruments and without anaesthetic. Instead he closed his eyes and imagined Revenue Ranger streaking away across the sky in his canary-yellow underpants.

'I'll leave you to think it over. You've got my number; give me a call to let me know when would be a convenient time for us to go through the figures. Any time's good for me; Her Majesty's Inland Revenue never sleep.'

Martin quietly gnashed his teeth.

Gifford picked up the appointments register and headed for the door with it.

'Um, excuse me,' said Donna. 'Where are you going with that?'

'It's part of my investigation.'

'But that's got all our appointments in it,' she protested.

'I should hope so; that's what an appointments book is for.'

'But if you take that we won't know who's coming in.'

'You should always back up your data,' Gifford replied smugly.

'Don't try and teach me my job,' Donna replied sharply. 'For your information every appointment is entered on the computer.'

'Then you won't mind my taking your book.'

'But I haven't yet had a chance to log those appointments made this morning.'

'I'm sorry, but that's not my problem.'

Martin leapt up and blocked the door. 'How am I meant to survive when you are constantly interfering with my work?' he snarled.

'Try and prevent me from going about my legitimate business and it could have dire consequences for you, Mr Gray,' Gifford warned. 'If I feel like it I could have you apprehended and held indefinitely.'

'You can't do that. What about habeas corpus?' Martin yelled.

Gifford snorted disdainfully. 'This is the Inland Revenue you're dealing with, sunshine. We don't mess around.'

Martin let out a long, painful sigh and slumped against the wall, emitting a sound like water going down a plughole.

'I really think you're working too hard, Mr Gray,' said Gifford, pushing past him and walking out of the door.

# Chapter 3

Francis Drake and King Philip of Spain stood at the foot of Beachy Head.

'Jump! Come on, we haven't got all day, jump!' Drake called up to the would-be suicide poised on the very edge of the cliff.

'*Qué compasión,*'[1] King Philip muttered.

'What did you say? Why the hell can't you speak English?'

'*¿Inglés? ¿Crea que me mancharía los labios hablando la lenguaje de cerdos? Tuve que aguantar a un cerdo inglés basta malo.*'[2]

'God damn you, jump!' Drake called again.

'*Tiene paciencia como siempre. Bien sabe Dios como se había arreglado a terminar un juego de los bolos.*'[3]

'Will you shut up! Or at least speak in a language I can understand.'

'*La única lenguaje que entiende es de los bajos fondos. La corte entera de la reina, que se parece un reinona con una cara chupada, no era más de matónes y ladrónes. Y usted era peor*

---

1. 'Such sympathy.'
2. 'English? Do you think I'm going to soil my lips speaking the language of swine? It's bad enough being stuck with an English pig.'
3. 'Patient as ever. God knows how you ever managed to finish a game of bowls.'

*que nunca: un pirata autorizada. ¡Ah! ¿Maria, cómo habi-
amos perdido en contra de hombres por el estilo?*[4]

Francis Drake advanced menacingly on the king. 'If
you don't keep quiet, so help me, I'll—'

But at that moment, a figure in a cashmere coat
appeared between them.

'Frank, Phil, hi.'

Drake staggered backwards, amazed. 'Who are you?
What do you want?'

'Looks like your working relationship could do with
a little help. Maybe I can be of service.'

King Philip held out his hand. 'Pleased to meet you.'

Drake's eyes blazed. 'You *can* speak English! You vile
dissembling rogue!'

From above came a blood-curdling scream as Ben
Frimley, gas fitter and secret (and incredibly bad) poet,
whose wife had left him for her Open University tutor,
hurtled through the salt air to smash onto the pebbles
beside them, curtailing further argument.

'Look, guys,' said the man in the coat, 'I can see you're
busy. Perhaps you'd let me tag along and watch you
work?'

'Please yourself,' Drake snarled.

'Delighted to have your company,' King Philip said
graciously.

Drake yanked the bemused soul of Ben Frimley from
his body without ceremony and hefted it over his shoulder. 'Come on, scumbag.'

---

4. 'The only language you understand is that of the gutter. The whole court of
that hatchet-faced man in drag you called queen was made up of nothing but
thugs and thieves. And you were worst of all: a licensed pirate. Ah, Mary, how
did we lose against such men?'

Philip turned to the visitor in the coat. 'Such refinement. You see what I have to put up with?'

Martin Gray yawned and looked at his alarm clock – 7.20. The early morning light was peeping around the still-closed curtains, but he had another five minutes dozing time before he had to get up. He turned over and closed his eyes again. Then he sat up with a start. There was someone moving about downstairs in the kitchen. Instantly awake, he swung his legs out of the bed and stood up quickly. It was a mistake: his head was suddenly full of stars and he slumped to his hands and knees with a groan.

The door opened. 'I thought you'd be up by now.' It was his wife, Helen. She looked neat and summery in a linen dress, her blonde hair hanging loosely around her shoulders.

Martin looked up at her groggily. 'What are you doing here; I thought you'd taken my blessed in-laws back to their bungalow?'

'I came back to get some things. Why are you on the floor?'

'Life has brought me to my knees,' Martin said woozily.

'Nonsense, *you're* solely responsible for your situation,' Helen replied sharply.

'Thank you for your sympathy,' Martin replied, struggling to get up.

'Don't get up on my account.' Helen started going through the wardrobe, pulling out clothes and throwing them on the bed. 'I'm not staying; I can't leave Mum and Dad alone for too long.'

'Why not, don't they know how the kettle works?'

Helen ignored him.

Martin approached from behind and put his arms softly around her. 'Stay. I'll take the day off. We can go for lunch somewhere.' He nuzzled her neck. 'Just the two of us, like it used to be.'

Helen broke away. 'You just couldn't resist that, could you?'

'What have I done now?'

'You resented Mum and Dad's presence from the moment they set foot in this house.'

'I never mentioned them.'

'It's what you were thinking.'

'Look, I admit it wasn't easy sharing the house with Mr and Mrs Mussolini, but what I really objected to was them treating you like a skivvy.'

'They can't help being old.'

'They're *using* you!'

'No, they're simply hopeless at looking after themselves.'

'And I'm great at it, so you don't need to worry about me.'

'Now you're feeling sorry for yourself.'

'Yes, I'm feeling sorry for myself. My wife's deserted me in my hour of need!'

'It's not like that.'

'Well that's how it looks to me! Do you know, yesterday I even tried to—' But he stopped himself. He wasn't going to play the attempted suicide card, not yet anyway. He turned away and sat down on the edge of the bed.

Helen studied him closely. 'Tried to what?'

Martin shrugged. 'Nothing. All I'm saying is: a little sympathy wouldn't go amiss.'

Helen sat down next to him. 'I would be sympathetic, really I would, if you hadn't brought this upon yourself. Westerham offered you a way out.'

'Oh, not this again.'

'Yes, this again! I'm sure he'd still be willing to lend you some money.'

'So you're on his side now.'

'I'm not on anybody's side. I just don't see why you're putting yourself through all this when there's no need. But if you don't like the idea of asking Westerham, why not go and see his father? He might be able to give you a business loan.'

'Admitting to Westerham that I'm short of cash is bad enough; I am definitely not going cap in hand to some twisted old megalomaniac like Topsham Wilding. Do you think *all* the Wildings have daft names?'

Helen sighed irritably.

'I'm sure old man Wilding would offer me a very *reasonable* rate,' Martin continued. 'But then, that was how he made his fortune: moneylending.'

'He did no such thing; he was a City banker.'

'Is that rhyming slang?'

'Why can't you take this seriously!'

'I *am* taking it seriously! That's why I'm working a twenty-four-hour day! Look, I am not borrowing money from anybody. If I've made a mistake, I'll get myself out of it.'

Helen stood up sharply. 'And *we* can all go to hell!'

'*No!* That's not what I'm saying. Besides, the man's a gangster. If I ask him for a favour, one day he's going to come to me and ask me to do a little something for him in return – you've seen *The Godfather*. I wouldn't be surprised if he had me changing the teeth of corpses so they can't be recognized from their dental records.'

'You've got an overactive imagination.'

'All right, but you have to admit that Wilding senior is a little creepy.'

'He's just rich and successful. You've always been frightened of success.'

'I am *not* frightened of success!' Martin screamed, leaping from the bed indignantly. 'I just want to practise dentistry – I'm good at it! I enjoy it! Unlike Westerham, I actually care!'

'Hi, Dad.' Luke was standing in the doorway.

Martin suddenly became aware that he'd been bounding wildly around the bedroom in his underpants. He suddenly felt rather exposed. 'Oh, hello, Luke. Your mother and I were just—'

'Having a little chat.' Luke smiled without mirth. 'Yeah, I heard. I suspect the whole of Dartmoor heard.'

'All right, that's enough!' Martin snapped.

Luke shrugged and left the room.

'What's the matter with him?'

Helen looked at him incredulously. 'I suggest it's time you started to find out. I've told him he's staying here with you.'

'With me? I thought he'd be keen to join the surfing crowd in Rock. No, I don't think that's such a good idea.'

'Why not? This *is* his home and you *are* his father, despite your efforts to distance yourself from that responsibility.'

'But I'm busy. What am I supposed to do with him?'

'You don't have to *do* anything with him; he won't be expecting you to change the habits of a lifetime. He'll be quite happy sitting in his room with his computer.'

'I can't leave him here alone all day.'

'He's eighteen years old and quite capable of looking after himself. He's a much better cook than you.'

'But—'

'He's staying here.' Helen fixed him with a stare that could have bored through two-inch steel plate and Martin knew he was beaten.

The truth was, Helen was worried about Martin's state of mind and wanted Luke to stay around to keep an eye on him.

'I'll phone later on in the week.' She gathered up the clothes she'd laid on the bed and left the room.

Martin was alone again. He caught sight of himself in the mirror on the back of the open wardrobe door. He looked pale and flabby, his belly just beginning to overflow the waistband of his underpants. 'You got problems, kid.'

The hunched figure shuffled into the back of the church and slumped, sobbing quietly, in a pulpit near the font. Eschewing the hassock, he fell to his knees on the cold, hard floor, clasped his hands tightly together and prayed fervently for redemption.

The vicar, who was in the vestry, heard the man's muffled sobs echoing through the empty church and peeped out through a crack in the door. Seeing the lone figure huddled at the back of the church, he was gripped by a vague sense of dread. *Damn*, he thought, *another tramp, probably come in to sleep off a surfeit of cheap cider. Leave the door open for five minutes and the place fills up with the bloody homeless*. He looked at his watch. He had a christening this morning – a nice, young executive couple and their new baby; they'd be here any minute.

Tutting irritably, he opened the door wide and lifted his cassock to negotiate the steps down to the nave. As he neared the crumpled figure, the vicar's sense of dread increased and he suddenly felt very cold. The man seemed to be surrounded by a buzzing swarm of unease which was almost tangible.

'Can I help you?' the vicar enquired.

The man raised his tear-stained face to the churchman. 'No,' he said pitifully. 'No one can.'

The vicar immediately recognized the man's face; he'd seen it countless times, smiling out from the covers of a thousand tabloid newspapers. 'But you're . . . you're that businessman. The one with all the yachts . . . Garth Ferrers! That is you, isn't it?'

Garth nodded silently.

'Are you . . . in trouble?'

Garth laughed at the question, but the laughter soon died in his throat and he resumed his pitiful sobbing.

The vicar couldn't for the life of him imagine what sort of trouble a multimillionaire businessman might be in. A lost wallet, perhaps? He dismissed the idea immediately. Perhaps, as a consequence of his much-publicized womanizing, Garth had given himself an unpleasant disease. But neither of these scenarios seemed to explain the depth of suffering the man was obviously enduring. However, that wasn't really the vicar's problem right now – he had a service to perform and this blubbing millionaire was in the way. A baptism was supposed to be a happy event; he doubted the family would appreciate this wretched individual snivelling all over their baby, even if he was famous.

'Um, I'm due to perform a christening here in a few minutes,' the vicar began, looking pointedly at his watch, 'and as it's a private service, unless you are a relation or a friend of the family, I'm afraid I'm going to have to ask you to leave.'

'I see. "So shall it be at the end of the world: the angels shall sever the wicked from the just, and shall cast them into the furnace of fire: there shall be wailing and gnashing of teeth."'

The vicar was a little taken aback at having Matthew 13, verses 49 to 50 quoted at him. 'Er . . . oh . . . um, you're welcome to come back later if you'd like to have a chat. I'm free after lunch.'

Garth looked at the vicar with vacant eyes. 'It's no use. There's nothing you can do.' He stood up shakily. 'Don't worry, I won't spoil your service.'

The vicar watched Garth Ferrers, millionaire playboy – a man with everything – trudge hopelessly out of the church and into the sudden, bright light of the Plymouth day.

# Chapter 4

'You can stay here, in reception, as long as you don't get in Donna's way,' Martin instructed Luke when they reached the surgery.

'OK if I breathe?' Luke asked.

'Don't be facetious.'

'He'll be fine,' said Donna.

'Look.' Martin indicated a stack of ancient magazines on a small table. 'There's a whole stack of garbage there you can work your way through.'

Luke threw his hands in the air in simulated delight. 'Wow, Dad, you're just too good to me!'

Martin grabbed him roughly by the arm and shoved him into a corner, out of earshot of Donna. 'I'm really, really stressed at the moment, understand? So be nice, or I may do something I might regret.'

Luke regarded him coolly. 'Like what? Act like a human being?'

A red mist floated up in front of Martin's eyes, but this sudden *whoosh* of anger was too much for his overworked system. Stars ringed his vision and he leaned against the wall to stop himself from falling.

For once, Luke looked concerned. 'Er, Dad?'

'Just . . . just . . . just a minute.' Using the wall for

support, Martin groped his way along it until he found a chair, then collapsed into it.

Donna filled a plastic cup from the water cooler and handed it to him. 'Here, drink this.'

'Thanks.' Martin took it and drained it. Breathing deeply, he wiped his mouth and looked up. 'I'm fine, really.'

'Do you want an aspirin or something?'

'No, no. Could you make me a coffee?'

'Of course. You're sure there's nothing else you want?'

Martin nodded. 'I'm sure. Just caffeine – lots of it. Is Vicky here yet?'

'Yes, she's already in there.'

'Right, well, I'd better go in and make a start.'

'Why don't you sit there for a minute, until you feel more yourself?'

'No, no . . . I'm fine,' Martin said vaguely, standing and staggering towards his surgery.

Donna watched as he went in and closed the door behind him. She turned to Luke, who was still rooted to the spot. 'He works too hard.'

'Mmh,' Luke muttered, then pulled out his phone and started tapping away at its tiny keyboard while Donna started fiddling with the coffee machine.


Dentistry at least was a place where Martin could get away from his worries. He spent the morning lost in his work: mining glittering root canals and wandering like a marvelling tourist through cavernous buccal occlusions.

By lunchtime he was feeling much more himself, and resolved to try and be a little more open and understanding with his son.

'OK then, Luke. Where do you fancy for lunch?'

Luke finished the text message he was tapping into his phone before looking up. 'Yeah?' he said challengingly.

'Lunch,' Martin repeated, miming putting something into his mouth. 'Something to eat?'

'Oh,' said Luke at last. 'How about the pub?'

Martin hoped that sharing the sacred mysteries of the lunchtime pub visit would bring them closer together. 'Good idea.'

The pub on the green was crowded, as usual, and Martin wished that Gabriel was around to perform his heavenly trick of catching the barmaid's eye. 'What'll you have?' Martin asked.

'Brandy and Coke,' Luke replied.

'Ah, er . . . I can't say I really approve of a young lad like you drinking spirits in the middle of the day.'

'A young lad like me?' Luke scoffed. 'Mum always buys me a brandy.'

'I must have words with her.'

'Another nice friendly chat, like this morning's?'

Things were already going wrong. Martin looked at his son long and hard. 'I'll get you a pint.'

Luke looked skywards and uttered a sound like a braying horse.

'Take it or leave it,' Martin said.

'All right.' Luke scowled.

A quarter of an hour later Martin reappeared from the crowded bar, and father and son sat down on the grass in the sunshine with their drinks. 'Cheers, Luke.'

'Whatever.'

They drank.

'So,' said Martin, simulating blokeish bonhomie,

'how's life? We don't really get a chance to talk much these days.'

'We never did. Besides, we never see each other, now Mum's left you.'

Martin sighed. 'She hasn't "left" me; we're just giving each other some space, that's all.'

'I'm never getting married.' Luke shuddered.

Martin took several thirst-quenching gulps of the cool, bitter-sweet beer before replying. 'You know,' he said at last, 'when your mother and I first fell in love, we couldn't bear to be apart for a moment. We spent all our time together talking, holding hands, laughing. And when we weren't together we were thinking about each other. Now, in spite of appearances to the contrary, we still feel the same. We may fight and hurt each other from time to time, but I'm still crazy about her, and I know she still loves me. And that's what it's all about. Without her I feel like half a person. That's what happens when you find "the one": you complete each other. I hope it happens to you.' Martin finished with a wistful smile and took another sip of beer.

Luke sniffed sceptically. 'Well if she's still so crazy about you, why's she been going out with Westerham?'

Martin felt as though he'd been punched in the stomach. 'Westerham?' he asked in a small voice.

'Yeah,' Luke replied. 'He took us all out in his Jag the other day – it's really, really quick.'

Martin felt sick, and although his legs had gone strangely numb, he had a pressing need to stand up. He urged himself to his feet and stood shakily above his son, feeling like a newborn wildebeest on out-of-control matchstick legs.

Luke looked up at him. He knew he'd said something

he shouldn't have and he also knew it was too late to take it back. He waited for Martin to say something.

'I . . . I . . . I'm . . .' Martin turned and wandered off across the green, leaving Luke with the awful feeling he'd broken something that had no hope of ever being repaired.


After vacantly wandering the streets for the rest of his lunch break, Martin reappeared at the surgery wearing a strangely glazed expression. Working his way through his post-lunch appointments in a daze, suddenly, halfway through the afternoon, something in him snapped. Calmly putting down his drill, he took off his mask and removed his rubber gloves.

'Excuse me, Mr Walkington,' he said to the bemused patient in his chair, 'I've just got to go and rip someone's head off.'

Stalking angrily into reception, he ignored his son sitting contritely in the corner. 'Where is he?' he barked at Donna.

'Where's who?'

'That marriage breaker Westerham.'

Donna's face crumpled into a frown. 'He's still at lunch, why?'

Martin looked at his watch. 'Half past bloody three and he's still at lunch?' He turned and headed for the door.

Donna came out from behind the reception desk. 'Where are you going, Martin?'

'No more Mr Nice Guy,' Martin muttered darkly, slamming the door behind him.

Donna looked questioningly at Luke, but he turned quickly away.

Martin knew where Westerham would be: his club, situated in the select seclusion of the cathedral grounds. But as he entered the quadrant, Gabriel appeared in front of him.

'Get out of my way,' Martin snarled.

'This isn't going to do any good, you know,' Gabriel warned.

'You're wrong there. It's going to do *me* a power of good, but I can't say the same for Westerham.'

'Well, on your own head be it.'

'Suits me!'

Martin reached the small, unprepossessing door of the private club and rang the bell. The door was opened by an ancient, white-haired attendant.

'Yes? May I ask your business, sir?'

'Murder,' Martin replied, pushing past the old man and striding into the building. Ignoring the attendant's protests, Martin followed the sound of jolly conversation down a corridor and soon came to a vaulted dining hall. In the centre, at a long refectory table still littered with half-finished puddings and the craterous remains of a Stilton, he saw his quarry. Westerham sat amongst his friends, entertaining them with an amusing anecdote.

Although short of stature, Westerham was good-looking in an obvious sort of way. Martin deeply resented his even teeth, square chin and carefully coiffed hair; it was all too perfect. He found it hard to imagine how any woman, let alone one with a brain like Helen's, could possibly fall for this manufactured creature with his expensive suits and year-round tan.

He looked up when his colleague marched into the room.

'Oh, Martin,' he said unsurely, 'I didn't know you were a member.'

'I'm not a fucking member,' came the growled reply.

'Er . . . oh.'

Martin noted with dark delight that Westerham looked somewhat discomposed. 'You've been screwing my wife!' he boomed.

'Do you know this fellow?' somebody asked.

'So, what's it to be?' Martin stalked slowly round the table, never taking his eyes off the small man until he was standing right behind him. 'Are you coming outside or am I going to kill you right here?'

Westerham gazed helplessly at his lunch companions. 'Look, it's not what you think, Martin. Can't we discuss this in a civilized manner?'

'No!' Martin screamed. 'You are going to pay for ruining my life!'

Westerham smiled. 'You've got it all wrong, you know,' he said smoothly.

'I don't think so.' Martin yanked back Westerham's chair, depositing the little man on the floor. Pulling him to his feet by the throat, Martin was just about to punch him in the incisors when one of the other guests intervened.

'Put him down! You're twice his size!'

'You're right,' Martin replied. 'Let's even things up a bit.' Taking an ever firmer grip on Westerham's neck, Martin yanked him up and stood him on his chair. 'There, that better?' Before anyone could say anything, Martin's fist had crashed into his jaw. Westerham went down like a sack of laundry, collapsing onto the table and scattering glasses of vintage port.

'That felt good!' Martin exulted. 'Get up; I want to do it again!'

Westerham gurgled something incomprehensible and stayed where he was.

'All right, then, have it your way.' Martin leapt onto the table and straddled his colleague, pounding his head into the remains of a spotted dick while the hapless man attempted, unsuccessfully, to defend himself with his small, manicured hands. But the club servants soon came to Westerham's aid. Martin was lifted bodily off the table, dragged, raving, to the door and deposited outside.

Gabriel was waiting for him in the street. 'So, what did that accomplish?'

'It made me feel better,' Martin replied, removing a lump of cheese from his ear.

'Bravo. You've also got treacle tart on your tie.'

'Thank you.' Martin licked a finger and wiped it off.

'So that's how you solve all your arguments, is it?'

'You wouldn't understand – you lot are all for turning the other cheek.'

Gabriel nodded. 'It makes life less complicated – there's no comeback.'

'Comeback? What's that little weasel going to do?'

'Have you found out anything yet?'

Martin stopped and glared at him. 'Do you have any idea how complicated my life is at the moment?'

Gabriel nodded. 'Yes.'

'Then you will know I haven't even had time to shit, let alone think about *Endgame*, whatever that is!'

'Oh, right, sorry.' Gabriel smiled. 'I'd forgotten how important your troubles were compared to the little matter of the world's utter annihilation.'

Martin wagged a finger at him. 'Don't give me that holier-than-thou bollocks! I've had just about all I can take!'

Gabriel raised an eyebrow. 'Was that meant to be funny?'

Under the spell of those untroubled blue eyes, Martin felt his anger abate a little. 'All right, all right!' He sighed. 'I'll see what I can do.'

'Why don't you ask Luke to help – he's feeling very bad about what he said, you know.'


Martin was halfway through dealing with a tricky distal occlusion on Mrs Kidd's upper seventh when he heard Helen's voice in reception. A few moments later, Donna stuck her head around the door.

'Um, Martin, sorry to interrupt, but it's your wife.'

'Can't come now, Donna. She'll have to wait.'

'She's pretty insistent.'

'I'm busy!'

'OK.' Donna retreated.

'A little wider, Mrs Kidd,' said Martin, continuing with the procedure.

But then there came the sound of raised voices, and after a small pause, Helen burst into the room.

'Martin, I need to talk to you, now!'

Martin didn't even look up. 'Sorry about all these intrusions,' he said to his patient. 'It's like Piccadilly Circus in here today. I'll see you outside in a minute, Helen.'

Helen stood in the doorway clenching and unclenching her fists in impotent fury, finally withdrawing with an angry sigh.

Five minutes later, Martin walked into reception to see a smirking Luke, a dangerously fuming Helen and, cowering behind her, Westerham, clutching a bloody handkerchief to his nose.

'Hello,' Martin said cheerily. 'What's up; I thought you were down in Rock?'

'I was, until I got a call from Westerham.'

'Couldn't bear to be apart from you, how sweet.' He waved at Westerham, who shrank back fearfully.

'I don't know what your twisted little mind has dreamt up, but contrary to your mad fantasy, I am not having an affair with Westerham!'

'Well that's not what *he* thinks.' Martin addressed Westerham around his wife's shoulder: 'Is it, Westerham? With me out of the way, you seem to think you're in with a chance with Helen here, isn't that right?'

Westerham gurgled something and made himself even smaller.

Helen sighed. 'Westerham merely took us all out for lunch the other day.'

'Ah, but Westerham's always telling me there's no such thing as a free lunch. He was probably lining you up for dessert. Tell me, how does he do it? How does someone that stupid *and* that short get *anyone* into bed? Least of all someone like you. You've got a science degree for God's sake! But then again, I don't suppose it's your intellect he's been stimulating.'

Helen slapped Martin hard across the face. There was a collective intake of breath from those gathered in the reception area.

In the ensuing stunned pause, Helen tucked a stray wisp of blonde hair behind her ear before speaking. 'Westerham is simply being a good friend. And if you'd listened to him in the first place you might not be in your present predicament! It's probably too late now, as I doubt he'll feel inclined to help you out after this little episode. So it's up to you to make it up with him. I'll be with Mum and Dad for the rest of the week. Don't call me unless you have something positive to tell me regarding your financial situation.' She turned to go. 'Come along, Luke. Your father's not safe to be around at the moment.'

But Luke didn't move.

'Luke, come on!'

'I'm staying.' And for the first time in his life, Luke gazed up at his father with something approaching respect.

Helen looked from her son to Martin and back again. 'Oh, great. Five years in dental school and a list of qualifications as long as your arm leaves him completely cold, but smack a poor defenceless man around the head and suddenly you have his undying admiration. Why couldn't we have had a daughter!'

Helen stormed out, leaving Westerham without his shield.

Martin regarded his cowering colleague coldly and bared his teeth at him. The little man jumped, then fled reception and locked himself in his surgery.

Luke looked at Martin and nodded, a smile playing around his lips. 'I always thought maroon was a terrible colour for a Jag.'

# Chapter 5

'Stuck with my mother-in-law for all eternity! Oh, powers from Hell, grant me Nero's wish, that all women have but one head and if that head belong to the shrew who tyrannizes me; then grant me the pleasure of chopping it off!' moaned Donatien Alphonse François, Marquis de Sade.

'Stop complaining, you disgusting creature,' replied Madame de Montreuil. 'You've got what you deserve. This is your reward for all those years of debauchery; for feasting on ordure, despoiling virgins and corrupting the young. *And* for breaking my dear girl's heart.'

The soul standing between them, a nun belonging to the Sisters of Carmel who had until recently been working in the Quality Religious Goods department of that order, was catatonic with fear.

'Keep your eye on him, sister,' warned Madame de Montreuil. 'Turn your back and he'll be up your habit like a shot and knocking on your rear entrance.'

'You old hag,' de Sade snarled. 'You're just jealous that I had your two daughters and not you. You've been gagging for it since the moment you set eyes on me. Well let me tell you, you wrinkled old witch, I'd rather fuck my dog!'

'You *did* fuck your dog!'

'Monsieur le Marquis, Madame de Monteuil, sorry to interrupt.'

A man in a cashmere coat had appeared in front of them. De Sade and his mother-in-law stared at him, blinking in surprise.

'Tell me, on a scale of one to ten, how would you rate your working relationship?'


Back home in Windyridge, Martin and Luke stood in the kitchen and looked at each other.

'Want something to eat?' Martin asked.

'Got any pizza in the freezer?'

'Pizza?' Martin frowned. 'No, I was going to make something.' He opened the fridge. 'Let's see, what have we got? Hmm, what's this?' He opened a small foil packet, revealing an ancient chicken leg. 'Ah, well, I haven't had a chance to do any shopping for a while.' It went in the bin. A forgotten slice of vibrant-green ham and a weeping slab of something brown and furry followed it into the garbage. 'OK, meat seems to be off the menu, but what about vegetables?' He opened the drawer at the bottom of the fridge.

Luke peered over his father's shoulder. 'Dad, that bag's moving.'

At the back of the drawer a paper bag rustled ominously.

'Mushrooms seem to be off as well, then.'

After consigning most of the contents of the fridge to the bin, all that was left were one and a half pints of week-old milk, a lump of blue-tinged cheddar and four past-their-sell-by-date eggs.

'I can feel a cheese omelette coming on.'

'Um, d'you know what, Dad? I'm not really hungry. I think I'll go upstairs.'

'Oh, really? Goodnight then.'

'Goodnight.'

Martin watched his son walk out of the kitchen. He listened to the creak of footsteps on the landing above, then wandered through into the living room, turned on the television and slumped down on the sofa with the remote in the vain hope of finding something to watch that didn't involve Z-list celebrities demeaning themselves for 'charity', or house renovation with a crew of cheeky, cheerful cockneys.

After Luke had been playing Splinter Cell on his computer for about forty minutes, there was a muffled knock on his bedroom door. 'Come in!'

Martin entered, carrying two mugs. 'I brought you some cocoa.' He looked vaguely round the room for an available flat surface.

'Put it on the bookcase.'

'Oh, right.' Martin stood the mug on a half-empty shelf. 'Having fun?'

Luke grunted in the affirmative.

'I've just been watching a documentary about a Nepalese charcoal burner,' Martin continued.

'Sounds fascinating.'

'Watching rock erode would have been marginally more interesting.'

Martin casually scanned the bookshelf. It was stacked with CD-ROMs and DVDs: computer games with names like Alien Maggot Wars and Undead Urban Invasion. Martin pulled one out at random. 'Killer Slags,' he read. 'What's this one about?'

Luke looked up. 'What?'

'This game.' Martin waved the CD-ROM. 'What is it?'

'Dunno.' Luke shrugged and turned back to his computer. 'That's one of Henry's.'

'Henry?'

'You know, Henry Morgan.'

'Is he one of your school friends?'

'I wouldn't call him a friend.' A burst of gunfire came over the speakers of his computer. 'Oh, fu—' But, restrained by the presence of his father, Luke refrained from using an age-old and hugely popular Anglo-Saxon expression.

'What happened?' Martin asked.

'They found me.'

'Who found you?'

'The rebels. They used the sewer system to creep up behind me.'

'And you didn't smell them coming?'

Luke was not amused.

'Sorry. Does that mean you've lost?'

'No, but I've got to go back a level.'

'Sorry, that was probably my fault. Do you want your cocoa now?'

'OK.' Luke swivelled round in his chair. Martin handed him the steaming mug then sat down on the bed, facing his son.

Luke took a sip and smiled.

'What?' Martin asked.

'I haven't had cocoa for years.'

'I thought Mum always gave you cocoa.'

'Not since I was eight.'

Martin suddenly felt foolish and out of touch. 'You don't have to drink it if you don't want to.'

'No, it's quite nice – reminds me of being a kid again.'

'Yes,' Martin sighed, 'I know what you mean. *My* mum always used to give me cocoa at bedtime.'

They sipped their cocoa in silence, both of them remembering a time when life wasn't quite so confusing and frightening.

Martin suddenly had an idea. 'Have you ever heard of something called *Endgame*?'

Luke thought a moment. 'No, why?'

'Well . . .' But where should he start? With the angel Gabriel and his tale of the impending annihilation of the earth because of a little wager between Heaven and Hell? Or God wearing Pringle? 'No reason,' he said at last. 'Do you ever surf the Net?'

Luke shook his head. 'No, that's just for weirdos and wan—' He stopped himself again.

'Wankers, yes.' Martin smiled.

Luke flushed.

'Would you mind looking it up for me?'

'*Endgame*? On the Net?'

'Yes.'

Luke shrugged. 'All right.'

He swivelled back to his computer and typed the word into Google.

A moment later a page of results flickered up on the screen. Among numerous sites dedicated to chess and Samuel Beckett and, of course, the ubiquitous eBay advert, *Buy Low-Priced Endgame, big selection*, was an entry about a magazine called *Web of Fire* and a computer game it was promoting.

'Try that,' said Martin.

Luke clicked on it. In a matter of moments the *Web of Fire* home page came up – black type on a red background, with flames licking around the edges of the page.

'It's a magazine,' Luke said.

The headline read, '*Endgame*, the game to end all games: Kill or be killed.'

'Do you know anything about this?' Martin asked.

'Like I said, it's not really my thing. Henry would, though; he's into this sort of crap.'

'I'd like to meet this Henry.'

'No, you wouldn't.'

'Why not?'

Luke shrugged. 'He's weird. He's always giving stuff away, like computer games and CDs – he thinks it makes him popular. It doesn't. Everyone thinks he's a joke.'

'But you still take the stuff.'

'Yeah – some of it's cool.'

'His stuff's cool but he's not?'

Luke considered this a moment. 'Yeah, I suppose.'

'But he'd know all about *Endgame* and *Web of Fire* and things like that?'

'If anyone does, he would. He hasn't really got any friends. He spends all his free time on his computer, playing games or visiting weird conspiracy theory sites.'

'Such as?'

'Oh, you know – aliens are already among us and have infiltrated the government, stuff like that. He really believes it – it's sad.'

'I'd like you to ask him over.'

'What?'

'You just said he hasn't got any friends.'

'Yeah, and when you meet him you'll see why.'

'Invite him over tomorrow.'

'Aw, Dad, he's a jerk. He attaches himself like a leech to anyone who even says hello. If I invite him over I'll never lose him again.'

'Blame it on me. Say I'm thinking of upgrading my computer or something and I want his advice.'

Luke squirmed in his chair. 'It's really not a good idea.'

'Please, Luke, it's very important I find out everything I can about this *Endgame*.'

Luke was suddenly curious. 'Why are you so interested in a computer game all of a sudden?'

Martin drained his cocoa and stood up. 'You wouldn't believe me if I told you. But Henry might.'

'What does that mean?'

Martin yawned. 'I'm going to bed. Don't stay up too late; we've got another early start tomorrow.'

'Are you serious about Henry?'

'Deadly. Goodnight.'

Martin left the room. Luke thought for a while, then sighed deeply, turned back to his computer and clicked on the Outlook Express logo at the bottom of the screen.

# Chapter 6

The entrance to Heaven and Hell – officially titled *The Universal Life/Death Interface* but known variously among those who work there as *The Last Round-Up*, *Hallelujah Corner* and *The Final Curtain* – exists in a dimension outside time and space. Its physical location is actually Southampton Docks, but its spatial and temporal ambiguity ensures that it is universally accessible to all those who have 'shuffled off this mortal coil', wherever they may happen to have done so.

Some time ago now God handed over the soul franchise to Hell. This meant that the responsibility for collecting newly dead souls and escorting them to the Interface became Hell's alone. This was a useful move for both sides: it freed up the heavenly host to spend more time praising the boss, and also solved Satan's problem of how to keep a vast workforce gainfully employed. The only drawback to this arrangement is that it has caused consternation to many a good soul who, after leading a blameless life and passing away with the full expectation of everlasting bliss in the hereafter, is chagrined, to say the least, to be met on the other side by a grinning denizen of Hades.

The soul-fetchers, or Hell's Angels as they are known, are distinguished by their red caps, which sometimes sit incongruously on the costumes they once wore in life. Robespierre's, for example, balances precariously atop his wig, whereas Lenin refuses to wear his cap at all, insisting that it is a bourgeois affectation, and carries it tucked under his arm. Mao, on the other hand, loves his little red cap.

Just in case there was any danger of the soul-fetchers having an easy time of it, one of Satan's masterstrokes was to pair them up with their avowed enemies on earth. So, Frank Sinatra is permanently stuck with Peter Lawford, Trotsky with Stalin, Francis Drake with Philip of Spain, the Marquis de Sade with his mother-in-law, and so on . . .

Another of Satan's concerns is keeping the citizens of Hell busy enough to prevent them from organizing themselves into anything that might be construed as a trade union. Fortunately for the management, most of them, having been gangsters and other privateers used to working only for themselves, are deeply suspicious of anything that smacks of socialism. There are, of course, politicians of every hue among their ranks but, as in life, no one really takes them seriously.

The Interface itself comprises two escalators: one going up (a finely wrought, elegant affair covered in delicate filigree work and gold leaf) and one going down (dirty, covered in graffiti and usually broken). The down escalator is manned by a hooded ghoul, dressed in rags, who ticks off the name of each soul in the long, long queue on a clipboard he carries in his skeletal hand.

The entrance to Heaven, on the other hand, is more like business-class check-in at Heathrow: no queue and overstaffed. Since Hell was given the soul franchise, it's left the majority of Heaven's host with nothing to do, and bored angels regularly loiter around the bottom of the up escalator just for some action – even an angel can stand only so much perfection. On really slack days this can lead to friction as the angels taunt their netherworld colleagues about their working conditions, lack of a coherent pension structure, meagre health benefit schemes, etc.

Today, the Interface had a visitor. Lurking in the shadows behind the large rack of index cards next to the time clock, where the constantly coming and going soul-fetchers clocked on and off, stood a figure in a cashmere overcoat. He was scribbling in a small notebook, and he did not look happy.

After digging Luke out of his pit at the ungodly hour of half past seven and spoon-feeding cereal and coffee into him, Martin installed him in the Range Rover and set off for work. But on reaching the practice, he was just about to turn in to his parking space when he saw that it was occupied by a police car, next to which stood Revenue Ranger Gifford Wilkinson's brown Vauxhall Astra.

'Oh, shit.'

Martin knew instantly what had happened: Westerham had made an official complaint to the police and they were here 'furthering their enquiries'. The elation Martin had felt yesterday after pummelling his colleague to a bloody pulp had evaporated, and now he was suffering the dismal hangover of contrition. He really wasn't up to fighting with the police *and* Her Majesty's Inland Revenue just yet. He could imagine Gifford rubbing his podgy little hands with glee at the appearance of the boys in blue. It would be another black mark on Martin's sheet – a cross against the box marked 'good character'.

Martin cancelled the indicator and put his foot on the accelerator.

They were at the bottom of the hill, near the railway station, when Luke finally realized they'd driven past his father's place of work. 'Where are we going?'

'I've decided to take the day off. Where does your friend live?'

Luke looked at him oddly. 'You *never* take the day off.'

'Well, I think it's time that you and I . . . got to know each other a little better.'

'What?'

'You know . . . do that father–son buddy thing, like in the movies.'

'Oh, I love you, Dad.'

A warm feeling came over Martin. He smiled; he'd always longed to hear that phrase from Luke's lips but, aware of the fact he'd never done anything to deserve it, nor was ever likely to, had convinced himself that he never would. 'I love you too, son.'

Luke frowned at him. 'No. It's what every modern American movie is about: "I love you, Dad."'

'Oh.' Colouring slightly, Martin cleared his throat, clutched the steering wheel a little tighter and stared intently at the road ahead.

Luke stretched and rubbed the sleep out of his eyes. 'What were we talking about?'

'Oh . . . um, yes. I thought we'd go and see your friend.'

'Which friend?'

'You know, the nerdy one nobody likes.'

'Henry?'

'Yes, him. Where does he live?'

'We can't see him now.'

'Why not?'

'He'll be asleep.'

'Then we'll wake him up.'

Luke shook his head. 'I emailed him last night and asked him to come round this evening. He doesn't do mornings – he spends his nights on the Net.'

'Doing what?'

'You know: communicating with other sad people who don't have a life. And . . .'

'And what?'

Now it was Luke's turn to be embarrassed. 'You really don't want to know. There's all sorts of . . . weird stuff on the Net.'

'OK, we'll go for a coffee somewhere first.' Martin turned into the station car park and slid the big car into a parking space. 'This is good,' he said to himself. 'They'll never think of looking here, and if they do, they'll assume I've taken a train somewhere.'

Luke looked sideways at his father. 'Who will?'

'The police. It's all that bloody Westerham's fault.'

'Are you all right, Dad?'

Martin turned off the ignition and smiled strangely. 'Do contemplating driving off a cliff, talking to angels and beating up my business partner sound like the actions of a sane man to you?'

Luke shifted uneasily in his seat. 'Talking to angels?'

'It's different, though; I'll give it that.' Martin went quiet for a long moment and stared unblinking through the windscreen at the featureless wooden fence in front of the Range Rover's nose.

'Dad?'

'All right, let's go.'

'Where?'

'How about the Carved Angel?'

'That's miles away,' Luke moaned.

'It's only up by the cathedral.'

'But we'll have to walk all the way back up the hill!'

'The exercise'll do us both good. Come on.'

Martin eased himself into the sofa in the window overlooking the cathedral green. 'What'll you have, Luke?'

'A latte and one of those cinnamon things,' Luke replied without looking at the menu.

'Good choice. I'll join you.' Martin waved at a waitress who ambled over to them.

'Yes?' she said.

'Two caffé lattes and two cinnamon buns, please.'

'Two lattes and two cinnamon swirls,' she corrected. 'Anything else?'

'No, that's all, thanks.' Martin relaxed back into the softly upholstered couch. 'I feel like I'm playing truant. I haven't done anything this naughty since hiding in the cricket pavilion all morning to escape double French.' He looked uneasily around the cafe. 'I hope I'm not letting anyone down too badly. Donna will never forgive me, of course.' But then, what did it matter? What did any of it matter? It could all end tomorrow! He turned to Luke with a smile.

'Er, Dad,' Luke began tentatively, 'do you really think Westerham's set the police on you?'

Martin looked at him for a long time. 'It's just the sort of thing the little twerp *would* do,' he said at last.

'I've always thought he looked sort of soft and squishy – a bit like a cherub,' Luke observed.

'He's about the right size, too,' Martin replied. 'And

speaking of heavenly creatures . . .' A tall man in a long coat had just entered the cafe. The man smiled and waved at them, but Martin didn't wave back. He still wasn't absolutely sure that Gabriel was real, and he didn't want to alarm his son further by striking up a conversation with thin air. The tall man came over to the couch and introduced himself.

'Hello, you must be Luke.'

Luke looked up, amazed. 'Excuse me?'

The man extended his hand. 'How do you do, I'm Gabriel.'

They shook hands. Gabriel looked at Martin and smiled. 'You see, even your son is part of this hallucination.'

'I'm sorry, Gabriel. Would you like a coffee?'

'Love one.'

'Luke, move up,' Martin instructed.

Gabriel squeezed in between them, beamed at Luke and tapped him playfully on the knee. 'Welcome aboard.'

The corners of Luke's mouth twitched.

'Um, he doesn't know yet,' Martin explained.

'You haven't told him?'

'Not the whole story, no, but we *have* found out what *Endgame* is.'

'How exciting.'

'It's a computer game.'

'That's it?'

'That's all we know at the moment, but one of Luke's friends is a computer expert – we're hoping he'll be able to tell us more.'

'Not so much an expert, more of a geek,' Luke added.

Gabriel eased round in his seat and smiled at Luke. 'And exactly how much *does* this young gentleman know?'

Luke's uncertain half-smile had frozen into a grimace.

'Nothing,' Martin said.

'Would you like me to tell him?'

'Tell me what?' Luke asked.

Gabriel gazed at him for a long moment before he spoke. 'Your father seems to think you wouldn't believe what I have to say or, indeed, what I am. But I think he underestimates you.'

Luke was feeling more and more uncomfortable. It was still very early in the morning by his standards and this all felt like part of some weird, waking dream.

'Dad, who is this?'

Martin opened his mouth to speak, but Gabriel put a hand on his arm. 'Please,' he said, 'allow me.' The archangel turned his radiant face back to Luke. 'I,' he announced, 'am an angel.'

'Oh, right,' said Luke, convinced that in a moment one of two things was going to happen: either he would wake up and find himself back in his bedroom, or the men in white coats would appear and cart this madman away.

'No, you're not dreaming, and I'm not mad. I really am an angel and I've come here to ask your father for his help.'

Luke looked to Martin, then to Gabriel, back to Martin and finally to Gabriel again.

'Well, you wanted to know what was going on.' Martin smiled.

Luke swallowed. 'What do you mean you're an angel?'

'You know, sitting about on clouds, playing harps, singing with the heavenly choir. Although it's not quite so heavenly at the moment – we're a little heavy in the bass section. Tenors are like gold dust.'

The waitress appeared with their order. 'That's two lattes and two swirls,' she said, unloading a small tray.

'And could we also have a—' Martin began.

'And a cappuccino and a raisin Danish.' The girl put the coffee and iced bun in front of Gabriel.

'Yes?' she looked up at Martin.

'Nothing,' he said.

'Enjoy your coffee.' She left, clutching the empty tray.

'How do you do that?' Martin asked.

'How do I do what?' said Gabriel, innocently.

'You know, order without ordering.'

'Oh, it's all down to attitude of mind. Faith can move mountains, you know.'

'It's a cheap trick.'

'Whatever, but it works.'

Luke seemed to have gone into a strange, trance-like state. He sat, eyes wide, mouth open, staring intently at the angel.

Gabriel was about to tuck into his raisin Danish but, seeing Luke's predicament, thought it better to try and reassure the boy first. 'Luke, I know this is all rather strange,' he began, 'and I would much rather have broken it to you gently, but we don't have time to mess about with lengthy explanations. So, I'm sorry, but I'm an angel and the end of the world is nigh. OK?' Gabriel tucked into his pastry.

'End of the world?' Luke repeated faintly.

'I thought you were going to *explain*,' Martin said. 'Luke, don't panic just yet. The end of the world is only a *possibility* – it's not a sure thing.'

'Sorry,' Gabriel muttered, spraying crumbs, 'I should have made that clear. The pastries here are *fabulous*,' he added unnecessarily.

73

'You see,' Martin continued, 'it's all down to who wins the bet – God or the Devil.'

Luke looked appalled.

'Now *I'm* not explaining it very well. Gabriel, help me out here.'

With a sigh, Gabriel put down his breakfast and gave Luke the bare facts of the situation – the bet, the comet and *Endgame*.

'You left out golf and Waitrose,' Martin said when he'd finished.

'Huh?' Luke said.

'Never mind. So that's why we need to find out as much as we can about this computer game, and why we need to talk to Henry.'

Luke let everything he'd heard sink in for a moment. It was far too weird to assimilate coherently; his mind kept veering off at a tangent whenever he approached it directly. Just to get a peek at this new set of ideas, first he had to pretend it wasn't there, then sidle up to it and, at the last moment, jump up onto its back and cling on for as long as he could before inevitably being thrown off into the dust. What he'd just been told was even further out than one of Henry's creepy, alien-infested scenarios.

'This isn't, like, some elaborate practical joke?' Luke queried.

Gabriel smiled at him benignly. 'Trust me.'

Gazing at the angel's serene visage, all Luke's doubts receded. 'Henry is going to go wild when he hears about this.'

'But no one else must know – we don't want to start a panic,' Gabriel warned, wiping his mouth with his napkin. 'Shall we go?'

'Go?' asked Luke.

'Go and see your friend.'

'He's a bit weird, and he's not really a friend . . .'

'Acquaintance, then, if you prefer.'

'He won't be awake yet,' said Luke, licking his fingers.

Gabriel rose. 'Let me worry about that. I have ways,' he added mysteriously. 'Besides, from what I'm beginning to gather about Henry, I rather think our little story will be right up his street.'

Luke shrugged. 'OK.'

Martin edged out of the seat and moved across to the small pay desk.

'We had two lattes, two cinnamon things—' Martin began.

'A cappuccino and a raisin Danish,' the young man behind the counter finished the sentence for him. 'It's already been paid for.'

Martin spun round to look back at Gabriel.

'How do you *do* that?'

The angel smiled back at him inscrutably. 'Like I said, I've been in this game a long time.'


Henry Morgan lived in a terraced house in the Burnt-house Lane area of Exeter, a run-down estate on the edge of the city. Rubbish overflowed the bins standing in the small front garden and spilled out onto the pavement, where cats and rats had obviously been going through the garbage, picking out the choicest bits. Martin parked the Range Rover outside and killed the ignition.

'Very salubrious,' Gabriel observed.

'His dad lives abroad,' Luke explained. 'Singapore or somewhere – he's loaded, apparently, but he only gives Henry and his mum a limited allowance.'

'Enough to cover the school fees and not much else from the look of things,' Martin muttered. Several thoughts flitted through his mind: *How do people live like this?* Closely followed by: *Is it safe to leave the car here?* And finally the chilling: *If I don't sort my current financial situation out, I could end up living somewhere like this.*

'Oh, I don't think it will come to that,' said Gabriel, soothingly.

Martin glared at him. 'Do you have to comment on every thought that goes through my head?'

'Sorry.'

They got out of the car. After making sure the windows were closed and the doors securely locked, Martin followed Gabriel and Luke up the trail of old tea bags, used tissues and baked-bean tins that led to the front door. 'So, over to you, Gabriel. How are you going to dig Henry out of his pit? Let's see your mystical heavenly powers in action.'

Gabriel smiled and rang the bell.

'That's it?'

'You have a better suggestion?'

They waited. Martin listened at the letter box. He could hear the soft, gentle mewing of a cat and the distant sound of a television.

Gabriel rang the bell again.

Luke took a few steps back from the door and looked up. 'He's there. I just saw his curtains twitch.'

Gabriel and Martin joined him, and the three of them stood gazing up at the bedroom window. The closed curtains were still swaying slightly.

Gabriel hurried back to the door and rang the bell, long and loud.

Eventually there was the muffled clump of feet on

stairs followed by a prolonged clicking and clunking as various deadlocks were sprung, door chains undone and bolts withdrawn. At last the door creaked open and one bloodshot eye peeped warily out at them.

'What do you want?' said a voice, thick with sleep.

Luke stepped forward. 'Hi, Henry. Can we come in?'

Henry opened the door a little wider. He was wearing a pair of dirty underpants and a T-shirt bearing the image of a skull, a rose between its teeth and a mace embedded in its shattered cranium above the legend Love Me to Death. His black and greasy hair was sticking out at strange angles and, just visible beneath this thatch, was a squashy face with two piggy eyes set either side of a bulbous nose. Blearily, he took in the group standing on the doorstep, then made a quick scan of the empty street.

'Come in, quick,' he said suddenly, opening the door wide.

The house smelt of cat urine and stale cigarette smoke. A morning television game show host's rapid delivery sprayed like machine-gun fire out of a half-open door beyond the foot of the stairs and echoed up the bare passageway.

'How do you do, I'm—' Gabriel began.

'What are you doing here?' Henry interrupted, ignoring him and addressing Luke. 'I thought I was coming round to see *you*. You can't just drop in unannounced like this – what if somebody was watching?'

'Yeah, sorry, Henry, but we're in a bit of a hurry.'

Henry looked suspiciously from Luke to Martin to Gabriel. 'Hurry?'

'We need your expertise,' said Martin.

'With computers,' Gabriel added.

Henry screwed up his eyes and stared at the tall man. 'Do I know you?'

'I don't think we've ever met.' Gabriel smiled.

'You look familiar. Are you sure?'

'In another life, perhaps.'

Henry scrutinized him further. 'You're about the right height for a Pleiadian.'

Luke rolled his eyes. But Gabriel's smile didn't falter for an instant. 'Oh, people are always telling me that.'

'Um, hello, Henry,' said Martin. 'I'm Luke's father.'

Henry turned his porcine gaze onto him, regarding him coldly for some moments. 'Yeah,' he said at last. He turned back to Luke. 'So, *what* is it you want?'

'We need to pick your brains about something called *Endgame*.'

'Web of Fire promo Internet game,' Henry shot back. 'A simple FPS using the engine from Cold War Fantasy but with better graphics.'

'FPS?' Martin queried.

'First-person shooter – it's all seen from the gamer's viewpoint.'

'You've actually *got* it?' Gabriel asked.

'The first two parts, yeah. It's old-fashioned, but not bad for a freebie.'

'Can we have a look?' Martin smiled.

Henry screwed up his eyes again and regarded Martin for several seconds before turning back to Luke. 'Yeah, you can have a look, but not here.'

'You said somebody might be watching you?' Gabriel queried.

Henry looked at the floor and tried to hide under his hair. 'Yeah, well, it's just that . . . my mum . . . she –' he dropped his voice to a whisper, '– she watches everything

I do . . .' His eyes flicked in the direction of the door at the end of the passageway.

Gabriel followed his gaze and just caught a glimpse of pink housecoat disappearing around the half-open door.

'It's really restricting.'

'I see,' Gabriel whispered back.

'How about *your* place?' Henry said to Luke.

'OK.'

'Give me a minute.' Henry started back upstairs.

'We'll wait outside,' said Martin, eager for some fresh air.

'Good morning, Mrs Morgan!' Gabriel called down the passageway. A shadow moved in the thin crack between door and frame and there was the sound of a chair scraping on lino.

Everyone was relieved to be outside. Martin turned to Luke. 'What's a Pleiadian?'

Luke sighed. 'What you have to remember with Henry is that everything is either a conspiracy theory or an alien. The Pleiadians are supposed to be some form of alien life that visited earth two millennia ago. I only know this because Henry once insisted on expounding his complicated theory about earth's colonization from space one excruciatingly embarrassing English class. I can't say I remember the whole thing in detail, but Pleiadians I do remember – they come from the Pleiades.'

'Oh.'

The small group clustered outside Henry's house began to wonder if they'd done the right thing in dragging this strange creature out from under its rock and inviting it into their midst. But it was too late to turn back now.

\*

When they arrived back at Windyridge they hit their first problem.

'Ah,' sighed Henry, looking critically at Luke's computer.

'What?' Luke asked.

'I thought you'd have something a bit more up to date.'

'It's only two years old!' Martin protested.

Henry stared at him with ill-disguised contempt and spoke slowly, as if to a young child. 'Precisely: the graphics driver isn't going to be up to it.'

'Is that bad?' Gabriel wondered.

Henry sucked his teeth. 'It's going to be very slow. *If*, that is, I can ever get the thing to load. But we'll have a go.'

After booting up, Henry inserted the first *Endgame* CD-ROM into the computer.

After several moments of whirring, a box came up asking if he wanted to load *Endgame*, *Yes* or *No*?

He clicked *Yes*. The whirring from the computer shifted up a gear and another box appeared asking him if he agreed to be bound by the terms of some long and complicated contract.

He clicked *Agree* and the box disappeared to be replaced with one bearing a long slot along which a green bar moved slowly.

'Will this take much longer?' Gabriel asked.

Henry shrugged. 'It's an old machine.'

Eventually, after several minutes of excited electric chuntering and a succession of boxes and further green bars, the game was loaded.

The monitor screen went black, and from the small speakers came the wailing of a synthesized bassoon and a thudding bass line reminiscent of marching feet. Then, out of the darkness, a rivet-studded steel door slowly appeared. Gunfire barked, sharp and sudden, and the word *Endgame* was picked out on it in bullet holes. The door creaked on its virtual hinges and fell over. Zooming in through the open entrance, a small, darkened room was revealed, empty save for a large chart pinned to the far wall behind a low wooden dais.

Yet another box opened, steel-studded and combat dirty, inviting the player to enter his name. Henry quickly typed in: 'Scimitar'.

'Scimitar?' Gabriel queried.

'My gaming name,' Henry muttered.

It was hard to imagine anyone less scimitar-like than Henry.

Staring intently at the screen, Henry began to tap away at the keyboard.

'What are you doing now?' Gabriel asked.

Henry clicked his tongue irritably. 'I'm configuring the game to my gaming style.'

'Really?' Gabriel smiled uncertainly.

'Yeah, the classic is W-A-S-D.'

'Ah,' said Gabriel, nodding sagely, trying to give the impression that computer game configuration was the sort of thing he did every day before breakfast. It was not a convincing performance.

Henry sighed long-sufferingly. 'They're all keys next to each other on the left-hand side of the keyboard. W to move forward, A to go left, D to go right and S to look around. I can manipulate them with my left hand while using the mouse with my right. It just makes it easier to navigate, OK?'

'Excuse my ignorance.' Gabriel beamed.

The on-screen image now zoomed into the map on the back wall, underneath which the message *Choose country* began to flash.

Henry turned to Gabriel. 'Who do you want to be?'

'Oh, the good guys, of course.'

'Not sure it's quite that cut and dried,' Henry murmured.

Martin peered at the map. 'Where is that?'

Henry's reply was edged with disdain. 'Well it's obviously the north Pacific.' He stabbed at the map with a pudgy finger. 'That's Russia, that's China, that's Korea and that's Japan. And right across the narrow band of the Bering Strait lies the United States in the shape of Alaska.'

Martin nodded. 'So, basically, it's East versus West.'

'Congratulations. OK, we'll be the white hats.' Henry clicked on Alaska and a grid appeared with a list of options: *Morning Patrol, Midnight Raid, Operation Ice Floe.*

'What are they?' asked Gabriel.

'Different missions. There aren't that many on this level. You have more to choose from on the second level.'

'Second level?'

Henry sighed again. 'If we complete a first-level mission successfully, we go up to the second level. The game gets harder, there are more obstacles to overcome, but ultimately it's more rewarding.'

Gabriel nodded doubtfully. 'I see.'

'OK, let's start with a fairly basic one.'

Henry clicked on *Morning Patrol.*

Lines of white type scrolled up the screen:

*The time: the near future. America has moved further to the right, Russia is once again retreating into isolation and para-*

*noia, and China continues to grow in strength and power. Add to this the continuing troubles in the Middle East and you have a situation as unstable as at any time during the height of the Cold War. New and fragile alliances forged through tireless diplomacy are beginning to break down as old enmities re-emerge . . .*

In the small on-screen room, an American general entered through a door in the back wall and took the stage. Martin, Gabriel and Luke huddled closer to get a better view.

The general addressed his officers: 'At ease, gentlemen. You are no doubt aware that during the past few weeks there have been several incidences of incursions of hostiles into our territory. We believe our defence capability is being tested. Those seeking to destabilize us must be made to understand that we're no pushover. As the cream of our ground-based defence corps it's your job to deliver that message.'

The image closed tightly on the general's strange, angular face as he turned to camera.

'Your mission is to seek and destroy those who would subjugate the American people and take away our God-given freedoms. Our boundaries must remain secure.'

The general saluted and exited through the door.

At the bottom of the screen a *Play* button appeared. Henry clicked it and the scene changed immediately to an arctic wasteland.

A message crackled over the speakers: 'Red Base to Red Leader, we have reports of hostiles bearing north by north-west. Seek and destroy.'

'Roger that, Base,' Henry said to no one in particular. Then, a little more loudly, 'Red Patrol, move out!'

Gabriel glanced sideways at Martin.

Henry pressed W, and Scimitar and his men moved off across the ice at a trot. After the small troop had been jogging along uneventfully for some moments, Martin was struggling to see the point of it all.

'Is this all there is to it?' he asked.

Henry groaned. 'See that wall of ice?' Off in the distance a jagged white wall was coming jerkily into view. 'That's where we're heading. There might be a hostile encampment beyond it. In fact I know there is.'

Martin was impressed by Henry's prescience. 'That's amazing. How do you know that?'

Henry closed his eyes; he may even have counted to ten before replying. 'Because I've played this game before.'

'Oh.'

Reaching the ice wall, Scimitar and his men scrambled up it to the top. On the other side, in a small valley far below them was a group of black dots.

'There they are, men.'

Gabriel squinted at the screen. 'There are *what*?'

Manipulating the mouse, Henry cycled through the various options available to him, and as he did so small icons flashed up at the bottom of the screen: compass, rifle, pistol, grenade launcher, binoculars. Clicking on this final icon brought the distant dots nearer within the familiar Hollywood-style incomplete figure of eight. It was indeed a small encampment. Men in full arctic combat gear wandered aimlessly about on the ice or sat on wooden crates around a campfire.

'Red Leader to Red Base, hostiles sighted,' Henry drawled into an imaginary mouthpiece. It was clear that in his own mind Henry was no longer a podgy Devon teenager; he was now Scimitar, super-fit Green Beret and Purple-Heart-winning war hero. 'OK, men, get ready to move out. We're going to blow those commie bastards back to Hell.'

Martin squeezed Luke's arm. Gabriel was beginning to wonder if they'd got the right man for the job.

Suddenly there was a sharp *crack!* and an American voice started screaming through the speakers: 'Red Leader, we're under fire. Take aversive action!'

'Is aversive a real word?' Martin wondered.

Scimitar and his men hugged the ground while bullets whistled all around them.

Curling his lip, Henry snarled, 'Here we go!' and clicked on the grenade launcher. With a sound that went *ptoom!* a grenade sailed gracefully through the air and landed in amongst the little dots. There was a flash, a *boom!* and several of the dots stopped moving. Swapping his grenade launcher for a rifle, Scimitar leapt up with a scream, 'Death or glory!' and charged down the hill towards the enemy, firing from the hip.

'Aaarghh! I've been hit!' The soldier on Scimitar's right grabbed his side and went down.

Pausing only to yell 'Medic!' so loudly that Gabriel, Martin and Luke winced, Scimitar continued his precipitate career down the hill. 'I'll come back for you, Bob!' he called back over his shoulder.

'Bob?' Martin wondered.

Then the screen flashed red and Scimitar stumbled. 'What now?' Gabriel asked.

'I've been hit.'

Scimitar went down, his left thigh oozing blood.

Gabriel bit his lip. 'Does this mean we've lost?'

'Nah, we've got three lives. Watch this – this is fun.'

Henry clicked on a small red cross near his mission status bar at the bottom of the screen. Scimitar sat up and pulled a small first-aid kit out of a zip-up pocket. Opening it, he took out a syringe and plunged it into his thigh, then wrapped a bandage around his injured limb and tied it tight.

'Every soldier is equipped with field dressings,' Henry explained.

'Handy for injured fields.' Martin chortled.

Henry swivelled in his chair and stared at Martin. He didn't say anything, he just stared. Martin's laugh died in his throat. Then with a grunt Henry went back to the keyboard, and Scimitar eased himself to his feet. 'OK, Boris, now it's your turn to suffer.'

Martin was becoming increasingly confused. 'Who's Boris?' he whispered.

Smiling sadly, Luke laid a comforting hand on his father's shoulder.

Bullets whistling past on every side, Scimitar strode unflinchingly towards the foe.

'You've made a big mistake,' Henry snarled. 'You shouldn'ta made me angry!' He clicked twice on the grenade launcher option. *Ptoom! Ptoom!* Two grenades arced across the heavens and landed in the centre of the enemy camp.

*KA-BLAM!* The sky lit up in an angry explosion, and bodies flew through the air.

'Take that, borscht-eaters!'

It was becoming clear to everybody why Henry had no friends.

Scimitar and what was left of his men hurried towards the enemy, guns blazing. When they eventually arrived in the enemy camp, the wounded and dying were dispatched with a pistol shot to the head.

Gabriel grimaced and looked away.

'Couldn't this all have been sorted out a little more diplomatically?' Martin wondered.

'I'm not a politician,' Henry growled; 'I'm just a soldier with a job to do.'

A strange, unnatural silence fell in Luke's bedroom.

Henry clicked on a small helicopter icon. 'Red Leader to Red Base, enemy camp neutralized. I've got injured men so we'll need a chopper to bring us in.'

Everyone watched in silence as a white helicopter appeared and picked up the wounded soldiers. As the aircraft *thocka-thocka-thocka*'d off into the distance, Henry relinquished his role as Scimitar and became plain old Henry Morgan again, spotty and slightly overweight Exeter teenager. He swivelled round in the chair and spread his hands wide. 'That's it. It's OK, but I wouldn't call it terribly sophisticated. Like I said, it's basically a glorified shoot 'em-up game.'

Gabriel nodded. 'Yes, I see. What's the next level like?'

'Basically more of the same. It's much harder, of course: there are more hostiles and they're equipped with more sophisticated weapons.'

'So that's it?' Gabriel asked. 'That's the game?'

'Basically, yeah.'

'Oh.' Gabriel was disappointed. He had hoped that, if this *were* part of some dark plan to destroy the world, Satan's intentions would become immediately apparent on simply playing the game. But at the moment it was looking like the information he'd received through the Interface was inaccurate.

'Do you want to try the next level?' Henry asked.

Gabriel smiled sadly and shook his head. 'I don't think that's necessary.'

'OK. Do you want to have a look at the second disk, then?'

'We might as well.'

Henry swapped the disks in the computer and again went through the long process of loading and configuring. At last the game itself opened, this time on . . . another desolate, icy wasteland.

'The conflict has gone to the next level,' Henry explained. 'China and Russia are both up in arms about US interference in North Korean affairs. The military bases in the area have been heavily reinforced – nobody trusts anybody any more.'

'Sounds familiar.' Gabriel sniffed.

Henry looked up at him. 'Whose side do you want to be on this time?'

'Oh, I don't know . . . Let's be Russian for a change.'

'OK.' Henry tapped at the keyboard.

On-screen the panorama moved through 180 degrees towards a group of buildings huddled on the ice field, then zoomed in on one of them – a long, low construction with a red roof. The building dissolved and the view changed to the inside of the structure itself. It was basically the same room from the first part of the game, but this time the general taking the briefing was wearing the uniform of the Red Army.

Again, lines of white type scrolled up the screen, setting the scene:

*Hostilities have escalated; skirmishes between Russian and American forces are a daily occurrence. So far loss of life has been low but, because of the critical situation, the United*

*States has increased its level of readiness from Defcon 3 to
Defcon 2.*

Gabriel frowned. 'What does that mean?'

Henry pressed P to pause the game. The Russian general stood patiently in the doorway next to the small stage, occasionally looking at his watch. 'Defcon 3 is readiness above normal readiness. Defcon 2 is a further increase in force readiness, but less than maximum readiness. Clear?'

Gabriel frowned again. 'Crystal.'

Henry resumed the game and the general mounted the podium.

'Comrades, the time is at hand. At last you will be able to put into practice all you have learned. Our most glorious objective now is to put out the Western aggressor's spying eyes by attacking their easternmost base. For too long we have suffered the prying of the Western imperialists; now it will end!'

The general turned and spoke straight to camera.

'*You* will lead the attack. Six Mi-24 Hind attack helicopters will be under your command. You will annihilate the decadent American base – no trace of it must be left. Good luck. For the glory of the Motherland!'

The general left the briefing room.

'The decadent American base?' Luke scoffed.

Henry shrugged. 'It's a little old-fashioned, granted, but that's just its Cold War roots showing.'

Martin scratched his head. 'But it doesn't make sense – what with spy satellites and all the sophisticated surveillance stuff they have nowadays. Knocking out the American base would just be an act of senseless aggression.'

Henry turned on him angrily. 'Do you want to play this game or not?'

Martin looked hurt but said nothing.

'I think,' Gabriel soothed, 'what Henry is trying to point out is that while we're in the virtual world of gaming we must put our normal critical faculties to one side and enter the realities of the game itself.'

'Exactly,' Henry snarled.

Martin glanced sideways at Luke, who looked back with *I told you so* in his eyes.

'OK, here we go.' Henry stabbed angrily at the keyboard.

The sleek black helicopters stood in readiness on the compacted snow, their blades turning. This time Henry had chosen to be Viktor, Soviet hero and proud recipient of the Order of Lenin, but he seemed less at home as this character than he had as Scimitar.

Viktor led his men out onto the snow. The soldiers immediately split into six units and leapt into the waiting helicopters, with Viktor and his group taking the lead.

In the bottom left corner of the screen a small window opened to reveal an overview of the battlefield with the Russian helicopters displayed as a bunch of green dots. The American base was, as yet, still off the map. Adjacent to this window was a grid containing various symbols: binoculars, bombs, rockets and, at the very bottom of the screen, bars of various colours, informing the player about the number and status of his own and the enemy's resources.

'Right, now the game starts.' Henry looked up at Gabriel. 'You want to have a go this time? It's pretty easy – you just use these keys and the mouse.'

Gabriel shook his head. 'I'm happy to watch.'

Henry smiled a secret smile. 'Yeah, I know what you mean,' he murmured.

Martin looked questioningly at Luke, who shook his head warningly and mouthed: Don't ask.

'So, this is us.' Henry pointed to the green dots on the map. 'And the Americans, strangely enough, are red.' With a few mouse clicks, Henry brought up a large map of the area, showing the relative positions of the two sides. It also showed a few red and green dots moving around in the Bering Sea.

'What are those?' Gabriel asked.

'Battleships. If I want, I can call in covering fire from them to soften up the Americans before we get there. The trouble is, if the fire they lay down isn't accurate, it will alert the enemy to our presence prematurely and they'll be waiting for us.' Henry scanned the faces in the room. 'Ready?'

Everybody nodded.

'Move out!' Henry tapped the keyboard and the helicopters took off. On-screen, Viktor demonstrated the various views available to him: from the cockpit, from above, from below, even infrared and thermal. The rear view afforded an image of the other helicopters, following behind in tight formation.

'We're keeping low to stay under their radar,' Henry announced over the sound of the helicopter rotors thudding through the speakers.

On the small window at the bottom of the screen, the green dots representing this small airborne force could be seen moving over the terrain: skimming first over a barren, icy landscape, then the patchy blue and white of ice floes and, finally, the wide open sea.

At last, in cockpit-view mode, a distant icy landscape began to take shape.

'You see that gulley?' Henry shouted, pointing at the gap between two large wind-sculpted ice features. 'We're going in through there. If you look at the map, you'll see the objective is about five kilometres further on. The gulley will shield us from view for about three of them, but the last two will be across open ground and we'll be vulnerable – that's when the fun really starts.'

Henry tapped something else into the keyboard.

'What are you doing now?' Gabriel asked.

'Calling in an advance barrage from our ships.'

As the group of helicopters cleared the end of the gulley they caught a glimpse of their objective for the first time. A collection of huts lay dead ahead of them across the barren expanse of ice.

'There they are!' Henry yelled.

As the others crowded round to look, flashes lit up the sky. Henry clicked on the binoculars icon and the scene immediately became clearer. The American base was being heavily battered by the Russian bombardment.

'Looks like they're on target for once!' Henry boomed. 'Good luck, comrades!'

The helicopters swooped low over the ice, shells and bullets exploding and whizzing all around them as the Americans began to organize themselves and return fire.

'You'll see from the map that the enemy are beginning to fan out across the ice.'

Little red dots were spreading across the map like ants.

'We've got to contain them, so I'm going to initiate a flanking manoeuvre.'

After a few more taps on the keyboard, two of the following helicopters broke formation and sped on ahead in a wide pincer movement. Then, after a few more taps, another helicopter broke away in an even wider arc.

'He's going to circle round behind the enemy to cut off their escape route – he'll be like my wicketkeeper.'

Martin brightened. 'Do you play cricket, Henry?'

'No.'

'Oh.'

'My remaining forces will tackle the enemy head-on. Tally-ho!'

'I'm not sure that's very Russian,' Martin complained.

'Here we go, men, for the glory of the Motherland!' Landing his remaining helicopters, Viktor leapt out and led his soldiers into the fray.

Suddenly, fighting seemed to be going on everywhere at once. Amongst the explosions, men were blown in two or cut in half by machine-gun fire. Viktor himself seemed to be shooting everything that moved. Gabriel, Martin and even Luke were finding it hard to follow what was happening. 'The confusion of war,' Henry said gleefully.

The battle was fierce but over very quickly. At one stage the Americans made a run for it, but came face to face with Henry's 'wicketkeeper'. None of them escaped alive.

Almost as soon as it had started, the conflict was over. After systematically going through the enemy camp, killing anything that was still moving, Viktor gathered up his troops, circled his helicopters over the American base and pounded it with rockets, completely flattening the whole area. Moments later the victorious soldiers were heading for home, skimming back across the sea, singing old Russian folk songs. Martin noticed that one of the troops on board even had a bottle of vodka.

'Look at that.'

'Yeah, if you take the American side, the successful GIs pass the Jack Daniel's around,' Henry explained.

'We've come a long way since Pong,' Martin said wistfully.

Back at base, the men were congratulated by a jubilant general, who debriefed them: 'Men, today you have secured a great victory. The forces of the revolution have given the fat, degenerate backside of the United States a good kicking, but this is only the beginning. The Motherland will go on to greater things. The Americans will retaliate, of course, but we shall be waiting for them, and of one thing I am sure: we will triumph! Long live the revolution!'

'Is it possible to have a degenerate backside?' Martin wondered.

Gabriel put a hand on Henry's shoulder. 'Well done. That was most impressive.'

Henry shrugged. 'Well, I have played it a few times.'

Gabriel sighed. 'It seems I was wrong. I see nothing earth-threatening in this admittedly violent but ultimately harmless entertainment. I'm sorry, everybody, but I've wasted your time.'

'Shall I put the kettle on?' Martin said brightly.

'Good idea.' Gabriel beamed.

Both of them were already heading for the door.

'Actually there's another instalment.'

They stopped and turned to look at Henry, who hadn't left his station at the keyboard.

'Another instalment?' Gabriel repeated. 'You mean there's more?'

'Yeah –' Henry scratched his belly, '– the third and final part of the game. It comes out at the end of the week.'

Gabriel looked quickly from Martin to Luke, then

stared thoughtfully at the floor for some moments. 'Henry,' he said at last, striding back into the room, 'do you have any idea what this final part is about?'

'No, except that it's multiplayer.'

'Multiplayer?' Gabriel queried.

'You can go online and play against other people,' Luke explained.

'It should be fun,' Henry continued. 'The way the conflict seems to be progressing, it can only get global.'

A dreadful thought had occurred to Gabriel. 'Oh no,' he murmured, sitting down heavily on the edge of the bed. He'd turned as white as a sheet.

'Are you all right?' Martin asked the angel.

Gabriel looked up at Martin, his once-clear eyes now clouded with dread. 'What if the Devil has found a way to do just that?'

'Do what?'

'Launch World War Three in the guise of a computer game. If he's worked out a way to electronically manipulate the missiles, he wouldn't need to push the button himself. People like Henry here would do it for him.'

Henry swivelled round in his chair. 'Did you say *the Devil*?'

Gabriel got up off the bed suddenly and started pacing again. Underneath his long coat, his wings twitched visibly. Henry watched the movement of his hidden pinions with interest.

'But how could he do that?' Martin asked. 'Nuclear missiles are well protected by all sorts of mechanisms to prevent anyone gaining control of them, aren't they?'

'Yes and no,' said Henry.

All eyes went to him.

'If the missiles were completely protected, it would be

impossible to launch them. That's why the military originally set the security code to 0000000.'

'I'm sorry?'

'The American military didn't want security procedures getting in the way of their being able to launch their own missiles whenever they wanted to, so they set the universal security code to seven zeroes – it's easy to remember.'

'My God!'

'They've changed it now.'

'Well that's a relief.'

'But any channel of communication is always going to be an Achilles heel and, if you were determined enough, it might just be possible to get into the system.'

'Are you saying that an outsider could launch these missiles?' Gabriel asked.

'Unlikely . . .' Henry left the word hanging in the air, while looking disconcertingly enigmatic.

'Carry on,' the angel encouraged.

'OK,' Henry continued. 'Take the American example: they've got missile silos strung out all over the country, pointing at Russia and China. If there were to be an escalation in hostilities, then there are a series of seven different alert conditions, or Lertcons that can be called. These are broken down into five defence conditions and two emergency conditions.'

'And they are?' Gabriel asked.

'Defcon 5 is the lowest stage of alert. The level ramps up as the numbers get smaller. The highest the US has ever been is Defcon 2 – during the Cuban missile crisis. Once you get beyond Defcon 1 and into the two Emergcons, you're in a nuclear war.'

'I knew it! I knew it!' Gabriel started pacing again.

'How easy would it be to take control of a missile silo?' Luke asked.

'Almost impossible. The LCCs in control of the missiles—'

'LCCs?' Martin frowned.

'Launch control centres.'

'Thank you.'

'The LCCs themselves are totally autonomous – they're capable of launching the missiles all by themselves.'

Gabriel had stopped pacing for the moment and was now staring intently out of the window. 'So all you would need to do is seize control of one of these LCCs?'

'Er, no. The LCCs can only launch missiles in tandem. If, say, a bunch of terrorists were to get hold of a single LCC and try to launch its silo's missiles, a fail-safe delay mechanism would kick in until the order was checked out. It takes two LCCs working together to launch a flight of ten missiles. Which means that any would-be attacker would have to coordinate the taking over of two LCCs simultaneously.'

Luke was intrigued. 'How do you *know* all this stuff?'

'It's all out there on the Net.'

'You're a very sad man,' Luke replied.

Henry smiled. 'Only the president can authorize deployment – he's the man with the codes and they're changed every day.'

'So, let me get this straight.' Gabriel leaned over the computer, resting his chin on top of the monitor to look Henry in the eye. 'If I wanted to start a nuclear war, I would need to get hold of at least two of these LCCs in order to launch any missiles?'

'Right – after you've input the launch codes.'

'Which the president always carries with him.'

'Right again. Which ensures that any decision to launch *has* to come from him.'

Gabriel seemed to be calming down. 'I see, I see. So in actual fact it would be quite difficult for any would-be terrorist to coordinate such a move.'

Henry nodded. 'There are too many people and procedures involved.'

The colour began to return to the angel's cheeks.

'But the Russian system,' Henry continued nonchalantly, 'now that's a completely different kettle of pickled herring.'

Gabriel's heavenly complexion took on the colour of goose fat once more. 'Really?' he said faintly.

'The Russians have centralized everything. There are the usual checks and balances in the system, as in America, but the whole operation can be overridden by one man from a control room in the Kremlin.'

Martin's jaw dropped open. 'So, one mad Cossack could launch an attack against the rest of the world?'

'Yeah, then there are the Chinese – no one is exactly sure what their nuclear capability is – and, most mysterious of all, the North Koreans. No one outside Pyongyang knows what kind of weapons system they have or what level of readiness they're at. What *is* certain is that they've got at least two nuclear missiles, but probably more.'

In the ensuing gloomy silence, Gabriel stood in the middle of the room, inwardly wrestling with a matter of great moment. A whole range of expressions flitted across his face from blank despair to buoyant optimism and back again. At length, the determined set of his jaw declared that he had come to a resolution.

'I am going to see him!' he proclaimed to no one in

particular. 'I know what he'll say, but he must be made aware of what's going on.'

'Who?' Henry asked, innocently.

'God,' said Gabriel.

'Ri-ight.'

Martin held up his hands. 'Hang on a minute; let's not be too hasty. At the moment all we've got is a couple of computer games. We've no actual proof that the Devil's involved at all.'

'I know, I know,' said Gabriel, pacing the room again and wringing his hands, 'but it's better to be safe than sorry. He's not going to like it, of course – he hates anyone telling him what to do. But I think he needs to know about this.'

Luke looked worried. 'But won't you get into trouble? What about all that stuff you said about him forbidding you to get involved in mankind's affairs?'

Gabriel smiled kindly back at him. 'Thank you for your concern, but it can't be helped. If there's the slightest possibility that the Devil is able to manipulate the world's nuclear weapons, something has to be done. When this whole ludicrous bet scenario happened, the earth was young and sparsely populated. Now there's just too much at stake.'

'Um?' Henry was looking thoughtful.

Gabriel turned to him. 'Yes?'

'Did you really say you were going to see God?'

'Yes,' Gabriel replied. 'The third part of this game – when does it come out?'

'This Sunday.'

The angel clapped a hand to his forehead. 'Of course!'

'What?' Martin asked.

'Heaven's closed on Sunday!'

'Closed?'

'No one works on a Sunday – it's a law that God strictly enforces. Don't you see? If you wanted to do something awful, like destroy the earth, Sunday would be the perfect time – when Heaven's blinds are drawn. What day is it today?'

'Friday.'

'We have no time to lose; I shall go and see him immediately.' Gabriel drew himself up to his full height and closed his eyes.

But Henry looked troubled. 'Excuse me.'

Gabriel opened his eyes. 'What?' he said testily.

'What's going on?'

'Armageddon – the final conflict. The Devil is about to lay waste to the world, so, if you'll excuse me, I have to go and tell God all about it.' Gabriel disappeared in a puff of smoke.

Henry, Martin and Luke all stared, blinking, at where the angel had once stood.

Henry was the first to speak. 'Cool,' he said.

'Not a word to a soul,' Martin warned.

# Chapter 7

It was business as usual at the Interface when Gabriel rushed in. The soul-fetchers came and went in a never-ending stream, bringing more souls to add to the steadily lengthening queue at the down escalator, which today had a sign hanging off it saying OUT OF ORDER.

Gabriel called across to the cowled figure of Death manning the Hell check-in. 'Haven't you got that thing fixed yet?'

'Do you know how difficult it is to get an engineer out at the weekend?' Death replied.

'Overworked and underpaid, as usual,' Gabriel quipped.

'Such is death.'

The rotund, red-capped figure of Goering appeared, accompanied by General Franz Halder, dragging a reluctant soul between them.

Goering was not in good spirits. 'If you'd kept your mouth shut at Nuremberg about the Reichstag fire, I might have got away with it!'

'And be remembered as an apologist for the Nazi regime? *Nein danke*.'

'At least then you might have *been* remembered!'

'Ooh, look, here comes the Bavarian Blimp,' cried one of the angels hanging around the heavenly escalator.

'One day you will go too far,' Goering growled.

'What, like the Eastern Front?' the angel retorted.

A dour-looking Nero and his mother, Agrippina – her bearing haughty despite being dripping wet – tramped in, arm-in-arm with a rather nervous-looking soul.

'Sing us a song, Nero!' shouted an angel.

'Oh, don't tempt him,' groaned another.

Snarling, Nero deposited the soul at the up escalator. 'This one is for you.'

'Ooh, a customer!' trilled one of the angels. 'You're our first today,' he said, putting an arm around the bewildered soul who had devoted her life to looking after her sick mother. The other angels gathered round as well, fussing and twittering and guiding her onto the first step. The poor soul was so moved she burst into tears – no one had ever looked after *her* before.

Hitler and Molotov entered and escorted their terrified charge to the back of the long queue at the down escalator. Goering snapped to attention. '*Sieg Heil!*'

'These working conditions are intolerable!' Hitler barked at no one in particular.

'Tch, tyrants,' said an angel. 'They're all the same. They can dish it out but they can't take it!'

Gabriel smiled. 'How many angels does it take to man an escalator?' he said, pushing through the press around the foot of the moving staircase.

'Eleven! One to actually man the escalator, and ten to tell him how heavenly he looks while he's doing it.'

Much as he enjoyed these bantering sessions, Gabriel couldn't hang around; he was on a mission. He wasn't looking forward to his forthcoming meeting. He knew how God would react: he'd tell him to relax and stop being so paranoid.

As Gabriel paused at the foot of the gold-plated steps moving endlessly upward to disappear into the clouds high above, out of the corner of his eye he caught sight of a figure in a cashmere coat standing in the shadows and observing the busy activity of the Interface with interest. The shadowy individual looked vaguely familiar, but Gabriel had no time to waste on trying to place him now. He had pressing business with the Almighty.

Setting his jaw, his long legs taking the steps two at a time, the archangel rushed up the moving staircase, hurrying past the lately arrived soul on her long and lonely way to Heaven.

God lived in a large, Lutyens-style mansion on the edge of an eighteen-hole championship golf course. Behind imposing golden gates lay wide, level fairways and greens as smooth as a billiard ball.

A bored-looking Peter greeted Gabriel with a smile as he rushed up. 'Hello, Gabe. Looking for the old man?'

'Yes,' panted Gabriel.

Peter hauled open the heavy gates 'What's up? You look a little . . . anxious.'

'No time to talk now, Pete. I'll catch you on the way down.'

Gabriel rushed off towards the big house. He was halfway towards it when Peter called after him: 'He's not in!'

Gabriel stopped suddenly, turned round and spread his arms wide in a *Well, where the hell is he then?* gesture.

'You'll find him on the twelfth!'

Gabriel bowed his thanks, then raced off towards the

distant twelfth hole, leaving Peter thoughtfully stroking his chin.

Gabriel found God, as Peter had said, on the twelfth green, surrounded by a group of sycophantic saints and angels. But as he rushed towards him, Gabriel was intercepted by Saints Paul and Mark, who explained, in whispered tones, that God was about to take a very difficult putt and was on no account to be disturbed. Groaning with frustration, Gabriel watched the creator go into a long-drawn-out pre-putt routine.

The ball was lying just off the green on the lip of a sand trap, and care had to be taken not to inadvertently nudge it with a co-respondent golf shoe and send it toppling down into the bunker itself. God plucked a blade of grass, held it at arm's length and let it drop.

Gabriel puffed out his cheeks and exhaled noisily.

There was a slight breeze blowing across the green from left to right, a fact that would have to be taken into consideration and entered into the complicated calculations of force and direction applied to the ball. Clambering down into the bunker, God got behind the little white sphere and squinted carefully at its awkward lie.

Gabriel rolled his eyes. 'Oh, for goodness' sake,' he muttered.

God looked up.

'Ssh!' Paul hissed.

At last, God was ready. With his right leg braced in the sand at the top of the bunker, and his left foot level with the ball at the edge of the green, knee slightly bent, he took a couple of practice swings. Then, shuffling his brown and white tasselled brogues into position, he adjusted his stance for the real thing. Peering first at the hole, then at the ball, then back to the hole, then once more at the ball, he pulled back his club and let it swing. The head of the putter struck the ball with a satisfying *clok!* and it raced away across the manicured green. He'd certainly given it a pretty solid knock, but did it have the line? The green fell gently away to the right, which meant he'd had to push the ball quite far out to the left.

The ball, rapidly losing momentum, now became subject to the effects of gravity and began to be pulled downhill. Closer and closer the little white dimpled ball approached the cup. The tension among the watching host was palpable – even Gabriel found that he was holding his breath.

The ball edged ever nearer, but soon it became clear that God had miscalculated: the shot was too short.

The crowd let out a sigh of dismay.

But then a small bump on the green nudged the ball back on line.

'Ooh!' went the crowd.

But it was too little, too late. The ball clipped the lip of the hole only to be swung around and sent careering back up the hill.

'Ahh!'

The ball slowed and stopped. For a moment it remained impossibly poised on the sloping green. But then gravity came into play once more and the ball rolled slowly back down the hill, gathering speed until, with a triumphant clatter, it plopped into the cup.

The sounds of dismay turned to cheers and the entire throng burst into spontaneous applause.

A smugly smiling God retrieved his ball and accepted the ovation with a modest bow.

An applauding Gabriel rushed up to him. 'Well done, my lord. Well played.'

'Cut the crap, Gabriel; I know you hate golf.' God smiled.

Gabriel blushed. 'I, er . . .'

'What is it?'

Gabriel suddenly looked thoughtful.

'Well?' God said impatiently.

'Sorry, I was just wondering. Did you . . . you know, just then? Not that I'm suggesting you did, of course, but, er . . . It didn't look like the ball was going to go any-where near the hole, and . . .'

God glared at the angel.

'Silly idea. Of course you didn't,' Gabriel stammered. 'Um, can we talk?'

'*Now*? I'm halfway through a game!'

'It's rather important.'

God sighed. 'We can talk on the way to the next tee, but make it snappy. I've got Matthew really worried – he shot a bogey on that last hole, and I'm three under par.'

God was a big man with bright, sparkling blue eyes, wide shoulders and thick, flowing hair. His once-long grey beard was now trimmed to something more man-ageable so that it didn't interfere with his swing. Today he was wearing a yellow Pringle sweater over a salmon shirt, and black-and-white check plus fours, topped off with a matching cap.

The Almighty strolled over to his motorized golf trol-ley and slipped his putter back into the bag.

Gabriel followed close behind. 'It's like this,' he began. 'I think Satan's up to something.'

God turned and glared at the angel. 'Not this again, Gabriel. When will you learn to leave things alone?'

'My Lord, I admit I may have been a little hasty in the past, but I believe that this time there is a real danger. I'm convinced that Satan is about to start World War III!'

Pursing his lips, God grabbed the handle of his golf trolley and steered it over towards the nearby thirteenth tee, with Gabriel in hot pursuit.

'Please, you have to listen to me. I think that he's about to release a computer game – but it's not a computer game, it's actually a program that's going to launch the world's nuclear weapons.'

God stopped his trolley at the edge of the tee and pulled out a four wood. 'How?' he asked.

'Sorry?'

'How is this computer program going to do that?' God started nonchalantly swinging his club.

'I . . . er, I'm not exactly sure, but there's this computer magazine that's giving away this free thing called a multiplayer game and it's all about World War III, and everybody's going to get it and start playing each other and launching virtual missiles and blowing each other up without realizing that's exactly what they're doing!'

God paused between practice swings and looked Gabriel square in the eye. 'Listen to yourself, you sound like an episode of the *X-Files*.'

'No, but really—'

'Gabe,' said God, putting a hand on the archangel's shoulder, 'we've been through this a thousand times. First it was killer asteroids, then some unstoppable worldwide plague. Since then we've had pollution, depletion of the ozone layer, global warming, deforestation, genetically modified crops and now this. You know how I feel, and you know the rule: no interference.'

'I know the comet's return is only days away,' Gabriel

insisted, 'but wouldn't that just be like the Devil – to leave it until the last moment? It's just his style.'

God sighed. 'Gabriel, Lucifer has tried, oh how he's tried to put one over on me, but he's failed. Mankind has proved me right. The Serpent's time is almost up. So leave it alone, please. In a week this will all be over and Satan will be history.'

Gabriel cast his eyes down.

'Don't give me that hard-done-by look, Gabriel. You and I go back a long way. You know how fond of you I am, and I appreciate the warning, I really do, but nothing's going to happen, all right?' God chucked him under the chin. 'You know your trouble? You work too hard. Why not grab a stick and hit a couple of balls around? It's a great way to relax.'


Gabriel trudged wearily back towards the golden gates. As he was about to pass through, Peter stopped him.

'Was he still wearing that yellow sweater over a pink shirt?'

Gabriel looked up. 'I, er . . . didn't notice.'

'It's ridiculous, the creator of the universe wandering around looking like a fairy cake. So?'

Gabriel frowned. '*So* what?'

'So, what's the story?'

'Apparently I'm imagining things.'

Peter raised his eyebrows. 'Oh, another of your "end of the world" scenarios?'

'I know how it must sound, but this time it's different. This time it's . . . sneakier somehow. I think Satan's cracked it.'

'How do you mean?'

'Somehow he's managed to develop this computer game which is actually going to destroy the world. It's really very clever, and the amount of organization it must have taken is quite something.'

'Hmm,' said Peter thoughtfully.

Gabriel frowned at the gatekeeper. 'What does "Hmm" mean?'

'Well it's just you saying that Satan's done something clever. I agree that he's sneaky all right, but *clever*? If he was clever he'd never have got himself kicked out in the first place.'

Gabriel sighed and turned to go, but Peter hadn't finished.

'*If*, as you say, Satan's done this clever thing which has taken a lot of organization, then it stands to reason there are going to be others involved, doesn't it?'

Gabriel stopped and turned to look at him. 'What are you getting at?'

'It may be nothing, but . . . I shouldn't really be saying this . . .'

'You haven't said *anything* yet.'

'It may be nothing,' Peter repeated, 'and you have to remember this is in the strictest confidence . . . There's no telling what sort of trouble I'd get into with His Lordship if he ever found out . . .'

'Get on with it!'

'All right. You know I take all God's calls on a Sunday?'

'Yes.'

'Well, the other day I heard something strange.'

'I'd have thought that, listening to the innermost thoughts of several billion people, that would be an occupational hazard.'

'No, but this was different. There was this prayer from someone we hadn't heard from for some time.'

'People are always coming and going in the Church.'

'People are always *leaving* the Church, yes. Those coming back in are few and far between, especially the *successful* ones.'

'Successful?'

'Yes. Usually it's only those who've been a complete failure – who've been soundly kicked in the teeth by life, so to speak – who come back into the fold. But this chap is a very successful businessman with everything going for him, and yet there he was, on his knees begging for salvation amongst the old dears smelling of mothballs and Parma violets.'

Gabriel pulled his earlobe thoughtfully. 'Perhaps he just realized that money can't buy him happiness?'

'Well, yes, that's a possibility, but Christianity's so unfashionable these days. Most people like him usually opt for some kind of free-form spirituality – you know, the sort that offers couscous and free condoms. Very rarely do the middle classes rejoin the Church, especially when things are going well for them.'

'What did he say?'

'"Father, forgive me. Lord, forgive me. Oh God, forgive me . . ." over and over again.'

'Forgive him for what?'

'He didn't say. But then *this* happened.' Peter turned to a little plastic box sitting on a table by the gate pillar. 'Because he's been so busy with his bloody golf this week – he's challenged Matthew, Mark, Luke *and* John to a best of three – he's asked me to record everything so that he can listen to it all tonight. And yesterday, as I was giving the gates a quick once-over with the duster, this came in.'

He flicked a switch and the small white plastic box crackled into life.

*Beep! 'You have ten million, five hundred and seventy-two thousand, eight hundred and thirty-one messages,'* the box announced.

'Tch, he's not going to get through half of them,' Peter muttered. 'Hang on.'

Peter pressed the SKIP button several hundred times.

'Is this going to take long?' Gabriel wondered aloud.

'Just have a bit of patience.' Peter kept on skipping through the messages until . . . 'Ah, here we are. Listen to this. Now, bear in mind that this was on a Friday – he's on his knees, in church, on a *weekday*. He's desperate all right.' He pressed PLAY and a despairing voice came pleading through the small speaker.

*'Oh Lord, I have sinned. I am beyond redemption. Please can you see it in your mercy to forgive me?'*

'Is that him?' Gabriel interrupted.

'Shh, listen.'

*'I've done a terrible, terrible thing. It was stupid, I know, but I was young; I didn't know what I was getting into. But now the fires of Hell beckon and I don't know what to do . . .'*

'Is that it?'

'Yes, that was when the vicar came up and told him to move on – family christening.'

Gabriel began pacing. 'The fires of Hell?'

'Of course, a lot of supplicants use the phrase figuratively, but if this feller's somehow got himself involved with the Devil, he might be employing it in a more literal sense.'

'And you think he might have something to do with setting up this computer game?'

'You never know.'

'What's his name?'

'Oh, I can't give out that kind of information.'

'Don't play games with me, Pete.'

Peter smiled. 'You'll be surprised.'

'Just tell me who it is!'

'What's it worth?'

'Peter!'

'All right. Garth Ferrers.'

Gabriel looked puzzled. 'Who's Garth Ferrers?'

Peter was stunned. 'Who's Garth Ferrers?'

'That's what *I* just said.'

'You've never heard of Garth Ferrers – millionaire publishing tycoon? The man who caused a scandal by sailing round the world with a ship-load of beautiful women?'

Gabriel shook his head. 'Should I have?'

'Don't you read the tabloids?'

'No.'

'No wonder you never have any gossip.'

'Wait a minute . . . You said publishing? That would fit. What else do you know about him?'

'Only what I've read in *Hello!*. He's good-looking, has houses all over the world – the one in St Kitts is fabulous – and seems to have the Midas touch when it comes to business.'

'Garth Ferrers,' Gabriel repeated, beaming at the heavenly gatekeeper. 'Peter, you're an angel. I won't forget this.'

'All I ask in return is that you find out who his interior designer is.'

# Chapter 8

By what stroke of ill fortune Satan's personal telephone number ended up on Garth Ferrers' cold-calling list all those years ago we may never know. It may have been a misprint – Mandy, the office secretary, was a notoriously bad typist – or perhaps it was simply a bit of mischief by one of Satan's bored minions. But, however it got there, the call Garth made that distant September morning changed his life.

For a company that advertised itself as 'Devon's Premier Double-Glazing Specialists', Westlight's business premises were surprisingly unprepossessing. Situated on an industrial estate outside Plymouth, head office consisted of a small prefabricated unit shared with a mail-order lingerie company.

Including Garth – office junior and general dogsbody – there was a total of only three staff. Westlight's CEO was Trevor Bere – a large, round man with curly, flyaway hair that he plastered to his scalp with copious amounts of gel. Garth only ever saw him in one suit – a dark grey pinstripe with fraying turn-ups, shiny elbows and greasy cuffs. The final member of the trio was Trevor's secretary – a middle-aged woman called Mandy Swinburne. Mandy had dyed-blonde hair and a fondness for the colour pink. She too was rather large, a fact emphasized by the clothes she chose to wear. She was forever trying to fit herself into a size 14 when, to be honest, she was an unreconstructed, no-holds-barred 16. Her ample waist overflowed the waistband of her skirt, and her arms, kept in check to the elbow by her collection of candy-pink short-sleeved blouses, ballooned gratefully free at the forearm to wobble about like two plucked chickens. Although approaching fifty, she still behaved like a schoolgirl, with her girly voice and high-pitched giggle. Garth had secretly nicknamed her Miss Piggy.

Trevor also had a wife, a shadowy figure who never actually came in to the office but would ring up from time to time and berate him for some real or imagined wrong. Trevor seemed to take it all with good grace and spent these conversations cooing into the receiver, 'I know, I know. I'm sorry, my pet. You're quite right, of course . . .' whenever she called in one of her passions.

Trevor's wife's real problem, whether she knew it or not, was Mandy. She and Trevor had been conducting an affair for years, and indeed were still pursuing it with vigour – they could hardly keep their hands off each other. Every lunchtime they would withdraw into the office's cramped lavatory for some stolen moments of passion. Garth always found an excuse to go out for lunch.

But one particular September morning, back in 1985, returning to the office after posting a load of mailshots, Garth discovered that Trevor and Mandy had started their lavatory rumpy pumpy prematurely. Mandy's high-pitched squeals and Trevor's grunts could be clearly heard through the thin wall. Garth was just about to turn around and start his lunch break early when he heard Trevor's voice boom through the paper-thin partition. 'Garth!' he panted, 'there's a list of telephone numbers on your desk. Work through them and see if you can't drum up some extra business!'

Grimly, Garth turned back into the room and walked over to his tiny desk, perched in the corner between the small, loudly humming fridge and the sink with its plug-hole permanently clogged with used tea bags. He looked down at the sheet that Mandy had typed out with her accustomed inventive flair – she couldn't even spell double-glazing, which was a bit of a drawback in her line of work. Trevor had even gone to the trouble of pro-viding Garth with a script – full of Mandy's spelling mistakes and typing errors – with the instruction 'Britely' at the top of the page. Garth sat down with a sigh as Trevor and Mandy's lovemaking shifted up a gear, the thumps and yelps emanating from the lavatory sounding more akin to murder than tenderness.

Gritting his teeth, Garth picked up the phone and dialled the first number on the list. Someone picked up at the other end and, doing his best to sound 'Brite', Garth began reciting his lines.

'Hello, this is Westlight, Devon's premeer dubbel-gliz-ing . . . er, double-glazing speshalists. Weer going to be in you're area in the next few weaks, and wundered if you'd like to take advantige of our once-in-a-lifetime offer. We can call at you're—'

The man at the other end muttered 'Bollocks' and the line went dead.

Garth went on to the next number, and this time only managed to get as far as 'double-glazing speshalists' before he heard the click of the receiver being replaced.

Garth carried on down the list, feeling less and less 'Brite' with every unsuccessful call, as Trevor and Mandy continued to grunt and gasp and scream with uncaring abandon only feet away. He had to hand it to Trevor; he certainly had stamina. Then Garth reached telephone number 01822 870666. It only rang twice before a man picked up. 'Hello?'

'Hello, this is Westlight, Devon's premier double-glazing specialists—'

'Who is this?' the voice at the other end enquired sharply.

'I, er . . . This is Westlight Double-Glazing,' Garth repeated, 'and we're going to be in your area—'

'I very much doubt that,' the man interrupted. 'How did you get this number? It's ex-directory.'

'Oh, I'm sorry, I . . . You see, I was given this . . . Er, it was on my calling sheet, and—'

'Cold-calling, yes, I am familiar with the practice. A job reserved solely for the desperate and moronic.'

Garth was completely thrown. 'Well, I . . .'

'Would you call yourself intelligent?'

'I beg your pardon?'

'Would you like me to repeat the question?'

'No, but—'

'I think you've already answered it. Indeed, why else would you put yourself in line for such abuse?'

Garth felt the blood rising to his cheeks. 'Now look here—'

'No, you look. It was you who called me, remember. I didn't invite you into my life; you intruded yourself, which, as it happens, gives me an idea.' The man's voice suddenly took on a friendly, wheedling tone. 'What's your name?'

'Um, Garth.'

'Garth. Did you know that Garth means someone in charge of a garden?'

'Er, no.'

'How's life treating you?'

Garth was finding it hard to keep up with the twists and turns of this conversation. 'Life?'

'Yes, you know, that thing that you sit and wish away in your idle hours, and yet beg for more of when your time's up.'

'Well . . .' Mandy let rip an orgasmic scream that rattled the lipstick-marked teacups on the sink drainer, then she and Trevor fell back into a low, rhythmic panting. 'It's—'

'Not living up to expectations, is it?' the man continued. 'Let me see, your life . . . You're a young man, with all a young man's fantasies – sun-kissed women with long legs pandering to your every whim, a Ferrari in the double garage with a remote up-and-over door, a yacht moored in St Tropez, a private jet, properties all over the world – and yet here you are stuck in a dead-end job with no prospects and the only thing to look forward to a cheese and ham sandwich and a half of lager at lunchtime. How am I doing?'

It was a surprisingly accurate picture both of Garth's innermost longings and the depressing reality of his existence. His life was a tedious black and white documentary and yet he longed for a wide-screen Technicolor experience with breathtaking special effects. 'Well, to be honest, I do sometimes wish I had a little more excitement in my life.'

'Excitement, yes! Racing around the streets of Monaco in a Formula 1 car; flying a microlight across the great white wastes of the Antarctic; skydiving from the edge of space. Sound like fun?'

'Er, yeah.'

'Do you know anything about publishing?' It was an odd question.

'No, not really. Why?' Garth said slowly.

'Never mind, you can learn on the job.'

'Job, what job?'

'Sorry,' said the man's voice, 'am I going a little too fast for you?'

'Well . . .'

'I don't know how you got this number and, frankly, I don't care. But this, Garth, is your lucky day. It just so happens that I'm looking for someone with your qualifications—'

'Qualifications?' Garth's only qualification was an NVQ in metalwork.

'You're alive, aren't you?'

'Er, just about.' Garth laughed.

'There you are then. Meet me in half an hour where the Torpoint ferry leaves, just off Park Avenue. Do you know it?'

'Er, yeah.'

'Don't disappoint me now; this is the opportunity of a lifetime.' The line went dead just as Mandy reappeared, adjusting her skirt. Trevor followed her out, zipping his fly and sweating profusely. The room was suddenly filled with warm, animal smells. Garth wanted to throw up.

'Erm,' he said suddenly, 'I have to go out.' Without saying another word, he got up and ran through the door.

'How'd you get on with that list I gave you?' Trevor called after him.

Although the rest of Plymouth was basking in bright sunshine, on the Torpoint ferry slipway Garth found himself enveloped in a thick mist. Unable to see where he was going and not wanting to fall into the sea, Garth was about to retrace his steps when he heard a car horn. Dimly, through the gloom, he could just make out a set of red tail lights.

'Garth!' came a voice out of the darkness. 'Over here!'

Garth walked tentatively towards the lights, the sharp sound of his metal heel plates on the stone cobbles the only sound in the deadening mist.

'That's right, follow the sound of my voice!' It was the same voice that Garth had heard on the phone. 'I'm so glad you could make it,' the voice continued. 'I can see you're a young man who's not afraid to buck convention. Not afraid to take a risk. Faint heart never won fair lady, eh?'

Now Garth was near enough to make out the form of a man standing by the open door of a large black saloon parked on the slipway. He was in full evening dress: top hat, white tie, gloves and opera cape, and he carried a silver-topped cane. 'We meet at last,' said the man, removing a glove and extending his hand.

'Er, pleased to meet you,' said Garth, taking it. Close up, the man looked ancient: his face was lined like a walnut, and yet his jaunty manner belied his obvious age.

'Nice to meet you too, Garth. Oh, but how rude of me, I haven't introduced myself, have I? I'm –' he paused a moment '– De'ath,' he continued brightly. 'Señor De'ath.'

'Señor? Are you Spanish, then?'

'Ah, Garth, what a quick mind you have. Yes, indeed, why shouldn't I be Spanish? Spain, with its dark and brooding soul – a magnificent country. There is life, passion, violence – bloody violence – and death. And the

Spanish character? It's there in the drama of the bullfight. The spectacle is all: sumptuous costumes, proud men proving their manhood by sticking gaily coloured sticks into murderous creatures merely to impress outwardly simpering, inwardly smouldering dark-eyed beauties. Oh yes, the Spanish soul is a work of art.' Señor De'ath indicated the back seat of the limousine. 'Shall we?'

'Er, oh. OK.' Garth got in and slid along the blood-red leather upholstery. Señor De'ath got in alongside him and tapped the glass partition immediately behind the driver with the top of his cane. The car moved off along the slipway towards the sea.

'Um, shouldn't we turn round?' Garth wondered nervously.

'Fear not, young Garth, I am taking you to your future.'

'My . . .?'

'Wait and see. Just sit back, relax and enjoy the ride.'

Garth settled back in the deeply upholstered seat and gazed out of the window. Outside, the fog grew thicker, but the driver, seemingly oblivious to the impenetrable mist, urged the large car faster and faster along the uneven slipway. Then, suddenly, there was a lurch and they started to head smoothly downhill.

Garth wasn't sure how long they'd been driving, but at last the fog began to thin and a pair of large wrought-iron gates appeared out of the swirling mist in front of the car. The gates opened as the limousine approached, and the car's tyres scrunched on gravel as it began to climb a long drive leading up to an imposing Gothic mansion which loomed like a landlocked galleon out of the darkness, lights blazing in every window. Darkness? Garth had left the offices of Westlight Double-Glazing in bright sunshine, and yet now he seemed to have arrived here in the middle of the night. Something wasn't quite right.

Beside him, Señor De'ath sensed his discomfort. 'Who needs the day when the night is so much kinder to the complexion?'

Garth turned to him and gasped in shock. In the gloom of the limousine's interior, the man's eyes glowed like red-hot coals.

'You really have nothing to fear, my friend,' Señor De'ath continued. 'All your wishes are about to come true.'

Garth turned back to the window and gazed out at the large turreted house they were drawing near. 'Um, this job you mentioned . . .' he began.

'What does it entail?'

Garth nodded, his eyes fixed on the house. 'Mm hm.'

'You'll be working for one of the most generous employers in the business; you can choose your own hours; you'll have all the help and support you need, an army of servants at your beck and call; women will fall into your arms; and the salary is out of this world. Any questions?'

Garth stared at Señor De'ath. Surely the man was putting him on. He narrowed his eyes. 'What exactly—'

'Do you have to *do*? Good question. The world of publishing has produced many rich men. The public seems to have an insatiable appetite for the trivial, and you will feed that appetite.'

'But I don't know anything about publishing,' Garth protested.

'Nor do most of the people in it. I, however, am an

expert, and will teach you everything you need to know. All I ask in return for this once-in-a-lifetime opportunity is something very small, something, indeed, you may not even be aware you possess.'

Garth's eyes were like saucers.

Señor De'ath smiled back at him. Garth felt a bit like a fat, juicy cricket being eyed up by a lizard. 'But we'll get to that later.'

The limousine came to a halt in the turning circle immediately outside the house, and Señor De'ath leaned forwards and addressed the driver. 'Thank you, Mephisto, that will be all. You may take the rest of the day off.'

The chauffeur nodded in acknowledgement as a gaunt, hollow-eyed butler emerged from the house and opened the car door.

'My Lord,' said the butler in a voice as dry and parched as a desert wind, 'and young Master Ferrers, welcome.'

Confused, Garth turned to Senor De'ath. 'How does he know my name?'

But Señor De'ath merely smiled and urged Garth out of the car. Garth's feet crunched on the gravel as he looked around. The air had a strange, sulphurous tang and – apart from the house, ablaze with light – everything was in darkness, the surrounding landscape completely shrouded in mystery.

Señor De'ath addressed his butler, 'Thank you, Lothar. I trust Signora Amati is ready.'

The butler nodded. 'Pitch perfect, My Lord.'

'Good, good. So, Garth, I expect you'll be wanting to freshen up before dinner. Lothar will show you to your room.'

'Dinner? I can't stay for dinner; I've got to get back to work.'

'Tush, tush.' Señor De'ath put an arm around his shoulder. 'My dear boy, your loyalty is admirable. Indeed, I only hope you show me the same dogged constancy in all *our* dealings. But, *honestly*, Garth. Here I am, offering you the world and you're eager to get back to your lowly position as office dogsbody? Where's your spirit of adventure? Don't worry. I'll sort everything out with Westlight and Mr Bere.'

Garth frowned suddenly and turned to look at him. 'I never told you his name.'

Señor De'ath winked at him in a sly, reptilian way. 'Oh, I know all about you, Garth. I know all your innermost secrets. For instance, remember that little prank at school when you put peanut butter in Tim Smith's sandwiches? It only took half a teaspoon to bring on a devastating allergic reaction that nearly killed him. And all because he reported you for spying on the girls' changing rooms.'

Garth went cold, cringing at the memory.

'Don't get me wrong,' Señor De'ath continued. 'I'm not judging you. I think your actions reveal a certain feistiness. Take, for instance, the time you punished your chemistry teacher for giving you a D– by slipping a small phosphorous rock in her handbag as she was getting into her car. The subsequent fire caused her to swerve into the path of that oncoming lorry. She was lucky to escape with just a broken leg.'

'I was young,' Garth protested. 'I didn't know what I was doing.' He looked at Señor De'ath suspiciously. 'Besides, no one ever found out I'd done it.'

'We all like to think we have secrets, Garth. But it's all written down in the Ledger of Life, believe you me. Every little lie, every stolen bag of sweets, every unpaid bus fare – it all gets recorded.'

'Ledger of Life?'

'We'll talk more later. Lothar! Show Mr Ferrers to his room and get him a drink. I have a feeling he needs one.'

'This way, Master Ferrers.' Before Garth knew what was happening, the butler had ushered him into the house and was showing him up an elegant, sweeping staircase, past a full set of armour, complete with murderous broadsword. The banisters reminded Garth of something, but he couldn't think what.

'I've laid out your evening dress, sir.'

'Dress?'

'For dinner. Milord always dresses for dinner.'

'Oh.'

Lothar opened a door off a corridor on the first floor of the mansion to reveal a large room dominated by an elaborately carved, dark-oak four-poster bed, a full evening suit laid out on its counterpane.

'But . . . how did you know my size?'

The butler ignored the query, smiled and softly closed the door.

Garth was left alone. Although the room was big, it was over-furnished in a claustrophobic, Victorian way. Two large armchairs faced the fireplace, and sofas covered in tasselled cushions and silk throws lined the walls. Small tables, draped with lace tablecloths, were scattered about the Persian carpets, and every available flat surface, from the mantelpiece to the windowsill, was covered in little porcelain figures and cut-glass vases. Garth found it very hard to breathe.

Edging his way through the clutter to the large sash window, Garth heaved it open and inhaled deeply. The air was warm, and up here the smell of sulphur was much stronger than it had been at ground level. Garth told himself this was just because of the fog which still swirled around the house, thick and impenetrable. But who'd ever heard of warm fog?

Garth's brain teemed with questions. What was this place? And what had Señor De'ath meant when he'd said it was his *future*? Who was this Señor De'ath anyway, and how did he know so much about him? But as the only kind of questions Garth was used to grappling with were of the *Cheese and onion or salt and vinegar?* variety, all this thinking soon exhausted him. He had just slumped down in a large wing chair when there was a knock at the door. It was Lothar, carrying a cut-glass tumbler half-full of an amber liquid, and a small glass jug of water on a silver salver.

'Whisky and water, sir. I'll leave it on the bedside table.'

Gingerly balancing the tumbler and jug on top of a teetering stack of books on the small table, Lothar stepped back, like a conjuror having performed a feat of the utmost dexterity, and announced, 'The recital is at seven o'clock, and dinner will be served immediately after.'

'Recital?'

Lothar smiled enigmatically, bowed and exited the room once more.

Clambering laboriously over the gratuitous furniture, Garth made his way towards the alcohol like a man in a desert might hurry towards an oasis. Although hard liquor wasn't usually his thing, in the present circumstances he thought he'd make an exception, and he gulped the burning liquid down greedily. It felt good. It felt even better when it reached his brain. The more he drank, the less space any doubts and anxieties about his present circumstances occupied at the forefront of his mind, receding instead to a distance where he could wave at them cheerily and blow raspberries.

The glass seemed to be enchanted. Every time he drained it, it miraculously refilled itself. He must have got through about three tumblers, and his worries had become a distant speck on the horizon before he sat down on the bed and wondered what to do next. He looked at the big, old-fashioned alarm clock ticking loudly on the bedside table. In his inebriated state it took him a little time to work it out, but after a concerted effort, straining his eyes at the dial, he interpreted its hands as reading 3.30. The 'recital', whatever that was, wasn't for another three and a half hours. What was he going to do until then? His body would have been happy for him to lie down and sleep, but there was a little bubble of devilish excitement deep inside which urged him to go exploring. His innate British reserve was crumbling in the face of the whisky, and the prospect of finding some answers to his questions was becoming more and more appealing.

But just then there was another knock at the door.

Staggering clumsily towards it, he yanked it open. At first he thought he was seeing double, because standing in front of him were two young women wearing identical see-through baby-doll nighties. He rubbed his eyes, but the double image persisted. They smiled at him.

'Hello,' said one.

'Aren't you going to invite us in?' asked the other.

'Ung,' Garth replied after a stunned pause. Then he stood aside and waved them into the room.

Giggling, they ran straight past him and leapt onto the bed. Garth watched them, feeling strangely detached.

They were beautiful. Both had long dark hair and were clearly naked beneath their skimpy nighties.

'Wha . . . whe . . .' Garth tried to frame a question but he wasn't sure what to ask or whether, indeed, it was necessary to ask anything at all. But feeling as if he ought to say *something*, he eventually managed a slurred, 'Woo . . . would you like a drink?'

The two girls looked at each other and burst out laughing. Then both turned their dark eyes on him. If he'd had any willpower to begin with, it would instantly have evaporated under their gaze. As it was, he happily gave in to the compulsion to join them on the bed. One, he noticed, had slipped off her nightie and was now kneeling on the counterpane naked, her large breasts invitingly pert. The other, without his noticing, seemed to have removed his belt, and was now yanking down his trousers . . .

Garth and his two new friends – Raven and Cassandra – arrived, happily glowing, at the bottom of the stairs just as the grandfather clock in the echoing hall struck seven. There was still something vaguely worrying about the banisters, but Garth couldn't for the life of him figure out what it was.

As the contented threesome hit the last step, Lothar appeared bang on cue and escorted them across the airy hall, with its intricately tiled floor, towards two large doors set into the ornately carved panel work. Pulling these open with a flourish, the butler stood aside deferentially and Garth and his escorts entered a long room decked out like a small theatre. From a centre boss in the high ceiling hung a crystal chandelier, filling the room with dancing, sparkling rainbows of light. And around a plaster frieze, high up on the walls, satyrs with impossibly large phalluses chased nubile nymphs, their timeless beauty forever just out of reach. At the far end of the room, directly above the small stage, hung the classic theatre motif: the intertwining masks of comedy and tragedy, although Garth was almost sure he'd never seen them with horns before.

On the stage, in front of plush red velvet curtains warmed by unseen lights, stood a simple gilt three-legged stool, while in the body of the hall were three ornate chairs, facing the stage.

Lothar ushered Garth into the centre seat, and his female companions took their places on either side.

Immediately the glittering light from the chandelier went out, the curtain-warmers dimmed and, out of the ensuing darkness, a spotlight snapped on, illuminating the single golden stool. The curtains parted and Señor De'ath appeared, leading by the hand a small, shapely, pale-faced woman in a black dress. Raven and Cassandra burst into applause and Garth followed suit.

Smiling and acknowledging the applause, Señor De'ath led his partner centre stage and sat himself down on the stool. Reaching under the seat, he produced a bow and, looking up at the small, nervous woman, smiled gently. Then something unbelievable happened. Garth gasped in amazement. Before his eyes, the most astonishing transformation had taken place. Trying to make sense of it, Garth went over again in his mind what had happened. Señor De'ath had reached out to take the woman's hand, then had suddenly whirled her around, simultaneously pulling her down towards him. But it was not the form of a woman that now rested between Señor De'ath's legs, it was a cello.

Señor De'ath placed the bow lightly on the strings and began to play. The most exquisite sound filled the air as he launched into the opening bars of Bach's Suite No.1 in G major. The tone of the instrument was almost human – it had a plangency that seemed to express all the exquisite sadness inherent in the human condition, although, if pressed, that's probably not how Garth would have expressed it. But he *was* moved by it. He closed his eyes and let the marvellous noise wash over him.

As the last, magical notes reverberated around the room, Señor De'ath lowered the bow and closed his eyes. Then he stood up and was once more hand in hand with the woman. The small audience burst into applause.

'Who is she?' Garth whispered to Cassandra.

'Ellena, wife of Nicolò Amati, the man who taught Stradivari.'

'He wanted to be the best violin maker in Italy,' Raven chipped in, 'so Daddy arranged it.'

'A plague ravaged Cremona in 1630, wiping out all the competition,' Cassandra continued, 'so Nicolò got his wish.'

'All his cellos were modelled on his wife's proportions.'

'So Daddy thought she'd be a fitting price to pay for his success.'

'That, and having his reputation completely overshadowed by his pupil,' Raven concluded.

But all Garth had heard was the one word: *Daddy*.

'Senor De'ath is your father?' he asked in a whisper. The awful thought that he had reduced to matchwood some kind of etiquette boundary by enjoying his host's two daughters completely veiled the terrifying and obvious truth about his current situation which had, for some time now, been attempting to force its way into his perception.

But Garth had no time to explore this feeling, for Señor De'ath and Ellena Amati were preparing for an encore.

Again came the magical transformation, and again the extraordinary, almost human sound of the Amati cello filled the room, as the bow touched the strings and the dramatic opening of Zoltan Kodaly's Sonata for Violoncello, Opus 8 (*allegro maestoso ma appassionato*) filled the room.

When the recital was finished, Señor De'ath and his instrument stood and took the applause, then the soloist led the now drawn and exhausted-looking woman off the stage and back through the red velvet curtains.

As the house lights came back up, Lothar appeared and ushered Garth and the girls through to the dining room, where a long oak table was laid for dinner. The room had a large bay window but, as from upstairs, the view outside was obscured by the all-enveloping fog. And although it was early autumn, a fire blazed in the grate. It was almost unbearably warm and Garth was sweating like a pig. In the middle of the table stood a large tank filled with bubbling water in which the dark blue shapes of lobsters scuttled about.

While Garth was studying the menacing creatures, Señor De'ath entered the room looking flushed. Garth and the two girls burst into applause.

Señor De'ath received his ovation with a modest bow of the head. 'Thank you, thank you.'

Lothar was immediately at his side with a tall glass filled with a blood-red liquid. Señor De'ath took the glass, drained it and smacked his lips. 'Lothar makes the best

Bloody Mary – the real thing,' he added with a leer, handing the empty glass back to his manservant.

Garth suddenly went cold and that undigested thought which had threatened to surface during the recital began to knock on his conscience once more, this time waving flags and blowing a whistle.

'Shall we?' Señor De'ath sat down at the head of the table. 'Garth, you're here.' He indicated the place immediately to his left. Cassandra sat herself next to Garth, and Raven took her place opposite. 'I must say,' Señor De'ath continued, 'if I'm allowed a modicum of vainglory for a moment, I thought I played rather well. Do you know, Garth, I sometimes think I missed my vocation. Ah, the musical life!' He opened his elaborately folded napkin with a flick of his wrist and laid it across his lap. 'How I long for like-minded individuals with whom to play and discuss music.' He turned to Garth. 'I don't suppose you play, do you?'

'No.'

'Never mind,' he sighed. 'It's not true what they say, you know – the best musicians always get dragged upstairs. All I ever seem to get are blues men and conductors. Signor Paganini, of course, is a notable exception, but playing with him is impossible. He's addicted to improvization; he never follows the notes!' Señor De'ath suddenly took Garth's hand and beamed at him. 'So, how are you feeling, Garth? How have my daughters been treating you? I do hope they've been keeping you entertained.'

Garth's heart did a sort of jig in his chest and he went beetroot red. 'Er, oh yes. They've been very accommodating,' he said, withdrawing his hand. 'We've . . . I've . . . They've looked after me very well.'

Cassandra's and Raven's eyes met and they giggled.

'Um, where's your instrum— Er, I mean the lady you were . . . playing?' Garth faltered, rapidly changing the subject.

'Ellena? Oh, she's very temperamental. If it's too hot her fingerboard warps, too cold and she can sound like a strangled cat. I've left her to have a little lie-down; recitals always leave her exhausted.' He smiled at Garth. 'I'm a very demanding player. With me it's all or nothing.'

Cassandra looked approvingly at her father. 'Daddy plays with a passion that she sometimes finds almost over-whelming.'

Señor De'ath smiled darkly at his daughter. 'If you are going to do something, do it to the utmost of your ability; that's always been my motto. I see no point in doing anything half-cocked.' He turned to Garth. 'Wouldn't you agree?'

Garth went a deeper shade of red and looked down at his lap.

'The trouble with Daddy,' Raven ventured, 'is that he's a frustrated performer.'

'She's right, Garth. Do you know, I would have given anything to be a professional? I still have a fond dream that one day I will play at one of the great houses: Carnegie Hall, La Scala, the Albert Hall . . .' Señor De'ath stared wistfully into the middle distance for some moments, then turned back to Garth. 'But I expect you're hungry. I hope you like venison.'

'Oh, I've never—'

Señor De'ath clapped his hands and Lothar appeared at the head of a hitherto unseen army of white-coated servants bearing large silver platters.

'Would you care to choose your fish course, sir?' Lothar asked an increasingly bewildered Garth.

'Sorry?'

'Your lobster,' Raven suggested helpfully, pointing to the tank in the middle of the table. 'Pick one you like the look of.'

'Oh.' Garth studied the lobsters carefully. He didn't really like the look of any of them. They all seemed rather vicious, circling each other and posturing aggressively. He was sure that were it not for the stout rubber bands around their claws they would be happily tearing each other apart. 'Er, that one.' Garth pointed to a rather dopey one sitting dazed in a corner of the tank.

'Nonsense,' said Señor De'ath. 'That one looks as if it's about to roll over and die. Choose one with spirit. The most aggressive make the best eating.' He stood to get a better view, then jabbed a finger decisively towards the meanest-looking lobster in the tank. 'That beast there. The one with the glint in its eye.'

Lothar rolled up his sleeve and plunged in his arm. Moments later Garth was face to face with the creature, its tail flapping angrily, as the butler displayed it for his approval. It had only one eye, the other having been lost in an altercation with one of its colleagues over half a rotten sprat, but its single orb glared at Garth with a malevolence that he found distinctly disconcerting.

Señor De'ath took the lobster from his butler. 'But, for the finest flavour it must die a *quiet* death. Too much adrenalin spoils the flesh.' He proceeded to stroke the creature's belly, cooing gently to it. To Garth's astonishment the crustacean relaxed to such an extent that Señor De'ath was able to lie it flat on the table, on its back, even balance it on its head without the least resistance. When he had finished displaying the lobster's docility, he tossed it back to Lothar and then picked his own. When Cassandra and Raven had also chosen, Lothar withdrew with the selected beasts and the white-coated servants served the first course: foie gras.

'Are you a wine drinker, Garth?' Señor De'ath had a bottle in his hand, the label towards his guest.

Garth shook his head. 'No, I can't really say I am. I mean, Mum sometimes used to buy a bottle of fizzy for special occasions, but I can't say I'm really a fan.'

'You'll learn. There is so much good wine around these days it would take several lifetimes to acquaint oneself with every single one. So, for the moment, we'll confine ourselves to the best.' Señor De'ath poured an amber-coloured liquid into Garth's glass. 'Château d'Yquem, 1945,' he announced. 'An unexpected but perfect partner for foie gras.'

'Oh, fancy that.'

'Have a little taste,' Señor De'ath instructed.

As Garth raised his glass to his lips he noticed it was very cold. 'Cheers.' He smiled lopsidedly. Then he took a sip. As the wine hit his palate, Garth experienced the most extraordinary sensation – his head was suddenly filled with the scent of wild flowers. And on his tongue was a taste like honey – no, not honey, more like . . . nectar. But even that didn't do it justice. It was . . . Unfortunately his oenological vocabulary was not yet up to describing the sensation in any detail. 'Wow!' was the best he could manage.

Señor De'ath regarded him over the rim of his own glass. 'Do you like it?'

Garth looked into the depths of his wine with astonishment. 'It's amazing!' Then he put it to his lips again and drained it, holding out his empty glass for a refill.

Señor De'ath raised an eyebrow and refilled Garth's glass. 'Best to take it steady if you're not used to it. It's got quite a kick. Tell you what, this time try a little foie gras first, then have another sip. Just a sip, mind.'

Garth already had his second glass halfway to his lips, but looking round the table at the smilingly indulgent faces of his host and two daughters, he sheepishly put down his glass and picked up his knife and fork. Or he would have done if he'd known which particular set of cutlery to choose from the many available. He looked up into Raven's eyes.

She helpfully mouthed at him, *From the outside in*, demonstrating this herself by picking up the knife and fork set furthest from her plate.

Garth did likewise, then looked at what had been placed before him: a small misshapen mass of something brownish-pink which looked distinctly unappetizing. Not wanting to offend, he cut off a small corner. It had a texture like lard and a vaguely offally flavour, like nothing he'd ever tasted before, but it complemented the wine perfectly.

'Um, what is this?' Garth tentatively enquired.

'Goose liver,' Señor De'ath replied. 'It's made by force-feeding the geese on corn. Their enforced overindulgence causes the liver to swell and gives it this unique texture.' He cut off a large chunk and raised it to his lips, closing his eyes to relish the taste.

Garth felt ever so slightly queasy. He put down his knife and fork and took another sip of wine.

Señor De'ath looked at Garth's unfinished plate. 'Not hungry?'

'Um . . . not really used to rich food.'

'You'd better get used to it, Garth, because this is how you're going to be eating from now on.' Señor De'ath wiped his mouth with his napkin and raised his glass. 'Here's to a long and fruitful collaboration.'

Garth followed suit, muttering, 'Long and fruitful collaboration,' without knowing what it meant.

After Señor De'ath's toast, the plates were cleared and the second course was served. Much to Garth's regret, his half-full glass was removed and replaced with a fresh but empty one. However, he needn't have worried; there were more vinous delights in store.

Garth looked down to see the lobster he had chosen, which not fifteen minutes ago had been so malevolently alive, now lying on his plate split in two. Suddenly his appetite completely deserted him.

Tucking his napkin into his shirt collar, Señor De'ath instructed Garth to 'Eat and enjoy' and attacked his own lobster with gusto.

Garth did his best, but he really couldn't say he was a big shellfish fan. The wine accompanying it, however, was another eye-opener. It was a crisp, clean glass of non-vintage Veuve Clicquot, completely unlike the cloyingly sweet Asti Spumanti that his mother used to buy at Christmas. After his second glass, Garth began to feel just a little light-headed, and any misgivings with which he'd started the evening were now a dim and distant memory.

Next course was woodcock, served with a 1953 Mouton-Rothschild, which was followed by venison with a stunning 1966 Haut-Brion, which to Garth's mind smelled like the inside of his school pencil box filled with vanilla ice cream. It tasted delicious though. As the plates were removed and dessert (a rich devil's food cake) was served, Garth felt he ought to give voice to the warm and affectionate feelings towards his host brewing in his breast.

'Mr, um . . . Señor,' Garth began. 'Thank you. I've never . . . ever . . . The most . . . and the food – marvellous!' He belched. 'I'm very full.'

Señor De'ath waited a while to see if Garth was going to continue, but it seemed that his dinner guest had exhausted his invention.

'I'm touched.' Señor De'ath smiled, laying a hand on Garth's. 'How about a digestif?'

Small cups of startlingly strong coffee were served, along with a fine old Armagnac. Garth was floating on a pink fluffy cloud. Happily clutching a glass of the exquisite liquor, he relaxed back in his chair, smiling inanely.

Señor De'ath beamed at him. 'And now, although it seems a shame to talk business after such a meal, we should get the paperwork over with.'

'Paperwork?' That old niggling doubt in Garth's mind raised its ugly head again. 'What paperwork?'

'Oh, just a formality.' Señor De'ath clicked his fingers, and Lothar produced a parchment scroll from an inside pocket and laid it on the table.

Garth scanned the document in front of him. There was a lot of dense legal language to begin with which even if he hadn't been drunk he wouldn't have understood, but there, towards the bottom, was a phrase which was completely unambiguous: 'I, the undersigned, do hereby grant exclusive rights to my soul to the Devil, otherwise known as Satan, the Dark Lord, Lucifer, the Beast, Señor De'ath, Beelzebub, etc. . . . '

Garth was suddenly stone-cold sober and gripped by a tingling dread. The thought which had been circling him all evening was now smacking him over the head with a mallet and yelling, 'I told you so!'

Garth looked up slowly at his host, whose bloodshot eyes burned with intensity. 'You're . . . the Devil?'

His host smiled. 'Oh, Garth, don't tell me you hadn't worked that out. Go on,' he urged, 'read the rest of it.'

Garth continued reading: '. . . in exchange for a life of luxury, success, untold wealth and sex with any woman I want, for as long as I want (see para 6, section c: special conditions relating to duration of erections).'

'It's all yours, Garth, and all I ask is a small thing, something you've probably never given any thought to until now. It's formless, odourless and weighs a whisker under twenty-two grams – your soul. Believe me, you're better off without it; the freedom you'll feel once you hand over its welfare to my care is immense. Just think what could be yours: an island in the Caribbean, your own private jet to get you there and a bevy of beautiful girls to look after you – in fact, Paradise. Money worries will be a thing of the past; never again will you have to endure a dreary day in a seedy, dead-end job because you need to pay the rent. You'll be able to buy and sell scrawny little companies like Westlight – put them out of business if you want to. What we're talking about here, Garth, is choice: the choice to do what you want to do, when you want to do it, the fulfilment of a life's dream. But I have to warn you, this is a strictly limited offer. To take advantage of this once-in-a-lifetime opportunity you have to act *now*. Say no and we'll shake hands and it will be as if we had never met: what you laughingly call your life will carry on as normal. You'll go back to sweaty Mr Bere and his amorous secretary and continue living in your grimy little bedsit on Union Street beneath the abusive drunk and his snivelling wife. It's up to you.' Satan leaned a little closer. 'So what's it to be: the grey monochrome of your current existence or the glorious Technicolor of a new dawn? Go on, Garth, think of your future. Sign on the dotted line.' He handed him a quill pen.

Garth hesitated. 'Well, I . . .'

Satan addressed his daughters. 'What do you think, girls? What should he do?'

'I think Mr Ferrers would be missing out on so much if he didn't,' said Cassandra, easing closer to him, sliding her hand over his thigh under the table and gently massaging his crotch.

Raven got up and moved round the table to his other side. 'Mr Ferrers isn't stupid; he knows what's best for him,' she said, stroking his neck and pressing her breasts into his shoulder.

'I expect you're feeling like a bit of a lie-down, Garth,' Satan leered. 'Just sign on the dotted line and you can go upstairs . . . to bed.'

Raven whispered something obscene in his left ear. 'Ah . . .' Garth gasped. 'There . . . there's no ink.'

'Lothar!'

The butler grabbed Garth's left hand and deftly nicked his index finger with a sharp knife.

'Ow!'

Producing a pewter inkwell, Lothar squeezed Garth's finger into it until it was half-full.

'So much more convenient than cartridges, don't you think?'

Cassandra was now fiddling with his fly, but just as Garth was about to plunge the quill into the inkwell, he noticed a line of very small print at the bottom of the parchment document. 'What's this?'

'Hm?' Satan feigned indifference.

Garth momentarily broke free from Raven and Cassandra's amorous embraces and squinted at the tiny row of type. 'It says that the signatory forfeits his or her life at age fifty.'

'Oh that,' said the Dark Lord. 'It's a standard clause, stipulating the length of the contract. After all, I'm about to make a considerable investment in you, and I need to have some guarantee of return. I think fifty is rather generous.'

To Garth, who had just turned twenty-two, the fact that he might already have lived almost half his life was a bit of a shock. 'But *fifty*?'

'For a young man like you, Garth, I should imagine fifty is hard to envisage, so let me paint the picture. For the average man fifty marks the beginning of the end, if, that is, he hasn't already been carted off by cancer or a heart attack. His chance of a painful and lingering death due to prostate cancer increases tenfold; hair – what's left of it – begins to turn white, skin sags, muscles that used to hold things firmly in place give up the struggle, allowing a flabby belly to droop towards arthritic knees. Bodily functions once taken for granted can no longer be relied upon; the back pages of the *Telegraph*, advertising stair-lifts and discreet incontinence pads, suddenly become necessary reading. Let's face it, the average fifty-year-old is lucky if he can still get it up! And since taste is but a dim and distant memory, eating is simply a chore to be endured, and overcooked pap, which is the only thing his clacking dentures can manage, is consumed without pleasure. But his sluggish digestion can't cope with even the blandest of food, and the pain of trapped wind is as sure to follow as night follows day. This isn't living, it's a slow, lingering death. But here's the clincher.' Satan leaned in confidentially. 'Did you know that fifty is the age at which most men take up golf?'

'No!' Garth gasped.

'It's an established fact. A man hits fifty and suddenly all he thinks about is pulling on a pair of check trousers and a yellow V-necked sweater. Not only that, but when buying a car he no longer asks about cubic capacity, nought-to-sixty times and how to turn the traction control off. The only thing a fifty-year-old male is interested in is how many bags of golf clubs the boot can swallow. I can save you from all that. Sign this contract and I guarantee that you will remain fit and healthy, with *all* parts in perfect working order, right up until the very last moment. And, instead of a slow descent into drooling senility on the golf course, a quick and dignified death.'

Garth sat with the pen poised over the blood-filled inkwell. Raven continued to nibble his ear and whisper gentle obscenities, while Cassandra now had her hand *in* his trousers. 'OK, OK!' he said suddenly and, plunging the quill into the gore, scratched his name across the document. Garth's blood seared into the parchment, sending up a curl of acrid smoke.

As soon as the deed was done, Satan snatched up the document and tucked it inside his jacket. 'Welcome to the family,' he said.

Then something absolutely terrifying happened. Señor De'ath's eyes began to glow like two red-hot coals and, rearing up on his hind legs, he unfurled monstrous leathern wings. He seemed to be everywhere at once, filling the room with his hateful presence and a stench like bad drains. Garth gasped and turned to Cassandra. But she too had undergone a hideous transformation and was now nothing but a grinning skull draped with rotting flesh. Garth, recoiling in disgust, his gorge rising, rose from the table and came face to face with Raven, whose face was a seething mass of maggots. Garth couldn't help himself: he was violently sick, the crimson tide of his vomit flooding the table. But as he watched, to his horror, everything he had eaten at that sumptuous banquet reassembled itself and came back to life: the lobster, the woodcock, even the goose liver took on a life of its own and started slithering towards him across the tablecloth. Fighting his way to the door he felt something moving in his trousers and looked down to see the dry sticks of Cassandra's forearm protruding from his open fly, her bony hand still massaging his rapidly deflating erection. In trembling panic, he yanked the bones from his trousers and threw them in Cassandra's wide, grinning skull's smile. Fumbling madly with the door, he somehow managed to wrestle it open and ran out into the echoing hall. Looking around wildly for a way out, in his haste and terror he tripped over the bottom step of the wide staircase. Grabbing at the banisters to steady himself, he realized with an awful shock what those strange banisters really were: human thigh bones. And the floor – those intricately laid little white tiles were pieces of human skull. The room began to swim. The last thing he remembered was Cassandra's shrill, unearthly laugh. Then . . . blackness.

Garth woke suddenly, bathed in sweat.

'Oh, thank God, thank God.' It was only a dream. He reached out an arm and groped for his alarm clock on the bedside table. But it wasn't there. He told himself that he must have knocked it onto the floor. But, as his senses gradually became more alert, he began to realize that the mattress he was lying on was suspiciously comfortable. He lifted his head and peered into the gloom, and suddenly went cold. This wasn't his bedsit in Union Street; this was a large room he didn't recognize. And this wasn't his knackered old bed, either; it was a sumptuous, canopied four-poster. Throwing back the bedclothes, he strode across the acres of soft carpet to the window. Yanking open the curtains he was presented not with his usual view of the grey, 1960s-brutalist streets of Plymouth, but with green rolling hills and fields full of gambolling sheep.

'Oh my God!' he gasped. Then it was true. He had sold his soul to the Devil. He might have spiralled further into panic and despair if, at that moment, there hadn't been a soft knock at the door.

'Who is it?'

The door opened slowly and a beautiful young woman he'd never seen before slid into the room. She looked deliciously sleepy in slightly rumpled pink silk pyjamas. 'Oh,' she said sadly, 'you're up. I was hoping to catch you before . . .'

'Before . . .?'

'Yes, you know . . .' She looked sideways at the bed and smiled coyly at him.

'Oh,' said Garth, understanding. But the gross and disturbing image of Satan's daughters was still fresh in his mind. Even the thought of sex made him want to retch. 'Um, sorry, but I'm not really up to anything at the moment . . . Possibly later?'

The girl looked disappointed. She stuck out her lower lip and slumped sadly out of the room.

Garth turned back to the magnificent view from the

large bedroom window. *Oh God, oh God, oh God, what have I done?*

There was a discreet knock at the door, following which a man carrying a breakfast tray entered, a copy of the *Telegraph* tucked under his arm.

'Ah,' said the man, seeing that Garth had already risen. 'I thought you might like breakfast in bed, sir, but if you'd prefer, I can serve you downstairs.'

'I'm not really hungry, thanks.'

'I'll leave the tray here, sir, in case you change your mind.'

The man placed the tray at the bottom of the bed and laid the newspaper on the counterpane.

'Who are you?' Garth asked.

'I'm Tuttle, sir. Your butler.'

'I've got a butler?'

'You're looking at him, sir.'

'What happened to Lothar?'

'Lothar is Milord's personal servant, sir. If you don't find me suitable a replacement can be arranged.'

'No, no.' Garth shook his head. 'I'm sure you'll do fine.'

Tuttle smiled. 'Thank you, sir. I wasn't sure if you'd prefer tea or coffee, so I took the liberty of preparing both. Or if you'd prefer chilled champagne . . .?'

Garth was in serious need of a drink.

'Er, yes, Tuttle. I think I would prefer that, thank you.'

'Very good, sir.'

Tuttle left the room and returned some moments later with an ice bucket containing a bottle of Pol Roger 1966. He uncaged the cork and grasped it between gloved finger and thumb. It left the bottle with a gentle *phhuuutt!*. Pouring his master a glass of the exquisite, honey-coloured wine, Tuttle placed it on the bedside table.

'Will that be all, sir?'

'Yes, I suppose it will.'

'Very good, sir.'

But there was one more thing that Garth simply *had* to know. 'Er, Tuttle?'

The butler stopped in the doorway and turned back to his master. 'Sir?'

'Whose house is this?'

'Yours, sir.' Tuttle smiled gently and withdrew, closing the bedroom door behind him.

Garth looked down at the laden breakfast tray. There was half a grapefruit, a toast rack crammed with both brown and white toast, various pots of steaming liquid, a large jug of cream, an even larger one of milk, a bowl of cereal and a plate of perfectly cooked bacon and eggs nestling under a domed silver cover. But none of this was of any interest. Garth picked up the glass of champagne and drank. The icy-cold and gently pétillant wine was exactly what his overloaded brain needed. He was soon on to his third glass, and beginning to feel a little better about the situation.

*Well, I may have sold my soul to the Devil, but look what I've gained: a mansion in the countryside and a butler!*

Garth got back into bed and opened the copy of the *Telegraph* that Tuttle had provided. A long white envelope fell into his lap. After a slight pause Garth picked it up. It was embossed with a seal which closer inspection revealed to be a representation of a man with horns and a tail buggering a donkey.

Garth drew down the corners of his mouth in disgust.

He poured himself another glass of Pol Roger and took a long sip before opening the envelope.

The blood-red notepaper inside was headed with the same seal as on the envelope, but made even more graphic by the fact that it was in full colour.

*My dear Garth*, it began, the words picked out in gold.

*Hope you are enjoying your new life as a success and that Tuttle is to your liking. He's a good man and can be relied upon for sound advice in a crisis.*

*Now then, you've got a busy day ahead of you. Did I mention that you were now the proprietor and CEO of Hoofprint Magazine Publishing? Well, you are. Titles include:* The Step-by-Step Guide to the Occult, Satanism for Virgins, Witch Which *and* Housewives' Monthly. *Turnover of only three million pounds a year, but all that's about to change. This is the dawn of the information revolution. The World Wide Web, which at the moment is the sole preserve of geeks and freaks, is about to change people's lives in ways we, from our limited viewpoint, can only imagine. To that end, at your meeting with the board of directors this morning, you are going to suggest publishing a magazine dedicated to the Internet. You will meet resistance from the old stick-in-the-muds, who will protest that it is of interest only to a tiny minority, but hold firm and push your ideas through. This is the world of business, Garth – only the strong survive. Besides, you've got me behind you. Just do as I say and everything will go swimmingly.*

*Now, this is how you will address the board . . .*

There followed a whole load of business-speak which Garth didn't really understand. It was peppered with words and phrases of whose meanings he had only the slimmest grasp: *profit margins, performance targets, market share, pre-tax profit forecast* and the soon-to-be-hackneyed *information is the new black.*

The letter finished, *Remember, you're the boss. What you say goes. Now, enjoy your breakfast and, by the way, her name's Jasmine.*

After pouring himself another glass of champagne, Garth considered the contents of the letter. The only bit that really made sense to him was that final phrase.

On the bedside table was a large, old-fashioned telephone. Garth picked it up. Tuttle answered immediately.

'Sir?'

'Oh, um, I was just wondering if Jasmine was still around?'

'The young lady is just finishing breakfast, sir.'

'Good. Would you send her up when she's done, please, Tuttle?'

'Certainly, sir.'

In moments, Jasmine reappeared in Garth's bedroom. 'You wanted me?' she breathed, pushing out her chest so that her nipples showed through the sheer silk of her pyjama top.

Garth, feeling happily mellow, gazed appreciatively and without shame at her softly rounded body. 'Now that's what I call room service.'

'Are you feeling better now?' she asked.

Garth smiled lopsidedly. 'Much.'

'Oh, good.' Jasmine slipped seductively out of her pyjamas and slid into bed next to him. 'You're cold,' she said, running her hand over his chest. 'Let me warm you up.' She kissed him on the lips, then worked her way slowly down his body, softly mouthing his neck, shoulders, chest, belly . . .

*This isn't so bad*, Garth thought. *I mean, I could*

*certainly cope with twenty-eight years of this.* Then, as she took him into her warm, soft mouth, all thoughts of the future evaporated and he allowed himself to melt into ecstasy.

Later that morning, at Hoofprint Publishing's gleaming, steel-and-glass headquarters in the brand new Exeter Business Park, Garth set in train a publishing revolution which in a very short time would see Hoofprint's market share rise to an astonishing 60 per cent, and its stock price hit four figures.

The name Garth Ferrers was suddenly on everyone's lips. His rapid rise to power and fame gave him an entrée into the most elevated social circles. He was invited to watch the Monaco Grand Prix from Prince Rainier's personal box; attended Royal Ascot as a guest of the Queen; caused a stir when he took part in the Trans-Pacific yacht race with an all-female crew in his ship *Borrowed Time*.

Life for the young tycoon seemed blessed. He had a lifestyle envied by pasty-faced adolescents everywhere: a year-round tan; a fleet of exotic machinery comprising several executive jets, helicopters and a complete collection of Ferraris; and, to top it all, he could call on the services of a small army of beautiful women.

But now, twenty-eight years after the young, innocent Garth Ferrers had signed that terrible piece of parchment, he awoke in the grey morning light consumed with dread. His fiftieth birthday – the day he had hoped would never arrive – was fast approaching, and he was terrified.

# Chapter 9

As Heaven had been designed with no exit, the long journey back down the up escalator was always tiring, especially as the only time the escalator was ever stopped was on Sundays, or when God wanted to visit earth, which he did less and less frequently nowadays, especially after what had happened to his son.

Gabriel paused at the foot of the moving staircase to catch his breath, and overheard a conversation between two Hell's Angels enjoying a smoke between soul-fetching forays. One was dressed as a British redcoat, the other in the uniform of a patriot from the time of the American War of Independence.

'We won because we had God on our side,' the American asserted.

'Oh yes?' the British soldier replied.

'Yeah!'

'Then how come you ended up working for Old Nick?'

The American considered the question, taking several puffs on his cigar. 'It's because,' he began after a long pause, 'I'm not a musician: I don't play the harp.' He seemed immensely pleased with his answer.

The redcoat slapped his hand to his forehead. 'Of course! That'll be it, yes. If you'd been a harpist, you'd have been hoiked upstairs and into the heavenly orchestra like a shot. Stands to reason – sorry, stupid of me.'

The American, impervious to British irony, was somewhat taken aback to have his age-old enemy suddenly agree with him. 'I'm happy we understand each other at last, sir.'

'Surprising though . . .' The redcoat paused tantalizingly and puffed on his clay pipe.

The patriot was intrigued. 'What's surprising?'

'Well . . . No, I don't want to upset you.'

'No, please, go on.'

'Well, the thing is, I heard that God had ditched harps and was getting a kazoo band together instead.'

Realizing at last that he was being mocked, the American stood up indignantly. 'You, sir, are no gentleman!'

'And you're full of shit!'

A red-skinned ghoul, fork-tailed and smeared with ordure, appeared and jabbed them with his pitchfork. 'Back to work!' he screamed.

'No peace for the wicked,' the redcoat observed, tapping out his pipe on his boot heel. The patriot sullenly stubbed out his cigar and tucked it in his waistcoat pocket. Picking up their muskets, the two soldiers went over to the big card index, took out a ticket, argued briefly about who should time-stamp it, and disappeared through the veil in search of their next customer.

Gabriel, having finally recovered his breath, was about to set off to find Garth Ferrers when he glimpsed the shadowy figure in the cashmere coat yet again. There was something annoyingly familiar about this individual, but where Gabriel had seen him before was a mystery that would have to wait a little while longer for an answer. Because, in the meantime, the archangel had to deal with the slightly more urgent matter of saving the world from destruction.

Although it was still morning, and despite the fact that Garth Ferrers' mansion was a blaze of light, the remains of the previous night still clung tightly to it, giving the big square house the appearance of a stout Victorian widow dressed in black bombazine. Gabriel stood in the front porch and shivered. Elsewhere it was a calm, warm day, but around the house itself a chill wind was blowing.

Slipping invisibly through the front door, the angel rematerialized in the high-ceilinged entrance hall, which, with its stark white decor and glittering marble staircase, was no cosier than the porch. He had no clear idea what he was doing there, nor what he might find. Indeed, other than Peter's vague suspicion that Garth Ferrers was somehow involved in the Devil's plot, he had no reason to be there at all. Peter could be a bit of an old woman sometimes, and may well have been overreacting. After all, hanging out with the saintly day in, day out didn't exactly make you an expert on sinners. As the archangel stood, occupied with these thoughts, a door in a blank white wall opened, and a butler emerged carrying a tray covered with a linen cloth.

Hastily dematerializing, Gabriel observed the man as he crossed the airy hall, his boot heels echoing off the black and white floor tiles. Suddenly the man stopped and sniffed the air – something seemed to be troubling him. He looked around, his eyes settling on the spot where the transparent Gabriel stood. The angel froze and held his breath as the butler took a step towards him and scrutinized the seemingly empty air, only inches from his invisible nose. But after a moment or two, the black-suited manservant shrugged, turned and moved towards a pair of tall wooden doors in the wall beyond the foot of the stairs. Gabriel breathed a sigh of relief and, as the butler opened the doors, edged sideways to peer past him into the interior of the room. In front of a blazing fire was a figure slumped in a wing chair, brandy glass in hand.

The butler approached the figure and spoke a few words in a low tone. It was obvious that at first the man neither heard nor understood what was being said because the manservant had to repeat himself several times before he got a response, which was a dismissive wave of the hand.

Gabriel slid a little closer for a better view of the man he assumed to be Garth Ferrers. The butler was trying to tempt his master with something to eat. Removing the cloth from the tray he revealed a basket of freshly baked muffins, and their sweet fragrance filled the air. It took all of Gabriel's willpower to stop himself from going into the room and grabbing one there and then. But Garth wasn't interested. Ignoring the basket of delectable baked goods, he helped himself to another snifter from the brandy decanter resting on the small table at his elbow. From Garth's shaking hands, red-rimmed eyes and quivering lip, Gabriel surmised that he had been crying. Maybe Peter was on to something after all – it was certainly clear that Garth's millions hadn't brought him anything like peace of mind. As Gabriel mulled over this, Garth broke down completely. His glass slipped from his fingers and rolled away across the large Persian rug, trailing a darkening stain of spilt brandy.

Placing the basket of muffins on the small table, the butler stooped to retrieve the glass. Producing a spotless handkerchief from an inside pocket, he wiped round the rim, refilled it from the decanter and placed it next to the muffins, hoping that their proximity to the alcohol would prove an irresistible temptation. With a small bow, he then withdrew from the room and closed the double doors, leaving his sobbing master alone with his terrifying thoughts.

Gabriel watched the butler recross the hall and disappear whence he'd come before himself slipping, unseen, through the closed doors into the drawing room. He could have settled everything there and then by asking Garth outright if he was in league with the Devil. But such a direct course of action was dangerous on two counts: one, if Garth told the Devil about Gabriel's visit, he could plead heavenly interference and would then win the bet by default; and two, if God found out, he'd give the archangel hell.

At that moment, Garth's chin dropped onto his chest and he started snoring.

'Garth?' Gabriel whispered.

No reply.

He shook him gently. 'Garth!'

But Garth's snoring merely increased in volume.

Gabriel looked down at the troubled man with compassion. He definitely wasn't going to get anything out of him now. Then the angel glanced at the basket of muffins. *Well, if you're not going to eat them.* He picked one up and bit into it. *Ah, vanilla – my favourite.*

Gabriel made his way back towards the front door, dropping crumbs. *Well, Pete,* he thought, *it looks like you might be on to something.* But what should he do now? All he had was a suspicion; what he needed above all else was proof, something concrete to prove he wasn't merely being paranoid. But what?

Gabriel looked around the large, empty hall for inspiration. Apart from the solemnly ticking long-case clock, the only other furniture was a hatstand and a small half-table screwed into the wall near the front door. *Can't see why Pete was so impressed with the decor*, Gabriel mused. *I don't see what all the fuss is about. It's probably some new fashion: nouvelle boring. Oh, well, there's nothing more to do here.* Finishing the last of the muffin, he licked his fingers and prepared to go, but just as he was about to leave, something about the small table by the door drew him over to investigate further.

On it was a stack of unopened mail. There were what looked like statements from various financial institutions, a brown envelope from Her Majesty's Inland Revenue, an invitation to become an American Express Diamond-Encrusted Card member and, right at the bottom of the pile, a large brown envelope with 'Hoofprint Publishing' printed across it.

Quickly checking that the coast was still clear, Gabriel rematerialized and, wiping his fingers, carefully slid the envelope out from under the rest of the mail. Teasing it open, he slid out the contents. It was a magazine. Attached to its front cover by a paper clip was a covering letter.

*Dear Garth,*

*Please find enclosed the proof of the latest edition. Let us know asap if you have any changes/corrections.*

*Best wishes . . .*

Gabriel's heart was pounding. *Latest edition of what?* he wondered.

Folding back the letter, Gabriel revealed the front cover of *Web of Fire*.

*Yes!*

Just underneath the title, in a slightly smaller, but garishly bright red typeface, was 'Final instalment of *Endgame!*' And there, stuck to the bottom left-hand corner by a glob of plastic goo were two glittering disks in a clear plastic sleeve.

*Henry will be pleased*, Gabriel thought, slipping the magazine back into the envelope and tucking it inside his coat. He could always talk to Ferrers later, if necessary, but what was most important at the moment was what he had nestling in his left armpit.

He was just about to wing his way back to Martin's house when he remembered Peter. The heavenly gate-keeper had done him a good turn and, as the saying goes, one good turn . . .

Putting his feet up in his quarters with the latest *Buttling Times*, one of Hoofprint's less successful titles, Tuttle was surprised to hear the front doorbell ring. Mr Ferrers wasn't expecting visitors, and Milord never arrived un-announced.

Tuttle's first thought on opening the door was to wonder how this strange man had made it through the heavy security surrounding the Ferrers mansion, and his hand went immediately to the small red panic button set into the door frame. This would alert Garth's small army of bodyguards to the fact of an intruder. 'Can I help you, sir?'

'Forgive me for bothering you like this,' Gabriel began, 'and I know this may seem like a strange request, but a man of wealth and taste like Mr Ferrers – a man for whom only the finest things are good enough – must have an interior designer.'

Tuttle frowned.

'It's just that it's an interest of a good friend of mine: interior decoration.' Gabriel flashed him a broad, gleaming smile.

'I see,' Tuttle replied, jabbing desperately at the panic button. 'I believe that from time to time Mr Ferrers employs the services of a company called Pink Inc. of Lancing, if that answers your question.'

'It does, it does. Thank you so much,' Gabriel replied.

'Not at all,' Tuttle said. 'And may I ask who *you* are, sir?'

'Me?'

Tuttle nodded. '*You*, sir.'

'Gabriel.' He smiled.

Tuttle looked sharply at him.

'Mr Gabriel,' the angel corrected himself.

Arranging his features into a tight smile only half a degree from a leer, Tuttle wished Mr Gabriel good day, and closed the door.

When the phalanx of black-suited, square-built bodyguards eventually made it, breathing hard, to the front door of the mansion, the intruder was nowhere to be seen. Nor did a careful sweep of the grounds turn up any sign. The mysterious individual had simply disappeared.


Materializing back in Luke's bedroom, Gabriel found Henry still seated at Luke's computer. 'Here!' he said breathlessly, handing the sparkling silver disks to the slightly wary teenager.

'What's this?'

'Last part of *Endgame*.'

'Cool. How did you get it?'

'I stole it. Where are Martin and Luke?' Gabriel asked.

'Downstairs making more coffee.' Henry studied the two disks he'd just been given. 'I wonder why there are two of them? Oh, well, we'll soon find out.' He slipped the first disk out of its plastic sleeve. 'This is a DVD.'

'Is that bad?'

'No, but this computer isn't up to it.' He looked up at Gabriel. 'You really stole them?'

Gabriel nodded.

Henry narrowed his eyes. 'What about "Thou shalt not steal" and all that stuff?'

'You mean the Ten Commandments? Oh that was just Moses' clever ploy to keep the Israelites in check.'

'Really?'

'Well, imagine you're leading a bunch of unruly ex-slaves through the desert. You've no support, you're worried about dwindling supplies, and while you're trying to concentrate on where you should be going, your charges are all busy jumping into bed with each other's wives, coveting oxen they shouldn't be coveting, and murdering each other; believe me, the Israelites were an unruly lot. There you are, responsible for this rabble, wandering around the desert in circles because instead of having the word of God in your ear, all you've got are complaints from cuckolded husbands and the entreaties of widows hungry for revenge!' Gabriel shook his head. 'No wonder it took Moses forty years to find the Promised Land – a lesser man would have given up. So, what do you do to keep this lot under control?'

Henry was rapt. 'What?'

'Well, what Moses did was to shin up the nearest mountain with a chisel. Of course, while he's away tapping at the tablets, the children of Israel find a new diversion – idol worship. So, Moses comes back, makes a dramatic entrance – breaking the tablets was a real coup de théâtre in my opinion – and tells them what "God" has commanded.'

'Did it work?'

'Like a dream. The Israelites were as nice as pie after that: all please and thank you and after you – no, after you. When Moses began to get a bit doddery they even made him a sedan chair to carry him around in. But enough Bible stories; we have work to do.' Gabriel went to the door and called downstairs. 'Hello! I'm back, and I've got a surprise!'

'Um, you *are* an angel, right?'

Gabriel turned in the doorway to find that Henry was scrutinizing him closely. 'What makes you think that?'

'Well, there's the story you just told me for one thing, then there's your little trick of disappearing in a puff of smoke . . . reappearing in a puff of smoke . . . and the fact that your wings are showing.'

Gabriel looked down at his ankles. All his hurrying to and fro had caused the hem of his long coat to ruck up, and there were six inches of snow-white wing showing beneath it. 'Ah, rumbled.'

Henry regarded him with wide-eyed wonder. 'So, you'd know all about Jesus, yeah?'

'I am familiar with the name,' Gabriel conceded.

Henry dropped his voice to a confidential murmur. 'He was from the Pleiades, like you, right? And Mary Magdalene was his queen, wasn't she?'

'Um . . .' Gabriel was a little nonplussed. 'Well . . . she

and Jesus were very close, it's true . . .' But before he could continue, Martin and Luke hurried into the room.

'What is it?' Martin exclaimed.

'OK, we'll finish this later,' Henry said to Gabriel. He turned to the other two and held up the disks. 'Gabriel got us the next part of the game.'

'Where did you get them?' Martin asked, intrigued.

'From the publisher,' Gabriel replied. 'I doubt he'll miss them – he has a few other things on his mind at the moment, like whether you get any time off eternal damnation for good behaviour.'

'Well, shall we play?' Martin said cheerily.

Henry looked at him as if he was something that had just emerged from a swamp. 'On this computer? You're joking, right?'

'What's the matter with it?'

'It's ancient. The graphics card is positively prehistoric.'

Martin retreated into sullen silence.

'No,' Henry continued. 'What we need is something a little more up to date.'

'What about yours, then?' Luke said.

Henry was shocked. 'Are you crazy? We can't go to *my* house.' Then he stared at the floor and mumbled, 'Mum's not very well.'

'What about the surgery?' Gabriel suggested.

Martin glared at him. 'What about it?'

'Well, presumably you've got a computer there.'

'Yes, but—'

Henry immediately started firing off questions: 'What sort of memory has it got? I assume it's got a DVD drive?'

'I don't know. Westerham bought a whole new system six months ago – it cost a fortune.'

'Great.' Henry slid the two DVDs in his pocket. 'Let's go there now.'

'But we can't just . . . I mean, there'll be people . . . and police . . . and . . . I'm hiding.'

Gabriel put a hand on Martin's shoulder. 'It might be time to face the music. *"If it were done when 'tis done, then 'twere well it were done quickly . . ."'*

'I don't think *Macbeth* is quite appropriate,' Martin observed.

'Let's hope not,' said Gabriel, making sure the hem of his coat was now straight and heading for the door.


In the car on the way to the surgery, Martin felt decidedly anxious about what he might have to face there, and his feelings of unease weren't at all soothed by the conversation that Henry and Gabriel were having in the back.

'What fascinates me is how the world governments have been able to keep it secret for so long,' Henry was saying. 'I mean, they couldn't have done that without help, right? So the order not to tell everyone must have come from *your* people, yeah? To stop a worldwide panic.' He shook his head appreciatively. 'Wow, you must have a lot of power if you can get all the governments on earth to do as you ask.'

Gabriel looked blank. He turned to Luke for enlightenment.

'"They are among us . . ." and all that,' Luke whispered.

Gabriel looked even more puzzled.

'Aliens . . . you know?'

'Oh,' said Gabriel, the penny dropping. 'Well, now, there's been a lot of nonsense talked about space travel . . .' But looking down at Henry's upturned face, so bright with trust and the desperate desire to believe, the angel faltered and immediately changed tack. 'Um, for instance, a lot of people assume that it's exciting. But really it's not. It's . . . extremely boring. Especially the long journey here from . . . where I come from . . .' Gabriel turned to Luke for help once again.

*The Pleiades*, Luke mouthed.

'The Pleiades, yes,' Gabriel continued. 'It can take . . . ooh . . . hours, especially if there's traffic.'

Henry was impressed. 'Hours, wow! Four light years in hours – amazing! What kind of craft have you got?'

'Well now, it's a lovely . . . shiny one . . . with lights.' Gabriel was seriously out of his depth.

'Saucer or cigar?'

'Cigar? No, I don't smoke.'

Henry laughed. 'An alien with a sense of humour! No, seriously, what shape is it – saucer or cigar?'

'Oh, yes . . . definitely.'

The light of understanding dawned in Henry's eyes. 'So they *are* the same thing – they can change shape! And this "God", he's your leader, right?'

'Ri-ght,' Gabriel said slowly.

'And he's on the mother ship, yeah, controlling operations?'

'I think *controlling* is putting it a bit strongly. But, broadly speaking, he is in charge, yes.'

'So, are you going to tell me the biggie?'

Gabriel frowned. 'Biggie?'

'Yes: when Jesus is going to come back.'

'Ah . . . right. Well now . . .'

'I know *where* he's going to appear,' Henry said smugly.

Gabriel seemed surprised. 'Really?'

'Oh yeah, I've worked it out.'

'I'll bet you have. So, tell me the location – let's see if you're right.'

'You first.'

'Sorry?'

'You tell me *when*, I'll tell you where.'

'Right . . . Well, if you've already worked out where he's going to appear, then I don't suppose there's any harm in you knowing when, is there?' Gabriel cleared his throat. 'Jesus is going to reappear sometime in two thousand and –' he paused while he thought of a number that Henry might accept '– twenty-four!' he finally announced. 'Yes, that's it: two thousand and twenty-four.'

'I knew it!' Henry exploded. 'It fits perfectly – that'll be two thousand years, almost to the day, that he was taken up to the mother ship after the Romans killed him. Or at least thought they'd killed him.'

'They didn't kill him?' Martin asked.

Henry smiled. 'Gabriel knows all about that, don't you, my friend?'

For the archangel, being addressed by a spotty eighteen-year-old as 'friend' was a new experience. 'I do?'

''Course. Jesus took a drug before being crucified that slowed down his pulse rate to below a discernible level. They took him down before he was dead, gave him the antidote and whisked him away in the mother ship – it's obvious.'

Gabriel nodded slowly, a half-smile on his lips. 'There's not much you don't know, is there? Now it's your turn.'

'Hm?'

'Jesus' second coming? The secret location where the son of man is going to reveal himself to mankind?'

'Oh, yeah – Jerusalem.' Everyone seemed rather disappointed by such an obvious answer, but then Henry added, 'But not Israel.'

Luke looked puzzled. 'But Jerusalem's *in* Israel, isn't it?'

Henry shook his head, radiating smugness from every pore. 'It suited the aliens to make everyone *think* it was, so that no one would interfere with its real location. And they've done a brilliant job, even manipulating ancient texts to point to what we now call the Holy Land. But if you look at a modern-day map of Jerusalem, you'll find there are certain discrepancies between the biblical description and its actual topography. Jerusalem isn't Jerusalem.' He turned back to the angel. 'Isn't that right?'

Gabriel opened his hands in a gesture of submission. 'I wouldn't dream of contradicting you.'

'So, come on, where is it?' Luke urged.

'Very well.' And Henry announced the real location of the Holy City, a city sacred to three religions and a site kept secret for over 2,000 years.

'Rotherham.'

No one dared speak for the rest of the journey.

Arriving at the surgery, Martin was relieved to see that the police car and Gifford's Vauxhall were no longer there. He drove past slowly and parked on the street, then addressed his passengers.

'Give me a few minutes to square things with Donna. I'll let you know when the coast's clear.'

Martin got out of the car and ran back up the road.

When he reached the gravel parking area in front of the surgery, he crouched – commando style – and surveyed the area. Satisfied he could not be seen, he remained in crouching mode and edged slowly across the no-man's-land between himself and the building. Peeping in through the window he could see the reception area was full to overflowing with a mutinous-looking crowd of patients. This wasn't going to be easy. Taking a deep breath, Martin slipped around the building and in through the back door.

Seated behind the reception desk, Donna was just about to get up and start making yet another placatory cup of coffee for everyone when she heard a noise that sounded like escaping gas.

*Psst!*

She looked around, puzzled. Then she heard it again, this time a little louder and more insistent.

*Psst!*

The sound seemed to be coming from the vicinity of her left ankle. She looked down and stifled a small scream when she saw Martin's head peering around the corner. He placed a finger to his lips, then gestured for her to meet him in the kitchen.

Donna rose to her feet uncertainly. 'Er, would anyone like another coffee?' There were a few assenting grunts from the resentful patients, and Donna bravely went among them gathering up mugs before joining Martin in the small kitchen just off the reception area.

Sliding the door closed behind her with her foot, she turned to Martin. 'I've been trying to ring you all morning. Where have you been?' she hissed.

'I'm really sorry, Donna, but it's a long story.'

'The police were here,' she whispered urgently, lowering an armful of dirty mugs into the sink.

'I know.'

'They said something about charging you with assault.'

'Yes, they probably did. Where are they now?'

'They couldn't wait any longer – they want you to go down to the station.'

Martin nodded.

'And that awful tax inspector was here too.'

'What happened to him?'

'I don't know; he just melted away. You know what he's like – mysterious.'

'He'll be back. Where's Westerham?'

'Called in sick. Did you really hit him?'

'I'm afraid so.'

Donna patted him on the back. 'I never knew you had it in you. But you've not done yourself any favours – he's shifted all his appointments for today onto you.'

'Ah, now, Donna,' Martin began slowly. 'This is a lot to ask, I know, but I need you to get rid of everyone.'

'What?'

'Send everyone home; clear the place.'

'I can't do that – they'll lynch me.'

'Possibly. Look, I can't explain now, but it's vitally important that I have the place to myself. Promise them free appointments for a month. Promise them anything, only get rid of them!'

Donna looked at him strangely. 'Are you all right, Martin? I mean . . . I hope I'm not talking out of turn, but I know things haven't been going terribly well for you at home. Is there anything I can do to help?'

'Yes, you can get rid of all the patients!'

'All right, all right. I'll see what I can do.'

Chewing her lip thoughtfully, she slid the door open and went out to face the seething crowd.

Five minutes later, after the last of the patients had stomped out of the surgery, Martin, who'd been listening at the kitchen door, finally slid it open. 'Donna, you're a genius. Go home.'

'I deserve a week's holiday.'

'Absolutely.'

'What?'

'Take a week's holiday.'

'Are you serious?'

'Why not?' said Martin, beaming at her in a way that she found rather disconcerting. *After all*, Martin was thinking, *if the end of the world is nigh, why shouldn't she be at home when it happens?* 'Go on,' he urged. 'And you can tell Vicky and our resident tooth-whitening operative that they can go, too. While you're at it, you can tell the sales-girls in our dental hypermarket next door to go home as well.'

When at last the building was clear, Martin led his waiting team into the surgery.

'Right,' said Henry, sliding into Donna's chair in front of the computer. 'Do you know what kind of graphics driver you've got?'

Martin looked at him and smiled weakly.

'OK, we'll just have to hope for the best.' Henry opened the computer's disk tray, laid the first of the DVDs containing the third part of *Endgame* on it and watched with satisfaction as it slid smoothly into the machine.

Curious as to why this part of the game should come on two DVDs, and not a single CD-ROM like the others, Henry had a swift peek behind the *Endgame* graphics. 'Well *this* is different.'

Gabriel stared at the undecipherable hieroglyphs which covered the screen. 'What's that?'

'That's the code the game's written in . . . It's really interesting.'

Gabriel looked at him expectantly.

'Well, for a start there's an awful lot of it and, without going into great detail—'

'Please don't,' Gabriel pleaded.

'You see, the game itself is written in something like Java C++, which is exactly what you'd expect. But *this* is really ancient.'

'By that I suppose you mean over a year old,' Martin growled.

'It's like what they were using in the eighties.'

'Oh, *that* old,' Martin sighed.

Henry screwed up his squashy features and peered at the screen. 'But to run this program on a modern computer you'd need an emulator.'

'Emulator?' Gabriel had completely lost track of this conversation.

'Basically it's a program that allows modern computers to run old languages. You can easily download one. In fact –' Henry scrolled through the lines of code '– yeah, this one's got an instruction to do just that.' Henry crossed his arms and stared at the screen. 'That's weird.'

Gabriel looked at Martin and Luke, who returned his vacant stare.

'The thing is,' Henry said at last, 'if this program's got an instruction to download an emulator built into it, that means it was written recently. But why bother? Why not just write the program in an up-to-date language? I don't get it.'

Henry slumped back in his chair in a slack-jawed reverie.

'Um,' Gabriel said, after a pause. 'You said this was going on *underneath* the actual game?'

Henry looked up at him and blinked, as though coming back from a long way away. 'Yeah?'

'So, as we're on rather a tight schedule, would it be possible to see what the actual game involves and worry about this emulator thing afterwards?'

Then the dawn of understanding suddenly flashed in Henry's eyes. 'Wait a minute. I know what this is. Oh, wow!' He turned back to the computer and started typing.

'Henry, can we just play the game?'

But Henry wasn't listening. He was gazing enraptured at the computer screen. 'This is amazing! Hah hah! Somebody's actually done it!'

Gabriel, Luke and Martin all gazed blankly at each other.

The angel tapped Henry on the shoulder. 'Done what, Henry? You're not making any sense.'

'This is dynamite! Gold dust! And it's on some crappy magazine freebie! Unbelievable!'

'Henry!' Gabriel snapped. 'Will you please calm down and explain!'

Henry smiled up at him. 'You will not believe what we have here.'

'Try me,' said Gabriel patiently.

'Well, I was wondering why this part of the game should need two DVDs, when parts one and two came on bog-standard CD-ROMs. DVDs have a huge capacity, much more than you'd ever need for a simple game like this, but— Hah!' Henry broke off and hugged himself with glee.

Martin turned to his son. 'What's he talking about?' Luke shrugged.

They all glared sternly at Henry.

'Sorry, sorry. You know, it's kind of beautiful . . .'

Gabriel looked at the screen but found it hard to find anything lovely in what he saw there. 'What's beautiful about it?'

'Amongst hackers there's always been talk about some mythical überprogram which no firewall can withstand, against which no system, however well protected, would be safe. But no one seriously believes it actually exists, or ever can exist. It's like the Holy Grail of hacking: the very idea of it spurs you on to greater things.'

'And?'

'This is it.'

'Are you really that seriously into hacking?' Martin asked disapprovingly.

'Oh, don't be so twentieth century,' Gabriel retorted. 'Henry, will you please tell me in terms I can understand what this actually is?'

'This –' Henry pointed at the computer screen, '– is a key to unlock any system, *anywhere*. I doubt there's a computer that could withstand it. Put simply, this program allows us access wherever we want to go. We could even reprogram the stock market if we wanted to.'

Everyone stared at the screen in awed silence for some moments.

'It's a masterpiece of software engineering. But I still

don't understand why they didn't use something a little more modern.' He frowned.

Gabriel was beginning to get interested. 'Would there be any advantage in using this particular language?'

'Dunno, it must have taken ages to write. But whoever's done it has been very clever.' Henry stopped scrolling and flexed his fingers dramatically. 'Right, pick a system.'

'I'm sorry?'

'To hack into.'

Gabriel and Martin looked blank.

'OK. Say, for instance, that I hacked into the regional examination board computer, Luke and I could see what grades we got for our GCSEs.'

Luke suddenly became animated. 'Yeah, and if we don't like what we see, we could maybe manipulate the results a little.'

'Just what I was thinking.' Henry started work on the keyboard.

'Absolutely not,' Martin said sternly.

Luke looked pained, 'Oh, Dad!'

'Come on, Mr Gray, it's not every day you get an opportunity like this.'

Martin had a sudden thought. 'You know, Henry, you're right. Here we have in our hands the ability to do good, to right wrongs and put an end to suffering. Hack into Exeter traffic control system.'

Gabriel gave him an old-fashioned look.

'Personal project of mine,' Martin explained. 'You see, I have this theory . . . Oh, never mind. The thing is, we need to test this program, don't we? To see if it really is as good as Henry says it is. Better we test it on something that's not going to cause too much trouble.'

'Exeter traffic control?'

'Believe me, whatever we do we can't make things worse. Go on, Henry: do your stuff.'

Henry sighed, 'All right,' and tapped something into the keyboard. The screen flickered but remained the same. 'Well, I kind of expected that.'

'Expected what?' Gabriel smiled tightly.

'The program's password-protected. We can't get into it.'

Gabriel clapped his hands in frustration. 'So we can't find out if it works?'

Henry smiled deviously. 'I never said that.'

Gabriel was beginning to find Henry's little games rather tiring. 'Henry,' he said sweetly, 'can you stop pissing about and get to the point?'

'All right, keep your wings on. All we have to do is guess the right password.'

'Oh, easy.' Martin scowled. 'With only several million words in the English language to choose from we'll get it in no time.'

Henry shook his head. 'It's really not that difficult. Most programmers usually go for the names of family members or their pets, or words that have something to do with what the program's actually about. Take this one: it's a hacking program, right? So the password could be something like Open Sesame.' He typed it in and pressed the Return key, but the cursor simply jumped a line and kept on flashing. 'No.'

'What about Doorway?' Luke offered.

'OK, let's try it.'

Nothing happened again.

'Um . . . Entry?' Martin suggested tentatively.

No luck.

'OK, let's try a different tack. The game's about world

conflict, right? So maybe the password's more along those lines.'

Henry typed in Conflict. Still nothing and, despite the many inventive suggestions put forward by the team, such as Battle, Annihilation, Megadeath, even the prosaic, and it has to be said, desperate: Kill Everybody in the World, the program stubbornly refused to open its doors.

Then a light came into Gabriel's eyes. 'Try Beelzebub,' he said.

In a matter of moments, they were in.

Henry rubbed his hands together with glee. 'OK, so where shall we go? Top secret Whitehall files? The Swiss banking system?'

'Traffic control,' Martin reminded him.

'Paris? Rome? New York?'

'Exeter.'

Henry sighed. 'All right, all right.' His stubby fingers tapped the keyboard without enthusiasm.

Eventually Henry raised his hands in triumph. 'Like a dream!' he exclaimed.

The others crowded round to look. On-screen was a map of Exeter city centre, showing the locations of all the traffic lights and their controllers.

'Luke,' said Henry, 'go outside and watch the lights at the top of the road. Tell me what colour they are.'

'OK.' Luke ran out of the door and stood in the street, while Martin opened the window.

Luke watched the traffic slow as it approached the traffic lights at the junction fifty yards away. 'They're red!' he called through the window.

Henry worked the keyboard: *tap*, *tap*, *tap*.

'Now they're yellow! Now green! Now they're red again!'

*Tap, tap.*

'Green! Red! Green again!'

The lights flashed on and off out of sequence, while the queue of traffic shunted forwards, stopped, moved off again, then screeched to a halt a moment later.

'You're doing it!' Luke laughed. 'Yellow! Red! Yellow! Red! Green! Red! Green!'

The pedestrians waiting to cross the road stepped tentatively off the pavement, then back on again as the green and red men flashed crazily on and off. There were soon raised voices and the angry blaring of horns as tempers frayed.

Henry was thoroughly enjoying himself. 'Now let's try something else.' *Tap, tap, tap;* his fingers moved over the keyboard once again.

After a few moments there came the distant sound of car horns – something was happening away in the centre of town.

'What have you done?' Gabriel asked.

Luke ran breathlessly back into the building. 'They've gone out now.'

Henry looked up at the faces gathered around him. 'I've just taken out all the traffic lights in Exeter. Amazing feeling, all this power.'

'Well, don't let it go to your head,' Gabriel warned.

'Have you really taken out all the lights?' Martin asked.

'Yes.' Henry smiled.

'Hang on a minute. Don't do anything till I get back.' Martin headed upstairs.

'Where are you going?' Gabriel called after him.

Martin ran to the top of the building and peered out of a third-storey window. From here he could see the junction over the Exe, where the A377 meets the B3212.

Usually the big roundabout was choked with slow-moving traffic, as the lights, standing guard like implacable bouncers at the door of an exclusive club, prevented the majority of cars from getting on to it. It had been a cause of frustration to Martin for many years and he'd written several letters to the council about it. But now, with the lights out, cars and lorries moved smoothly and swiftly around the big circular junction. Martin nodded with satisfaction. 'I knew it!'

'Well?' Gabriel queried as Martin came back into the room.

'Henry, just leave the lights as they are for the time being, will you?'

'OK, Mr Gray.'

Gabriel looked at Martin curiously.

'Just proving a point.' Martin smiled.

'I see,' the angel replied. 'And now that everyone's had a little play, can we get on, please?'

Everyone stared blankly at him.

'The game?'

'Oh, right.' Henry opened the computer tray and inserted the second DVD.

Whizzing swiftly through the pre-game rigmarole, Henry brought up the opening screen. This time it showed the action hero ducking and diving and firing off shots at an imaginary enemy. But once Henry clicked on the *Start* button, the familiar slow, dramatic music came over the speakers and, through a swirling white mist, several lines of type appeared:

*The situation in the north Pacific has escalated. What was merely a skirmish has developed into a major conflict. Russia,*

# Endgame

*China and North Korea on the one side, and America and the Nato alliance on the other, are eyeball to eyeball across the narrow strip of the Bering Sea. Diplomacy has broken down, as all political attempts to end the crisis have failed. In desperation, the world's powers are resorting to their last remaining option: espionage. The third and final phase of the game – Endgame – has begun.*

The image on-screen collapsed and was replaced by a map of the north Pacific showing all the countries involved in the rapidly escalating dispute.

*Choose country* flashed up at the bottom of the screen.

'Who shall we be today?' Henry asked.

'Espionage? What does that mean?' Martin asked.

'Dunno.' Henry thoughtfully excavated his left ear with a finger. 'I suppose we'll find that out once we start playing.'

'All right, let's be American,' Gabriel urged.

Henry opened his mouth to speak, but the angel interrupted him. 'Boringly conventional, I know, but I can't cope with any more "glorious Motherland" speeches.'

Henry exhaled, 'OK.' Moving the mouse pointer over North America, he left-clicked and the computer asked another question: *Multiplayer* or *Single player*? 'We'd better choose *Single player*.'

'Sorry, Henry,' Gabriel said with an apologetic smile, 'could you run that by me again?'

Henry turned to him. 'There are two ways you can play this game: either against the computer in *Single player* mode, or against other people online. But as we're the only people who have this game at the moment, the *Multiplayer* option is going to be a bit lonely.'

'And I think it's possibly safer if we stay offline, anyway,' Luke added.

'Good thinking,' Gabriel agreed.

Henry clicked on *Single player* and, in a matter of moments, the now-familiar briefing room appeared, this time furnished with a table behind which two US five-star generals sat side by side.

Through the speakers came the sound of a door opening, and the perspective moved to a high angle as a third man marched into the room and stood to attention in front of the two officers.

'At ease, Scimitar.'

Martin was incredulous. 'How does he know your name?'

Luke looked embarrassed. 'Dad!'

'Simple voice synthesis program – it recognizes whatever gaming name you put into it,' Henry explained easily.

'Shh! We'll miss the plot!' Gabriel hissed.

'It's time to show the world who's boss,' the virtual general continued. 'For too long the military's hands have been tied by the spineless liberals in government, but even they now see that if we're going to survive this situation we have to get tough. The time has come to stand up to the commies. Now we have the chance to wipe the red stain of communism from the earth once and for all.'

Martin was shocked. 'I didn't think you were allowed to say stuff like that any more, not in public anyway.'

'Will you be quiet!' Gabriel said testily.

The other general took up the theme. 'The world stands poised on the verge of a devastating war, the consequences of which would be far worse than of any conflict in history.' The general leaned forward into the pool of light falling across the middle of the table. 'And yet, the desperate nature of the time may be turned to our advantage. If we are successful, we will see our enemies' final, crushing defeat.'

The perspective changed again, to an over-the-shoulder viewpoint, just behind Scimitar's right ear.

'Rather than just sit here and wait for the reds to fire their missiles at us,' the general continued, 'we're going to act. Your mission is to obtain the enemy's nuclear missile launch codes and upload them to our communications satellites. Once their weapons are under our control, we will then be able to launch a pre-emptive strike from that same country against its own allies. What will follow will be a nuclear exchange between Russia, China and North Korea, leaving the US totally out of the loop.'

Martin gasped. 'That's insane!'

'It was once very nearly official US policy during the sixties,' Henry offered.

Martin gawped at the teenager but thought it would probably be better for his sanity not to pursue the matter.

'Once in the field you will be on your own, and the dangers you will face are many. But, Scimitar, your previous record shows you to be the best man for the job. Succeed and you will gain the undying admiration of all the peoples of the free world; fail and we are likely to be plunged into darkness. It's up to you.'

'I'll be proud to take this mission.' Scimitar's low, gravelly voice was pure Hollywood tough guy.

The generals both stood and saluted.

'Welcome aboard, Scimitar. All that remains is for you to choose your theatre of operations.'

The perspective changed again, this time zooming in

between the two generals and moving to a close-up of a map on the end wall of the briefing room: the same map of the north Pacific familiar from the previous two games.

Henry addressed the small group clustered anxiously around the screen. 'So, which particular "red stain" are we going to wipe from the face of the earth?'

Gabriel shrugged. 'Which do you suggest?'

'I'd go for North Korea,' Henry replied. 'It's not as organized as either China or Russia, and so should be that much easier to get into.'

'Very well.'

Henry clicked on North Korea, and its boundaries were immediately highlighted in red.

The voice of one of the generals came over the speakers: 'The target you have chosen is North Korea. Good luck.'

'This is very different in tone to the first two parts of the game,' Martin observed.

Henry was thoughtful. 'Yeah, it's much . . . deeper.'

'And darker,' Gabriel muttered.

The map was replaced by an image of a deserted mountain plateau. The words *North Hwanghae Province* slowly emerged on-screen, then dissolved. There was the sound of a helicopter, and soon the chopper itself could be seen, flying in low between two mountain peaks. It hovered over the plateau and a rope dropped out of the open door. A single soldier – Scimitar – slid down the rope and crouched in the sparse vegetation as the helicopter flew back through the mountains, the rapid *thocka-thocka-thocka* of its rotor retreating into the distance.

'Now what?' Martin asked. Scimitar waited, alert to any approaching danger. Then the perspective changed abruptly to FPS mode. Scimitar was now completely in Henry's hands: the game proper had begun.

'First we look for our objective,' Henry explained. He scrolled through the various options available to him. A pistol appeared at the bottom of the screen, closely followed by a grappling hook, a rifle, a grenade, a knife, a computer disk and a pair of binoculars. Henry left-clicked on the binoculars and the distance between Scimitar and the far hills disappeared.

'What are we looking for?' Martin asked.

Henry shrugged. 'We'll know it when we see it.'

He then did a 360-degree scan of the horizon. 'There!' He jabbed a finger at the screen.

Martin, Luke and Gabriel all gathered round.

'Do you see? Just below that mountain peak.' Henry pointed to a grey-black smudge on the side of a mountain.

Martin was unsure. 'Do you think so?'

Henry sighed irritably.

'OK, OK, you're the expert.'

Henry pressed W and Scimitar took off across the scrubby plain.

'He can move really fast,' Martin observed.

'He's a Green Beret, he's super-fit!' Henry snapped.

Martin resolved to keep his mouth shut until he had something constructive to say.

At the edge of the plain Scimitar encountered his first problem: a sheer drop from the small plateau down to a narrow gulley far below.

Henry was thoughtful. 'Hmm.' Looking around, he saw a ridge a little way off to the left, connecting the plateau with the very mountain he was heading for. 'Well, we could try and traverse that ridge, but it's pretty obvious and probably guarded. It's also very exposed; if we take it we might end up as a sitting duck. Whereas the gulley . . .' Henry panned down to take in the vertiginous drop to the ground far below. 'They won't be expecting an attack from that quarter, and we'd be shielded from view until we're right underneath our objective.'

Gabriel put a hand on Henry's shoulder. 'We're in your hands.'

'OK.' Henry clicked on the grappling iron and suddenly Scimitar was securing its metal hooks between two sturdy rocks at the edge of the plateau. Once he'd made it fast, he hurled the attached rope over the edge of the cliff. The rope flew out into space, then fell back against the sheer rock face, writhing and snaking its way down towards the ground. 'Here goes,' Henry muttered.

Pushing himself off with his US armed forces-issue combat boots, Scimitar abseiled expertly down the cliff. Once on the ground, he released himself from the rope and stood awaiting Henry's next instructions.

Henry did a quick pan to ascertain Scimitar's position. The mountainous walls of the gully rose up on either side, disappearing into thin clouds high above. 'Now we really have to keep our wits about us.' Henry moved Scimitar off at a slow walk.

After a time, the virtual Green Beret came to a kink in the narrow gulley which completely obscured his forward view. 'This could be a danger point. They may well have this area covered by surveillance, and possibly snipers. We'll have to be careful,' Henry warned.

Martin cleared his throat.

Henry sighed irritably and took his hands off the keyboard.

*Sorry*, Martin mouthed in response to Luke and Gabriel's sharp looks.

After a pause to gather himself, Henry's fingers re-assumed their positions and Scimitar, flattening himself to the rock wall, edged slowly forward. The narrow path between the parallel grey granite bluffs rose gently, leading directly to a set of large steel blast doors in the side of the mountain.

Scimitar put the binoculars to his eyes.

'What are you doing now?' Gabriel whispered.

'Scanning for information-gathering devices. Although it's quiet at the moment, anything could happen – we should be prepared.'

Martin just managed to restrain his urge to murmur: *Dib dib dib*.

'Ah!' Henry had seen something. He clicked on the *Zoom* icon, and a distant black speck on the mountain came suddenly into sharp focus. 'There – a camera fixed to the rock just below that ledge.'

The others squinted at the screen. Henry was right. Attached to the mountain was the elongated box of a CCTV camera.

Martin couldn't resist – 'I suppose they get a lot of street crime out here' – but his smile soon faded under the withering glances he received. Retreating in sullen silence, he collapsed onto the upholstered banquette under the window and picked up a dog-eared copy of *Hello!*. Turning the pages, he gawped blankly at the glossy individuals inside. *Who the hell are all these people? It seems anyone can be a celebrity these days – all you have to do is bare your bum on television. We used to have real celebrities, like Laurence Olivier and Vivien Leigh, Richard Burton and*

*Elizabeth Taylor*. He sighed. *Now who have we got? Posh and Becks, and Richard and Judy.* He shook his head sadly.

'I'm going to take out that camera.' Henry clicked on the rifle icon, lining up the small cross hairs in the middle of the screen with the angular shape of the CCTV camera. *BLAM! BLAM! BLAM!* The rifle's report echoed off the high granite cliffs. The camera fizzed, burst into flames and hung limply from its cable. 'Nice audio,' Henry remarked. 'Now we have to move very quickly – they'll probably send troops out to investigate.'

Henry hurried Scimitar along the gulley.

Brought out of his reverie by the sound of shooting, Martin ambled back over to the computer to see what was going on. The scene on-screen didn't appear to have changed: the same old unrealistic, awkwardly angled granite mountains. *God, what do people see in these games?* he thought. *You'd have to be desperate to get into them* – he looked at Henry – *or sad.*

Up ahead, the thin black line down the middle of the steel blast doors was beginning to widen: the doors were opening.

Henry pushed Scimitar as fast as his virtual legs would take him.

In front of the huge steel doors was a large, level area like a parade ground and, as a platoon of armed guards rushed out of the still-opening doors, Scimitar dived and hugged the ground. As the guards fanned out, Henry noticed a small ditch skirting the parade ground off to the right. Scimitar rolled into it.

But he couldn't stay there long. Lifting his head slowly, Scimitar could see two guards heading straight for his position. Bent double to keep out of sight, Scimitar set off again, following the ditch in a long curve, eventually coming to rest behind a large rock to one side of the half-open doors.

Here, for the time being, Scimitar was safe. Henry exhaled and massaged his keyboard hand.

'Good work, good work,' Gabriel muttered.

'Now we have to get inside.' Henry's fingers took up their positions on the keys once again, and Scimitar peeped round the safe haven of his rock. Not two yards in front of him was a guard, presumably stationed there to prevent anyone trying to do exactly what Scimitar was about to attempt.

Henry clicked on the knife icon. 'This isn't going to be pretty.' In a flash Scimitar had leapt from his hiding place and stabbed the guard in the kidneys. The soldier turned, fell to his knees with a small groan, then collapsed onto the ground in a spreading pool of blood.

*Ah, the old 'guard with his back turned' cliché*, Martin thought. Rolling his eyes he went back to the mystery celebrities in his copy of *Hello!*.

But what happened next was definitely not a cliché. As Scimitar slipped in through the steel blast doors, he was suddenly assailed by a cloud of black, fluttering shapes. But it wasn't only Scimitar who found himself engulfed by this living fog; a turbid stream of bats burst from the computer screen and started flying around the room.

'Bats!' Martin exclaimed in wonder.

They poured out of the monitor in a never-ending torrent, swirling around the neat reception area, squeaking and chirruping, flapping around the heads of the group gathered around the computer. Then, just as suddenly as they had appeared, they were gone.

Martin, Luke and Gabriel all stared wildly at each other.

They turned to Henry, who was so engrossed in the game he didn't seem to have noticed. 'OK,' he said, 'now all we have to do is find the control centre.'

Martin, his interest in computer games suddenly and miraculously rekindled, put *Hello!* gently back on the table and joined the small cluster around the screen.

Scimitar was now in what looked like the set of a James Bond movie: a vast hangar, all shiny steel walls and gantries. Away from the entrance, where a certain amount of daylight spilled in through the half-open blast doors, the inside of the hangar retreated off into ever-increasing darkness. Disappearing into the shadows behind a handy pillar, Scimitar looked around. Square-section ducting ran along the ceiling, and the steel walls were pierced here and there with double doors under red and blue flashing lights. There didn't seem to be much activity. Several military vehicles were parked in the main body of the building, but the only signs of life were a couple of guards sitting in the cab of a caterpillar truck, smoking cigarettes.

Then there was the sound of a door opening and closing and footsteps on the gantry above. Scimitar looked up and, through the perforated walkway, could make out a figure in a white coat. The scientist, clipboard in hand, descended the stairs, turned, walked straight past Scimitar's hiding place, turned again and disappeared through a set of double doors to one side.

'I think we need to be up there,' Henry observed.

Slipping out of the shadows, Scimitar crept up the staircase, but as the soldier reached the elevated walkway, yet another white-coated scientist appeared. Scimitar reacted quickly and, with a few deft moves, broke the man's neck.

'Was that really necessary?' Gabriel grimaced.

'It was him or me,' Henry growled.

Dragging the scientist's body through the door from which he'd recently emerged, Scimitar found himself in a small atrium opening onto a low-ceilinged room humming with electrical equipment. In this room a number of identically attired scientists sat behind a bank of computers facing a huge map of the world on which Korea was highlighted in green and festooned with flashing red dots.

'Korea's missile silos,' Henry explained. 'This must be the control centre. But where are the guards?'

Scimitar pulled off the dead scientist's white coat, slipped it on, then bundled the corpse into a handy broom cupboard.

'Wish me luck,' murmured Henry. Scimitar strode confidently into the control room.

'Better look as if we know what we're doing.' Henry manoeuvred the soldier to a vacant position behind the computer bank. No one paid him any attention. 'So far so good.'

'Don't say that,' Martin pleaded.

On the virtual computer screen in front of Scimitar was a menu:

MISSILE STATUS
MISSILE TARGETING
LAUNCH MISSILES
MISSILE TRACKING

'Launch missiles?' Martin asked incredulously.

'Hmm, I know what you mean,' Henry agreed. 'It's a bit obvious. I'm going to select *Launch* anyway and see what happens.' Henry moved the flashing cursor down from MISSILE STATUS to MISSILE TARGETING and pressed *Enter*.

Up came another screen: INSERT OPERATOR'S SECU-
RITY CARD.

'Ah, well they do have *some* security, it seems.' Shifting
Scimitar's point of view, Henry looked over at the scientist on his left. 'Now then, where would you keep a
security card?'

Everyone crowded round the screen to have a good
look.

'What's that he's got round his neck?' Luke asked.

The computerized scientist was wearing a credit card-
sized tag on a long chain.

'I think you get the prize for observation, Luke. Well
done,' Henry said patronizingly. Flicking Scimitar's view
back to the computer console in front of him, Henry
studied the image closely. 'Now then, where does it go?'
Alongside the virtual screen was a thin black slit resem-
bling a floppy disk drive. 'That must be the place.'

'But we haven't got a security card!' Martin was beginning to panic.

'Calm down, Mr Gray. Our dead scientist will have
one. All we have to do is go back and get it.'

'Won't that draw attention to ourselves?' Gabriel wondered.

'No one's noticed us so far – no one's even looked at
us. It's going to be a bit dull if we never get challenged.'
Henry was clearly finding it hard to stay in character without the threat of opposition.

He took Scimitar back to the cupboard where he'd
stashed the body, and removed the code card from around
its neck. Slipping it over his own head, Scimitar went
back to the computer console and inserted it into the slot.
Once the card was accepted, Scimitar removed it, and a

question came up on-screen: INITIATE MISSILE LAUNCH SEQUENCE, YES/NO?

'Hmm. Well, we could simply launch the missiles and start the war, but that would put us right in the middle of it. No, we have to get out of here first.' Henry clicked *No*.

Up came another option: CHANGE LAUNCH SECURITY CODES, YES/NO?

'I think this is what we're looking for.' He clicked *Yes*.

A list of seven-digit numbers flickered up, a flashing cursor under the first number of the first line.

'This looks like a pretty comprehensive list.'

'Now what?' Martin asked.

'Now we simply take them away with us.' Henry scrolled through Scimitar's options until he came to the computer disk, and clicked on it. The disk was inserted into the virtual computer and Henry dragged each of the numbers in turn down to the CD drive icon. It was a long and laborious process.

Martin's heart was beating fast. 'Will this take much longer?'

'We have to make sure we've got everything,' Henry said. 'We won't be able to come back. Don't worry, Mr Gray; I've done this kind of thing before.'

Once Scimitar had all the information he needed, he slipped the disk out of the virtual computer and pocketed it, left the control room and crept stealthily out of the mountain fortress, shedding his white coat on the way. He was halfway back along the gulley and safety was almost in reach when a bullet ricocheted off the granite wall. He looked up to see a line of troops on a mountain track high above him.

'Halt or you die!' came the unequivocal order in cod Korean.

'Now we have to hustle.' Henry urged Scimitar along the gulley as fast as he could go. Gunfire barked and bullets whistled around his head, some bursting out of the computer screen and thudding into the walls of the reception area.

'Get down!' Gabriel yelled.

Everyone dived for cover except Henry who, now completely back in character as the Purple Heart-winning Green Beret, ducked and dived and rolled his way along the gulley, occasionally turning and firing off the odd shot, even taking out a couple of the pursuing Korean guards. Hauling himself tirelessly up the rope and back onto the plateau, Scimitar lay prone in the scrub until the helicopter arrived to pick him up. Once safely inside the aircraft, he pulled out a laptop, inserted the disk into it and started uploading the codes to his base via satellite. Once this was complete, a message crackled over the speakers: 'Good work, Scimitar. Codes received. We have control. Moving to phase two of the operation: arming the missiles.'

The inside of the helicopter was replaced with a map of the area, Scimitar's flight tracked by a flashing red light and, underneath this at the bottom of the screen, a virtual console with a blue loading bar. Right in the middle of this console was a red button above which was a single word in bold: LAUNCH.

'Now we have the codes, we have complete control of the missiles, and once they're fully armed, we can target any country we like,' said Henry with a certain amount of satisfaction. 'Who do you want to get rid of? Russia? China?'

'Steady on,' Martin warned.

'There'll be no comeback,' Henry continued. 'We're the only ones playing. We can take out any part of the world we like. It'll be like being God.'

Gabriel cleared his throat pointedly.

'Sorry.'

Martin shuddered. 'I know it's only a game, but it gives me the willies. It feels almost real.'

If the small group gathered around the Exeter dental receptionist's computer terminal had known just *how* real the game they were playing actually was, they would have broken off immediately. For, unbeknown to them, on the other side of the world the crews of several North Korean nuclear missile bunkers were in a terrifying flap. Their control consoles were lit up like a Christmas tree. The missiles seemed to be arming themselves and there was nothing they could do to stop them.

The 'hot' missiles were immediately picked up by the network of early-warning satellites circling the earth, sparking a major panic amongst the world's nuclear powers. The US president had to be woken from a deep and satisfying sleep, the president of Russia was dragged out of a state banquet commemorating the heroes of the revolution and the head of the Chinese communist party's visit to a tractor factory was interrupted by the news that World War III was about to begin. There followed a flurry of frantic diplomatic activity, with four-way conference calls between Beijing, Washington, Moscow and Pyongyang. The North Koreans insisted they had no hostile intentions, and instead accused the US of infiltrating their missile defence system in an attempt to discredit them in the eyes of the world.

While diplomats were deployed to sort out the rapidly unravelling situation, the entire nuclear defence systems of Russia, China and the USA were ramped up to the highest state of alert.

Meanwhile, in a darkened operations room in the bowels of Hell, preparations were being made for the big day. At one end of the room was a wall-sized screen, and at the other, on a black leather sofa, sat the Devil, toying tunefully with Signora Amati. Next to him, behind a table stacked with dozens of beige plastic boxes interconnected with miles of cable, sat a strange lumpen figure, tapping away at an ageing keyboard. A projection of a map of the world flickered on-screen. The Devil nodded with satisfaction.

'So far so good,' he muttered.

The strange creature's dirty, cracked nails *clicked* and *clacked* on the keyboard, and little orange dots blinked on, indicating the locations of all the world's nuclear missiles.

'Excellent.'

'And now, my lord, if we press F7, the screen will display the missiles' level of readiness,' the creature explained in a guttural, eastern European accent. 'Orange is the default colour, green indicates a missile being launch-prepared, and red shows that the missile is launch-ready. Of course, you won't see any change yet because no one is playing,' the creature added.

'Let's just check that, shall we?' the Devil put down his bow and twirled Signora Amati off his knee. 'Run along now, my dear. Why don't you go and have a lie-down?' The strange, nervous woman walked unsteadily out of the room as the Devil slid along the sofa and hit F7. To his and his colleague's evident surprise, a wave of flashing green dots swept across the screen.

The Devil glared at the creature next to him. 'What's going on, Max?'

'Your crepuscular Majesty,' Max replied, sweating in the darkness, 'it is merely a glitch. Some small hiccup in the colour-coding program. Just give me a moment.' Max started typing furiously.

The screen flickered, went black, then came back on again – but the missile sites were still green. Max tried something else.

The Devil rose and strode around the back of the sofa to stand menacingly behind his minion. 'If your program fouls things up for me tomorrow, I'm sure you don't need me to tell you that I will hold you personally responsible.'

Max wiped the perspiration from his brow.

'Your Darkness,' Max began, 'as we are merely using the system in an observational capacity, whatever happens should not affect the outcome of your master plan.'

'*Should* not? I deal only in certainties. Let me give you an example: if anything goes wrong you will *certainly* suffer for it. All right?' He paused and frowned at the screen. 'What's that?' The counter inset in the bottom left-hand corner, which displayed the number of gamers online, had clicked round to *00001*. 'Max?' he growled threateningly.

'A glitch, O mighty one, only a glitch!' cried Max, still tapping maniacally at the keyboard.

'How can someone be playing? The game doesn't get distributed until tomorrow.' The Devil called for his manservant: 'Lothar!'

The butler appeared immediately and almost tripped over a cable gaffer-taped to the floor. 'Watch out, you fool!' his master screamed at him. 'You could upset the whole thing.'

'I apologize, Magnificence. What is your bidding?'

'Get that idiot Ferrers on the phone. I need to check he hasn't done anything stupid.'

'Sire.' The butler bowed and left.

Satan turned back to Max. 'No one should be playing until Sunday, when those meddling fools in the other place aren't looking. If this goes off too soon and God gets to hear of it, that's it! It's over! I'm history – consigned forever to the inky blackness of post-celebrity!'

The Devil gripped Max's shoulders a little too tightly and whispered hoarsely in his ear, 'I'd just like you to know, Max, that if I am cast into eternal oblivion, you are going to keep me company. It'll be really cosy: just you, me, a skewer, a blowtorch and an oven glove – for eternity.'

Max swallowed. 'The system I have been forced to work with is operating at the very edge of its capabilities; there are bound to be a few problems to iron out. Don't worry, I will soon have it working again.'

The fact was, Hell was a technological nightmare. Having sown the seeds of the electronic revolution back in the 1980s, Satan had equipped his home with all the latest technology of the time: mobile phones the size of house bricks, clunky Betamax video recorders and the most up-to-date computer system that money could buy, complete with green screen monitors. Above ground, things had moved on: the electronics industry had become more sophisticated, the gadgets smaller and more efficient. Max had tried from time to time to suggest that it might be a good idea to upgrade the computer system, but tight-fisted Satan didn't see why he should replace something if it still worked. The Lord of Misrule had shelled out thousands for something that had once been the very apogee of silicon technology, and he was determined to get his money's worth. So it was that Hell's computers were all hopelessly out of date, and the only things to watch on video were the complete third series of *The Dukes of Hazzard* and a couple of fading episodes of *The Mary Tyler Moore Show*.

Max had done his best with what there was, but his ingenuity had been sorely tested by the prehistoric equipment. Programming took three times as long as it should because the complicated operations he was trying to get the system to perform had to be written in an ancient computer language which was all the out-of-date machines could understand. The game itself had been composed by an earthbound computer programmer and, so as not to overload Satan's already creaking system, the multiplayer aspect of it was run from a central, above-ground server. But for security reasons Max had written the long, complex hacking program himself. He just hoped that enough people would have computers with large enough memories to handle it.

Another of Max's worries was that someone would do exactly what Henry had already done: have a peek behind the game and find the code-breaking program. But as long as operations above ground were carried out as per Satan's plan and the magazines delivered at their appointed time and not before, that shouldn't really be a problem. Besides, with his boss's insistence on keeping the domestic budget to a minimum, there was no way round these difficulties. Max sighed and rubbed his eyes.

Having worked for the East German Stasi during the Cold War, he was used to hardship and poor equipment, but never had he attempted anything so complicated nor so significant on equipment so ill-suited to the task.

As for the act of worldwide monitoring on which the system was presently engaged, the strain of processing the vast amount of information it was receiving from satellites and ground-based monitoring stations had pushed Max's carefully constructed electronic house of cards to its very limit. The system was teetering on a knife-edge; he just prayed that it wouldn't crash.

What Max didn't know, of course, was that his system was working perfectly and, just as it was indicating, the world was indeed poised on the brink of nuclear war.

The North Korean missiles were rapidly approaching launch-readiness, and the terrified soldiers and technicians watched this inexorable process helplessly, impotent in the face of satanic forces about which they knew nothing.

Activity in the Pentagon had reached fever pitch and the president, now wide awake but still clad in his Stars and Stripes pyjamas, sat behind his desk in the Oval Office. Right across America – in Kansas, Nebraska, Alaska – missile silos were standing by, ready to discharge their contents like the ripe pustules on the acne-covered face of an eager teenager.

The president was waiting for the latest intelligence from his spy satellites. Once the North Korean missiles were fully powered up, he had less than three minutes to make a decision. He could wait for them to launch first and risk the USA being blown back to the Stone Age, or he could hit them with a pre-emptive strike which would reduce a large portion of Asia to radioactive charcoal and risk starting a global chain reaction which would successfully remove most life forms from the planet. The decision was his alone, and alone was exactly how he felt.

In northern Russia, ancient Soviet technology creaked into gear and clouds of super-cooled oxygen coiled dramatically around missiles hidden deep in the remote and frozen tundra, as their rocket engines were fuelled to overflowing.

But as these terrifying international developments unfolded, the small group gathered around the computer in an Exeter dental practice remained in blissful ignorance of the desperate panic they were causing amongst the world's top political circles. Until, that is, a small thought which had been buzzing like a mosquito around the back of Henry's mind became annoyingly insistent.

'Mr Gray,' he began, 'this new computer system that you recently installed . . .'

'Yes?'

'How many computers are we talking about?'

'Oh, dozens. Westerham bought one for every bloody room in the place – there's even one in the loo!'

'Are we talking individual, autonomous stations or network?'

'English please, Henry.'

But Luke was way ahead of him. 'Oh fuck!'

'Luke!' Martin frowned.

'What is it?' Gabriel asked.

'If the computers are connected up to a network, there's a chance that they have been playing this game too. And, as they presumably still have Internet access, there's a distinct possibility that they could be online.'

'Fuck!' said Gabriel, echoing Luke's sentiment.

'Gabriel!' Martin chided.

'Turn it off!' Gabriel yelled.

Luke was already running up the stairs. 'I'll go and see what's happening on the other computers!'

Henry moved the cursor down to the *Close* button at the bottom of the screen. 'Hmm.'

'What?' Martin asked, his face a frozen mask of terror.

''Snot responding,' Henry muttered.

'It's not . . .?' But Gabriel's mouth refused to finish the sentence.

The steadily growing blue bar at the bottom of the screen was showing that the missiles were now approaching launch-readiness. Henry poked at the keyboard with his stubby fingers.

Gabriel was doing a good impression of a kangaroo with bladder trouble. 'Why won't it turn off?'

'Dunno,' Henry replied, baffled that all his computer expertise had been unable to find an answer to the problem. 'Hang on.' He pressed Ctrl+Alt+Delete – the computer operator's last resort. For a hard-wired computer nut like him it was demeaning to stoop to such a hackneyed solution, but he had to admit that it usually worked. Except in this case.

Luke's voice came bellowing down the staircase: 'It's on every bloody machine!'

'What do we do?' Gabriel's wings were trembling like a trapped moth's.

Henry scratched his head.

'Where's the OFF button?' Martin began searching

around the back of the computer. 'Why the bloody hell can't they make it obvious?'

'I've tried that,' Henry informed him casually. He jabbed at the disk eject button, stabbed **Esc** several times. But nothing he did had any effect.

'Why don't we pull out the plug?' Martin suggested.

'Good idea!' Gabriel leapt to the wall socket.

'Wait!' Henry warned.

Everyone froze as Henry considered his options. He hated being frustrated by the machinery like this and was sure there must be another way . . . but he just couldn't think of it at the moment. 'All right,' he said at last, 'go ahead.'

Gabriel yanked the plug out of the wall. The bar reached the end of its travel and the message *Missiles armed and ready for launch* flashed on-screen.

'Must be residual charge in the system,' Henry explained to the stunned faces around him. 'It'll stop in a minute.'

A voice crackled over the speakers: 'Scimitar, you have done well. To you now comes the honour of neutralizing our enemies. Press the red button to launch.'

'Aaarrghhh!' Gabriel was frantic.

Luke reappeared in the waiting room. 'I can't turn them off. I even pulled the plug on one!'

'We know,' Martin informed him.

'Wait a minute!' Henry yelled.

Gabriel stared at him, his face a rictus of panic.

'This is a wireless system, right? So, all we need to do is find the LiveBox!'

'Don't be technical!' Gabriel screamed.

'The wireless Internet server,' Henry explained carefully.

'If we can find it and disconnect it, it will disable the Internet connection.'

All eyes went to Martin.

'Dad, where is it?'

'I don't know!'

'Fuck!'

'Luke, language!'

'Oh, please,' said Gabriel. 'Do something useful and look for your live bait thing!'

'LiveBox,' Henry corrected.

'Precisely. What does it look like?'

'It's a plastic box, about this big –' Henry held his hands about a foot apart '– with red flashing lights on it.'

'OK,' said Martin. 'Spread out – take a room each.'

The group dispersed throughout the building.


Meanwhile, amid the panic, the North Koreans set about finding out exactly who it was that had hacked into their defence system. The US was top of their list of suspects, of course, and although they didn't have the vast array of intelligence-gathering equipment possessed by the Americans, their kit was just about up to tracing a phone line, and they were looking forward to putting a big dent in the stainless steel image of the 'world policeman'.


'Henry, I think we've found it!' Martin called from the foot of the stairs.

The flabby, pasty-faced teenager, who had just opened a drugs cupboard in a second-floor surgery and was contemplating how much his friend Dave would pay for a box of the exciting-looking little glass phials it contained, was brought suddenly back to the task at hand.

'Coming!' he yelled, and loped down the stairs.

Martin led the way into the small kitchen and pointed to an open cupboard under the sink.

Henry stooped and looked inside. 'That's it all right.'

'Why's it in there?' asked Gabriel, peering round the door.

'It's pretty central – probably the best place for a signal.' Henry pulled out the white plastic box and yanked out the lead connecting it to the phone socket. 'That, hopefully, is that.'

On the other side of the world, the North Korean missiles suddenly came back under their commander's control and were deactivated immediately.

When this news reached Moscow and the United States, weapons systems capable of turning the earth into a lifeless asteroid ten times over were gratefully stood down, and everyone breathed a huge sigh of relief.

Once they had recovered their breath, the North Koreans found, to their surprise, that the trace they had run on their mystery hacker ran all the way to Europe. But that was all they'd been able to ascertain in the time available.

Lothar came carefully back into the room carrying a telephone on a long lead. 'Mr Ferrers for you, My Lord.' He handed the receiver to his master.

Satan was about to launch a tirade against the hapless tycoon when all the lights on the large screen turned from green to orange. 'Oh, never mind,' Satan said, and passed the receiver back to his manservant.

Max breathed easily again, and offered up a silent prayer of thanks to Lenin.

'So now we know Satan's little game,' said Gabriel. 'The end of the world by proxy.'

But Martin was keen not to get too carried away. 'We don't actually have any proof of that.'

'Oh, come on! Bats and bullets pouring out of a computer screen is perfectly normal, is it?' said the angel. 'And what about your anarchic city-centre traffic solution?'

Martin got defensive. 'It could have been a mass hallucination,' he said lamely. 'I mean there's nothing – other than your paranoia – to say that anything happened here except the playing of a computer game.'

'Oh, I'm paranoid now, am I?' Gabriel was becoming rather tight-lipped.

'Well . . .' Martin began.

Henry thought it was time he intervened. 'I've never seen a computer go on running after its plug's been pulled, Mr Gray. *And* I've never come across one I couldn't shut down before. That was no ordinary game.'

'Thank you, Henry.' Gabriel turned back to Martin. 'At least someone's on my side.'

'I just think we should go a bit carefully, that's all.'

'Carefully?' Gabriel exploded. 'The world is going to end tomorrow and he wants to go carefully!'

'Gabriel's right, Dad,' said Luke. 'If there's the slightest possibility that this game could lead to World War III, we have to do something about it.'

'See! Even your son supports old Mr Paranoia here.' Gabriel sniffed.

'All right, all right. Let's just all calm down and think about what we're going to do, shall we?'

Henry piped up, 'I've been thinking.'

Everyone turned to look at him.

'We could pre-empt anything bad happening at all.'

'Go on,' Martin urged.

'Using the code breaker we could—'

'No,' said Gabriel firmly. 'No more messing with computers. The power of this code breaker is terrifying – it's playing with fire. And we don't know what other tricks Old Nick has up his sleeve.'

'But—' Henry pleaded.

Gabriel was firm. 'No. We're poised on a knife-edge here – it's too dangerous.'

'So what do we do?' Martin asked.

Gabriel looked tired and drawn. As an angel he wasn't really equipped for stress; he should have been reclining on a cloud, strumming a harp. Although these days you were much more likely to see one of Heaven's host wearing plus fours and swinging a mashie-niblik.

'We have to stop this game being distributed,' Gabriel said at last. 'If no one has a copy of it, then no one can play.' Everyone had to agree that the angel's logic was faultless.

Garth was packing. He knew it was probably futile to attempt escape, but he had at least to try. Maybe if he didn't tell anyone where he was going, perhaps if he just took off without a plan? After all, if *he* didn't even know where he was going, then how could Satan? It was worth a shot.

As he turned back to his wardrobe, he was startled to find a tall man in a long raincoat standing there. 'Ah!'

'Don't panic,' Gabriel soothed. 'I'm here to help, if I can.'

'Who are you? How did you get in here?'

Gabriel looked around the room. 'What colour do you call this?'

'April Sunset, why?'

'It's very nice.'

'I chose it myself. You still haven't answered my question: who are you?'

'Like I said, I'm here to help.'

Garth looked a little closer at the strange man. Something about his clear blue eyes and golden hair made him gasp. 'You're . . . you're an . . .'

Gabriel nodded. 'I *am* an angel, yes, but—'

'So my prayers have been answered!'

'Um . . .'

Garth fell to his knees and began kissing the hem of Gabriel's raincoat.

'There's really no need for that.' But Garth had already worked his way down to Gabriel's bare feet. 'Please stop – you're tickling.'

But Garth wouldn't stop and covered the angel's toes in thankful kisses.

'Look,' said Gabriel sternly, taking a step backwards, 'I suppose you could say I'm here under false pretences.'

Garth detected a certain edge in the angel's tone. 'False pretences?'

Gabriel looked troubled. 'Yes, you see . . . Oh this is

very awkward. The thing is, I shouldn't really be here. If God found out there'd be hell to pay.'

Garth gazed up at the angel. 'He didn't send you?'

'I'm sorry, Garth, but in cases of soul-selling – if that's what you've done – God doesn't usually intervene. It gets in the way of free will, you see. Besides, it violates the Heaven–Hell treaty.' Gabriel put on his best heavenly smile. 'I can put in a good word for you if you like . . .'

Garth got back to his feet resignedly. 'I see.' After a pause during which he studied the burnished uppers of his handmade shoes long and hard, Garth suddenly looked up and fixed Gabriel with cold grey eyes. 'You've got a nerve.'

'I'm sorry?'

'You dare to come here and offer me a glimpse of hope only to snatch it away again?'

Gabriel shuffled uncomfortably. 'Oh, but I never—'

'How cruel can you be? How incredibly heartless. You're worse than him down below. If Heaven's full of people like you, maybe I'll be better off where I'm going. Now, if you'll excuse me, I have things to do.' Garth pushed Gabriel out of the way and grabbed another armful of clothes from the wardrobe. 'What a fool, to think that God would save me. I'm beyond salvation!' Something about that particular word made Garth pause. Tears welled up in his eyes and he slumped down on the bed and started sobbing. 'Oh God, oh God, oh God, what have I done?'

'There, there,' said Gabriel sitting down beside him. 'Do you want to tell me all about it?'

Through his tears, Garth started to tell Gabriel about his time at Westlight Double-Glazing and that fateful telephone call. He'd just got to the bit about meeting the Devil at the quay when Gabriel interrupted.

'Um, this is all really fascinating stuff, and I don't want to appear unfeeling, but I am a little pressed for time. Do you think we could fast forward to the whole *Endgame* saga?'

Garth sighed, then quickly recounted the salient events: the pact with Satan, his taking over of Hoofprint Publishing, the publication of the most recent edition of *Web of Fire*, ending with his present state of abject terror at his imminent descent into Hell – his fiftieth birthday being on Sunday.

When he'd finished, Gabriel was thoughtful for a moment. Then he spoke. 'Well now, I can't promise anything, but God has occasionally been known to show clemency in these matters, especially when the subject is particularly penitent.'

'I am, I am. I'll do anything to prove it,' Garth sobbed.

'Anything?' said the angel.

'Anything!'

'Right then –' Gabriel smiled, '– you can start by giving me details of your distribution network.'

# Chapter 10

If the world really was going to end, Martin wanted at least to have spoken to Helen before it happened. He wanted to warn her, but then, apart from making her anxious, what would that achieve? Besides, why should she believe him? Talk of angels and the Devil would only confirm her suspicions that he was losing his mind. Nevertheless, he did want to make contact, if only to hear her voice one last time.

The phone rang several times before it was picked up.
'Hello?'

Martin's stomach sank when he heard the crisp, dry voice of Helen's father.

'Oh, hello, John. Can I speak to Helen, please?'

'Well now, Martin, I don't know about that.'

*Why can't he just say no if he means no?* Martin thought.
'Is she there? I'd like a word.'

'I'm not sure she wants to speak to you, Martin.'

John had never really taken to Martin. Before their first meeting, to overcome his nerves, Martin had consumed several pints in a local pub, and when John had told the story, in deadly earnest, of how he had once rescued his wife's pet budgie from the roof, only to have it fly out of his hands and straight under the wheels of a passing refuse truck, Martin had burst out laughing. It hadn't really endeared him to his prospective father-in-law.

'Please, John, I'd like to talk to Helen.'

There were muffled voices as John put his hand over the receiver and conferred with someone. Eventually he came back on. 'I really think you've done enough damage, Martin. You don't want to upset her any more, do you?'

Martin could feel his rage rising. '*I've* done enough damage? If it wasn't for you we'd still be together! The moment you moved in you started poisoning her mind against me. You –' There was a click and the line went dead. 'Bastard!' Martin yelled pointlessly at the handset.

Gabriel needed an army. Hundreds of thousands of magazines had already been distributed the length of the country – some were in warehouses ready to be loaded onto lorries and delivered the next morning, some were waiting in the back rooms of newsagents in time to be put on the shelves on Sunday. If he was to stop a nuclear holocaust, Gabriel needed to account for every single edition of *Web of Fire*. It was a mammoth task, and he would need help.

In Caesar's Palace, in the middle of the Nevada desert, a male figure in a long grey mackintosh was playing the slots. He inserted a quarter in the first of a line of brightly coloured flashing machines and pulled the handle. The reels whirred and clicked to a stop one by one: watermelon, watermelon, watermelon. With a sigh, the punter placed a canvas holdall under the chute as an avalanche of coins poured out. When the last quarter had clinked into his bag, he moved on to the next machine.

The reels spun round in a blur, then came to a staggering halt: Bar, Bar, Bar. Once again he hefted the heavy canvas bag and held it under the chute as the coins tumbled out. Moving on to the next one in line, he had just inserted a coin and pulled the handle when someone called his name: 'Michael!'

The angel spun round and found himself looking at an almost carbon copy of himself, right down to the ankle-length raincoat. 'Gabriel! What brings you to the Nevada fleshpots?'

'I need your help. Can we go somewhere a little less public?'

'Just a minute. Grab a handle will you?'

Gabriel took one side of the heavy canvas holdall and the two angels held it under the money chute as the spinning reels juddered to a stop: 7 7 7. Soon the weight of the bag had increased dramatically.

The sight of one strangely attired individual winning the jackpot on every machine was suspicious enough, but two identically dressed customers bleeding every machine dry was too much for casino security.

Noticing that they were slowly being ringed by men in dark suits and mirror shades, Michael turned to Gabriel. 'I think it's time to go.' Swinging the money bag between them, the angels headed for the exit. But, as they approached the smoked-glass doors, a six-foot square of expensively tailored muscle blocked their path.

'Excuse me, gentlemen . . .'

Michael passed his free hand over the man's face. For a moment the security guard looked puzzled, as though he couldn't quite remember what he had been doing.

Andy Secombe

Then, suddenly smiling, he opened the door and saluted smartly. 'You have a nice day now.'

Stepping out of the air-conditioned interior of the casino and into the blaring heat of the Nevada day, Michael looked up and down Las Vegas Boulevard. At first he seemed unsure of which direction to take. Then he smiled. 'This way,' he said, and led Gabriel down towards Flamingo Road.

In the shade of a footbridge linking Caesar's Palace with the Barbary Coast, a sad, shabby man was slumped on the sidewalk. 'Are you homeless?' Michael asked. It was an unnecessary question, considering the state of his clothes and the aroma of overripe Camembert which enveloped the man.

It took him a little while to focus, but eventually the derelict managed to get his bloodshot eyeballs to fix on the angel's face. 'Homeless,' he breathed.

Both angels recoiled from his whiskey-tinged breath.

'Homeless, hopeless and in Hell,' the man added with a wry, wheezy laugh.

Michael turned to Gabriel. 'We can put it down now.'

The angels gratefully lowered the heavy bag onto the sidewalk alongside the drunk.

'Sober up, get yourself a wash and a good meal, buy a car and get out of this town.' Michael patted the bag, which chinked pleasingly.

The drunk had no idea what was happening. He frowned up at the angel, then slowly turned his attention to the holdall. Peering inside, his eyes widened at its glittering contents. He looked up once more to offer his thanks, but his saviours had disappeared.

'Wealth redistribution,' Michael explained as the two angels walked on up the baking street. 'He probably has a family somewhere, came to Las Vegas to make his fortune, but lost everything instead and now can't get out. You see so much of it here.'

'How do you know he won't just take that money back into a casino and blow it all?' Gabriel wondered.

'It's evens he'll do just that, but I'd say the odds are worth the punt. But you didn't come to see me to talk about my outreach programme.'

'No,' said Gabriel, 'I need your help.'

In some respects, Michael was nearer to God than Gabriel was. He had a wide rebellious streak, but God treated him like a wayward son, and more or less let him do what he wanted. He was definitely easier on Michael than he was on his own son, who wasn't allowed to get away with anything, poor chap. It was bad enough having to bear the burden of being the son of a famous father, but he was also expected to follow his dad in everything he did. It was heart-rending to see him trailing his old man around the golf course, glumly swinging a club and dressed like Ronnie Corbett.

Michael had taken advantage of his special relationship with the creator to do his bit for the world's deserving. Recycling casinos' money in Las Vegas was only the latest in a long line of schemes in which he'd been involved: he'd helped set up Oxfam; whispered the idea of Amnesty International into the ear of Peter Benenson; and had a hand in Band Aid (if you look closely at the group photograph of the stars who sang on the original 'Do They Know it's Christmas?' you can just see him, peeping round Paul Young's left ear). He was like the black sheep of the family but loved even more because of it. And if there was one person in the heavenly host who'd understand Gabriel's present dilemma, it was Michael.

'So you see,' said Gabriel, 'it's pointless me trying to talk to him; he never listens to a word I say. But if nothing is done, then earth is doomed.'

They were standing under the starkly unforgiving sun in the middle of the Nevada desert. Having draped their raincoats on the arms of a handy cactus, they were slowly beating their great wings to provide a cooling breeze. Unfortunately this had the effect of intensifying the heat, like a fan oven, but it did give them something to do. Wing beating was the angels' equivalent of head scratching or chin stroking: it helped them to think.

'So,' Michael said after a pause, 'what can *I* do?'

'We have to stop the magazines reaching the shops, and it has to be done before the newsagents open on Sunday.'

Michael's wings froze in mid-beat. 'Tomorrow?'

'Yes.' Gabriel relaxed his pinions too and became thoughtful. 'Have you noticed,' he observed, 'that it's cooler if we don't flap?'

'What sort of numbers are we talking about?'

'Thousands. Probably hundreds of thousands.'

Michael's wings began to beat again, faster this time, stirring up little dust devils around his ankles. 'That's impossible. How are the two of us going to dispose of that many magazines in a single night?'

'Not just the two of us,' said Gabriel, who was standing in the superheated draught from Michael's wings. The temperature was fast approaching the perfect heat for roasting beef – not very conducive to productive thinking. 'Sorry, can you stop a minute?'

'Oh, forgive me.' Michael rested his wings.

'Thank you. No, of course we'll need help, which is why I came to you. The thing is, they're sick and tired of my so-called doom-mongering upstairs. God's so fed up with me that whenever he sees me coming he dives into the nearest bunker. Whereas you seem to be able to wrap him around your little finger.'

Michael shook his head. 'Nothing I can say will make him change his mind on this subject. You know how keen he is on all this free will nonsense.'

'*He* may not listen to you, but the others will; they're all a bit in awe of you. If you turn up, switch on the charm and say you need their help, they'll be falling over themselves to come to your aid.'

Michael thought for a moment, his snow-white wings twitching involuntarily as he considered Gabriel's request. 'If he finds out what's going on, he'll put a stop to it,' the angel said at last. 'Knowing him, I wouldn't be surprised if he just handed Heaven and Earth over to Old Nick, saying that the bet was forfeit because we'd cheated in his name. Sometimes I wish he didn't have such an overdeveloped sense of fair play – it's the Devil he's dealing with, for Pete's sake!'

'This evening,' said Gabriel.

Michael looked intrigued. 'What?'

'He's got a huge backlog of prayers to listen to. If we sneak upstairs while he's locked in his study with the answerphone, we can get everyone together without him even knowing. Up to his armpits in requests for money and forgiveness, he won't notice a few missing angels.'

Michael nodded slowly and put his fingers to his lips. 'Of course, you do realize he'll find out eventually.'

'I know,' Gabriel sighed, 'but we'll cross that bridge when we come to it. The most important thing is that we stop this terrible thing happening.'

Michael thought for a long moment, staring hard at

the ground while moving slowly round in a circle. Then suddenly he looked up at Gabriel, his jaw set. 'I'm in.'

Gabriel smiled and grasped Michael's hand.

'Welcome aboard.'


Back at the surgery, Gabriel outlined his plan to Martin and the rest of the gang.

'So tonight, once he's safely ensconced in his study, Michael and I are going to round up as many angels as are willing and, with the distribution schedule I got from Garth, dispose of all the magazines.'

'What are you going to do with them?' Henry asked.

'The warehouses we can simply set fire to.'

'Isn't that a little dangerous?' Martin wondered.

'Heavenly fire,' Gabriel explained. 'A phenomenon you might know as spontaneous combustion.'

Henry's eyes lit up. 'So it really does exist?'

'Oh yes. It's caused by the soul of the departed being ripped out of the body too quickly by an impatient soul-fetcher, rather like a match head being struck against the side of a matchbox. The body instantly flares up but, because it's a fire that exists between dimensions, it's pretty weak. The body can be completely consumed, but the surrounding area is left untouched. It's a little more complicated to get it to work on inanimate objects, but it can be done. One has to dematerialize, permeate the stack of magazines or whatever it is, then leave the magazines and rematerialize at almost the same instant. Timing is all.'

Henry's mind went into an ecstatic orgy of wonder.

'Besides, warehouses are usually located on industrial estates and away from built-up areas, so if anything does go wrong and the building goes up, it won't set the town on fire. The newsagents could be more problematic. We're probably going to have to physically remove the magazines from them, and for that we'll need transport. But I'm hoping Chris can sort that out.'

'Chris?' Martin queried.

'Saint Christopher.'

'Of course.'

'Now, then. I suggest you all get some sleep.'

'Sleep!' Luke exclaimed. 'How are we going to sleep?'

'I can sleep,' said Martin, his eyelids already feeling heavy.

'I need you to be sharp for tomorrow,' Gabriel instructed. 'There's nothing for you to do tonight, but who knows what the day may bring?' He pointed at Henry. 'You have to be online first thing. If we've done our job properly, you should be the only player. If not, you're going to have to think of something really, really clever.'

'No problem.' Henry shrugged.

As Gabriel had predicted, Michael's reappearance in Heaven was greeted with great excitement. The two angels had waited until they were sure that God would be fully occupied before presenting themselves to Peter at the golden gates.

'Michael!' Peter exclaimed. 'Long time no see. You haven't changed a bit!' Saint and angel embraced.

'It's good to see you too, Pete. How's the security business?'

Peter rolled his eyes. 'Sometimes I don't know why

I'm here – we hardly have any passing trade. All we seem to get these days are nuns and librarians.'

'Look, I'd love to have a proper chat, but we're in a bit of a hurry. Where's the old man?'

'In his study, listening to guilty secrets, pleas for forgiveness and requests for large amounts of cash.' Peter looked hard into the angels' faces. 'Is this about that business in North Korea?'

Gabriel looked worried. 'Did God see that?'

Peter shook his head. 'No, when it happened he'd just sliced his ball off the thirteenth tee. He spent the whole time of the crisis looking for it amongst the trees. It put the wind up everyone else though. A lot of them have come round to your way of thinking – except Thomas, of course.'

'About time,' Gabriel snorted.

'So, are any of the lads around?' Michael asked.

'Saints James and Andrew are sharing a wineskin in the clubhouse bar, and Matthew and Mark have gone to see Son of. I think they're trying to persuade him to talk to his father. If you ask me, they should have gone to his mother first – she's the one with the real power.'

'Looks like we got here at just the right time,' Michael concluded.


At a hastily convened meeting in the pro shop, overlooking the first tee, the assembled throng of angels, saints and assorted divine entities listened to what the two archangels had to say.

After outlining the situation, Gabriel handed the floor over to Michael.

'Brothers and sisters,' Michael began, 'we have to act.

We must stop this terrible tragedy from happening, and the only way we're going to do that is to get our hands dirty: go down to earth and intercede on God's behalf.'

St John the Divine piped up, 'If anybody had paid attention to what I'd said, we wouldn't be in this mess now. It's all there in my Revelation chapter thirteen: "*And I stood upon the sand of the sea and saw a beast rise up out of the sea—*" '

'Thank you, Brother John,' Michael interrupted.

An ancient creature with a long white beard, standing by a rack of yellow and pink Pringle sweaters, shook his head sadly. 'Never even got to see the Promised Land and now it's all going to be blown up.'

'All right, Moses, let's just stick to the point, shall we?' Michael pleaded.

'Can I go home now?' Lazarus asked. 'I'm not feeling terribly well.'

'Please!' Gabriel implored. 'Time is running out. We have to reach some kind of consensus before Satan destroys the world!'

A discontented grumble ran around the room. One of three men in rich attire, standing together beside a rack of putters, raised his hand.

'Brother Balthazar!'

'But God's forbidden us to interfere. Are we to go against his wishes?'

'Let me paint you a picture of what happens after Satan's trashed the earth,' said Gabriel. 'If he's successful, there's going to be a new addition to the heavenly choir: the Beast will be back, sitting at the top table and sneering at you all. There goes the neighbourhood! Is that what you want?'

A thoughtful silence fell upon the crowd. Eventually

an attractive, dark-haired woman in the front row raised her hand.

'Yes, Sister.'

'I didn't mind Satan,' she said, her dark eyes flashing. 'I thought he was quite cute.'

The crowd turned on her furiously.

'Now, now, now,' Gabriel shouted over the baying throng. '"*Let him who is without sin . . .*" etc., etc. . . .'

The angry multitude fell back into sulky muttering.

Michael was getting more and more frustrated. 'Look, the longer we spend here arguing, the more we're playing into Satan's hands.'

'Quite right,' Gabriel agreed. 'We've wasted enough time already. All those in favour say aye!'

There was silence as the mass of saintly personages decided which way they were going to vote. Eventually Solomon, standing in the very heart of the multitude, shouted out a clear and distinct 'Aye!'

Then came another: 'Aye!'

More and more of the heavenly host followed suit in a haphazard and uncoordinated chorus of agreement.

Eventually a lone voice at the back shouted, 'I'm Spartacus!'

'Thank you, James —' Gabriel smiled – 'but *I* do the jokes.'

'Right,' said Michael. 'Those against?'

'Well, I'm not sure . . .' came a voice.

'Oh, Thomas!' chorused the crowd.

'All right, all right. I'm allowed to have an opinion, aren't I?'

'The motion is carried by a majority!' Gabriel rejoiced. 'Now then, here's the plan . . .'

\*

As darkness fell on that fateful night, Heaven's army of angels, saints and do-gooders spread themselves out across the land, each one armed with nothing but a copy of Garth's delivery schedule and an *A–Z*.

As lights clicked off in bedrooms up and down the country, the heavenly commandos went to work. Silvery-winged figures and people dressed like the cast of a nativity play cruised the silent streets in white Transit vans searching for the shuttered newsagents on their clipboard lists, while piles of magazines stacked in echoing ware-houses mysteriously burst into flames, producing neither heat nor smoke to trigger the silent fire alarms.

That night, in every town in England, Wales and Scot-land, thousands, tens of thousands of the magazines, the innocuous-looking DVDs of death glittering on their covers, were taken from newsagents by shoplifting angels and driven to remote locations – lochs, lakes, rivers, estu-aries, the sea itself – to be dumped into the cold, dark waters.

It was a miracle that more of the vans weren't stopped by the police. Generally speaking, the drivers of the vehi-cles were unfamiliar with driving anything other than sheep, and that, coupled with the strain of trying to read tiny *A– Z* street maps by dim interior light, contributed to a rash of breaches of the Highway Code.

John the Baptist was the worst offender. Fed up with constantly having to refer to the *A–Z* on the seat beside him, he had a brilliant idea. Without even leaving his position behind the wheel, he removed his head and wedged it on the dashboard, the *A–Z* open in front of it. This gave him a perfect sight of the map, but unfortu-nately completely obscured his sight of the road. He drove straight through a red light and into a lamp post.

A police car was soon on the scene, but when the investigating officer opened the door of the van to be confronted by a headless man groping around on the floor for his dislodged head, the poor policeman fled in panic.

The operation was a near-total success. Before sunrise, every one of the offending magazines was accounted for. Only one small problem remained: the van driven by apostles James and Andrew had slipped backwards into Loch Maree, in Wester Ross, while they were unloading. Unfortunately the resulting splash had attracted the attention of a patrolling gamekeeper, and the police had been called. James and Andrew fled, but the van and what was left of its cargo were recovered and taken into police custody.

It was a very sheepish-looking pair of apostles who reported the incident to Gabriel and Michael.

Michael was furious. 'Didn't you check that there was no one else around?'

'It was the middle of nowhere. No one in their right mind would have been out there at that time of night,' James pleaded.

'I see you're unfamiliar with the Scots,' Gabriel murmured.

'It's not our fault,' Andrew yelped. 'We did everything we should have done.'

'Yes, you did everything brilliantly, except for handing over a whole stack of magazines to the police!' Michael exploded.

Gabriel tried to calm the situation. 'It is a problem, admittedly, but every problem has a solution. Now then, Andrew, James, you did follow the van and see exactly where the police took it?'

The apostles gazed up at the angel with a look of growing horror.

'Ah. Now we *have* got a problem.'

Michael was jumping up and down. 'You don't know where the magazines were taken? Do you have any idea how big Scotland is?'

The brothers shook their heads.

'It's big! You,' said Michael, jabbing a finger at Andrew, 'should have known better!'

'I do have a name,' the apostle bridled.

'Yes, and you're also patron saint of Scotland! Don't you take any interest in your constituency?'

'It was dark,' James whined. 'We couldn't see.'

'Of course it was bloody dark; it was the middle of the night!'

'Shouting at each other isn't going to get us any-where,' Gabriel said gently. 'Andrew, could you at least find the place where you left the van?'

'I could show you on the map.'

Gabriel smiled benignly at the apostle. 'If you wouldn't mind.'

Near the spot on the map where the van had reversed itself into the loch was a small town: Kinlochewe. And, joy of joys, there in its centre was a black triangle, denoting a police station.

'Well, I suppose it's a start,' Michael said grudgingly.

'But if the magazines are locked up in a police station, how do we get them out?' James asked.

'Good point,' Michael conceded. 'It's going to be a lot trickier breaking a stack of magazines out of police custody than it is from a newsagent.'

'We're just going to have to go in and ask for them back,' Gabriel suggested.

'Not too familiar with police methods, are we?' Michael sneered.

Gabriel glared at him. 'Do you have a better suggestion?'

Michael clenched and unclenched his jaw. Eventually he looked at the ground and muttered, 'No.'

'Right,' said Gabriel, with a hint of satisfaction, 'off we go then – to bonny Scotland.'


Sergeant Angus MacFarlane, a large and ruddy-faced man, looked up from his *Evening Herald* at the four strange men who had crowded into the small public vestibule at the front of the station. His policeman's eye took them all in and summed them up in an instant. *Southerners*, he thought distastefully. Two were tall, wearing almost identical raincoats, the other two – bearded, swarthy-looking – were of foreign appearance, and dressed in flowing raiment. Closing the newspaper and taking a long, satisfying draught of his whisky-laced mug of tea, Angus rose unhurriedly from his comfy leather chair and crossed, with an easy swagger, to the front desk to see what they wanted.

'Good evening, gentlemen. Isn't it a little late to be wandering abroad?'

One of the tall men smiled. 'Officer, we're so sorry to trouble you at this hour, but we believe you may have something of ours.'

'It's vitally important that we retrieve it,' the other raincoated individual added.

Sergeant MacFarlane eyed them steadily. 'I see. Well, let's start with some details, shall we?' He opened a ledger on the desk and picked up a biro. 'Would you mind telling me what this thing is that you are so anxious to recover?'

'A white van,' said Archangel Michael.

'Loaded with magazines,' Gabriel added.

The sergeant sucked his teeth. Putting down the pen, he leaned heavily on the counter. 'And what makes you gentlemen think it might be here?'

'We know you've got it because we saw you drive it away!' James blurted out.

Angus MacFarlane stared hard at the apostle. 'Don't I know you?'

James blushed and shook his head. 'I . . . I don't think so, no.'

The sergeant's eyes bored into him. 'Your face looks very familiar. It'll come to me, don't worry.' This last was uttered like a threat. He picked up his biro again. 'Now then, I suggest you start by giving me your names.'

Michael clicked his tongue. 'Oh, we don't have time for this.'

The sergeant directed his flint-like gaze at the angel. 'It's for *me* to say whether or not you have time. You may or may not have committed a serious offence – that of polluting a loch – something we do not take lightly around here, believe you me.'

'Then you *have* got it!' Gabriel cheered.

'Got what?' Sergeant MacFarlane said mysteriously.

'Oh, come on,' said Michael irritably. 'Don't play games. Look, we know you've got the van. I'm sure we can conclude this matter swiftly and amicably.' Michael leaned towards the policeman. 'You look like an intelligent man. How much would it take for us to get our property back?'

Angus's eyes turned from flint to steel. 'Are you bribing me, sir?'

'Yes,' Michael replied. 'Couple of thou' do you? Not bad for a night's work, eh?'

The sergeant smiled and stroked his chin. 'Hmm, two thousand you say?'

Michael nodded.

'That would come in very handy, very handy indeed. Why don't you come through and we can discuss it?' Lifting the flap in the counter, he ushered the four individuals into the rear of the station.

Michael winked at Gabriel and smiled. 'Works every time.'


Gabriel glared at Michael across the small cell. 'Works every time? I suppose this is your famous familiarity with police methods, is it?'

'I don't understand – it always works in America.'

'This isn't America, this is Scotland; they do things differently here. People who have nothing are usually more honest.'

'All right, all right. I was trying to short-circuit the process, that's all. We could have been there all night answering questions.'

'Instead we're going to spend all night in here!'

'Why doesn't one of us do a bit of a recce,' James suggested, 'just to make sure that the magazines are actually here?'

'Yes,' Andrew added, 'anything to stop you two sniping at each other.'

Gabriel pursed his lips. 'Point taken,' he conceded.

'I'll go,' Michael said. 'I won't be a minute.' The angel

dematerialized and wandered unseen through the small police station. He soon found the magazines in a squat, grey stone building off the parking area where their white Transit van was parked in a puddle.

'Well, so much for police security,' said Michael, returning to his colleagues. 'They've stored the magazines in the loo.'

James exploded. 'You're joking! You mean all we had to do was nip round the back and take them? This has all been for nothing?'

Gabriel rounded on him. 'Don't you start – it's your fault we're here in the first place.' He turned back to Michael. 'How do we get them out?'

'The van's there; we could simply load it up and blow.'

'If it'll start,' Gabriel warned, looking darkly at James and Andrew. 'It has been swimming, remember.'

The two apostles shifted uneasily in their seats.

'It's got to be worth a go,' Michael continued. 'Sitting here's not really getting us anywhere, is it? Or has earth's imminent destruction ceased to worry you?'

Gabriel stood up furiously and banged his head on the low ceiling of the cell. 'Ow! I am quite aware of the urgency of our mission, thank you very much. It was me who discovered it!'

'Come on, then, follow me,' said Michael. 'And mind your heads,' he added with a smile.

Getting the magazines out of the loo and back into the rear of the Transit van presented no major problems – the sergeant seemed to be the only policeman on duty and, now into his third mug of heavily fortified tea, was sinking steadily and happily into alcoholic oblivion. For all he cared the end of the world could be nigh (which, in fact, it was).

Michael, who had often watched car thieves in action in the States, had picked up a little about engines, and gave the Transit's power plant the once-over. Gabriel watched with reluctant admiration as his angelic colleague removed the carburettor, wiped out the bowl and blew through the jets to clear any remaining beads of water.

'It should start now,' Michael said, climbing behind the wheel. He reached down to turn on the ignition. 'Ah, no key. It must be inside the station.'

Gabriel looked worried. 'Well, we've no time to look for it now. What do we do?'

Michael smiled, reached under the dashboard and pulled out a bundle of wires. 'This shouldn't be too difficult.'

Within minutes the heavenly troupe was bowling along the A832 singing 'Ye Holy Angels Bright' in four-part harmony, and within half an hour their satanic cargo had been consigned, once and for all, to the depths of Loch Maree.

Back at the lonely police station, Sergeant MacFarlane, completely oblivious to the fact that his prisoners had pulled off an audacious escape and committed a breathtakingly daring act of larceny right under his nose, reached down under his chair and pulled out his latest acquisition. He pictured the smile on his young nephew's face when he handed it over to him. He was sure the lad would love it. To him, of course, it made no sense at all, and he was almost certain that wasn't because of the large amount of Famous Grouse he'd consumed that evening. The thing was written in an alien language; it was full of words like *downloads*, *Google* and *podcasts* – he could make neither head nor tail of it. Sighing, he picked up his mug of tea and replaced the slightly water-damaged copy of *Web of Fire*, its complimentary copy of *Endgame* still attached to the cover, back out of sight under his chair.

# Chapter 11

Following Gabriel's advice, Martin, Luke and Henry had all bedded down for the night. As the surgery wasn't really equipped for sleepovers, they had decamped to Martin's house, taking one of Westerham's expensive computers with them. The house was much more comfortable and, besides, Martin didn't want to be available for any out-of-hours dental emergencies.

Sunday morning dawned bright and clear. Martin had set the alarm for five o'clock and was already busy in the kitchen making a large pot of coffee when the sun rose over the great brooding hump of Dartmoor, pushing purple shadows along its valleys and turning the tops of its granite crags to gold.

If Henry was anything to go by, any self-respecting computer nerd would rather be flayed alive and rolled in tin tacks than get up before midday. But, just in case there was the odd maniac out there who had happened to stay awake all night so that they could be first in line to claim their copy of *Web of Fire* from a local newsagent that Gabriel and the boys had somehow overlooked, Martin thought it was as well to be up and ready for them.

\*

Henry was deep in a wood of towering trees. At his feet, the ground was punctuated by dark, gaping holes from which a deep, rhythmic sound emanated. It was like the snoring of great beasts, and Henry knew he had to keep absolutely silent. At the slightest sound the terrifying creatures that lived in these underground lairs would spring awake and tear him limb from limb. Just out of reach, across the other side of the largest of these pits, a bag of gold hung from a small tree. If he could only reach it he could get out of this awful place and move on to the next level. He looked around and there, at his feet, was a long stick – a fallen branch. Gingerly he reached down to pick it up, but before he had even touched it, it sprang up and put itself into his hand. Carefully, he edged the stick across the mouth of the monster's lair towards the bag of gold. From deep underground came a sudden snort, and a plume of fire shot from the cavern. Henry froze, holding his breath. But after a pause, the great animal's breathing fell back again into its rhythmic cadence. Collecting himself, Henry reached out once more. Balanced on tiptoe, straining every muscle, he inched the stick painfully across the yawning chasm. Finally, just as he thought he might topple headlong into the darkness below, the bag of gold leapt from the tree and attached itself to the end of the stick. Yes! He'd done it! All he had to do now was leave the wood without waking the monsters, and then find the path to the next level. Unhooking his glittering prize, he attached it to his belt and looked around for the way out.

But just then came a shattering sound: 'Good morning!'

The words of the wizard he'd met in the village came

back to Henry in a sickening rush: 'Beware the approach of the brekkie man.'

Now the ground was moving beneath his feet. The monsters were waking! All around him the trees rustled and swayed. The forest itself seemed to come alive and he found himself in the eye of a storm of whirling leaves and branches.

'Wake up, Henry!'

No! No time to run as giant reptilian legs armed with fearsome claws began to emerge from earthy pits all around. Huge bloodshot eyes fixed on him malevolently as the monstrous creatures leapt from their sleeping-tombs and moved, shrieking, towards him, their mouths gaping hungrily.

'Henry!'

'Wah!' Henry sat up suddenly and gazed at the un-familiar wallpaper. He shook his head and groaned. 'No!'

Martin was standing at the foot of his sleeping bag, a mug of coffee in his hand. 'Are you all right?'

'I never get to the second level. I could have done it this time if you hadn't interrupted me, I'm sure I could.'

'Sorry, I have a habit of doing that.' Martin handed him his coffee. 'Drink this. Then you'll need to boot up, or whatever it is you people do, and see what's happening online.'

Even as Henry was dragging himself out of his role-playing dream, expectations in Hell had reached fever pitch. After belting through his own arrangement of Elgar's Cello Concerto accompanied by a rather good but, it must be said, thin orchestra of blues guitarists and harmonica players, Satan wiped the sweat from his brow and embraced a startled Signora Amati.

'My dear, you were magnificent! Such tone, such passion!'

'Bravo! Bravo!' Max and Lothar applauded.

A grinning Satan bowed low. 'Thank you. Thank you.' Then he turned and addressed his orchestra. 'Tonight, gentlemen, we shall play in Paradise! There, or the Albert Hall – take your pick. The whole of creation shall be our oyster!' He stroked Signora Amati's long, elegant neck. 'And you, my dear, must be tired,' he cooed. 'Lothar! Take Signora Amati back to her room and give her a rub-down with a handful of rosin – she's earned it.'

Dismissing the ragbag orchestra, Satan turned to Max. 'Is everything prepared?'

'I need to run a systems check, O malodorous one.'

'Do what you have to do.'

Bowing low, Max settled himself into the leather sofa behind the table laden with computer equipment and started booting up the antiquated system. A map of the world flickered onto the wall screen and the Devil eyed it hungrily.

'Soon, soon, Max, it will all be mine! As we speak, Sunday morning is dawning over an unsuspecting Britain. Presently, strange pasty-faced men with bad skin and unkempt hair will emerge from their crusty bedsits and trek down to their local newsagents to collect their eagerly awaited copies of *Web of Fire* and its last and most potent instalment of *Endgame*, little suspecting that they are about to bring a dramatic end to their sad, pointless existence. The meek shall inherit the earth? Hah!'

Max's fat fingers *clicked* and *clacked* on the keyboard

and the player's online counter appeared at the bottom left-hand corner of the screen, reading: *00000*.

Satan paced the room excitedly. 'I can't wait to see the look on that overstuffed baboon's face. Call himself omnipotent? I can't believe how easy it's been to pull the wool over his eyes!'

Max silently crossed his fingers for luck. He was thankful at least that Satan had not decided to release the game worldwide, which would have stretched the antiquated system far beyond its capabilities. Satan said this was because he wanted to keep everything low-key: the more people who became involved, the greater the likelihood of God finding out about it. But the real reason was the Devil's meanness. Not only would releasing the game globally have been a logistical nightmare, it would have cost a fortune to set up.

'Systems check complete, your foetidity; the equipment seems to be working perfectly.'

Satan threw his arms dramatically wide. 'Let the game begin!'

After the rigours of the night, Gabriel and Michael had eschewed the company of the heavenly host, who had retired to a favourite bar to celebrate, and gone for a long walk on the moor. Angels didn't sleep, and although there was nothing more they could do, they couldn't just sit still and wait for morning.

'I haven't been here for years,' said Michael, gazing out over the wide expanse of Dartmoor slowly being brought to life by the rising sun. 'I'd forgotten how beautiful it was. Nevada has the weather, granted, but it's got no scenery, not really, not unless you like sand. Whereas this . . .' he spread his arms wide '. . . this is *real* countryside.'

Beside him, Gabriel breathed in the early-morning scents of gorse and heather as the ground warmed up under the sun's gentle persuasion. 'I know.' He nodded sadly. 'I just hope it's not all going to disappear in a fiery conflagration.'

Michael looked down at the ground. 'How does it go again? *"And there were voices, and thunders, and lightnings; and there was a great earthquake, such as was not since men were upon the earth, so mighty an earthquake, and so great. And the great city was divided into three parts and cities of the nations fell . . ."*'

Gabriel looked pained. 'Do you think St John the Divine was right?'

'I don't know.' Michael shrugged. 'John always sees the black side of everything. But if he *is* right, I suppose we can take comfort from what happens next in Revelation: the victory of the Lamb and Satan being bound for a thousand years.'

'Little consolation for those poor devils already blown to smithereens.'

Michael nodded thoughtfully and studied the ground once more. Then he suddenly looked up brightly. 'I don't know about you, but I'm feeling a little peckish.'


Back at Martin's house, while Henry connected up all the equipment and checked that nothing had got damaged in transit, Martin had made himself busy in the kitchen. Just as he pulled the perfectly crisped bacon out from under the grill there was a knock at the door. He opened it in his pinny.

'Martin,' said a smiling Gabriel, 'I'd like you to meet an old friend of mine. Martin Gray, this is Archangel Michael.'

Martin shook hands politely with the angel. Somehow he wasn't particularly fazed. It wasn't that he was becoming blasé about meeting famous angels, it was just that, coming on top of recent events, it no longer seemed *that* extraordinary. 'Very nice to meet you. I've heard all about you, of course.'

'All good, I trust?' Michael smiled warmly.

'Come in, the kettle's on. How did it go last night?'

Gabriel glanced sideways at Michael. 'It was touch and go for a while, but I'm glad to say that our mission was a complete success.'

'Brilliant! Well done, both of you!'

But Michael added a cautionary note: 'Let's not be too hasty in congratulating ourselves, we still have today to get through. Do I smell bacon?'

When Henry and Luke finally made it downstairs they found two angels seated at the breakfast table tucking into bacon sandwiches.

'Luke, Henry,' said Martin, pulling more bacon from the grill as the toaster popped up, 'meet Archangel Michael.'

The angel waved a hand. 'Just Michael, please,' he mumbled, his mouth full.

Henry pulled up a chair and sat down next to him. 'You're Michael?'

The angel nodded.

'You can eat earth food?'

Michael looked at Gabriel helplessly – he'd just taken another large bite and couldn't speak.

'Well, strictly speaking, we don't need to eat at all,' Gabriel explained. 'But there are so few vices left to us. Food is the only area in which we can really indulge ourselves.'

Michael finally swallowed. 'And if there's one thing I can't resist it's bacon. You can keep your manna – I'd rather have a bacon sarnie any day. You must be Henry – how do you do?' Michael wiped his greasy fingers on his raincoat and they shook hands.

Henry was transfixed. A thousand questions whirled around his excited brain, but he couldn't put one into a coherent sentence. He just gazed at Michael in wide-eyed wonder.

'We'll talk later,' Michael said, going back to his sandwich. 'You can ask me anything you like then.'

'Um,' said Gabriel, looking hopefully at Martin, 'I don't suppose you've got any eggs?'

When the angels had eaten their fill and the breakfast things had been cleared away, everyone went upstairs to Luke's room and gathered round the computer. They watched in silence as Henry loaded the game and went online.

'Now we'll see if it's all been worth it,' Gabriel muttered.

'And if it hasn't, it was nice knowing you,' Michael added.

'Look! Look!' The Devil pointed a long bony finger at the player's online counter. It had clicked round to *00001*. 'Someone's playing!' He hugged himself with glee. 'Oh joy! Soon God's little experiment will be a nothing but a barren rock and I will regain my rightful place in Heaven.'

Max sat silently on the sofa. It was true that one player could set the whole nuclear line of dominoes toppling all by themselves, but dedicated gamers would want to wait for someone else to go online before playing. Needless to say, that wasn't something Max felt comfortable about sharing with his employer, especially not when the boss was in such a good mood.

Satan pranced around the room. 'Let me tell you, Max – when I get back up there, when I reclaim my seat at the old man's left hand, there are going to be some changes. Oh yes! I'm going to rip up all the greens and build a For-mula One racetrack down the fairways – bring some excitement back to the place! Golf – hah! A game for old men. What Heaven needs is youth – pit-lane lovelies with long legs – young flesh . . . young, smooth, nubile flesh . . . ahh.' Satan closed his eyes and shuddered in ecstasy. 'Watch out, angels!' he yelled at the ceiling. 'Old Nick's coming home and he wants to party!'

But Satan would have a long wait before his little online shindig took off. When Lothar appeared with his ten o'clock coffee, there was still only one player show-ing, and the Lord of the Underworld was becoming rather anxious. He padded nervously to and fro in front of the large map.

'What's happening, Max?'

This was the moment Max had dreaded. He sat next to his lord on the leather sofa, drenched in sweat. 'Dark-ness, what you have to understand about people who play these sort of games is that they are not usually early risers. Most play games through the night. The whole concept of morning is one they are not particularly comfortable with.'

The Devil seemed to buy this explanation, for the moment at least. Besides, the alternative was to accept the unacceptable: that he had failed, and that the last few decades spent setting the whole thing up had been a complete waste of time.

Henry yawned and looked at his watch. It was mid-morning and he was still the only player online. Scimitar, meanwhile, crouched in readiness on the mountain plateau. At the moment, Henry held the advantage: he'd chosen the terrain, which meant that anyone who wanted to compete would have to follow him into the North Korean arena. In effect, he controlled the game.

Gabriel, Michael, Martin and Luke were also beginning to relax. It seemed that they'd done it.

'It's probably too soon to congratulate ourselves—' Gabriel began.

'Don't,' said Michael.

'Don't what?'

'Don't tempt fate.'

Henry looked up into Michael's face. 'Angels are superstitious?'

'Only in cases where the future of the world is at stake.'

'Um, what's that?' Luke pointed at the bottom left-hand corner of the computer screen.

Everyone stared. The little counter had clicked round to *00002*.

'Oh, bum,' said Michael.

Gabriel suddenly looked drawn and tired. 'It's all been

for nothing,' he moaned. 'All that effort, all that organization . . .'

Henry, on the other hand, seemed fired up by the challenge. 'OK, mister, let's see what you've got.'

'What's going to happen now?' Martin asked nervously.

'Well, that all depends on how the other guy wants to play it. He could opt to be any one of several characters from any of the countries in the game. He's not going to choose to be American – there'd be no point in playing if we're both on the same side. He *could* choose to be a North Korean general and mobilize his forces to prevent me getting into the base. But then, once he's neutralized me, it's game over: he's got nowhere to go. No, if I were him I'd try to stop me, and then, with the opposition out of the way, break into the American defence system and launch against Europe.' Henry stroked his chin. 'Or, then again, he could be really scary.' He nodded silently.

Gabriel looked at him sharply. 'Tell me,' he ordered.

But before Henry could answer, there came the approaching *thocka-thocka-thocka* of a helicopter and, between two distant mountain peaks, a small black dot appeared, growing bigger with every second.


Angus MacFarlane was not in a good state when he turned up for Sunday lunch at his sister Eileen's. He was hungover, it was true, but he was used to that. No, his real problem was that he had allowed four suspects to walk out of his jail, taking with them almost all the evidence. His superior had not been amused, especially when he'd found the empty bottle of Famous Grouse under Angus's desk, and had suspended him immediately pending an investigation. It was very bad timing: retirement was looming and Angus's pension no longer looked like the sure thing it once had seemed.

'Would you like something to drink?' Eileen asked. 'Whisky?'

Angus winced at the word. 'Just a cup of tea, thank you, hen.'

Eileen nodded her understanding of the delicate situation.

'I brought something for the boy,' Angus continued, sitting down gingerly on the sofa and handing his nephew a plastic wallet containing two sparkling disks.

Young Ian took the gift without enthusiasm.

'I took it off the cover of one of those computer magazines. I know you're into computer games, so I thought you might like it. I'm only sorry I couldn't give you the whole thing, but that magazine is the only evidence we have left.'

'What do you say, Ian?' Eileen prompted.

'Er, thanks Uncle,' Ian replied. The truth was he'd stopped playing computer games years ago, having discovered other interests since starting university, like girls.

The three of them settled into an uneasy silence. Eventually Eileen rose. 'Well, I'd better see how lunch is getting along.' She paused in the doorway to the kitchen. Her brother badly needed his mind taken off his problems, and if he wasn't going to drink . . . 'Ian, why don't you play the game for Uncle Angus? I'm sure he'd like to see it.'

'Oh, Mum . . .' Ian protested. He never stuck magazine freebies into his computer – you never knew what was on them. But he could see that his Uncle Angus was troubled, and he wanted to cheer him up. Besides, his mum's eyes were boring into him like laser beams. 'OK, come on, Uncle Angus.' Ian led him up to his room and dutifully turned on his computer.

Although he hadn't played since going up to university, as he went through the pre-game rigmarole, all Ian's old gaming skills came back to him. It was like putting on an old pair of shoes – out of style maybe, but comfortable in all the right places.

'How do you understand all this stuff?' Angus marvelled at Ian's expertise as he swiftly configured the game to suit his particular gaming style.

By the time Ian got to the point of choosing which country he was going to represent he was beginning to get into the mood and was somewhat disappointed to see that there was only one other player online.

'Oh.'

'What – is it no good?' Angus asked anxiously.

'No, it's just that this is meant to be a multiplayer game.'

Angus frowned.

'That means you play against other people online. At the moment there's only one other person playing, and it's more fun when there are a few more people logged on. But that's OK; we can still play one against one.' Ian studied the screen. 'Now who shall we be . . . let's see? This guy's waving the Stars and Stripes. So, there's really only one choice.'

Ian left-clicked on the Kalashnikov icon, and the game began.

Angus was amazed at how lifelike it all was, even if he couldn't quite follow the complicated plot.

'We're going to make things a little hot for the president, but first we've got to neutralize the infidel who's ahead of us,' Ian explained.

Ian's soldier got into the helicopter and set off in pursuit of his virtual foe.

'OK, we've got trouble,' Henry announced. 'He's chosen the al-Qaeda option.'

Gabriel peered at the screen. 'I didn't know there *was* an al-Qaeda option.'

'An operative on a suicide mission doesn't need to get out of the country to avoid being wiped out in a retaliatory strike – what with seventy-nine virgins waiting for him in Paradise. He can go in and launch straight from the North Korean bunker. And here he comes now.' Henry nodded towards the screen.

As Ian's helicopter drew near, carrying his virtual soldier – code name Ahmed – Henry took Scimitar to the edge of the plateau and abseiled him down into the gulley leading to the missile bunker. Racing along the passage between the rocks, Scimitar came to the small angled bend. Swiftly taking out the CCTV camera with a shot from his rifle, the virtual soldier slipped around the rocky curve and looked back. The enemy was already halfway down the cliff. 'This guy's good – we may be in trouble. He's going to try and take us out, so at some point we're going to have to fight. The one thing in our favour is that *we've* played this game before – we know what we're doing. But for him, this is the first time. Experience is on our side.'

The tension in the room ratcheted up a notch and every eye was glued to the on-screen progress of the virtual Green Beret as he hustled along the simulated gulley towards the steel doors of the bunker.


Satan was furious. 'What do you mean we can't watch the game?'

'My Lord,' Max explained, 'the equipment is barely up to processing the information it is already receiving. The graphics driver alone is more than twenty years old. If we tried to look in on the game, the whole system would inevitably fail.'

'But I want to see what's happening!' the Devil wailed. 'Can't you open another window? You know, like they do in the football – I've seen it on Vinnie Jones's telly. You can watch the European Cup from several different angles at the same time!'

'Mr Jones has Sky.'

'Sky?'

'Satellite television – a highly advanced system which offers many different and interactive options for the way you watch television.'

'Well, why haven't I got it?' Satan stamped his foot petulantly.

'All that cutting-edge technology comes at a price.'

'Oh.' Satan thought for a moment. He narrowed his eyes. 'How much?'

'For the full package I believe there's a monthly fee of forty pounds.'

'Forty pounds! Good God, people must have money to burn. All right, all right, so we won't watch the game. We'll just have to be content to watch the effects of the game.' Satan sat down heavily on the sofa. 'Forty quid?'

he muttered. 'A month?' He shook his head sadly at the wasteful nature of modern society.

Having fought his way though the cloud of bats, Scimitar was already inside the missile base.

'We're going to have to take this guy out before he gets into the missile control room.'

Henry pulled Scimitar back into the shadows under the walkway. 'All we have to do now is wait.'

After several temple-pounding minutes, the sound of gunfire could be heard from outside.

'Here he comes.'

It all happened very quickly. Something black and round came sailing through the air and landed at Scimitar's feet. It was a development that Henry had not foreseen.

'Grenade!'

Scimitar hit the dirt but it was too late. There was a *boom!* The screen flashed red and shrapnel fragments hit Luke's bedroom wall.

'Jesus!' Martin yelled.

'I've been hit!' Henry wailed.

Gabriel examined the teenager's face. 'Where?'

'Not me, Scimitar!'

'Oh.'

The stricken commando could barely drag himself upright. His 'life force', indicated by a green bar at the bottom of the screen, was reading almost zero. And as if that wasn't bad enough, as Scimitar struggled to his feet he came face to face with the shrouded and mysterious Ahmed.

'Now you will die, infidel!' Ahmed screamed, lunging at the Green Beret with a broad-bladed knife.

Scimitar went down again.

Henry started tapping on the keyboard and the screen went black.

'What are you doing?' Martin panicked.

'I'm leaving the game.'

'You're leaving the game? You're leaving the game!' Martin danced wildly round the room. 'He's leaving the game!'

Michael placed a restraining hand on Martin's shoulder. 'Thank you, Martin; I think we get the picture.' Then he turned to Henry. 'Why are you leaving the game?'

'He's won. *He's* not restrained by the need to survive, so all he's got to do is get into the control room and launch against America. It's pointless our still being in the game – we've got to think of something else to stop him.'

'Like?'

'I'm working on it.' Henry continued clattering the keyboard.

Gabriel started chewing his mac.

Martin felt helpless. He thought he should be doing something useful. But what? This probably wasn't the time to start making biscuits.

'OK!' Henry yelled.

'What now?' Gabriel peered at the screen. On it had appeared a map of the world.

'I've hacked into the US satellite monitoring system. From here we can keep an eye on the world's nuclear missile sites, so if any of them launch we'll know about it. Now for the difficult bit.' Henry's fingers flew over the keys once again, and the world map was reduced to a window at the bottom left of the screen. 'I should have done this earlier, when I had the chance,' Henry muttered. 'I only hope I've still got enough time.'

Several red dots started flashing on the world map. 'This guy's fast,' Henry said appreciatively. 'North Korean missiles now launch-ready!' he announced to the room.

No one even breathed. The only thing that anyone could hear was the sound of their own heartbeat.

Then came the news they had all been dreading. 'Confirmed missile launch from North Korea.'

*So this is it*, thought Martin. He felt strangely detached as he watched Henry sweating at the keyboard. He had looked into the face of death before: on the morning he'd first met Gabriel. But then he'd been in control of his own destiny – or at least under the illusion that he was – and facing death alone. Now his entire species was on the brink of annihilation and, although not exactly comforted by that fact, he suddenly felt enormous camaraderie with his fellow beings – even Westerham. He put his arm around Luke. 'Sorry,' he murmured.

Luke hugged him back. ''S all right.'

'I wish your mum were here.'

'Yeah, so do I.'

Michael came round from behind and embraced them both.

Gabriel, still crouched by the computer, looked up at the three of them as they shared a group hug. 'What's up with you lot? Why aren't you helping?'

'Do *you* know anything about computers?' Michael asked him. 'Let Henry work it out.'

For a moment Gabriel's features contracted into a scowl, then relaxed. 'You're right,' he said and went over to join them.

The irony that the future of the world was now the sole responsibility of an overweight adolescent with personal hygiene problems and a liking for amateur pornographic sites wasn't lost on them, and they lapsed into a sort of fond reverie as they watched Henry as he beavered away feverishly at the computer keyboard.

Satan was already thinking about what he should wear to make his grand re-entry into Heaven.

'Nothing too flamboyant, and yet I don't want everyone to think I've lost my sense of style while I've been away. Something understated but well cut. And white. It *has* to be white.' He threw his arms wide. 'It's going to be the event of the millennium. The prodigal returns – Part Two!'

On the sofa, Max was studying the incoming data from the earth monitoring satellites. 'Hmm.'

Satan stopped strutting up and down the room and turned to him. '*Hmm?* What does *hmm* mean?'

'It's probably nothing, your foulness, but—'

'But?' The horned one glared at Max. 'But? But what?'

'These missiles are behaving rather oddly.'

Satan stared blankly at the screen and its array of flashing dots and incomprehensible symbols. 'Is that bad?'

Max shrugged. 'As I said, it's probably nothing, but their trajectory is . . . curious. They are in danger of falling short of their intended objective.'

'Well, that doesn't matter. As long as they come down somewhere. After all, America's a big enough target.'

'Ye-es,' Max said slowly.

Satan narrowed his eyes. 'You're worrying me, Max.

I've worked hard for this moment. Through sheer bloody graft and determination – not to mention my genius at having had the idea in the first place – I've actually managed to get a cluster of two-hundred-kiloton nuclear devices poised over the earth. You can't tell me that something can go wrong *now*.'

Max wished he'd kept his thoughts to himself. His concern was that North Korea, having never done a full-scale nuclear test, may not have perfected its missile guidance systems. The arc of the missiles' trajectory was too steep, and if they kept on their present course, there was a danger of them either going into orbit or running out of fuel and falling short into the cold waters of the north Pacific. The result would be the same in either case: World War III would fizzle out like a damp squib before it had even begun.

'We needn't be overly anxious at the present moment, your stenchiness. We are only talking about a handful of weapons. There are many, many more all over the earth, and all primed and waiting to go.'

Satan reached across, took Max's hand and squeezed. Max went cross-eyed with pain. 'Don't panic me. I can be very unpleasant when I'm panicked. People have even told me I become a little unpredictable. And, believe me, unpredictable is not good – in fact it's very bad. Is that understood?'

Max nodded; there were tears in his eyes.

'Good.' Satan released Max's hand. 'From now on I want only good news, OK? Otherwise old Mr Unpredictable here might do something you'll regret.'

As Satan rose and started to work on his heavenly acceptance speech, Max bowed his head silently and, massaging his throbbing hand, brooded on the awful possibility that he had overlooked something.

In a sombre White House war room, the president came off the phone to North Korea. 'The son of a bitch says he knows nothing about it. Even had the gall to blame us, saying we broke into his missile system and launched his weapons to discredit him in the eyes of the world. Can you believe it?'

The president looked up at the electronic map which covered one entire wall of the room. A small group of blinking lights was emerging from the eastern edge of the Asian continent and heading out across the narrow band of the north Pacific towards the USA.

Every face in the room now turned towards the supreme commander. He knew what they were waiting for. This was the moment he'd always dreaded, the moment he'd hoped he would never have to face. Now it was here. His options had just run out. It wasn't really a comfort to know that he hadn't started it, and that all he was doing was responding – the outcome would be the same. The leader of the free world was about to plunge it into a nuclear holocaust.

His face etched with tiredness, the president looked up at his chiefs of staff and uttered one simple word: 'Launch.'

'We have a problem!' Henry's voice was shrill with excitement.

Everyone gathered round.

'America has responded!'

No one could quite believe what was happening. Outside it was a beautiful, soft Devon day: the sun was shining and the air was full of birdsong. But the computer told a terrifying story: on the other side of the world several thousand tons of nuclear hardware were airborne and about to set in motion a chain of events which would reshape the world in ways as horrific as they were unimaginable.

'Um, it may not be as bad as it looks,' said Henry, in response to the obvious dismay in the room.

Martin was a little sceptical. 'Oh, really?'

'Yes. I've had an idea.'

'Oh, so you're going to deal with the entire nuclear arsenal of the most heavily armed nation in the world with a couple of mouse clicks!'

Henry stood up furiously and offered Martin his chair. 'You want to see if you can do better?'

Archangel Michael put a soothing arm around the scowling teenager. 'Martin didn't mean it, Henry. We're all a little tense. What you're doing is brilliant, but so complicated that we can't always follow what you're up to. Forgive our ignorance, but you're our only hope. You're the world's only hope.'

Martin smiled hopefully at the dishevelled boy. 'I'm sorry, Henry; I'm just a little . . . jumpy. You really are doing brilliantly.'

'All right, then,' Henry muttered and reluctantly sat down at the keyboard once again.

Angels and humans gave the sweating teenager room to let him get on with it; Henry was becoming increasingly fragrant with every anxiously passing minute.

'Can we open a window?' Martin asked finally.

'Good idea.' Michael pushed open the casement and

looked out over green fields populated by little cotton-wool blobs of sheep.

'OK,' Henry shouted. 'If I can get to the US missiles before they reach apogee we're still in with a chance.' Henry attacked the keyboard again.

'But you don't have a lot of time!'

'Even if I don't, it's no big deal,' Henry muttered.

'No big deal?' Gabriel spluttered. 'Millions of people will die!' He paced the carpet, his arms flapping. 'Why oh why wouldn't he listen to me, instead of sticking his head in a bunker?'

'If you'd let me finish what I was saying . . . America has actually been rather restrained and only launched two missiles. If everyone just keeps their heads the worst thing that could happen is that North Korea gets obliterated.'

'Oh, that's all right then,' said Martin.

'But what about the Korean missiles?' Luke wondered.

Henry smiled. 'Take a look.'

On-screen, the little block of dots representing the North Korean missiles had halted in its steady progression across the north Pacific and seemed to be hovering just off America's West Coast.

'What's happening?' Martin asked.

'They're going straight up!' Luke cheered.

'I reprogrammed them,' Henry explained. 'Once they're free of earth's gravity they'll just carry on going. But I've also engineered a little surprise into the system.'

Gabriel raised an eyebrow. 'Surprise?'

'Once in space they're programmed to detonate. It'll be the biggest fireworks display ever.'

But Gabriel was still worried. 'And the American missiles?'

Henry gave him an old-fashioned look. 'Oh ye of little faith.' He pointed at the screen.

The tracks of the US missiles had also come to a stand-still.

'I had no time to reprogramme the American missiles individually, so I introduced a virus into their guidance system software. Now, every American missile that becomes launch-ready will be infected with the virus, overriding its original programming and telling it to head for the stars.'

'Brilliant!' Martin cheered. 'Why did CND never think of this?'

The president of the United States was on the hotline to Moscow. 'I'm begging you, Vlad, please don't do it . . . No, of course I didn't launch at you . . . Take a look at what your early warning systems are telling you . . . I know North Korea is your friend, but what are we sup-posed to do, just stand by and watch the rockets come down on us? . . . Do you think I feel good about this?'

The secretary of state was waving at him.

'Hang on a minute, Vlad.' He put his hand over the mouthpiece. 'What is it, Don?'

'Our missiles seem to have . . . stopped, sir.'

'Stopped?'

'In mid-air.'

The president looked at the wall-sized map. The traces of the American missiles were paused midway across the north Pacific. 'What's going on?'

The secretary of state was equally perplexed. He gazed out over the activity in the war room. Lines of men and women sat working at computers, while the commanders of the armed forces stared up at the large map on the wall trying to make sense of it all. 'We're not sure, Mr President.'

'Don't go away, Vlad,' the president muttered into the red phone.

'Sir!' A young man in a crumpled white shirt ran up, a computer printout in his hand.

'What is it, son?'

'It seems the guidance systems have been compromised, sir.'

The president frowned at the young man. 'Can you give me that in English?'

'The guidance computers on the missiles have been reset. They're heading straight up into space.'

'Could it be a fault in the hardware?' the secretary of state asked.

The young man shook his head. 'No, sir. It seems that someone has deliberately tampered with the control systems.'

The president was horrified. 'Are you saying that a terrorist has managed to break into the US nuclear missile system? How is that possible?'

'We, er, don't yet know if it's terrorists, sir.'

'Don't get politically correct with me, son. In my book, anybody messes with my missiles, they're a terrorist.' He turned to his secretary of state. 'How did this happen?'

But before he could reply, another man ran up clutching a computer printout. 'It's a virus, sir!'

'I beg your pardon?'

'A virus has been inserted into the missile network and has spread through the entire system. It's quite a piece of work.' The man smiled appreciatively at the ingenuity of the mind behind it.

The president was not amused. 'This isn't a game, son.' He put the red phone back to his ear. 'Vlad, I want you to look closely at what your intelligence is telling you about the progress of our missiles . . . Yes, that's right; they're going straight up. So you see, you're not in any danger. Now, what I need – what we all need – is your assurance that you're not going to launch . . . By all means keep the missiles launch-ready, just don't set them off . . . Of course you can do it, Vlad, you're top banana . . . No, it's just an expression . . . I know, I know, but the future of the world is at stake, godammit! . . . Thank you, Comrade . . . Yeah, you too. Stay by the phone.' The president put the receiver back in its cradle and looked up at the secretary of state. 'Don, find out where this virus got in, and more importantly find who the fuck is responsible.'

'Yes, sir.' As the secretary of state ran off to engage in urgent talks with the secret services, the president brooded darkly on what he would do to those who had dared breach homeland security, once he had hold of them.

'We're going to lock you motherfuckers in a deep, dark hole and throw away the key. Where you're going will make Guantanamo look like a holiday camp.'

Ian had been quiet for some time. Angus tried hard to make sense of what was on the computer screen but it might as well have been Chinese to him.

'What's happening, Ian?'

'The Korean missiles I launched at America haven't

come down. These mass-manufactured freebies are cheaply made and they're not always very reliable.'

'Sorry. I thought it might be a bit of fun for you.'

'Well, to be honest, Uncle Angus, I haven't played computer games for a long time now.'

'Oh.' Angus suddenly felt very old, and secretly added the heinous crime of patronizing his nephew to the growing list of his recent offences.

Ian felt his uncle's awkwardness and wished he hadn't said anything. 'Of course, it might not be faulty,' he said hurriedly. 'I've just not played it before.'

Angus put a hand on his nephew's shoulder. 'It's all right, Ian. You don't have to play it on my account.'

'No, no. Let's try something else.' Ian's fingers clattered on the keyboard and a list of options flashed up on-screen.

'Where's my war?' Satan was jumping up and down in front of the damply nervous Max, who was checking and rechecking the worrying intelligence he was now receiving through the flawed medium of his ancient computer system.

'O darksome magnificence, there appears to be something we may have overlooked.'

The Devil glared at him with eyes that were burning coals, and Max could feel his throat tightening.

'A fault in the missile systems, O essence of evil. The genius of your idea was nothing short of perfection. Everything has gone to plan, except—'

'Except . . .?' As Satan breathed the word, it seemed to take on a life of its own, reverberating around the room and echoing inside Max's skull till it made him dizzy.

'The . . . the missiles should have already come down,' Max said hoarsely. 'It is inconceivable that they are still airborne. Half of North America and the entire eastern seaboard of Asia should have been destroyed by now.'

The Devil was beginning to get angry. Unlike mortals, he didn't lash out blindly at the nearest thing to hand. No, his anger had focus and purpose; like a trained Rottweiler, once let off the leash and sent towards its intended target, it seized it round the throat and worried it until all the life went out of it, then worried it some more just for fun. The Devil was looking for a target. Punishing Max at this moment would serve no purpose – he was still potentially useful. Satan needed someone he could just crumple up and throw away.

'Lothar!' He called softly for his manservant, who appeared immediately.

'My Lord?'

'Get me Garth Ferrers.'

'What the . . .?'

Henry had been surprised by the sudden launch of a large number of missiles from northern Russia. Surprise too was on the faces of the commanders of the missile silos, who watched helplessly as their doom-laden charges blasted out from their underground bunkers and seared hungrily across the sky.

'What is it, Henry?' Gabriel asked.

'Mass launch from Russia. Our Koran-toting friend must have changed theatres and infiltrated the Russian system!'

'What do we do now?' wailed the hysterical angel.

Michael put an arm round him. 'Calm down. Let Henry concentrate.'

The teenager grunted and groaned as his fingers flew over the keyboard. The missiles' course could be clearly seen on the world map – the bulk of them tracking steadily over the Pole towards North America, with the odd one heading westwards towards Europe and the United Kingdom.

'We're all going to die!' Luke whispered.


'You're telling me that Russia's launched, too?' The president was furious. 'Get them on the phone!'

But the hot line was already ringing. The president picked it up angrily. 'What the hell's going on, Vlad . . . You're kidding me . . . You expect me to believe you didn't authorize this launch? . . . OK, OK, Vlad, calm down . . . Hang on a minute.' The president put his hand over the mouthpiece and looked over at his secretary of state. 'Looks like this virus thing could be a fucking pandemic. How far have you got with it?'

'We've identified where the security breach occurred, sir. Now we're working on a telephone trace.'

'A telephone trace?'

'The source of the virus is most likely a home computer.'

'Don't tell me that this fuck-up is the fault of some teenage terrorist on his home PC!'

The secretary of state ran a finger nervously around his collar. 'Er . . . well, he'd have to have a very sophisticated program, but . . . that seems to be a possible scenario, yes, sir.'

'Jesus! If we ever survive this I'm going to ban home

computers.' The president took his hand away from the mouthpiece. 'OK, Vlad, we're going to give you all the help you need. And don't worry about us – your missiles will be a good chance for us to test our Star Wars system . . . Of course you knew. We know about yours, too . . . Oh, come off it, Vlad, you think we were born yesterday?' He put the phone down and turned nervously to Don. 'Is Star Wars fully operational yet?'

'I wish you wouldn't keep calling it that, sir.'

'Aw, shit, Don – Homeland Security Anti-nuclear Satellite System is such a fucking mouthful.'

'It *is* the correct terminology, sir.'

'Does the fucking thing work? That's all I want to know.'

Don looked at the floor. 'We're hopeful, sir.'


Garth, his coat collar turned up, hat pulled low over his eyes, had just parked his car on the top floor of the Mary Arches Street multistorey in Exeter. He was heading for the bus station. He didn't know where he was going to go; he just knew that he couldn't stay where he was. His rational mind was aware that running was futile, and yet a deeper, primordial part of him was reacting to the stimulus of danger in the only way it knew how – it was fleeing.

As he wrestled his suitcase out of the boot and started towards the lift, Garth's mobile phone rang. He knew he probably shouldn't answer it, yet a strange compulsion forced his hand into his pocket. 'Garth Ferrers,' he mumbled.

'Happy birthday to you! Happy birthday to you!' crooned a familiar voice. 'You weren't at home, Garth.

Why's that – doing some last-minute shopping for your little sojourn with us?'

'Er . . . I . . . er.' Garth was trembling so much he dropped his suitcase.

'You don't really need to, you know. We have everything here you'll need. Not that you need much to endure an eternity of suffering.'

'I'm not coming! I'm not coming and you can't make me!' Garth said suddenly, and threw the phone over the car park parapet.

Running and stumbling towards the lift, he pressed the button. Thankfully, he didn't have to wait long. With a gentle *bong!* the lift doors slid smoothly open. Garth stepped inside. But, as the doors closed with terrible finality, the possibility dawned on him that he might have just made an awful mistake.

Without warning the lift plummeted downwards at terrifying speed. Screaming in terror, Garth braced himself against the elevator's featureless steel walls. After what seemed like an eternity, with a hideous *kerrump!* the lift stopped and Garth hit the floor. After a short pause, the doors opened.

'Basement!' said a voice. 'Eternal hellfire, pain, torment and soft furnishings!'

Rising shakily to his knees, at first Garth could see nothing but swirling fog. But soon out of the mist emerged a hideously smiling face – the Devil in all his vileness. Garth gazed with terror at the true image of Satan: a face without the defining softness of flesh. Sinews and veins ran over the bare skull like cables. Teeth protruded startlingly from a lipless mouth, and lidless eyes bulged from beneath horns that dripped blood.

Garth shrank back, whimpering pitifully.

'You seem surprised to see me, Garth. Had you forgotten about our little arrangement? As I recall, it was a few years of living it up in exchange for an eternity of torment. It's not looking like such a great deal now, is it? You know, it never ceases to amaze me how willing you mortals are to sign on the dotted line. It's all now, now, now with you lot – you never think ahead. Well, *now* it's my turn. I've held up my side of the bargain, and it's time for you to make good on yours!'

Garth felt talons ripping at his flesh, as his skin burned and blistered in the infernal heat. His mind too was gripped by a terrible anguish as all hope was extinguished, not one spark of joy now to lighten his darkness.


Martin couldn't speak. He stared at the screen and the thin tracks of the approaching missiles. At any moment they would appear overhead. He knew exactly what would happen; he'd seen it on a Channel 4 documentary. There would be an awful, bright flash, followed almost instantly by the flesh-stripping blast, so fast-moving it would hit them before they'd even heard the explosion. They would die in silence, atomized soundlessly before the great boom reached them, which would then roll thunderously over a landscape already flattened and devoid of life.

But as Martin played this horrific scene in his mind's eye, he gradually became aware that, on-screen, the missiles were winking out one by one.

'Yes!' Henry was saying. 'Got you! And you! Take that!'

'Wha . . . what's happening?' Martin gasped and realized he hadn't drawn breath for some moments.

'Russian Star Wars. I'm into their Murmansk control centre. All I've got to do is shoot down the missiles with their own satellite-mounted lasers.' He left-clicked on the mouse. 'There goes another!'

Martin stared at the screen and the real-life game of Space Invaders going on. 'But the Russians don't have Star Wars technology. Part of their agreement with America was that they wouldn't develop it.'

'Get real, Mr Gray. The Russians knew that the Americans were developing their own system and they didn't want to be caught out. It seems to be very efficient, too. Using the mouse, all you have to do is line up the cross hairs on the target missile, and . . .' He left clicked again. 'Burn, baby!' Another missile blinked then faded from the screen. 'Do you want a go?'

'No, I do not want a go! How do you know all this stuff?'

'It's all out there on the Net. You've just got to know where to look.'

The missiles lit up the northern skies like an unseasonal display of the aurora borealis. Below, the Mongol people of the frozen tundra paused in their restless wanderings to gaze up in wonder at the strange lights overhead.


Meanwhile, in a small terraced house in Scotland . . .

'I don't get it,' said Ian.

'What's happened now?' asked his uncle.

'It's weird,' Ian muttered. 'Infiltrating the Russian bases was a piece of cake, but now the missiles seem to be blowing themselves up before they reach their targets.'

'Sorry, Ian,' said Angus. 'I've given you a duff one.'

'It's on the table!' Ian's mum called from downstairs.

'Come on,' said Angus. 'Leave it be and let's have something to eat.'

Everyone crowded around Henry to congratulate him, but he shrugged them away. He hadn't finished yet; he'd had an idea, an idea so audacious he wanted to keep it to himself, at least for the time being. He didn't want the bloodless timidity of the so-called grown-ups spoiling his fun. Not only was he intent on inserting the direction-systems-confusing virus into every nuclear weapon system in the world, he was also going to make sure they could never be used again.

Having expended a good deal of his anger on the unfortunate Garth, Satan was nonetheless still looking for ways to vent his frustration. With the imminent collapse of his carefully thought-out scheme, his aggravation levels had reached critical, and he needed fresh meat.

The Devil – Eblis; the Antichrist; the angel of the bottomless pit – stalked threateningly towards Max. 'Find out who did this,' he growled. 'Someone is going to suffer.'

Max nodded enthusiastically. 'I will get to work on it immediately, wickedness.'

Now that the outcome of the game was no longer of any concern, Max was able to downsize his computer operation and free up some memory in order to run a telephone trace. He'd done it often enough when he worked for the Stasi – it was one of the first things they taught you. But, because of the antiquity of the system he was currently working with, it might take some time.

All over the world it was the same story: presidents and prime ministers stood helplessly by as their nuclear missiles went up in smoke. The rockets armed and launched themselves, and those that had not already done so would soon be detonating spectacularly in deep space.

A stunned silence hung over the White House operations room. The president stared, slacked-jawed, at the wall-sized screen and the impossible story it told.

'We've got a fix!' The secretary of state's voice broke the crystal silence.

The president looked up with weary eyes. 'Where?'

'England.'

'England?'

'Exeter, in Devon County, to be precise. We've contacted the English authorities and told them to seal the area. Our own men are already on their way to the location.'

The president sighed and pressed the heels of his hands into his eye sockets. 'The fucking English, we warned them about this very thing, and did they take any notice? No, they called us anti-democratic. Shit, if it wasn't for us there wouldn't be any democracy left!' He picked up the hot line to Moscow. 'Vlad, you still there? . . . Good . . . No, we're not feeling too happy about it, either. Listen, we think we may have found the culprits. Rest assured, we will come down on them with the ultimate force of the law . . . Yeah, with pleasure – after we've had a go at them . . . No, Vlad, we're not protecting them . . . No, of course we didn't know . . . Now don't take that tone with me, Vlad . . . I beg your pardon? . . . Why, you Russki son of a bitch!' He slammed the phone down. 'Can you believe that? He accused us of being behind the whole thing just so we could get rid of his missiles! Fucking commie bastard! They may call themselves democratic, but scratch a Russian and underneath they're all as red as . . . as red as . . .'

'As the red flag, sir?' the secretary of state suggested.

The president smiled for the first time that day. 'Yeah, as red as the red flag.'

As Martin put the kettle on to make a celebratory cup of tea and the two archangels raided the fridge, Luke and Henry were left alone in Luke's bedroom. Henry was sprawled flat on the floor, eyes closed, while Luke stood at the window, staring up at the weird and violent flashes that still blotted the blue sky like splashes of multi-coloured ink.

Luke turned slowly and looked down at Henry's flabby form sprawled on the floor like a stain. 'What did you do?' he asked.

Henry opened his eyes and smiled slyly. 'What no one else on the planet could have done. I'm going to be famous.'

Luke frowned. 'For what?'

Henry sat up and yawned. 'For being the person who got rid of all the world's nuclear missiles.'

Luke's mouth dropped open. 'You didn't!'

'I did. Once I'd inserted the virus into the American missile systems, I thought, why stop there? Why not go all the way? No one has ever had, nor is likely to have again, the means to do such a thing. It was in my power to save the world from itself, so I did. Right now I expect the politicians are pretty pissed off, but in time, when they find out about me and what I did, they'll see that I was right. They'll all be grateful.'

'Um, Henry . . .'

Henry got up and stretched. 'Yes, my friend, what is it?'

Luke had turned back to the window. 'Did you by any chance close the Internet connection?'

'No, why?'

'I think the politicians may already know about you.'

The thudding of a helicopter could plainly be heard.

Henry moved over to where Luke was staring up at the sky. Not one but a whole squadron of black helicopters was advancing on the house.

'Probably coming to offer me the Nobel Peace Prize.'

Several black limousines screeched to a halt outside the front door and armed men wearing black flak jackets emerged and surrounded the house.

'I don't think it's peace they have in mind,' Luke said doubtfully. 'Get down!' A stun grenade flew in through the open window and bounced across the floor.

The last thing Henry remembered was tasting the dusty nylon pile of the bedroom carpet before being hit by something that felt like a large building, and blackness descended.

# Chapter 12

Helen Gray had not had a good night: her dreams had been full of awful images of death and destruction. But what had actually shaken her fully awake was the vague fear that Luke might be in danger. She couldn't really believe that Martin would deliberately harm his own son, but then he wasn't himself at the moment.

As she went about making breakfast for her parents – who sat at the table without lifting a finger despite their oft-repeated cry of 'Don't worry about us, dear' – her thoughts careered on, running increasingly out of control. *If Martin's capable of beating up Westerham, he's capable of just about anything . . . Luke's virtually an adult it's true, but he's still so immature in many ways. . .*

The news on the radio, which her father insisted on listening to even though he was reading the newspaper, did nothing to soothe Helen's feelings of unease. It was dominated by reports of large numbers of UFOs, which had been observed streaking across the sky, and weird, multicoloured lights in the heavens. Although many politicians were invited to speak on this subject, no one could get any sense out of them.

Helen picked up the phone and dialled. There was no reply from Windyridge. Replacing the receiver she chewed her lip thoughtfully. It was unlikely that Martin had taken Luke out for the morning on Sunday, as he was always on call for emergencies. It had caused no end of friction between them. She tried his mobile but had no luck there either.

'Are you all right, dear?' her mother asked as Helen burnt the toast for the third time.

'I'm . . . It's . . .'

'It's that bloody dentist, isn't it?' said her father from behind his *Sunday Express*. 'Do you know, I've always maintained that dentistry is only practised by people who aren't clever enough to be doctors.'

'I'm well aware of your prejudices, thank you very much. And I'd appreciate your taking my feelings into consideration when you start criticizing my husband!'

He peered over the top of his newspaper at her with his one good eye. 'Hoity-toity.'

'Don't talk back to your father, dear,' her mother warned.

Helen started taking off her pinny.

Her mother immediately looked worried. 'Where are you going?'

'To see Martin.' She wasn't going to share with them her vague fears about Luke's safety; that would only give them more ammunition.

'You're not going anywhere, my girl,' said her father with paternal finality.

'Try and stop me.'

Her father's rigid authoritarian mask started to slip; he suddenly looked old and vulnerable. 'You're going to leave us here all alone?'

'At our age?' A tremor had come into her mother's voice.

'Oh, for goodness' sake, you're perfectly capable of

looking after yourselves. The kettle's on the sideboard and there's food in the fridge. I'll be back at teatime.'

Gifford Wilkinson, after missing Martin at the surgery, had decided that Sunday would be a nicely unsettling time to call on him at home. He imagined with pleasure the look on his victim's face when he turned up on the doorstep. *He'll probably be in the middle of preparing lunch,* he thought. *Tch, these middle classes, they all think they can cook. It's pathetic. Men in the kitchen? It's like women in politics – they just don't belong there.*

Gifford had a feeling about Martin Gray: he was a wrong 'un, something in his gut told him so, and never in his long and self-satisfied career had he been mistaken – he knew his job. His technique was always the same: wear down the suspect, like water on stone, until they caved in. It worked every time. *No one defrauds the Inland Revenue, not with me around. When I'm finished with Martin Gray, he'll wish he'd never been born. I'm going to get that bastard. I'm going to flay him alive.*

But Gifford would have cause to rue this thought before the day was out. For, unbeknown to him, beneath his feet all the forces of Hell were massing. The underworld's antiquated communications system had finally managed to trace the exact location of the Internet connection which had caused the Devil so much trouble.

And Old Nick was livid.

When Helen arrived at Windyridge all her worst fears were realized. The doors were open, the place was a complete tip and Martin and Luke were nowhere to be seen.

She ran up the stairs, calling their names. There was confusion everywhere: drawers spilled their contents onto carpets covered in books and broken ornaments. It was as if a typhoon had hit the place.

With trembling fingers she tried dialling Martin's mobile phone again. Still no reply.

*Where the hell can they be?*

She was shaking violently and might have fallen apart completely had not she heard, at that moment, footsteps downstairs.

Going to the landing, she crept down a few steps and peered through the banisters. A large, crop-haired man was nosing around her kitchen.

'Can I help you?' she called down.

Gifford looked up when he heard her voice. 'Well now, that all depends.'

Helen descended and confronted the man. 'Who are you and what are you doing in my kitchen?'

Smiling smugly, Gifford drew from his pocket a small leather wallet and opened it in front of her face.

'Inland Revenue,' Helen read aloud.

'Well done,' said Gifford. 'Obviously an educated woman. One wonders what you were doing with a man such as Martin Gray.'

'What do you know about him?' she said sharply. 'Where is he?'

'That's a very good question, and one I'd like to find an answer to. Now then, if we can just go somewhere a little more comfortable, perhaps we can discuss this further.'

Gifford made as if to push past Helen and go into the living room, but Helen stood her ground and he was forced to retreat back into the kitchen.

'I don't know who you are or why you're here,' she said, 'but I don't like you, or your attitude.'

'Now, there's no need for any unpleasantness.'

'I'll be the judge of that. Tell me what you're doing here or I'm calling the police.'

Gifford sighed, his smile fading. He hated dealing with women – they couldn't be manipulated like men. And if you used strong-arm tactics they were liable to claim sexual assault. 'Very well. I'm here because your husband . . . I'm assuming he's your husband and not your fancy man—'

Helen slapped him hard around the face.

Gifford put his hand to his stinging cheek. *The cow!* He wasn't used to being treated like this. Adding his wife's little indiscretion to the long list of black marks next to Martin's name wasn't going to be enough. She deserved a slap, this one, and by heck he was going to give it to her. *She was hysterical; no jury would convict me.* He raised his hand to strike her back, and as he did so, the ground beneath his feet trembled. A fine rain of dust fell from the ceiling. 'Wha . . . what was that?' he said in a small voice.

Then it happened again – this time the quaking was stronger and more prolonged. The whole house shook; pictures fell from the walls; cupboards opened and glasses and plates tumbled out and smashed on the kitchen floor. The noise was deafening – Helen couldn't even hear herself scream. Cracks appeared in the walls from floor to ceiling, and Gifford dropped to his knees and crouched beneath the kitchen table in terror. As Helen joined him there, she had the strangest sensation that the house was being pulled down into the ground. Outside the windows day had turned to night. Was this an earthquake? Devon didn't get earthquakes. The odd tremor, perhaps, but nothing like this.

At last, after one final, quivering shudder, it was over. The silence was total. Helen opened her eyes and, through the swirling plaster dust, could just make out a dim red glow through the frosted glass of the back door. Then the door burst open and a strange smell assailed her senses like the stench of a blocked drain tinged with the aroma of burning flesh. There was the clack of claws on the stone flags of the kitchen floor as something strode into the room. It was difficult to make out, but Helen could have sworn it had horns sprouting from its head. Whatever it was spoke with a booming voice: 'Nice of you to drop in.'

'So who are you working for?' The flat, dry American voice came out of the darkness on Martin's left side.

He was handcuffed to a chair, a light shining in his eyes. The interrogation scene in *To Have and Have Not* came to mind, but Martin didn't feel anywhere near as brave as Lauren Bacall. Apart from the CIA agent grilling him, Martin could sense other people in the room, but he couldn't tell how many; beyond the light was a threatening pool of darkness.

'I'll repeat the question.' Now the voice came from behind. 'Who are you working for?'

'I'm a dentist,' Martin protested. 'I'm self-employed.'

Martin felt a hand on his shoulder. 'Don't play dumb; you know what I'm talking about.'

'I'm not working for any terrorist organization, if that's what you mean.'

There was a small pause. When the voice spoke again

it had a playfully superior tone. 'No one mentioned any-thing about terrorists.'

Martin sighed. 'But it's obvious that's what you're asking, isn't it? You're CIA, for God's sake – it's your job to search for terrorists.'

'So, you going to tell us?'

'I'm not a terrorist. Like I said before, I'm a dentist. I know why I'm here and yes, I admit it, I did have a hand in hacking into the missile systems and reprogramming them, but it was done with the best intentions. If any-thing, we were trying to *prevent* terror.'

'We know exactly what you did.'

'Then why are you asking all these questions?'

'Where'd you get the program?'

'I don't suppose you'd believe it came free with a com-puter magazine?'

Martin felt a sharp blow to the side of his head. 'Ow! What did you do that for?'

'That was for insolence.'

Something warm trickled down the side of Martin's face and he realized he must have been hit with something harder than just a fist.

'Look. I'd like to help you, I really would, but I warn you now, it's going to be hard for you to believe. It's hard for *me* to believe.'

'Try me.'

'OK, but no more violence. I really don't react well to violence.'

'You tell the truth, you have nothing to fear.'

*The truth?* Martin thought. *I have everything to fear from the truth.* 'All right. It all started with a dental emer-gency . . .'

*

Martin was led, shuffling, back to his cold, damp cell. The door was closed and locked behind him and he heard footsteps moving away. In the distance another door opened and closed, and then . . . silence.

He curled up, foetus-like, on the thin, hard mattress, his ears still ringing from the pistol-whipping he'd received. *If that's what you get for telling the truth, I'll never make that mistake again,* he thought grimly. *Next time I'll tell them what they want to hear: that I belong to an organization with links to a worldwide terrorist network.* 'Yes, I'm a terrorist!' he yelled suddenly. 'I'm responsible for saving the lives of billions of people!' He hugged himself pitifully and rocked gently to and fro.

'Martin?' The voice, this time, was soft and gentle.

Martin rolled over and opened his eyes to look into the serene face of an angel. 'Gabriel? Oh, it's good to see you.' He reached out to him and Gabriel took him in his arms.

'There, there. There, there.'

'All I did was tell the truth,' Martin sobbed.

'Some people can't cope with the truth.' Gabriel looked down at Martin's bruised and bloody head. 'Ooh, that looks painful. Let's see what we can do.'

As Gabriel took his achingly sore head gently between his hands, Martin felt an incredible warmth suffuse his being. The pain dissolved and the ringing in his ears subsided.

'Better now?'

Martin looked up at him and smiled. 'You're an angel.'

'That's more like it.'

Martin sat up and leaned against the wall. 'Is Luke all right?'

'Luke *and* Henry are both fine; Michael's keeping an

eye on them. These people are going a little easier on them because of their age, but Luke's coping well – you'd be proud of him. And they're rather impressed with Henry – I shouldn't be surprised if they offer him a job when all this is over.'

'Can you get a message to Helen? I want her to know we're all right.'

'You can tell her yourself if you like.' Gabriel produced Martin's phone from the pocket of his overcoat.

'You think of everything!'

'They left it lying about for anyone to pick up. They haven't even been through its memory yet. Very sloppy work – not at all what you'd expect from experienced agents. Now Herod's spy network, that was what you'd *call* a secret service – very thorough.'

Martin dialled a number. 'Hello? Helen?'

'Who is this?' said a voice at the other end.

Martin's heart sank. 'Oh, hello, Gloria. Is Helen there?'

Martin could feel Gloria's face hardening as she realized who it was. 'I thought she was with *you*,' came the terse reply.

'With *me*?'

'She's been trying to get hold of you all morning. Although God alone knows why . . .'

Martin cut her off and immediately began dialling Helen's mobile number.

'What is it?' Gabriel asked.

'Probably nothing, but Helen's not at home with her parents.' The phone rang once, twice, three times before it was picked up.

'Hello!' said a voice Martin didn't recognize. He went cold.

'Who is this?'

'Why don't you have a look?'

'I beg your pardon?'

'This is one of those newfangled video phones, isn't it?'

'Er, yes.' Martin's phone was a state-of-the-art piece of cutting-edge mobile technology. Westerham had handed them out to everyone who worked in the surgery, justifying the huge expense by claiming it was tax-deductible. Martin wasn't even sure yet how the video function worked. He removed it from his ear and stared at the small keyboard. Just underneath the screen was a button with VID on it. It was worth a try. He pressed it. 'Oh my God!'

On the phone's tiny screen had appeared an image of unspeakable ugliness: a horned creature covered in gore and slime, grinning up at him.

'Greetings from Hell, Martin! I've got a little bone to pick with you. But before we go into that, there's someone here who'd like a word.'

The picture panned across to a terrified figure strapped into a dentist's chair.

'Helen!'

'That's right, Martin, and unless you come and see me to explain exactly why you thought it necessary to upset my carefully laid plans, I'm going to remove her teeth one by one – without anaesthetic!'

Helen squirmed and whimpered in the chair, wide-eyed with fear.

'Say hello, Helen.'

'Martin, Martin, help!'

'You leave her alone!' Martin yelled into the phone. 'You don't give the orders down here, I do,' Satan growled. 'Let me show you what happens to people who think they know better.'

The picture panned again to a scene that was vaguely familiar – a bleeding man nailed to a cross. But closer inspection revealed that this was not the traditional wasted form of Jesus. This was a much plumper figure, and not only that – the wretched individual seemed to have been flayed alive. Martin recoiled in horror.

'Probably hard to recognize without his skin.'

The Devil raised the poor man's head. 'Smile for the camera, Gifford!' The inspector's rolling, frightened eyes filled the screen for a moment, then the connection was broken.

Martin dropped the phone and slumped to the floor of the cell, trembling uncontrollably.

'Martin,' said Gabriel, 'you probably realize this already, but if he's got hold of her, Helen's in an awful lot of trouble.'

Martin, struck dumb, could only nod his awareness of this fact.

Gabriel helped Martin back to his feet. While he tried to regain some sort of control over his quivering body, something deep within him stirred: an unfamiliar and terrible longing for what might have been and the vague feeling that his entire life had been leading up to this one moment. But what sprang from his lips surprised even him. 'I have to save her.'

Gabriel gazed earnestly into Martin's eyes. 'No. This is not the time for heroics. This is the Devil you're dealing with: the Prince of Darkness, the Antichrist. Besides, it could be just a trick – Helen may already be dead.'

'No, no, I'm sure she's not dead.' Now Martin knew with absolute certainty what he had to do. He straightened and a determined look came into his eye. 'I'm going to rescue her. She's terrified of dentists; it's how we met. I was the first one who didn't hurt her. If anyone goes near her with a drill, she'll flip.'

'But, Martin, do you have any idea of the danger . . .? What are you doing?'

'Removing your belt. I'm going to hang myself.'

'You can't do that!'

'Why not?'

'Suicide's a mortal sin!'

'Exactly. I'm assuming that's the quickest way to get to Hell.'

Having pulled the belt of Gabriel's raincoat free, Martin was about to attach it to a cable-housing running across the ceiling of his cell, but the angel grabbed it back.

Martin rounded on him. 'Gabriel, give it to me.'

But the angel had already slipped it round his waist and secured it with a knot.

'No.'

'Give it to me or I'll have to take it from you.'

'I'm not helping you to do such a stupid thing.'

Martin advanced on him threateningly. 'Give it to me!'

'Back off, Martin, before you force me to do something I'll regret.'

'You'll regret it if you don't give me your belt.' He grabbed at the belt and fumbled with the knot.

'Let go, Martin! I am not helping you to kill yourself. My job's to protect life!'

'Arghh!' Martin pulled harder. 'Give me the fucking belt!'

They struggled around the cell, bouncing off the walls. The tussle was finally ended by the sound of a key in a lock. Both of them started and looked towards the cell door.

When the guard entered, Martin was alone.

'Who were you talking to?' the man asked, his gun drawn.

'Ah . . . ah . . .' Martin stared back at him, unblinking.

The man shook his head. *They must have improved their interrogation techniques*, he thought. *It used to take longer than just a couple of hours for people to lose their minds.* Convinced now that Martin posed no threat, the jailer holstered his pistol. 'Come on, pal, they want to see you again. Put your hands behind your back and turn around like a good little soldier, so I can put the cuffs on you.'

Martin turned around slowly as the germ of an idea began to grow in his mind. When the jailer reached into his pocket for the handcuffs, Martin elbowed him hard in the stomach. The guard doubled up in agony and, before he could recover, Martin slid the man's gun out of its holster. Its weight surprised him: compared to the featherweight dentist's drills he was used to handling, the pistol weighed a ton.

Turning the weapon on himself, Martin pulled the trigger. But nothing happened.

'Come on now, sir,' said the guard, rubbing his stomach tenderly. 'Give me back the gun before one of us gets hurt.'

'That's the point, you berk!' Martin snapped. 'How does this bloody thing work?' Then two things happened at once. From the various gangster films Martin had seen, the phrase 'safety catch' suddenly came to him, and at the same moment the guard made a lunge for the gun.

'No!' Martin screamed. 'Let me take off the safety first!'

'I don't think that would be wise, sir,' the guard grunted.

As he and the guard struggled, Martin's fingers fumbled over the cold, hard surface of the weapon until they found a small catch. Martin shoved it with his thumb and it clicked. 'Yes!' Now all he had to do was get it pointing in the right direction. But the guard was strong, and Martin was already losing this tug of war. Just then something soft and squidgy brushed his cheek – the man's ear. Without thinking, Martin turned his head and bit into it, hard.

The guard screamed and released his hold on the gun, and in that split second, Martin pulled the trigger.

In the small cell the report was deafening. The guard staggered back, stunned. Examining his body for wounds, he was puzzled to find none. Then all became clear. Martin, smiling benignly, fell backwards, blood pumping frothily from a chest wound.

'Oh shit, oh shit, oh shit!' the guard wailed. 'I'll be right back. Don't die on me now!' he instructed, before running out of the cell and back along the corridor to get help.

As Martin lay there on the cold stone floor in a rapidly expanding pool of his own blood, he could feel his life ebbing away. He felt no pain, just a soft, warm drowsiness like the moments before sleep. He closed his eyes and before him a tunnel opened up, pulsing with light. Falling into it, he became weightless, drifting along towards a pure white incandescence.

'Well I hope you're pleased with yourself.'

Martin opened his eyes and sat up. Gabriel was standing over him.

'I don't understand,' said Martin. 'I feel fine.'

Gabriel reached out a hand. 'Get up; I want to show you something.'

Martin took the angel's hand and stood up. He felt as light as a feather.

'Now look down,' Gabriel instructed.

Martin followed Gabriel's gaze. It took him a little while to comprehend what he was seeing. 'But that's . . .'

Gabriel nodded. 'Yes, you did it.'

There, at Martin's feet, was his own body, flat out and cooling rapidly.

Suddenly there was the sound of feet in the corridor outside, and moments later the small cell was crammed with people crowding around Martin's body, while a doctor crouched to examine it. It didn't take long for him to make his diagnosis, one stark word: 'Dead.'

Gabriel looked sternly at Martin. 'Happy now? I told you not to do it. Now you're in real trouble.'

Gradually the cell emptied, until at last just two men were left, one kneeling beside the body, the other leaning up against the wall and smoking a cigarette. Both of them were wearing red caps. As the kneeling man looked up at him with his electric-blue eyes, Martin gasped, 'Frank Sinatra!'

Frank smiled and stood up. He was smaller than Martin had expected, but his suit was immaculate. 'Well it's about time,' he said. 'You've kept me waiting long enough.'

Martin glanced from Sinatra to the man smoking the cigarette. 'And you're Peter Lawford!'

'Pleased to meet you, Martin.'

'Aw, don't talk to that piece of shit!' Frank moaned. 'He'll steal your wallet as soon as look at you.'

'Hello, Frank, Peter,' interrupted Gabriel.

'Hey, Gabe, what're *you* doing hanging out with this cat?'

'It's a long story,' Gabriel sighed.

Frank turned to Martin. 'Ready, kid?'

'I suppose.'

'Wait,' said Gabriel. 'Before you go, Martin, you'd better have this.' He reached inside his coat and produced an ornately decorated sword hilt.

Martin didn't understand.

'Watch,' said Gabriel. Suddenly, flames shot from the hilt in a fierce jet. Gabriel brandished it with practised ease.

Martin was amazed. 'It's a lightsabre!'

'Er, not quite. It's the very sword used to chase Adam and Eve from the Garden of Eden.' The flames died and Gabriel handed it to Martin. 'Where you're going, I may not follow. It may come in useful when you meet . . . him.'

Martin examined the sword hilt closely. 'How do I make it work?'

Gabriel screwed up his eyes inscrutably. 'Use the Force.'

Martin frowned.

'Oh, all right, you press this button here.' Gabriel indicated a small red knob set into one side of the finely worked hilt.

'Hey, kid,' Frank was looking at his watch, 'I can't hang around all day; I'm on a schedule.'

Martin gazed up at Gabriel one last time.

'Go to her,' sighed the angel. 'You're a very brave man. Foolish but very brave.'

Martin gripped the sword. 'Thank you.'

Gabriel shrugged. 'It's the least I can do. Best keep it out of sight.'

'Oh, right.' Martin tucked it into the front of his shirt.

Frank cleared his throat. 'Come on, come on – you're gonna make us late for our next pick-up!'

Gabriel touched Martin on the shoulder. 'Good luck.'

Martin embraced the angel warmly, then turned to his escort. 'OK.'

Peter Lawford and Frank Sinatra each took one of his arms.

'Let's take off,' said Frank.

'To Peru?' Martin asked.

'Oh, a wise guy.' Frank scowled.

Gabriel watched as Ol' Blue Eyes and Lawford the lounge lizard escorted Martin through the wall of the cell. The angel had helped save the world, yes, but he could do nothing to save his friend. He thought about going to see God and pleading Martin's case, but Gabriel knew what he'd say: 'I'm sorry, Gabriel, but my hands are tied. To forgive this Martin character his mortal sin would send out quite the wrong message. Every transgressor could point to his case and demand to be let off too. And where would that leave us? Heaven would be full of sinners.'

*At least then it might be a little more fun,* Gabriel mused. But he felt bad about doing absolutely nothing. *I could go to the Interface and see him off. He's a brave soul, but it's a strange and disorienting place to those who aren't familiar with it. A friendly face might help him keep his resolve.* Then something Frank had just said came back to him: 'Come on, come on – you're gonna make us late for our next pick-up!'

*Yes,* Gabriel thought, *the soul-fetchers are always busy, charging to and fro, barely having time to pause between assignments. And the conditions: the heat, the filth, the incompetent middle management . . . And what do they have to look forward to? Nothing. They are stuck on a never-ending conveyor belt of suffering for eternity. And, to make matters worse, every time they come back with a new soul, there, mocking them, is the pristine, golden gateway to Heaven, staffed by angels with all the free time in the world.*

As Gabriel's thoughts dwelt on life at the Interface, the image of a certain cashmere-coated individual came back to him, and suddenly it all clicked into place. 'Of course!' he said out loud.

A sly smile played around Gabriel's lips as he formulated a plan.

Michael was crouched on the floor in the middle of telling Luke and Henry the *real* story of the Nativity.

'Now you have to remember that Jesus was born into an agricultural society, and it's probably because of that fact that the fourth wise man – Hamish – is never mentioned in the scriptures, because his gift to the baby Jesus was a sack of manure—'

'Michael!'

Gabriel suddenly appeared to them through the solid wall of their cell.

'Hello, Gabe, I'm just keeping the lads amused.'

'So I hear. Look, we have more work to do.'

'What?'

'I'll tell you on the way.'

Michael rose. 'Sorry, boys; duty calls, apparently.'

The angels made as if to leave, but Luke wanted news of his father.

'He's . . . He sends his love,' Gabriel faltered. Now was not the time to upset the boy with anything as messily disturbing as reality. 'Don't worry, we'll be back soon.'

The two angels waved goodbye and disappeared in a puff of fragrant smoke.

Henry turned to Luke. 'I'd love to know how they do that.'

# Chapter 13

As Gabriel and Michael arrived at the Interface, the angels around the foot of the up escalator greeted them with whoops of joy.

'Here they come – Super Seraph and Wonderwings!'

The archangels bowed graciously.

'Thank you, thank you,' said Gabriel. 'We come to ask a small favour.'

'Ask and ye shall receive.'

Gabriel and Michael gathered the angels around them in a small huddle.

'It's like this . . .'

When Martin eventually got to the head of the down escalator, he glanced across at the entrance to Heaven and was amazed to see Gabriel and Michael in conference with several other angels and a host of unlikely historical figures. Cromwell, Lenin and Robespierre he recognized straight away, but there were dozens of other strange-looking souls, some with great beards, some in sharp suits, some in nothing but loincloths, and all deep in conversation. One in particular seemed to be doing most of the talking, but Martin couldn't see his face because he had his cashmere-coated back to him. And no matter how much the attendant ghouls screamed and danced around this unlikely crowd, lashing out with their whips or jabbing with their pitchforks, the group stubbornly refused to break up.

'Name?'

Martin looked up into the hooded face of Death himself. He started. 'Ah!'

'This is nothing,' Death replied. 'You should see me after a heavy Saturday night. Now come on, give us your name.'

'Er . . . Martin Gray.'

Death scanned the list on his clipboard. 'Gray, Gray, Gray . . . ah, here we are.' He ticked the name with the stub of a pencil. 'Hmm, it says you're to be given the fast-track treatment.' Death took a long, rasping in-breath and yelled down the escalator, 'Will you keep to the left, please!' The souls tramping down the metal stairway obediently moved over. 'On you go – down the stairs and first right. I'm afraid you'll have to walk; the escalator's knackered. But then, so are you. Next!'

Martin found himself walking down the long, long stairway to Hell. Looking into the pit, past the line of poor souls on the escalator below him, he could see tongues of flame leaping out from great pools of molten fire, and hear the pitiful screams of those doomed to live in perpetual torment. All at once the enormity of his task came home to him. He was going, alone, to fight the forces of Hell. Fingering the hilt of Gabriel's sword through the fabric of his shirt, he realized how ill-prepared he was for this trip.

At the bottom of the long escalator, greeted by the appalling stench and scorching heat of the lower world, his ears assailed by the sound of a billion souls screaming in agony, he could bear it no longer. His trembling legs gave way and he fell to his knees on the sulphurous rocks. Immediately his trousers began to smoulder – even the ground was searingly hot. But he was given no time to indulge his terror. From behind him came a violent, angry howl – half animal, half human – and a pain like red-hot needles in his back. He turned sharply to see a grinning ghoul jabbing him with a pitchfork.

'Get up!' the creature screeched, thrusting the points into Martin's flesh yet again. 'Seek not comfort here! Vile human, abandon hope!' it wailed in a thin, high scream as it danced around him. 'Look around you and weep. Behold the abyss, Pandaemonium, the unquenchable fire of the bottomless pit! Ha, ha, ha, ha, ha!' it laughed maniacally.

Martin staggered unsurely to his feet. 'Um, I've got an appointment . . .'

The ghoul stopped prancing about and blinked. 'Is your name Gray?'

'Yes.'

The ghoul frowned, regarding him closely for some moments. Eventually it sighed resignedly. 'If you'd like to follow me,' it said, 'My Lord is waiting for you.' The ghoul led the way through an ancient, smoke-smudged archway.

Martin followed through clouds of choking, sulphurous fumes, past lakes of blazing brimstone where souls stood waist-deep, wailing in anguish. Everywhere was pain and misery. From the walls, souls impaled on long spikes screamed in unending agony. Elsewhere, lines of men and women in chains waited to be violently assaulted by the ghouls, some of which, Martin noted, had not one but two phalluses.

'Ouch!' he murmured.

'Nearly there,' said his guide, throwing open a large studded door. 'In here – and wait to be called for. Don't touch anything!'

Martin was thrust inside and the door slammed shut. He was in what might have looked like a church vestibule had it not been for the excrement seeping from the walls.

Martin retched – the stench was appalling – but he had to focus on what was about to happen. Soon he would meet the prince of Darkness himself and he had to be ready. But nothing in his long training as a dentist had prepared him for how to approach this hellish meeting. This time even Shakespeare let him down: not a single honey'd word of the great bard came to his aid. Then another door in the vestibule opened – he had already run out of time.

Martin was ushered into the gloomy and imposing front hall of a dilapidated Gothic mansion by a butler in a tailcoat. Relieved at least to be out of the foul-smelling vestibule, Martin nervously looked around. The dark wood panelling lining the walls was cracked and warped and festooned with cobwebs, and a full suit of armour, complete with murderous-looking broadsword, stood at the foot of the stairs.

'This way,' the butler instructed.

Martin followed him across the echoing hall and noted with terror that the floor tiles, laid in a herring-bone pattern, were made unmistakably from pieces of human skull. Likewise, the banisters of the staircase were human thigh bones.

The butler pushed open a set of double doors and ushered Martin inside. Once the doors closed behind him, Martin found himself in almost total darkness. Despite the heat of the furnace radiating from all sides, a fire leapt and crackled in the grate, and gradually, amongst the shadows, Martin was able to make out several shapes in the gloom.

'Welcome to my world,' said a voice.

Immediately a light snapped on, and Martin started back in shock and revulsion. Revealed in the stark glare of the single overhead light was a creature from the blackest depths of the unconscious – a figure from a nightmare. A hideous thing of slime and gore.

'Bit of a shock, isn't it?' The creature chuckled. 'But what did you expect – a man with a pointy beard and a long tail? The real thing takes some beating, eh?' He turned round slowly so that Martin could get the full effect.

Martin couldn't speak. The vision seemed to have robbed him of all thought, all action. Now he knew for certain he was doomed.

Satan clicked his fingers and another light snapped on, revealing the crucified figure of Gifford Wilkinson. If the sight had been bad enough on Martin's phone, the real thing was unimaginably awful. Martin wanted to be sick.

'Don't feel sorry for him; he brought it on himself. It's what he wanted to do to you. Gets you right here, doesn't it?' Satan rubbed his stomach. 'Better get used to it, Martin; you're going to be seeing a lot worse. But I expect you're wondering about a certain little lady.'

Yet another light snapped on, and there was Helen, strapped into the dentist's chair, catatonic with terror. Next to her head was positioned a rack containing a selection of drills on which her frightened eyes were fixed.

The sight of his wife stirred something in Martin's

soul and from somewhere he found the strength to utter a weak, 'Let her go!'

The Devil applauded. 'Bravo. Very courageous, I'm sure. I like a man with pluck, but unfortunately that won't help you down here.'

Martin had to move his mouth several times before he could get any more words to come out of it. 'You . . . you've got *me*, now let her go.'

'Oh, that's very touching. Did you actually think you could come down here and *bargain*? You're a little out of your depth, son. Have you forgotten who you're dealing with? Are you aware that one of my nicknames is the Father of Lies?' Satan gave a harsh laugh. 'No, no, no. Somehow you have managed to thwart one of my most complex, most carefully thought-out schemes. Do you know how long it took to plan this little enterprise? I had to invent the silicon chip *and* found Microsoft. Then, after making the computer indispensable to virtually everyone on the planet, I had to get them all hooked on the Internet! It took years of careful preparation, and you destroyed the whole scheme in a morning!' Satan reached out and grabbed the front of Martin's shirt, pulling him close. Martin reeled from the foul fiend's stinking breath. 'I don't know how you did it, you little shit, but you've caused me no end of trouble. Because of you I might be stuck down here forever! And that makes me rather angry. Correction: *very* angry. So, you see, somebody has to pay, and as you're responsible for causing me such grief, it's only fair that you should suffer the consequences. And, oh yes, you're going to suffer terribly. But I don't want to give you the impression that I'm a discourteous host so we'll let the lady go first.'

Releasing his hold on Martin's shirt front, Satan

clapped his hands and the room was flooded with light. A door opened and a rotund, bearded figure strode in.

'You probably know this man by reputation. Allow me to introduce Walter Sickert.'

The plump figure came to a stop in the middle of the room and bowed.

'Mr Sickert was an accomplished artist in his time, but that isn't his real claim to fame,' the Devil continued. 'No, Walter here is famous for quite a different sort of artistry, a kind that kept the London bobbies scratching their heads for many years. It gives me great pleasure to present to you, here, tonight, the one and only Jack the Ripper!'

Sickert revealed his teeth in a sickening leer and from his coat pocket produced a scalpel.

Despite the intense heat, Martin went cold as he watched the artist hold the scalpel aloft, its blade catching the light and making sharp darts of brilliance dance around the room.

Satan crossed to Martin and spoke confidentially. 'We're honoured tonight to be present at the inception of Jack's latest work – a bit of a departure for him. It's sort of performance art: a three-dimensional piece entitled *Helen's Final Act of Suffering*.'

Martin began to shake.

'And, in another departure,' Satan continued, 'he's going to eschew his favourite instrument – the scalpel – in favour of the dentist's drill. Who says you can't teach an old dog new tricks?' The Devil turned and addressed an imaginary audience. 'Mr Ripper works with neither anaesthetic nor safety net and therefore needs complete concentration. So can we have absolute silence, please? Thank you!'

The mutilator of women turned to the hysterically squirming figure of Helen held fast in the chair by wide leather restraints and selected one of the drills from the rack. Pressing a foot pedal brought it to life, and the instrument wailed with a shrill, siren-like scream. Sickert bent intently over Helen and, narrowing his eyes, pressed her head firmly into the leather of the chair with his left hand while with the other he lifted the drill high. 'A little wider please,' he said with a grin, and began to bring the yowling drill down towards her mouth.

This was the moment – it was now or never. Reaching inside his shirt, Martin withdrew Gabriel's sword and switched it on. A fiery blade shot from the hilt. Crossing the room in three strides, Martin brought the flaming sword up, slicing through the Ripper's wrist. The murderer screamed in agony as his hand fell to the floor still clutching the drill. Quickly releasing the straps binding Helen to the chair, Martin turned to face the Prince of Darkness.

Even Satan looked surprised at this turn of events.

'I'm impressed. Interesting little toy you have there. Do you know, it looks vaguely familiar. Let me think, where have I seen it before? Flaming sword . . . flaming sword . . . Why does that phrase ring a bell? Ah, I've got it! It's Gabriel's, isn't it? He lent you his little weapon – how thoughtful. So it's him I have to thank for this mess. That interfering busybody has been the bane of my life! But this time he's gone too far.'

While Martin held both Jack the Ripper and Satan at bay with the sword, with his free hand he helped Helen to her feet.

'Now,' he said, 'you're going to let us go.'

Satan smiled. 'But I can't do that; you've only just

arrived. I was looking forward to a bit of a chinwag. Lothar's made buns and everything.'

Martin edged Helen towards the door. 'We're going now and you can't stop us.'

'And how far do you think you'll get? You'll be cut down by my minions as soon as you leave this room. Besides, how are you going to get back out? It's a very long escalator and it only works one way – down.'

'It's broken.'

'Still?' Satan frowned. 'Tch, I must get someone to look at it.'

'And we don't mind a long walk, do we, Helen?'

She shook her head.

'Well, that's fine for her, but what about you, Martin? I'm afraid you belong here. You're mine now.'

'Martin?' Helen whispered. 'Tell me it's not true.'

'Yes, Helen.' The Devil grinned. 'You see, to coin a phrase, I used that ol' devil called love to attract your husband. It's rather sweet. Martin killed himself just so he could come down here to rescue you, all the time knowing that for him it was a one-way trip. How's that for devotion, eh?'

Helen touched Martin's face. 'You did that for me?'

Satan sighed impatiently. 'Look, this is all very lovely, and I hate to interrupt such a tender moment, but we really must get on.' He turned and barked, 'Lothar!'

From nowhere, the butler appeared, launched himself at Martin and grabbed him round the waist. Martin nearly went down, but after a short struggle managed to break free and lash out with the sword. Lothar squealed in pain and threw a hand up to the left side of his head. Quickly retreating out of range, the butler glowered at his opponent, dabbing at his torn and blistered ear with a handkerchief. Then, coming to a sudden decision, he left the room to return a few moments later armed with the two-handed sword from the suit of armour in the hall.

'Bravo, Lothar!' Satan cheered.

Lothar lunged at Martin, but he sidestepped and caught the butler on the other ear. Howling in agony, Lothar retreated to the fireplace.

'Well, well, well. It seems we have a bit of a contest on our hands. What do you think, Walter, fancy a small wager? I'll lay five guineas on Lothar.'

As Lothar prepared to come in again, Martin placed Helen safely out of range behind a large bureau and went to meet his opponent.

Raising the sword high, the Devil's manservant charged. It may have had a longer reach, but in comparison to Martin's light and finely balanced weapon, Lothar's was clumsy and unwieldy. As the great blade came swinging down, Martin once again sidestepped the stroke. The heavy sword crashed into the parquet flooring, sending up chips of shattered bone, and Martin lashed out swiftly, inflicting another wound on Lothar's leg. But this time the butler simply gritted his teeth and came straight back on the offensive, taking a swipe at Martin's head. The vicious blade sliced the air, whistling past so close to Martin's face he felt the breeze of it on his cheek.

Martin, in turn, swung his sword, but this time Lothar saw it coming and ducked out of the way, and the flaming blade passed harmlessly over the manservant's crouched back.

Martin retreated to a safe distance, and the two men glared at each other from opposite sides of the room.

Satan was beginning to look worried. 'Lothar, lose this match and I shall be five guineas down.'

Lothar roared and charged in again. Martin swiftly dodged to one side, and Satan's butler buried the great sword in the wall. As Lothar struggled to pull the blade free, Martin saw his chance. Raising the flaming blade above his head, he was about to bring it down on Lothar's neck when Helen screamed.

Turning quickly, Martin was faced with a grisly sight – Walter Sickert's severed hand, the dentist's drill still gripped between its fingers, had clawed its way up the front of Helen's dress and was now at her throat.

'Checkmate, I believe,' Satan announced. 'Come on, Martin, put down the sword or Helen here is going to get some extensive and unnecessary dental work. It'll be just like the old NHS.'

For a moment Martin wondered if he'd be able to dispose of Lothar and reach his wife before Sickert's disunited hand had a chance to do any harm, but he was forced to the uncomfortable conclusion that he'd never make it. He had no choice. Turning off the flame he dropped the sword to the ground and was immediately gripped in an armlock by a vengeful satanic butler.

The Devil advanced slowly. 'You played that very well, Martin. But now playtime's over.' Satan turned to the malevolent figure of Jack the Ripper. 'Kill her, Jack.'

The whine of the drill increased as Sickert's hand brought its tip nearer and nearer Helen's carotid artery.

'No!' Martin screamed, but at that moment the drill died and all the lights went out.

'Oh, typical,' Satan complained.

There was a wet *schlump* as Sickert's hand fell to the ground and scuttled back to its owner.

In the gloom the door opened and several dark shapes entered. A torch snapped on and a man wearing a cashmere coat led the group of new arrivals across the room. Illuminating his own face with the torch beam the man addressed the Devil. 'Are you Satan, also known as Lucifer; the fallen angel; the archfiend; Prince of Darkness; Antichrist; His Satanic Majesty; Old Nick; Diabolus; angel of the bottomless pit; Cloutie; Old Scratch; Shaitan; Apollyon; and king of Hell?'

'I have that distinction, yes.'

The man with the torch turned to his colleagues. 'Looks like we've got the right feller.'

'Who are you?' Satan enquired.

The man extended his hand. 'I'm Jimmy Hoffa. Nice to meet you.'

'Hoffa?' The Devil frowned. 'The union leader?'

'You've heard of me? That's good. You obviously keep abreast of what's going on upstairs.'

'I have what you might call a passing interest, yes. I believe you were friendly with Sam Giancana, the Mafia boss.'

'We had dealings, I admit, but strictly of a union nature.'

'What do you want? I'm right in the middle of something.'

'Well, Mr Satan, I've been doing a little research in the field, and it appears that there's a lot of dissatisfaction among your workforce – they don't feel very nurtured. Apart from the fact that you've been keeping the proposed takeover of the earth all to yourself – which we'll get to later – there's the little matter of working conditions, both for the soul-fetchers and pit personnel. Chief amongst grievances I've noted seems to be an insensitivity in the

way workers are paired up, but then, on top of that, there
are also the long hours, the short meal breaks, the lack of
air conditioning downstairs, and the total absence of any
accident and emergency provisions. It's a long list, and I
have to say I'm not impressed.'

'This is Hell,' Satan growled. 'It's run to impress
neither you nor the scum who inhabit it.'

'Now, you see, that's just the sort of attitude I'm talking about. Employer–employee relations seem to have
reached an all-time low. Some of us think it's time you
did something about it and that's why we've organized
this strike.'

Satan blinked, his mouth opening and closing several
times. 'Strike?' he said at last. 'Did you say strike?'

'That's right, your devilship.' Hoffa handed Satan a
sheet of paper. 'Until these demands are met, in full, the
power is going to stay off. And I've also called out
the soul-fetchers. There will be no more soul collecting
until this dispute is concluded to our satisfaction.'

The Devil studied the sheet of paper he'd been given
in the torchlight. 'Medical insurance? . . . Holiday pay? . . .
Maternity leave? . . .' Crumpling up the union leader's
demands, Old Nick glared at him with eyes that burned
like fire. He reached out and grabbed the lapels of Jimmy
Hoffa's handmade coat and pulled him close. 'Listen to
me, you villain. I am the Devil – Beelzebub. I don't make
deals, and Hell isn't supposed to be a holiday camp. So
you just take your thugs out of here and call this strike off
before I deep-fry your entrails.'

But Hoffa was unmoved. 'Cooking staff are out too.'

Satan began to swell up like a grotesque pufferfish,
filling the room with his malevolent presence, while a hot
violent wind swirled around him like a tornado. 'You will

burn for all eternity!' His head began to spin on his shoulders like a Catherine wheel and brimstone sprayed from his lips.

At once the room was full of molten fire. Martin broke free from Lothar and grabbed Helen, pulling her back further behind the shelter of the bureau. But those left exposed to the searing rain screamed in agony as the molten lava clung to their skin, burning their flesh.

But Hoffa persisted. 'You keep this up,' he yelled, 'this place is going to stay dark forever!'

The Devil's head ceased whirring, his body resumed its normal size, and the wind stopped.

Satan had never been in this position before. He wasn't used to being dictated to; he always had the last word. He didn't like it but he began to see that things were no longer under his control. If, as seemed likely, he was now stuck in Hell for eternity, he needed it to function. But acceding to Hoffa's demands went against every principle he'd ever stood by.

'No! No! *No!*' he wailed.

'You'd better believe it, buddy,' said Hoffa. 'Now, as to this proposed hostile takeover of Earth Inc., it's our view we should have been brought in from the start. As it happens, this time you were unsuccessful, but any future attempts at mergers, takeovers and the like are going to have to be done with the full cooperation of the workforce. I'm afraid, Mr Satan, the days of your doing whatever you like whenever you like without any consideration for your workers' welfare and security are over. But hey, look on the bright side: you get your workforce behind you, you're going to have that much more leverage.' He glanced at his Rolex in the beam of the torch.

'We'll give you twenty-four hours to think things over. Come on, guys, let's go play some poker.'

Hoffa led his people out of the room, leaving Satan feeling crushed and impotent. Out in the hall the grandfather clock chimed midnight. On the last stroke came the sound of the front door opening and closing, and a voice that bellowed, 'Where is he?'

'Now what?' Satan moaned.

Footsteps crossed the floor. In the flickering light of the guttering fire someone else could be seen entering the room. This time it was a large, bearded figure.

'You've got some explaining to do, Lucifer! Let's have some light on the subject, shall we?' The bearded figure clapped his hands and immediately the room was illuminated. 'Well, well, well,' said God, taking in the mess, 'had a bit of a party?'

'What are you doing here?' Satan snapped.

'You know perfectly well why I'm here!' God growled. 'Apart from the streets topside filling up with uncollected incorporeal souls, in strict contravention of the Heaven–Hell treaty, a little bird told me you'd been cheating!'

'Does that little bird happen to be over six foot tall and wear a mac?'

'That's the chap. He told me some nonsense about a computer game you'd developed which was going to destroy the world. But I said he must have got it wrong because that would be breaking our little pact, wouldn't it?'

The Devil stared at the floor.

'You have *absolutely* contravened the terms of our bet!' Satan's eyes flashed. 'Oh yeah? And whose little helpers have been swarming all over the earth trying to stop me, eh?'

'Don't change the subject. Admit it, Lucifer: you cheated!'

In the ensuing silence somebody groaned.

For the first time, God realized they were not alone. 'You never told me you had company.' He scanned the various faces dotted around the room. 'Now who do we have here? Lothar I know, of course, and the chap trying to reattach his hand looks familiar. Don't tell me . . . Walter, isn't it?'

Sickert nodded.

'Of course. I've got one of your pictures in my loo. Not going to be doing much painting for a while with that hand, are you?' His eyes came to light on the figure of Gifford on the cross. 'Tch, tch, tch. Not very original, Lucy. Who is he?'

'A tax inspector.'

'Oh, well, that's understandable. But, no, take him down and give him back his skin.'

Satan nodded to Lothar, who reluctantly crossed the room and started removing the nails that held Gifford fast.

At last, God's gaze lit on Helen and Martin. 'I don't believe we've met.' He turned back to the Devil. 'Aren't you going to introduce us?'

Satan pursed his lips and snorted. 'Helen and Martin Gray, meet God, creator of all things, lord and master of the universe, and fair-weather friend.'

'How do you do?'

Martin and Helen stood open-mouthed in shock as God shook them by the hand.

'Been here long? How are you finding it?'

'I, er, well, I shouldn't really be here,' Martin mumbled.

'Ah, that's what they all say.'

Helen at last found her voice. 'No, he's right; he shouldn't be here. He only came to rescue me.'

'Now that story sounds familiar.' God studied Martin hard. 'So we have an Orpheus here, do we, come to rescue his Eurydice?'

Martin nodded. 'Something like that.'

'But, as I remember, in the story it was Eurydice who died and the living Orpheus who descended into Hell. You seem to have it the wrong way round. Helen here, if I'm not mistaken, is still alive – am I right?' God glanced at Satan, who nodded curtly. 'Well, my dear, getting you out of this place shouldn't be too problematic.'

Satan rolled his eyes.

'But as for Martin here . . .' God shook his head.

'Please, Almighty Father, Martin only killed himself to come and rescue me,' Helen implored.

'Ah, a suicide. Case closed, I'm afraid. You see, however pure the motive, there are certain rules by which everyone has to abide. One of them being that if you take your own life you wind up down here. There can be no exceptions. My rules are not to be broken.'

After all he'd been through, something in God's smug tone was beginning to get right up Martin's nose. 'Except by you,' he murmured.

God blinked. 'I'm sorry?'

Martin spoke up a little louder. 'If your rules are unbreakable, then how come it's OK for you to shatter them?'

God was not used to being challenged, especially not

on a moral issue, and certainly not by a mere mortal. 'I, er . . . What do you mean?'

'I mean,' said Martin, now getting into his stride, 'making bets with your friend Lucifer here over the future of the earth, completely ignoring the fact that, had he won, billions of people would have died in agony.'

'But he *didn't* win.'

'Only because *he* cheated!' Satan screamed.

'I haven't finished!' Martin bellowed.

God and Satan stood guiltily mute like naughty schoolchildren.

'Just because you're God, you think you can do anything you like, but you have a moral obligation to your creation to set an example. No wonder earth's in the state it is if all you care about is your golf handicap.'

God blushed.

Martin turned to Satan. 'I'd expect this sort of behaviour from you. You're *supposed* to be evil. But you!' He swung back to the Almighty. 'I'm really disappointed in you. I always imagined you'd be above vanity and temptation. But it seems I was wrong, you're as fallible as the rest of us.'

From the direction of the entrance hall came the sound of a single person clapping. Everyone turned. Framed in the open doorway was the figure of Mary, the Madonna. 'Bravo!' she shouted. But this was not the demure, porcelain-complexioned, saintly figure of Renaissance art; this was a strong, dark-skinned Middle Eastern woman. Standing next to her, dressed in plus fours and a pink Pringle sweater three sizes too big for him, was Jesus.

God shrank visibly and glared at his son. 'You brought your mother?' he hissed.

'Don't blame the boy,' Mary shot back. 'He only came

along because I asked him to keep me company. Gabriel told me I'd find you here. He told me a lot of very interesting things.'

God groaned. 'How long have you been standing there?'

'Long enough to realize that the only one who's talking any sense here is this gentleman.' She indicated Martin.

'The name's Martin Gray,' he offered.

'Pleased to meet you.' Crossing the room, she confronted God. 'You made a bet with the Devil over the future of the earth? You old fool! After all the trouble you went to to get the place up and running in the first place, you were prepared to throw it all away because of an altercation at a cocktail party?'

'I have my position to consider. I couldn't let it look like Satan was getting one over on me.'

'So you were prepared to risk the earth just so you could look like the big man? Mr Gray's right, you *are* vain and weak.'

Satan smiled slyly at the Almighty.

Mary turned on him. 'And you're just as bad. What's all this nonsense about wanting to be back in Heaven? *This* is where you belong.' She stood back and surveyed them both, shaking her head, sadly. 'You and horny-head here just don't get it, do you?'

God and the Devil frowned.

'You *need* each other.'

God raised an eyebrow.

'You need the Devil as much as he needs you. So I suggest you master your feelings and start working with him.'

God was becoming rather confused. 'I'm sorry but

I—'

'Look,' Mary continued, 'if it wasn't for friend Lucifer here, how could people have the option to choose you? You're always yammering on about free will, and yet you have no idea what it really means in practice! If there were only goodness, the universe would be full of unconscious automatons all doing thy will. Satan here does a very good job of providing a useful counterpoint to your so-called righteousness. But at the moment there's nothing to tell between the two of you; you're beginning to look like New Labour and the Tories. No wonder people are confused. You've both got to get back in touch with who you really are and start behaving like grown-ups.'

God shuffled uncomfortably.

'And how many times have I told you to stop giving Jesus your golfing cast-offs? You've made him a laughing stock. He doesn't even like golf!'

God looked hurt. 'Don't you, son?'

Jesus looked at the ground. 'Not really, Dad, no.'

'What *do* you like, then?'

'I've always been rather fond of fishing.'

'Fishing?'

Mary's eyes burned. 'Excuse me, but I'm still talking!'

'Sorry,' God murmured.

'Now then, I want you and Old Scratch to make up.'

God was horrified. He pointed a finger at Satan. 'With him?'

Mary nodded. 'With him.'

'But I—' God began.

'Go on,' Mary urged.

'Oh, me,' God sighed, looking at Satan.

Satan looked at God.

'Friends?' said the Almighty through gritted his teeth.

'Friends,' Satan agreed, a little more readily.

Mary smiled. 'Good. Now give each other a hug.'

God grimaced. 'I'm sorry, but I really draw the line at physical contact.'

Mary pursed her lips.

'All right, all right.'

God and Satan moved sheepishly towards each other. Reluctantly, God opened his arms and Heaven and Hell embraced awkwardly.

'That's better. Now we'll have no more of this nonsense.' Mary narrowed her eyes at God. 'Betting indeed.' Then she turned to Satan. 'And you, stop goading him; you know it always ends in tears.'

Satan nodded silently.

'There,' said Mary. 'All better now. Come on, Mr Universe, let's go home.'

God joined his family in the doorway.

'Um, what about us?' It was Helen.

'Sorry, dear,' said God. 'I'd forgotten about you in all the excitement.' He looked warily at Mary before continuing. 'Of course *you* can have your life back, but I'm afraid Martin here—'

Helen was about to remonstrate with her maker, but Martin stopped her and addressed the creator himself. 'Look, I understand that it's too late for me, but *he* doesn't deserve to be here.' Martin nodded in Gifford's direction. 'He's never done me any favours, it's true, but he's got nothing to do with any of this. He should be allowed to live out the rest of his life.'

God considered this a while. He looked with ill-disguised revulsion at the rotund figure of Gifford, who was now off the cross but still awkwardly adjusting himself back inside his skin. It was a tricky operation – a bit like putting on a pair of socks, which can be extremely uncomfortable if you don't get the seams in exactly the right place.

God didn't like tax officials and normally would have brushed such a request for clemency aside, but in Mary's disapproving presence and considering the selflessness of Martin's request, he felt he ought at least to make a gesture. 'Oh, very well,' he said. 'He's more than welcome to go back to his dreary life as a tax collector.'

'Inspector,' Gifford corrected.

'Don't push it, son,' God warned.

'And what about Martin?' Mary reminded him. 'After all, he did help stop the world going up in smoke as a result of *your* pig-headedness.'

God eyed Martin thoughtfully. 'Well, I can't give him back his life, on that I'm immovable. And I'm certainly not going to let him in upstairs . . .'

Mary too was unmoved.

'He's a suicide!'

But the Madonna remained granite-faced.

'I . . . I can't . . . If I let him into Heaven I'll leave myself open to a tidal wave of litigation from all sorts of undesirables.'

Mary pursed her lips and raised an eyebrow.

God closed his eyes and inhaled noisily through his nose. 'I suppose I could say that he redeemed himself by pleading for the life of his persecutor.'

'Go on,' she prompted.

'And because of that I was able to offer him special dispensation for his sin.'

'Sounds fair,' Mary agreed. But just as God was about to head for the door once again, she stopped him with a sharp 'Ahem!' and looked pointedly in Satan's direction.

God got her drift. Sighing deeply, he addressed his one-time friend.

'And you, Lucy? As I seem to be handing out favours right, left and centre, is there anything I can do for you? I believe that just before I came in you were having a little trouble with the lighting. The natives getting restless?'

'That bloody Hoffa. But don't worry; I've made him disappear once and I can do it again. No, what I'd really like . . . and this may sound silly, but . . . well, I've always wanted to play the cello at a big venue like the Albert Hall.' He gazed at God like a child asking for an expensive Christmas present.

God's eyes twinkled. 'Of course, my friend. Anything you desire.' He addressed the ensemble with a beaming smile. 'Right then, I think we're all done here. Shall we go?'

# Chapter 14

Mary and Jesus, Martin, Helen, Gifford and God paused at the foot of the heavenly staircase at the Heaven–Hell Interface, where Gabriel, Michael and St Peter were waiting for them. A host of angels gathered excitedly around.

God frowned at both archangels. He was about to rebuke them for meddling in mankind's affairs *and* getting him into serious trouble with *she who must be obeyed*, when he caught sight of Mary's thunderous expression. Instead he forced his mouth into a smile, nodded faintly and muttered, 'Well done, boys.'

Mary beamed at him. 'Now you're getting the idea.'

Martin had a sudden thought. 'I wish Luke were here. I would have liked to have said goodbye.'

Helen tried to choke back her tears. 'I'll tell him how brave his father was. He'll be very proud of you.'

Martin put his arms round her waist. 'That's all I ever wanted. And you beside me, of course.'

Helen pulled him close and sobbed into his shoulder. 'Oh Martin, I'm so sorry. I thought you didn't love me any more. If I'd known that you cared that much I would never . . .'

Martin hugged her tighter. 'Maybe I didn't know it myself,' he murmured. 'I'm sorry too.' They kissed, clinging to each other one last, lingering moment.

God cleared his throat. 'Um, I hate to separate you two, but I'm afraid it's time for us to go.'

God ushered the heavenly party onto the escalator and then got on himself, with Martin beside him.

As the metal staircase began to move slowly upward, Martin turned back to gaze at his wife, standing forlornly, looking lost and alone. 'I'll be waiting for you!' he called.

Helen, her face streaked with tears, waved goodbye to her husband. He was, she now realized, the best of men, and she watched helplessly as he receded slowly, inexorably, further and further out of reach. It didn't seem right that, having just rediscovered the warm, loving man she had married, he should be taken from her like this, and deep inside she felt an exquisitely painful rage building: a mixture of loss and longing, as if this one parting resonated with all the bittersweet, painful partings the world had ever known. This feeling surged in a great writhing current within her, swirling round her belly, her heart, rushing upward until it finally burst from her lips.

'*I love you!*'

The escalator groaned and creaked with the sound of metal grinding against metal. The moving staircase shuddered, slowed, then stopped altogether. Mary had to cling tightly to Gabriel to stop herself from falling over, and Michael completely lost his balance and fell quite heavily, damaging a few of his primary feathers.

Love had triumphed once again.

'I hate it when that happens,' God grumbled.

'Helen!' Taking the steps two at a time, Martin was already running down the escalator towards her. At its foot, they embraced. Nothing was going to part them now.

Mary smiled smugly at God. 'Well? Now what are you going to do?'

Gabriel, Michael and even Jesus gathered round.

'All right, all right, don't crowd me! I . . . I suppose that in this one instance . . . I mean, to be honest, if it hadn't been for him we might now be welcoming Satan back into the fold . . . So, I suppose it's only fair that . . .'

'Yes?' Mary prompted.

'It's only fair that he should – that *they* should – have a happy ending.'

The angels all cheered.

Gabriel wiped his eyes. 'I love a happy ending!'

Michael put an arm round him. 'I know, I know.'

God surveyed the scene below. 'Now that the bet's been declared null and void, I suppose it's all right for me to interfere again – take more of an interest in mankind's affairs.'

'About time!' Mary was emphatic.

God raised his arm and gestured towards the mortals still standing at the foot of the escalator. 'It's time to draw a veil over this whole episode.' He pointed his famous finger at Gifford 'You, tax inspector, are absolved your appalling conduct. Go now and sin no more.' He turned to the happy couple. 'Martin, Helen, I won't be seeing you for a little while, so enjoy the rest of your lives together. And now, goodbye!' At a wave of his hand, Martin and Helen felt themselves moving backwards as if through a long tunnel, the Heaven–Hell Interface rapidly diminishing to a distant dot. And, as their vision of God and the heavenly host faded, so too their memories were wiped clean of all knowledge of angels and demons.

*

The medical orderlies loading Martin's body into the back of the ambulance were surprised to say the least when the 'stiff' suddenly sat up, stretched and yawned.

Those inside the temporary British CIA headquarters were also rather confused. They had two teenage detainees but no one could remember what they had been arrested for. Luke they released immediately, but Henry seemed to have a certain expertise in computing, a talent that they could put to good use.

Helen and Gifford gazed at each other across her kitchen table.

'Can I, er . . . help you?' She stammered. She was sure she'd been about to do something but couldn't for the life of her remember what.

Gifford was equally confused. 'I, er . . . I'm looking for . . .' *What was his name again?* He shook his head. One didn't like to lose face in front of the punters, so retreat was probably the best option in the circumstances. 'It appears I have the wrong address. Sorry to have troubled you. Good day.'

He got back into his car. Never in his long years of service in Her Majesty's Inland Revenue had such a thing happened to him before. He opened the briefcase on the passenger seat and rummaged round looking for clues. Martin's name stared up at him from a letterhead. *Martin Gray? Of course, I remember!* His sense of purpose rekindled, he was about to go back and start interrogating Helen about Martin's whereabouts, but an uncharacteristic thought stopped him. *Hang on, it's Sunday, isn't it? I can't go barging about disturbing people's Sundays. This can wait until the morning, surely?* The thought caught Gifford completely unawares but seemed to have an authority he couldn't question – like an instruction from a higher power. He closed his briefcase and drove away, feeling no longer entirely in control of his actions.

On his way back towards Exeter, he was passed by a big black limousine going in the opposite direction.

The limo turned down the small country lane leading to Windyridge and drew up outside the front door. Martin and Luke got out and bade the driver goodbye as Helen stood watching them from the doorstep. Martin thought she was the best thing he'd ever seen. They ran to each other and embraced.

'I've missed you,' Martin murmured.

'I've been an idiot,' she replied.

'And I've been blind.'

Luke stood awkwardly by, kicking the gravel. 'Um, shall I go and put the kettle on?'

Martin reached out to his son and drew him into a three-way hug.

'It's nice to be home,' said Helen.

# Chapter 15

One by one, the world's nuclear powers began to wake up to the fact that they no longer possessed their most cherished weapons. Every missile-borne warhead seemed to have vanished without trace, a fact as puzzling as it was disturbing. Understandably, this story never found its way into the public domain, as any country admitting to losing its entire stock of missiles would leave itself wide open to attack from a hostile power. But worse even than that: it would be extremely embarrassing.

With every erstwhile nuclear power now certain that it was the only country on earth not to possess such devastating firepower, the planet entered one of its most peaceful and safe eras. Countries that for years had been at each other's throats now reined in their animosity and went into diplomatic overdrive to try and patch things up.

And so it was with Martin and Westerham. He didn't really know why, but Martin's feelings had changed towards his colleague, and he'd had an idea which, with Westerham's help, might just resolve his financial predicament.

When Martin turned up at the surgery on Monday morning, it was apparent to everyone that a transformation had occurred. Gone was the old, worried, grey Gray and in its place was a cheerful and optimistic Martin, who wasn't even daunted by the arrival of his old nemesis Gifford Wilkinson.

The burly tax inspector trundled into reception just as Martin and Donna were staring at the computer screen, trying to work out who exactly was booked in for that day. Martin looked up and smiled. 'Hello there,' he said cheerily, 'and what can I do for you today?'

'Oh, ah, well . . .' Gifford handed Martin the appointments book he'd confiscated. 'I'm giving this back to you as I've concluded my investigation into it.'

'So soon?'

Gifford cleared his throat. 'Yes, and you might as well have this back, too.' He handed over Martin's red accounts book. 'As I've been unable to find any irregularities, I'm winding this investigation down.'

Martin was extremely relieved but somehow not surprised. 'Oh dear, I'll miss our little chats.'

'Goodbye,' said Gifford. 'I won't be seeing you again.' And without more ado, the big man turned and walked out into the sunshine. Some weeks later, having re-evaluated his life, he left the Inland Revenue and started up a business helping victims of corporate fraud to rebuild their lives.

Martin's day, however, didn't continue in the same happy vein. Almost immediately after Gifford's exit, Westerham turned up, flanked by two policemen.

'Ah,' Martin murmured to Donna, 'I think *"We have scotch'd the snake, not killed it"*.'

Martin greeted the policemen warmly. 'Gentlemen, good morning!'

Westerham shrank away and hid behind the larger policeman as Martin approached to shake hands.

'Shall we convene in my surgery – it's a little more private? Donna, put the kettle on. This way, gentlemen.' Martin swept out of reception with the policemen in tow. Westerham followed in their wake like a nervously bobbing dinghy.

As the two policemen, sombre and businesslike, walked into Martin's surgery they seemed to suck all the light from the room. One was tall and broad, the other shorter but equally wide. And with their dark uniforms and black belts festooned with truncheons, handcuffs, radios and other villain-nabbing paraphernalia, they looked somehow out of place indoors. These were definitely creatures of the street.

'So,' said Martin, 'what can I do for you gentlemen?'

'You know exactly why they're here, Gray!' Westerham piped up from behind the taller policeman's left knee.

The policeman looked down at the small man. 'Thank you, sir, but *we'll* handle this.' He turned to Martin. 'I think you are already aware why we're here, Mr Gray.' The officer raised himself to his full height and his shorter colleague followed suit, the leather of their belts creaking self-importantly. 'Assault and battery is a very serious offence.'

Martin smiled faintly. He was remembering an old schoolboy joke about a fight in a fish-and-chip shop: something about salt and battering.

The policeman caught Martin's shadow of a smile and he raised a questioning eyebrow. 'Something funny, Mr Gray?'

'Er, no, not really.' Martin quickly turned his smile to a frown. He had no idea how he was going to get out of this. The truth was, he was guilty as charged. He had gone to Westerham's club and attacked the man with no provocation. In Martin's eyes it was simply a *crime passionnel*, but he suspected British justice, in the shape of these two plods, wouldn't allow that defence – he doubted they'd even be able to spell it.

'So, do you want to tell us about it?' the tall one asked.

'About it?'

'Mr Wilding alleges that you made an assault on his person. We'd like to hear your version of events.' The taller policeman nodded to his colleague, who got out a notebook and looked around the room for a suitable perch. His eyes came to rest on the small chair provided for nervous mothers of small children, and he looked at Martin like a dog asking for permission to climb up on the sofa.

'Please, sit down,' Martin urged.

'Ah, thank you, sir.' The plump policeman's face broke into a grin and he eased himself into the seat in an orgy of creaking leather.

All eyes were now on Martin. What should he do? Throw up his hands and admit it was 'a fair cop'? That they'd got him 'bang to rights'? Did they still imprison people for doing what he'd done? That would be disastrous. Three months in jail would make life very difficult indeed; if he was ever to clear his debts, he needed to work. 'Um, well,' he began, 'I don't really know where to start . . .'

'I saw the whole thing!'

Everyone in the room turned to the tall man wearing a raincoat standing in the corner opposite the door. He seemed to have slipped in completely unnoticed.

'And who might you be?' the tall policeman enquired.

'I'm . . . Mr Gabriel, a patient of Mr Gray's, and I was at the luncheon club when the alleged assault occurred.'

Martin stared hard at the man. Although he couldn't place him, there was something about the golden hair, the fine features and the radiant blue eyes which stirred the ghost of a memory. He chased the thought for a while but it was like trying to catch a dream. Martin was almost certain this man wasn't one of his patients, but he wasn't about to admit that fact just yet. He would let Mr Gabriel have his say first.

'You say you were there, sir?' asked the tall policemen.

'Yes, indeed. I don't know if this is relevant, but . . . I mean, one hears a lot of talk at the club and most one can ignore, but the feeling is that Mr Wilding suffers from a bad case of professional jealousy. Mr Gray is an excellent dental surgeon, whereas Mr Wilding, although wealthy and well provided for by his doting father, would appear in comparison to be nothing more than a talented amateur.'

Westerham listened to this, open-mouthed.

The tall policeman looked over at his frantically scribbling colleague. 'Are you getting all this?'

The shorter man nodded.

'Carry on, sir.'

'I was at the luncheon club when Mr Gray entered. I was in the smoking room, in my usual seat by the window from which it is possible to see into the dining room where the alleged assault took place. The incident occurred over the small matter of the whereabouts of a certain key to a drugs cupboard.'

The tall policeman nodded meaningfully at the mention of the word 'drugs'.

'Mr Wilding's party had been causing a few raised eye-brows with their wild behaviour . . .'

Westerham stared incredulously at the stranger, won-dering what gave him the right to rewrite history.

'It was three o'clock in the afternoon and they were *still* at lunch. They had obviously consumed a large amount of alcohol and were becoming rather rowdy. Mr Wilding does have a reputation as a bit of a toper.'

'Could you spell that for me, sir?' asked the seated policeman.

'Certainly. T - O - P—'

'This is preposterous!' Westerham exploded. 'I've never seen this man before in my life, and I can assure you he is most definitely not a member of my club. For a start, he'd never be allowed through the door dressed like that!'

The taller policeman glared at Westerham. 'You'll have your say in good time, sir. Let's just hear the rest of the gentleman's story, shall we?' He turned back to 'Mr' Gabriel. 'Carry on, sir.'

'As I was saying, Mr Wilding's party was making a lot of noise and had already been warned by the stewards to tone it down when all hell seemed to break loose. As Mr Gray entered the dining room and approached the table, he asked Mr Wilding if he happened to have the cupboard key about him as he needed a phial of some drug or other to soothe the pain of one of his patients. At this, Mr Wild-ing leapt up and started verbally abusing Mr Gray. He actually clambered onto the table . . . You may have noticed Mr Wilding is rather short of stature . . .'

The two policemen glanced at Westerham and smirked at this reference to his diminutive frame.

'I can only assume he wished to be on a level with Mr Gray, who is a fine, upright man. Mr Wilding, inflamed by drink – of that there can be no doubt – stamped all over the table, spluttering oaths and sending the lunch things flying. Then a most extraordinary thing happened. Intoxicated beyond all sense, Mr Wilding threw himself at Mr Gray. Mr Gray sidestepped and Mr Wilding hit the floor. And that is how he got his bloody nose – it was entirely self-inflicted.'

Westerham was apoplectic with rage and hopped around emitting high-pitched squeals reminiscent of a mouse being attacked by a buzzard.

'Thank you, sir.'

'Not at all, I'm a fervent seeker after truth, and would do anything in my power to help prevent a miscarriage of justice.'

'Balls!' Westerham had at last found his voice.

The tall policeman frowned down at him. 'I beg your pardon?'

'It's absolute balls!' the short man spat. 'This fellow's making the whole thing up! Gray attacked me! He punched me on the nose! If the stewards hadn't pulled him off he'd have killed me!' He wagged an angry finger at Gabriel. 'This man is not a member of my club. I've never seen him before in my life! He's one of Gray's cronies! Can't you see that, you blundering plods?'

The short policeman stopped writing suddenly and the officers looked at each other.

'I demand you arrest this man immediately!'

'I think we'll be the judge of who needs arresting, sir.' The policemen's attitude had turned decidedly chilly.

'Oh, for God's sake! Look, I'll explain it to you in words of one syllable so that even you can understand. This man –' he pointed to Martin '– hit me. While this man –' he pointed to Gabriel '– is lying to protect his friend. They've cooked this up between them. It's obvious! A three-year-old child could see that! Don't they issue brains at Hendon?'

The short policeman rose menacingly. 'That's enough now, sir.'

'No, it most certainly is not enough! My father is a close friend of the deputy commissioner. If you two imbeciles don't do your job, i.e. arrest this criminal, you will find yourselves patrolling Dartmoor looking for sheep-shaggers!'

'I'd strongly advise you to remain calm, sir.' The tall policeman put a hand on Westerham's shoulder.

'Let go of me, you moron!' Westerham lashed out with his fist and caught the officer firmly in the groin. The policeman went cross-eyed and emitted a low groan.

'Right, that's it!' The shorter officer snapped his notebook shut and grabbed Westerham in an armlock. 'You all right, Paul?' he enquired of his stricken colleague.

Paul, bent double, nodded grimly.

'Head between your knees and deep breaths,' Martin advised.

After a few moments, Paul had recovered enough to speak. 'Mr Wilding, are you aware that assaulting a police officer is a very serious offence?' he said hoarsely.

'But . . . it was an accident.'

'I'm going to have to ask you to accompany us to the police station, sir.'

'But—'

'Take him outside and caution him,' Paul gasped, obviously still in pain.

The short policeman tightened his grip on Westerham. 'Now, now, sir, we're not going to cause any more trouble, are we?'

'*No!*' Westerham yelped as his elbow was forced up towards the nape of his neck.

'Come along, we're going for a little ride.' Westerham was escorted out of the surgery, through a reception full of gawping patients and into the waiting police car.

Paul straightened with difficulty and turned to Martin. 'Sorry to have troubled you, sir. I doubt you'll be hearing from us again. Have a nice day.' He saluted and followed his colleague, walking at a slow, measured pace.

Martin was left alone with a beaming Gabriel.

'Do I know you?' Martin frowned.

'Not strictly angelic behaviour, admittedly, but excusable in the circumstances, wouldn't you say?' Gabriel replied.

'I . . . I'm very grateful that you helped me out there, but . . . I'm at a loss . . .'

'Let's just say I was helping out a friend in need and leave it at that.' Gabriel sighed. 'I've enjoyed our association, Martin. You have a nice life now.'

As Martin watched, the man began to glow. Light streamed from him, shining out into the room in glittering shafts. He rose up slowly, and the air was full of the beating of wings and the sound of a heavenly chorus.

'Martin, your nine o'clock's here.'

'Huh?'

Donna was standing in the doorway.

'Wha— Where did he go?' Martin peered around the empty room.

'Who, Westerham? I assume he's helping the police with their enquiries.'

'No, the man in the mac.'

Donna narrowed her eyes. 'I never saw a man in a mac.'

Martin looked back to the corner where Gabriel had been standing. He tentatively stretched out his arm and felt the empty air.

'Are you all right, Martin?'

'Yes, I'm fine,' he said slowly. Actually, he felt better than he had for some time. He'd never really understood the expression before, but it seemed as if his heart really was singing. He turned to Donna and smiled. 'I really am fine.'

# Chapter 16

After letting Westerham cool his heels in Exeter nick until lunchtime, Martin went to see him to discuss a little business proposition. He was going to offer to give the little man his share of the practice for nothing, and on top pay rent for the continued use of his surgery. Becoming the sole owner of the entire building would be very appealing to a man like Westerham, and he could well afford the increased mortgage repayments. Meanwhile, this arrangement would free Martin up from the crushing burden of shelling out for two mortgages and help him to get himself straight. As an extra incentive, if Westerham agreed to these terms, Martin would, in exchange, appear as a character witness in Westerham's forthcoming court case on a charge of assaulting a police officer.

Westerham couldn't quite comprehend his sudden flip from victim to aggressor, but, confused and angry though he was, realized he had no choice. Under the watchful eye of the police guard in the interview room, he consented to Martin's conditions through gritted teeth.

Buoyed up by the success of this meeting, Martin reckoned he now had the courage to tackle his in-laws.

\*

Leaving work early, Martin drove the family Gray down to John and Gloria's bungalow in Rock.

Parking outside on the small, neat driveway, he told Luke to wait in the car while he and Helen went inside.

'Aw, can't I come?' his son pleaded.

'Certainly not,' Martin replied. 'Blood may be spilt.'

Although undeniably surprised to see him, Helen's parents feigned disinterest in Martin's sudden appearance. But they were in for a shock.

'John, Gloria sit down,' barked Martin as he strode into their living room. They'd never seen him quite so assertive before and something in his eyes made them think they'd better do as he said. Helen's parents sat side by side on their DFS sofa.

'Now then,' Martin continued, 'there's someone here I'd like you to meet.' He took Helen's hand. 'This is Helen. She is not your housemaid; she is my wife and, as such, her place is with me.'

'Doomed to life with a failure,' John protested.

'Shut your mouth – I haven't finished,' Martin snarled. John was struck dumb.

'Your days of free housekeeping are over. From now on, if you want someone to fetch and carry for you, you've got two choices: do it yourself or employ someone else to do it for you.'

John got up awkwardly. 'I'm not listening to any more of this.'

Martin pushed him back down. 'Oh yes you are. Otherwise, I'm going to let it be known at the local Conservative club that "Major" John Sullivan is a fraud: that he didn't get his injuries in the battle of Goose Green, but in Peckham where he used to run a grocer's, and where one day he slipped on a bag of frozen asparagus spears, causing him to fall down the shop's basement staircase and collide with a disused bacon-slicer.'

Martin was gratified by the answering look of terror in John's eye.

'You . . . you wouldn't?'

'Oh yes, I would.'

Beside him on the sofa, John's wife sat seething with rage. 'You can't threaten us like this!'

Martin turned on her. 'And you, Gloria, with your thinning hair and your ridiculous perm, how do you think the other members of the women's golf club would receive the news that the father of their current president was an embezzler who spent two years in Wandsworth?'

Gloria's face was now too a mask of fear and anguish. She instinctively reached for her husband's hand and they sat silently on the sofa looking like two frightened children.

'That's better. Now, I've made some enquiries, and here is a list of local agencies that specialize in caring for the elderly.' Martin handed them a leaflet.

John stared at the list. 'This will cost money.'

'You can afford it.'

'But we're old,' Gloria croaked.

'You're not too old to stride round eighteen holes every other day. And don't tell me that someone who's brought up three kids doesn't know her way round a kitchen. Now, we're leaving. If you're nice, we may even come and visit from time to time. Come on, Helen.'

'Goodbye, Mum, goodbye, Dad.' Helen kissed them both.

'You don't think of us like he does, do you?' Gloria asked in a small voice.

'I love you both very much –' Helen smiled, '– but you really are two difficult old sods. I'll be in touch.'

Martin and Helen withdrew from the living room, leaving Gloria and John sitting on their sofa, frozen in shock.

Closing the front door gently behind him, Martin smiled, savouring his triumph. 'I can't tell you how much I enjoyed that.'

Helen chewed her lip. 'We weren't too hard on them, were we?'

'They're as tough as old boots. They'll be fine.'

Luke was out of the car now and leaning back against the door with his hands in his pockets. 'How did it go, Dad?'

'Like a dream, son. Now then, Luke, you're the expert. Is there a decent pub around here? I think what's called for now is large brandies all round.'

# *Alpha and omega –*
## *the beginning . . .*

'So,' said Jesus, casting his fly expertly into exactly the right spot under the rushes on the far bank, 'what about the Devil? Did you grant his wish?'

'Hmm?' God replied, trying to untangle his line from the overhanging branch of a willow. 'I'll never get the hang of this bloody sport.'

'It's not really a sport, Dad; think of it more as a meditation.'

'Ngah!' God yanked on his rod. The line broke and snapped back into his face. 'Ow! This is more dangerous than hang-gliding!' He sighed heavily. 'What were you saying?'

'The Devil – did you grant his wish?'

A curious look came into the creator's eyes. 'Oh yes, I always keep my word. The Devil wanted the Albert Hall, and that's exactly what he got. Now then, help me tie another fly onto this line.'

## and the end . . .

The final bars of the courante from Bach's Suite No. 2 in D minor for solo cello soared around the ornate arches and porticoes of Prince Albert's great vision. The Devil put down his bow and lowered his head. There was a smattering of polite applause, then someone dropped a fifty-pence piece into the upturned hat at Satan's feet. In the queue for the Albert Hall box office, umbrellas were unfurled as the first drops of rain began to fall.

'Lothar!'

The Devil's manservant immediately opened an umbrella too, and held it over his master's head as lightning tore the night sky and thunder rolled over Kensington Gardens.

The Devil shifted uneasily on his three-legged stool; his eyes were dark with fury. *The Bastard*, he brooded. *He's done it again!* He threw back his head and screamed at the sky, 'You're going to pay for this!' Then he turned his attention to the queue and growled menacingly, 'You're all going to pay!'

'I've just paid, mate!' said the man who'd put the fifty pence in his hat.

There was laughter from the others waiting patiently in line.

The Devil groaned, took a deep breath, lifted his bow

to Signora Amati's strings and went into Paganini's Caprice No. 24, arranged for solo cello by Signor Paganini himself that very morning.

As he played the dark and complex music, Satan began to feel better. *Music. Music is the answer. Music can reach into a person's soul; music is subtle, persuasive; music has the power to transform . . . Of course!* A smile played around his lips. *My time will come*, he thought darkly. *Oh yes, my time will come.*

The rain lashed down as the lone busker sawed feverishly at his instrument. Some of those watching thought they could detect thin wisps of smoke rising from the strings, but it was probably just a trick of the light . . .

Visit **www.panmacmillan.com** to read more about all our books and to buy them. You will also find features, author interviews and news of any author events, and you can sign up for e-newsletters so that you're always first to hear about our new releases.